BEYOND
—THE—
AFTER

PRINCESS LILLIAN

C.M. Healy

Publisher's Cataloging-In-Publication Data
(Prepared by The Donohue Group, Inc.)

Names: Healy, C. M.
Title: Beyond the after. Princess Lillian / C.M.
   Healy.
Other Titles: Princess Lillian
Description: [Dallas, Texas] : Mercury West
   Publishing, LLC, [2015] | Interest age level:
   010-020. | Summary: Princess Lillian is the
   beautiful daughter of Snow White and Prince
   Charming. She has led a fairly uneventful life
   until a faction of rogue Drodic citizens
   threaten the lives of the people of the Valanti
   Kingdom, including its royal family--especially
   Lillian. As Lillian tries to discover who is
   targeting her, she must rely on the help of old
   friends and new, thus intertwining the lives of
   three famous queens and their eldest daughters
   in a way they couldn't have possibly imagined.
Identifiers: ISBN 9781948577007 (paperback) |
   ISBN 9781948577014 (hardcover)
Subjects: LCSH: Princesses--Juvenile fiction. |
   Battles--Juvenile fiction. | Friendship--
   Juvenile fiction. | Queens--Juvenile fiction. |
   Imaginary places--Juvenile fiction. | CYAC:
   Princesses--Fiction. | Battles--Fiction. |
   Friendship--Fiction. | Kings, queens, rulers,
   etc.--Fiction. | Imaginary places--Fiction. |
   LCGFT: Fantasy fiction.
Classification: LCC PZ7.1.H4315 Bel 2015 | DDC
   [Fic]--dc23

Second Edition ©2020

Beyond the After: Princess Lillian

By C.M. Healy

Copyright 2010 C.M. Healy

ISBN 9781948577007

For my beautiful wife, my princess, and my happily ever after.

Contents

Acknowledgements

The journey of writing my first novel has been long and arduous. One that I couldn't possibly have done alone, and would be amiss if I did not thank a few people who helped me along the way.

Foremost, my parents and teachers throughout my life, who encouraged my creativity and challenged me to be great. Dave Yackuboskey, my archery expert, who made sure my terms and description of the sport were correct. My "lunch lady" helpers, who gave me invaluable insight into the young teenage mind, and what really happens at sleepovers. A special thanks to Paul Boyd and A.M.H. who, actually took the time to read the whole thing and give me constructive feedback. My proofreaders Brooke Fugitt and Tiffany Chan who I could not pay enough for their expertise in making this book look and sound professional.

And of course my partner in crime, my wife Sondra, who was encouraging me every step of the way, staying up multiple late nights, and being my sounding board throughout this endeavor. You truly are my light and I can't wait for our next adventure together. I love you. I know we'll live happily ever after.

Azshura

Zoldaine's Castle

Menari River

Pool

Felloren Trib

Grove

Valanti

Guanaic Range

Kraneth Mountains

Tocarin Range

Twin Falls

Tocarin Lake

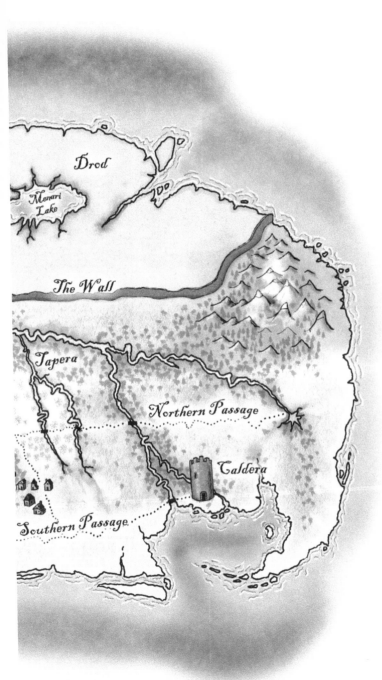

BEYOND

— THE —

AFTER

PRINCESS LILLIAN

Preface

The battle between good and evil is a tale that's as old as the universe itself. Both have always existed, coexisted if you will, but they are not always equal. In truth, equality between the two is rarely the case. Evil does have its moments, but good has always seemed to have an upper hand. Is it the edge of sacrifice versus selfishness? Loyalty opposed to treachery? Love over hate? Whatever the mysterious power, more often than not, good wins, and peace is established for a period of time. It might be a year. It might be a hundred years. However, when one evil is vanquished, another will arise, attempting to shroud the land in darkness again, for that is the natural order of things. It is a delicate shift of momentum between these two, much like the swinging of a pendulum. One can never be sure what situations will spawn sinfulness or what hardships will harbor heroics. And one can never be sure what the outcome will be. But one thing is for sure, it is during this fluctuation of powers, in which the greatest stories ever told take place.

Prologue

And they lived happily ever after. The End.

The End?

Such a strange beginning for a tale. Nevertheless, the ideal one for ours because it reminds us of where things left off. Because The End is never really the end. What The End means is that the current story being told has come to a relative finish. All the important events have been told, all the characters' problems have been resolved, and life continues on for these heroes and heroines as they live out their daily lives without much interruption. But as we all know, life rarely continues without interruption. Important events occur that must be told. The End really represents quite the opposite. The End indicates the beginning of a new tale. So, really, The End should be The End…, especially in this story, because for three very famous tales, there was more. There was the beginning of a new tale that followed the "happily ever after," the tale beyond the after, and that is exactly where this story begins.

Prologue I: History

Snow White, Cinderella, and Aurora (better known as Sleeping Beauty) all married their princes and became queens of their kingdoms. This is well known. But what is less well known is that their tales happened at the same time. During that time, evil ruled two of the five magic kingdoms on the continent of Azshura and was attempting to take over the remaining three.

The southeastern portion of Azshura at that time was made up of two kingdoms in the process of becoming one. The first kingdom was ruled by King Stefan and Queen Leah, who arranged the marriage of their newly born daughter,

Aurora, to King Hubert's son, Prince Phillip, to unite the two kingdoms. The rest of the story you know: evil sorceress, curse of eternal slumber, prince kills sorceress, and they lived happily ever after, reigning over the newly formed kingdom of Caldera.

Just to the west was the kingdom of Tapera, where Cinderella resided. Here, evil was in the works through her wicked stepmother. Fortunately, good had a strong hold in this kingdom by way of the king and, of course, the fairy godmother. That story I'm sure you know as well. The infamous glass slipper and Cinderella's marriage to King Louis Charming.

The next is the kingdom of Valanti, home to Snow White. Here, the evil witch queen (and stepmother to Snow White) ruled. The queen did not meddle too much in her people's affairs because the kingdom was rich in diamond mines, and as long as those diamonds supplied her with her every desire, life was at least livable. There was once, however, a dry spell when the queen turned citizens into pigs every day until a fortunate group of dwarves discovered a vast mine of infinite wealth. It was this discovery that actually made the queen happy enough to marry Snow White's father. Unfortunately, she killed her husband shortly after, only to use Snow White's tears for a potion of eternal youth (a practice she utilized regularly by inflicting different methods of cruelty upon Snow White). Ironically, the queen's vanity was her ultimate downfall, for it was prophesied that someday there would be one who would surpass the queen's beauty and be her demise. Snow White was such a plain child in youth that the queen dismissed her entirely until it was, of course, too late, and Snow White had blossomed into a beautiful young lady. Fairest in the land, if you recall. So, the queen had Snow White killed, or so she thought.

I'm sure you remember the rest of the tale, but it is important to focus on a small part. The part in which the hunter was supposed to kill Snow White but did not.

Everyone has a sense of good and evil. And everyone has a choice of which one to follow. But just because someone decides to follow one over the other does not mean that the other is completely lost. In other words, champions of good are quite capable, in a moment of despair or weakness, of making an evil choice. Just the same, there are villains of malicious intent, who can, in one instant, choose the path of righteousness and change the history of what could have been.

So it was with the Hunter. He was a man who, for most of his life, had chosen evil. He was the queen's right-hand man and the executioner of Snow White's father. But on that day in the forest, with his axe high above his head ready to end Snow White's life, he paused. No one can say for sure why he hesitated. Some believe it could have been Snow White's beauty. Others believe it was because she reminded him of his own daughter he had lost long ago. Either of these is quite possible, but the simple truth is on that day, the hunter chose good. No magic. No potion. Just a simple man, making a simple choice to do what was right, forever altering the events that followed.

Naturally, he was tortured without mercy by the queen for his insubordination. Yet the deed had been done, and the queen was eventually destroyed. An interesting part of this story you may not know, however, is that the prince who gave Snow White the famous kiss, Prince Harry Charming, is actually King Louis's younger brother. He was on a secret mission to kill the queen when he was love struck by Snow White's beauty.

The last of the once five magical kingdoms was Drod. Drod was ruled by Zoldaine, the evil king and sorcerer, older brother to both the late wicked queen of Valanti and the late sorceress of Caldera. Here, the land had not seen the rays of the sun for almost two hundred years. Evil had a strong hold on the land and its people. Despite what prince or knight attempted to defeat this evil, it would not relinquish its controlling grip. It is this kingdom you have not heard of because no one wants to tell or listen to a tale where evil triumphed and the handsome hero perished under its talons. Zoldaine ruled his kingdom with a twisted iron fist. He tormented his people in any way you could think of. Starvation, poverty, drought, flood. All to entertain his sick and demented mind. Why didn't the people just leave, you ask? Because Zoldaine had a wall built around the entire kingdom and enchanted it by a very ancient dark magic, killing instantly whomever should touch it. This enchantment made entering the kingdom very difficult as well. Difficult but not impossible.

Prologue II: A Change of Heart

It was shortly after the kisses and slipper that each newlywed king and queen did what any king and queen would do—start a family. Cinderella was first with her son Marcus, followed closely by Aurora with her son Jaccob, and then Snow White with Lillian. A few years later, Aurora gave birth to Avery, and Cinderella bore Olivia. Several years after that, Snow White had Andrew, and Aurora had Layla, who was a much-needed blessing, as you'll see later.

It was a few months after Andrew was born when Zoldaine made his first and only attack on the three kingdoms. He was hell-bent on controlling the entire continent of Azshura, and the passing of his sisters motivated his poisoned heart even more. Revenge is a potent toxin, capable of not only amplifying a nefarious presence but also

6

corrupting some of the most gallant heroes. Nothing good ever comes from revenge. Nothing.

So, with his twisted desire to rule Azshura and revenge set deep in his soul, Zoldaine led the first offensive attack against the Valanti Kingdom. Now, Zoldaine was no fool. There was a reason he had held his kingdom for the last hundred years. He knew the only thing more powerful than magic was information. Six months prior to the birth of Andrew, Zoldaine had sent out an informant to gather as much information on the three kingdoms as he could. Weapons, soldiers, magical beings, supplies, and most importantly, the royal families. The informant had been hideously deformed by Zoldaine but was still loyal to his master, if only for a desired lack of future torment. Zoldaine had even promised amnesty for him and his family. Zoldaine provided safe passage from Drod, and the informant began his assignment. In his deformed state, he was expecting those gawking stares and whispers just out of ears' reach. What he was not expecting was the lack of ridicule and the generosity of the people. The three kingdoms under the rule of good reacted in a way the informant was not used to. Even though he had no coin for food or residence, the kind citizens of all kingdoms offered him a warm meal and a soft bed. Now, the kingdoms were not without their problems or criminals—as I said before, good and evil coexist, it's only a matter of choice. But when one is almost always surrounded by goodness, it is hard not to follow suit.

So it was with the informant.

Maybe it was the smile from that pretty girl in the village. Maybe it was when that stranger had helped him up after he had fallen in the mud. Maybe it was the family that had shared their last piece of bread with a deformed stranger. For whatever reason, when the informant got back to Drod, he made a choice. He chose the path of good. He chose to mislead his master. The informant knew about the birth of

Andrew. And he knew the prince's birth would entail a royal coronation, which would require the audience of the other kings and queens, their royal guards, and most of the magical creatures of Azshura. Once the date was set, the informant went back to his master.

When Zoldaine invaded Valanti, he quickly realized the betrayal of the informant, but it was too late. The battle was quick, and Zoldaine was forced to retreat to avoid losing all of his forces as well as his own life. It was then that the kings and queens realized they could not allow this threat to fester any longer. This brazen attempt by Zoldaine while they were surrounded by loved ones put an urgency in their hearts. They had always discussed plans to overthrow Zoldaine and release his people, but now he had given them an opportunity they could not overlook. His forces had been cut in half, if not more, and Zoldaine himself was weakened by his encounter with the faeries. The rulers knew following him to Drod increased the risk, as he would begin to regain his strength, but it was worth the ultimate price if it meant a life of freedom for their families and kingdoms.

Prologue III: The Price of Victory

The kings quickly sent for all available knights to assemble in the Valanti Kingdom. Everything was prepared within a few days of Zoldaine's attack. Sir Aaron from Caldera led the band of troops. He had done some reconnaissance in Drod for a few months after the marriage of King Phillip and Queen Aurora to ascertain Zoldaine's power and if it was possible to rid Azshura of this evil once and for all. He didn't advise the attack then, but he did manage to map out most of Drod, including the location of Zoldaine's castle.

There was a small discussion of who was to go and who was to stay. Good-byes were said. Kisses were given. The soldiers and kings mounted up and waved farewell one last time before heading out on their quest.

The trek to the wall wasn't a long one, but the solemn mood of their purpose still took its toll on the crusaders. Too soon for some, they finally reached their destination. The faeries did their part and cleared the wall from any curses or wards. Next, the dwarves used their expertise of the black powder to clear a path through the wall for the troops.

Word spread quickly throughout Drod that they were there. Depending on who was doing the talking, the kings were either saviors or sinners.

Some fought, loyal to death.

Some left, eager to flee.

Some stayed, afraid to leave.

Now, I could go into the details of how the battle went. The close calls, mighty blows, the near misses. But that is a tale for another time. What concerns us at present is the outcome. Zoldaine was defeated, but not without inflicting a mortal wound of his own. King Phillip was struck by Zoldaine's enchanted sword. The wound was devastating in its own right, but it was also infected with the poison of dark magic. Try as they might, the faeries could not repair the injury, and King Phillip lay slowly dying after the battle's end. They finally resolved to put the king into a magical sleep, much like his wife had been in years before. This would at least preserve him until a cure could be found—if one existed.

News of Zoldaine's defeat spread quickly. Most of Drod's citizens left with what they could carry, many of them taking pieces of the wall as their own personal victory, and took up residence in one of the other three kingdoms.

Moods were cheerful but somber back in Valanti as Queen Aurora dealt with the news of her husband. The faeries assured her they would not rest until they found a cure. The dwarves offered to build a protective enclosure from diamond so no harm would come to the king before that time. King Louis and King Harry told her their kingdoms' resources were at her disposal as well.

She was very grateful for all the support. She smiled and accepted consoling hugs. She was hopeful on the outside, but dying on the inside. She had not wanted to burden her husband before going into battle, but she had needed to tell him something. Zoldaine's attack had interrupted her opportunity, but it did not change the fact that she was pregnant. And the thought of their new child, not to mention Jaccob and Avery, growing up without a father saddened her deeply.

But unfortunately, nothing could be done about the past. She and the rest of the inhabitants of Azshura had to push forward and hope that brighter days lay ahead in the years to come.

CHAPTER 1: Party Crashers
May 14

Before the sun had kissed the horizon, the celebration was in full swing, which was understandable seeing as half the Valanti Kingdom was in attendance. It was Princess Lillian's eighteenth birthday. The party was more of an informal celebration with the entire kingdom invited to give the princess their well wishes. Her actual birthday had been a few days ago, when they had held her official coming-of-age coronation to ensure that if something should happen to her parents, Fae forbid, she would become queen. A lot to take in for an eighteen-year-old, even though she'd been preparing for this moment since birth. It also meant her dating life was going to become more serious as well, which she was not too sure about.

Not only was the coronation an important rite of passage but also a time to join the royal families together, which was becoming hard to find time to do, now that the children were getting older. Royal guests included Queen Aurora, her children Avery and Layla, along with Queen Cinderella and King Louis with their daughter, Olivia. Both Marcus and Jaccob were absent. Not because they were too old for such things—quite the opposite. They had been away now for almost a year on an important quest searching for a cure for Jaccob's father, King Phillip. The princes had kept some correspondence and last said they had a promising lead on a reclusive wizard named Merlin on the continent of Britania who might be of assistance. In the meantime, they sent their best wishes to Lillian on her important day.

The royal party was a sight to behold. Carriages outlined in gold and decorated with the most luxurious fabrics were pulled by beautiful white horses down a sweeping drive that circled a great fountain at the end. Smiling valets opened doors and helped guests down. Stairs led to the fantastic double doors with the kingdom's great seal placed proudly in the center. These doors were slowly opened by doormen who bowed and invited all into the festivities. A symphony of sounds from musicians, games, laughing, and joking greeted the guests' ears. The great hall was a dizzying display of activity. Tricksters, jugglers, acrobats, dancers, magicians, people, and food. Oh, the tables of food! Aromas of the most succulent delicacies flowed over the crowd like a gentle wave. Exotic fruits from all over the continent. Roasted pork, chicken, and smoked salmon. Pastries, chocolates, and the sweetest sweets to temp the most diligent wills. A different bottle of wine to complement each type of cheese. Decorations garnished the hall and elaborate banners trimmed in gold stitching hung from every corner. Streamers flowed from column to column, accenting the glorious colors that adorned the hall. And, of course, the occasional confetti popper was heard from the children who were weaving in and out of the crowd. Laughs spilled out around the silly games being played like "Don't Sit on the Cake" or "Pick the Basket." An older group of children cheered on two others to see who could handle their Dragonfire Drops, a sweet yet intense candy that would enable a brave soul (if his tongue could last) to breathe a burst of fire from its liquid elixir encased inside.

Grayson, the resident wizard, had even managed to manifest a dazzling light show with his crackling stars that was nothing short of spectacular.

A good time was had by all until…

"Andrew!" Lillian chased her little brother with the ferocity that only an older sister could. However, Andrew was quick on his feet and made his way to his mother, Snow White, before suffering Lillian's wrath.

"Mom, help me, she's going to twist my ear off!" Andrew cried as he hid behind the queen.

"Come here, you little troll," Lillian fumed.

"I didn't do it, Mom, I swear."

"He's lying, Mom. This is the third time he's put cream in my hair, which now looks like a swamp rat," she explained as she lunged for Andrew.

"No, I didn't. It was Ethan this time!"

Snow White looked down at her son. "This time?" It was hard to hear the disdain in her voice as heavenly as it was, but her look conveyed the meaning perfectly.

Andrew realized he had unintentionally incriminated himself. "I mean every time. This was the first time, I mean. It's all Ethan's fault." Andrew was quickly failing at any plausible explanation to exonerate himself and was convicting his best friend at the same time. Usually, Andrew and Ethan romped around with Marcus and Jaccob during these engagements, which kept the younger boys out of trouble—mostly. But in the older boys' absence, Andrew and Ethan had become quite the pests as of late. Lillian had taken the brunt of their practical jokes, unfortunately, and she was ready to tear his ears off.

"Lillian, calm down, sweetie."

"But Mom, he…"

"I said I will handle this," Snow White reassured her. "Go upstairs and have Alondra help fix your hair. It will be fine."

Lillian gave one last disgusted look at her brother hiding behind the queen and turned to go upstairs. She hurried past her father, King Harry, who was conversing with his brother, King Louis, and his wife, Queen Cinderella, rulers of the Tapera Kingdom. King Harry almost asked Lillian what was wrong but thought better of it when he saw her face. He had seen that look before and knew Andrew was up to no good. The king caught the eye of his wife, who motioned to him she had things under control.

Lillian walked up the winding staircase, leaving the festivities of her birthday behind. *Some birthday*. She quickly walked to her room on the second floor and sat down on her bed almost in tears. It was a conflicting scene to see someone so beautiful in such a luxurious room so upset. Alondra entered shortly after, and Lillian wiped her eyes.

"Pardon, m'lady," Alondra apologized, "but your mom said you required my assistance?"

"Yes, yes." Lillian waved her in. "It's okay, Alondra, come in." Alondra walked over and joined Lillian on the bed. "I'm sorry, I'm just upset."

"About Andrew, m'lady?"

"Oh, to be certain, I'm angry with him, but this isn't about him. He just happened to be the raindrop that caused the flood. I just…I don't know. It's nothing—forget it. Let's just go back to the party. I am the guest of honor after all."

"Not before we get you looking like it. Now, let's see what that ornery brother of yours has done this time."

They walked over to the vanity, and Alondra did her best to remove the sticky mess from Lillian's hair. Lillian liked Alondra. She had been the maidservant to the princess since her birth. Alondra was someone Lillian respected and could talk to without getting a lecture about her duties as a princess. The older woman entertained Lillian with stories that always seemed to help Lillian through her difficult times.

"It's a boy, isn't it, Miss Lillian?" Alondra asked as she combed out some tangles.

"What? Of course not, it's just..." Lillian let out a sigh. "You always seem to know."

"It's Richard Burkhardt, isn't it? The merchant's son? The one who's been courting you for, what now, a month?"

"Six weeks," Lillian interjected.

"Six weeks. What has he done to get you so upset? He seems like a nice enough young man, and he sure is handsome."

"Alondra?" Lillian was surprised her maidservant took notice of such things after being married for so long.

"Sweetie, I may be married, but there's no harm in lookin'."

Lillian sighed. "He is nice. He treats me like a true gentleman would. Not like Reginald, who was only after my crown and the royalty perks. Can you believe he had the audacity to ask me if I would ask *my dad* if we could use the royal cottage to throw a party for his friends? He even wanted to take the royal carriage. What a jerk."

"Aye, I didn't see you shedding any tears over that one, handsome or not."

"I know. And Richard is very attractive, but..."

"What, sweetie?"

Lillian turned to face her friend. "It's just that... I don't feel what I think I should be feeling. He's nice. He's smart. He's funny. He's good-looking. He comes from a good and respected family. He's everything a girl should want, but I just get this sense like we're missing something."

"Why do you think that is?"

Lillian pointed to a portrait of her family hanging over the hearth. "My parents. They are so happy with each other. And the way it all came together almost seems magical. Like some greater force pulled them together because they were made for each other. And sure, Richard makes me happy, but

I don't know if I'm happy *with* him. Is any of this making sense? I just want what they have. A prince rescuing a princess, sweeping me off my feet, love's first kiss, the happily ever after. I mean, I'm a princess. Isn't that what's supposed to happen?"

Alondra took a deep breath. "Sweetie, every girl wants and deserves those things, princess or not. A magical relationship isn't just reserved for those of royalty. Take my husband and I, for example. Well before he was to become your father's head advisor, he worked in the stables. I had just been hired as your maidservant and had headed down to get some fresh milk for you. When I walked in, no one was there. I waited for a couple of minutes and had turned to leave when in walked Henry, with his shirt off no less. My heart skipped a beat, and I even forgot to breathe for a second, not to mention why I had come down there in the first place."

Lillian smiled.

"But I somehow managed to get out 'Milk.' He smiled that gorgeous smile of his and turned to help me get some. Unfortunately for him, he had forgotten where he had set some buckets and tripped over them, falling headfirst into a big pile of manure."

"No way!" Lillian said, wide-eyed.

Alondra held up her hand. "Truth to the faeries. So, not exactly your first-kiss-under-the-glass-lid kind of impression." Alondra winked. "I later heard from Elise in the kitchen that Henry had been just as flustered as I was. Apparently, the sun was coming in from a hole overhead 'illuminating me with a ray of heavenly beauty,' as he put it. After two weeks of shy exchanges of smiles and glances, he finally asked if he could court me. When I said yes, it gave him the confidence to talk to your father about some ideas he had, ultimately becoming your father's right-hand man. Eighteen years later, here we are, still as happy as ever.

Although there is always the inside joke of him being full of it after his plunge."

Both women laughed at this thought.

"But you know what?" said Alondra.

Lillian gave her an inquisitive look.

"My heart still skips a beat whenever Henry enters the room." Alondra blushed at the thought of it. "But not everyone's story is like that, sweetie. Most people go months before they get that feeling. Even I wasn't totally convinced about Henry until after we had been seeing each other for about six months. So, I guess my point is, it doesn't matter who it's with or what the circumstances are, but if you're with the right person, you'll just kind of know."

Lillian smiled.

"And however you meet, *that* will be *your* fairy tale. Your 'happily ever after'."

"Thanks, Alondra, I really…"

BOOM!

Lillian's statement was cut short as a thunderous blast from downstairs rocked the room.

CHAPTER 2: Resurgence

tems on her vanity shifted as the concussion was enough to shake several bottles and dislodge dust from the ceiling. Lillian immediately jumped up and raced to the door with Alondra close behind. The hallway was thick with smoke, but surprisingly the ladies didn't choke as they breathed it in. The party was in pandemonium as the great hall below echoed with screams, cries, and yells. Lillian and Alondra cautiously made their way downstairs, feeling along the wall for the banister. Then suddenly, the "smoke" was whisked away like it was being sucked up by a giant wind spinner. But instead of disappearing, it coalesced to form a message of two horrifying words, *Zoldaine Lives!*

Lillian raced down the stairs. She used the height advantage of the stairs to locate her dad in the hysterical crowd, who was now exiting the great hall through any door they could find.

"Dad!" Lillian shouted over the noise. "Dad!"

"Lillian!" King Harry pushed his way through the crowd toward the stairs. He met her three stairs from the bottom and embraced his daughter tightly. "Oh, Lily Pad, thank the Fae, you're okay."

Normally the king's use of her nickname from childhood would put a smile on her face. But only concern lingered there now.

"What happened? What was that?" Lillian asked, looking over her shoulder. Most of the guests were either outside or calming down, now realizing the threat was empty.

"It appears another rogue Dainian snuck into the party and released a shock bomb. Harmless really but still gets the job done. Panic and chaos."

"How did a Rogue get in here?" Lillian was stunned.

"That's what I plan to find out." The king turned and shouted for his advisor "Henry!"

A shorter stocky man raised his hand and weaved his way through the remaining guests. "Right here, Sire."

"Henry, please spread the word to the guests that things are under control and the party will resume shortly. Are there any injured?"

"Minor scrapes or bruises from the initial chaos, Sire, but nothing the faeries can't handle."

"Good. Make sure no one leaves until we account for everyone on the list. We'll have to interrogate them eventually, which I'm not fond of, but I don't want to ruin the celebration. We'll show them just how ineffective their ploy was."

"Yes, Sire."

"Tell the faeries I may have need of their services. And have Grayson put up the barriers."

Henry nodded his head and left to do the king's bidding.

The king turned back to his daughter. "Sweetheart, I am so sorry they ruined your birthday party."

"Don't worry about it, Dad. It was just the icing on the cake. I'll be fine. Do you think it would be terribly rude if I left my own party?"

"I'm sure if the birthday girl slipped out for a bit, I could cover for her," the king said with a wink and gave his daughter a big hug. "Just don't be long because—and you didn't hear it from me—your mom has another one of her cake creations to bring out soon."

Lillian groaned just a little. Her mom, Snow White, had always made it a point to make her children's birthday cakes personally. They were okay most of the time, edible at least. The times when she incorporated some magic for "flair" were when things got out of hand. One time, she tried to enchant a cake for Andrew's eighth birthday. It was *supposed* to sing "Birthday Merriment" once the candles were lit. Instead, it leapt off the table, almost catching the tapestries on fire while trying to eat him. It was definitely something one doesn't forget.

Lillian headed back up the stairs. She just needed some time alone to breathe and compose herself. She went back past her room and down another corridor to the right. Past another couple of doors there was a column that looked like all the other columns, except that it moved. That was one of the good things about living in a castle. There was always some secret way to get out somewhere. This particular passage would take her to the back of the castle close to the woods. A favorite place of Lillian's.

When she finally opened the other side of the passage, she had to squint her eyes against the sun beaming down. Even before her eyes adjusted, she traversed the terrain with ease just as she had before, even in the dark of night.

Not too many people ventured this far behind the castle because of its close proximity to the former Drod border. The dilapidated barrier wall was still a good half-day's walk away, but superstition was always closer. Over the last few years, there were rumors of a white ghostly figure with one red eye that roamed the woods. Story goes, it was a lost Drodic soul who had forfeited its life during the great battle and hadn't realized its death had come, still looking for freedom. Because its death had come before the true release of Zoldaine's power, it was doomed to stay close to the magic that had imprisoned it for so long. Forever wandering the forest, free from one gloomy grasp only to fall into another. Or so the story goes.

Lillian didn't believe in such nonsense. She had never seen the ghost, and she had been roaming these parts of the kingdom since she had discovered the passage when she was eight.

She found the passage quite by accident, as discoveries often go. She was playing hide 'n' seek with Alondra and had decided to hide behind a suit of armor standing beside a column. When she finally settled behind the legs, she felt a slight draft coming from the column. Lillian put her face up against the stone, and strangely, she could smell the woods coming through the small separation between the wall and pillar. And a small round pebble that didn't quite match with the rest of the stone wall tipped her off. Push. Click. All it took was a small shove to slide the pillar back into the false wall, revealing a spiral staircase going both down and up. She chose down. There was just enough light from some cleverly disguised slots in the wall. She descended the stairs cautiously, occasionally overhearing conversations from various rooms adjacent to the tunnel. Another quick search of the "dead end" at the bottom of the stairs revealed another matching pebble that opened up the door to the world outside the castle. Since then, she had ventured here often until she knew almost every stick and stone the nearby forest contained.

When she got to the small creek about fifty yards away, she slipped off her shoes and left them on her usual rock, hiked up her gown, and waded in the ankle-deep water that rippled by. The instant she stepped into the cool water, she felt her problems and tension start to wash away. The creek had no imbedded magic, it was just soothing. A couple of small fish seemed to play a game of weaving between her feet, occasionally tickling her foot with their tails. She crossed over through the soft mud squishing between her toes and onto the soft, moss-covered bank. Her hair, a dark brown that shimmered with gold, swayed playfully in the light breeze. She moved with her mother's grace as she slipped deeper into the forest. The canopy of trees slowly blocked out the sunlight, giving a warm glow to her surroundings. The forest's inhabitants didn't always flock to her the way they usually did to her mother, but they didn't flee either as they recognized their old friend. Rabbits munched on the vegetation. Squirrels scurried up trees with a treasure in their mouth. A pair of fawns and a doe looked her way before leaping off into the thicker part of the woods as if to say, "Come play with us." Yes, she knew her friends and surroundings well. She even knew the best thackleberry bushes to plunder and had become fairly adept at picking them. She hadn't gotten a scratch in nearly two years.

The berries' delicious flavor of honey, blackberries, and cinnamon all rolled into one made them sought after by both people and animals. But they were hard to come by because their thorns carry a poison that makes the skin swell and itch ten times worse than a stickle bug. Get too many scratches, and not only can you barely move but also you become very nauseated.

She found her regular patch of bushes and noticed the scarcity of berries. *That's odd. The animals usually only eat the ones that fall on the ground. It was a pretty hard winter, though.* Either way, she knew how to find more. She navigated her hand through the outside thorns like a weaver carefully threading a design. She felt a grouping of plump thackleberries, slowly plucked them from the stem, and pulled them out. Pulling them out was always much more difficult because now your hand was in a fist. Concentration was the key to not letting any distraction startle you. The slightest jerk could mean several scratches and dropping your reward. But as she had many times before, Lillian managed with nary a tickle and popped the first juicy, bright purple prize in her mouth.

She continued on only a little farther, knowing she must not be too much longer, as her absence would most assuredly be noticed. Especially when the cake was brought out. But she just wanted to visit her favorite place quickly before going back. She picked up her pace a little, careful not to harm her dress. After about a minute, she came into a clearing that separated the forest in half. Some time ago, the ground had split, causing a great chasm called Goblin's Gorge, effectively dividing the woods and allowing a tributary of the Menari River to run through. Someone, although she wasn't sure whom, had managed to create a narrow yet sturdy wooden suspension bridge joining the two parts of the woods. As far as she knew, time and people had forgotten all about it. And why should they remember, for there was a perfectly good stone bridge connecting the kingdom not too far away on the more traveled road where the chasm was not nearly as deep. That bridge, of course, had been built by the dwarves. Lillian still remembered the trepidation of her first step onto the wooden bridge. It had been scary at first, but now she knew every creak and groan of its wood and rope. Some of her favorite times were when she was on the bridge in the wind. Some people might have been fearful of falling. But standing on the bridge while the wind whipped around her made her feel like she was flying.

So, she walked out onto the weathered wooden planks with as much peace and ease as walking on any trail. She still tread carefully, respecting the old bridge, but relishing the sense of freedom that came over her body. She stopped right in the middle. The wind was just right today. Just enough for a sway, but not so much that she had to hang on. That was the perfect moment. She could close her eyes and imagine herself far away, high above her kingdom, soaring amongst the clouds. The feeling of gliding along the wind currents was almost indescribable. But suddenly something was wrong.

The wind quickly picked up, twisting the old bridge awkwardly. Lillian opened her eyes just in time to see the bracing ropes passing by her. The planks beneath her feet had finally given way after all these years. Lillian was not flying anymore. She was falling.

CHAPTER 3: Ghost in the Woods

rasping, frantically searching for anything to hold, but all Lillian found was air. After what felt like decades, Lillian finally dug her fingers into one of the planks beside her. Adrenaline racing, senses heightened, she dangled above the great chasm desperately looking for a way to pull herself up. Now the wind was not her friend, as it seemed to have picked up even more. It blew her body around, all the while flinging the bridge around like a swing, making it impossible for her to even attempt to grab the supporting ropes that hung just outside her reach. She thought of yelling for help but knew no one was remotely close enough to hear. Everyone was at the party. Waiting for her. How ironic. Left to die by her own birthday party.

SWOOSH!

Lillian felt a quick blast of air rush inches past the left side of her face. That was not the wind. She looked in that direction to find a small, silver-colored rope in front of her. Not wanting to relinquish her grip for a possibility, she tested the tension by leaning her head against it. Taut. She was running out of options and couldn't hang there forever, especially since the wind was growing stronger. She counted down. Three...two...one...*LUNGE*!

Her left hand grabbed the new line of salvation. She began hauling herself up slowly but surely. She heard several rips and tears redecorating her dress, but there was nothing to be done about that now. By the time she had hoisted her body onto the remaining wooden planks, the wind had died down. She gave herself just a moment to realize her safety and then quickly found her way to solid ground.

Once she caught her breath, she came to her senses. Someone had saved her. She examined the silver cord that had saved her life. It was taut for a reason. As she followed the rope with her eyes across the bridge, she saw it was attached to an arrow that was stuck deep into a tree. Back the other way, the rope had been tightly secured around another tree about ten feet behind the forest line. Now Lillian was no fool. Whoever made that shot was either very lucky to have missed her head or an expert marksman. She was betting on the latter. And the rope would have had to have been tied to the other tree before the shot. So, whoever made that shot not only positioned the rope perfectly past her head by mere inches, but also knew the exact distance from tree to tree. Lillian started to run through her head anyone she knew who could have made such a precise shot. There was Sir Alger, trainer of the royal archers, but he would be back at the castle. Her cousin Marcus was rather talented with the bow as well, but he was away with Jaccob. There was that one boy from town who had won the archery contest last year. What was his name? Ugh. She couldn't remember, but why would he be out here during the celebration? He wouldn't. Which still left the question, who?

Well, it was something she would have to ponder later because she desperately needed to get back. Lillian was sure her father was searching for her by now, having exhausted all means to delay her mother's grand unveiling of the birthday cake. She would also have to change, giving a glance down at her once-pristine gown now adorned with several tears and painted with dirt and grass stains. *Ophelia's going to kill me.* She hiked her dress up to keep from tripping and jogged back toward the castle. Along the way, she looked around, unable to shake the feeling of someone watching her, but she never saw anyone. She splashed her way through the creek and grabbed her shoes, not wasting time to put them on. As she reached the wall where the passage was, she bent down to hit the same familiar pebble in the stone. Slowly the weighted pulley system shifted and a portion of the once-uniform wall swung inward. Lillian took a step inside but couldn't shake a feeling of being watched. She turned to look one more time and couldn't believe what she saw. About a hundred yards away in the forest, something white floated a few feet off the ground. Then a small red eye twinkled at her right before disappearing behind a tree.

Lillian could not erase that image from her head as she started up the passage stairs. There was no way that she just saw the ghost, right? She had heard the stories and scoffed at them before, but now? There had to be a logical explanation. She couldn't remember hearing of anyone seeing the ghost during the daytime. Was it the ghost that had saved her? How could it have fired an arrow? And why would it choose to show itself to her now? She'd been in that forest a thousand times and had never felt like she had been being watched like today. Or had she? Now that she thought about it, there had been a few times that she had gotten the same prickly feeling on the back of her neck, but she had just attributed it to the wind or such. She didn't know now. But she'd have to think about it later, because she was nearing the top of the stairs.

She made it to her room and quickly decided on a light blue dress, and if anyone asked why she had changed, she'd say it was because there was cream on it from Andrew. As she went downstairs to rejoin the celebration, she caught her father's wide-eyed *Thank-the-faeries-you're-back* glance followed by *Come save me*! He waved her over, and she made her way through the crowd, who was back to enjoying the festivities.

"Sorry to be gone so long," Lillian apologized as she greeted her father with a kiss on the cheek.

"Not to worry, dear," the king reassured her with a wink, "your mother and I were just discussing that maybe this year you're too old for a cake. Faeries know there's already plenty of food."

"Ah, yeah, you're probably right," Lillian admitted, recognizing the game. Her mother had tried to do this for a couple of years now. The queen liked to baby her children, as anyone in the kingdom knew. Not that she spoiled them, but she was just not ready for them to grow up. Especially Lillian, her first. Snow White just wanted to be reassured that her efforts were wanted and that she was not imposing.

"I'm sorry, honey, I've just been so busy with the council and making sure your brother's keeping up with his lessons," said the queen. She knew the game too, but that didn't change the fact that she needed to be appreciated.

"It's okay, Mom, but just so you know, I was really looking forward to it this year, with me being eighteen and all. As long as the cake didn't try to eat me and burn down the kingdom." Lillian gave her mom a sly smile.

"Were you really looking forward to the cake?" Snow White asked.

Lillian knew what that meant. "Of course. I know it's something really important to you. Some of them are even edible." She started looking for the obvious entrance of a cake.

"Pierre!" the queen called for the head chef. That was the cue. Everyone started singing "Birthday Merriment."

Today is the day we celebrate your birth
We're all here to show just how much you're worth

Ghost in the Woods

Eat a piece of cake, play a couple games
Everyone rejoice in singing out your name
Lillian, Lillian, Merry Birthday, Lillian.

A huge cake rolled out from the back of the party. The crowd had to part about ten feet just to let it through. The towering pastry was a beautiful lilac-frosted confection with indigo-swirled trim and consisted of several layers. The outermost rose in a spiral all the way up to the top. So far, the only magic Lillian could make out was the eighteen candles rotating up the ramp, and once at the top, they dropped down into the middle of the cake only to reappear at the bottom of the ramp to start the whole process over again. It would definitely make blowing them out a trick. But as the cake slowly approached her, the candles slowed down too and finally stopped as the cake halted in front of her. Lillian looked at her mom who was beaming now, as apparently the cake presentation was going off without a hitch. Lillian leaned over to blow out the first candle at the bottom of the ramp, and to her surprise, the rest of the candles started to go out in succession. All the way to the top until the very last candle suddenly shot out a small display of fireworks. This drew a couple of cringes from the crowd and even the king, as they'd seen the queen's creations go awry before. But as the last firework fizzled out, everyone relaxed and eagerly anticipated tasting the queen's newest confection.

After thanking her mother for the beautiful and surprisingly tasty cake, Lillian rejoined her friends Jafria, Sophie, Elizabeth (who everyone called Lizzy), and Princesses Olivia and Avery. Lillian wasn't as close to the two princesses as her other friends simply because she didn't see them that often. Usually they stayed in touch only at occasions like this or through letters they would write back and forth. Forming a close bond with someone was hard if you had to wait a few days for a reply. But since the princesses were so close in age, they did share a lot in common, especially when it came to royal duties. Venting was hard to do to your regular friends who wanted nothing more than to trade places with you. None of them resented Lillian, mind you, they just couldn't find the problem with having to entertain dignitaries at various functions in fancy dresses eating fancy food. Especially when the dignitaries included Duke Taylor and Sir Chandler. Sure, they were nice to look at but were absolute bores when it came to conversation. So, Lillian found solace in writing both Olivia and Avery because they understood that being a princess was not all it was portrayed to be.

"What did your mom do to Andrew?" asked Jafria, always the nosey one.

"I'm not sure," replied Lillian. "I went upstairs to fix my hair. Did any of you get hurt during the chaos?"

Sophie didn't hesitate. "Sir Laurel pushed me into the doorway while trying to get out. So much for his chivalry."

"I'm sure he was pushed himself, Sophie," Lizzy defended her crush.

"He didn't even apologize though," Sophie retorted.

"I have seen him overlook a couple of ladies in need, in the times I've seen him," Olivia piped in. "Not that I'm judging, I'm just saying." Olivia saw Lillian more than Avery. One, because they were closer, and two, because they were family.

"Whatever. You're all just jealous that he fancies me over you," Lizzy concluded.

"He's all yours, Lizzy." Sophie winked at the others, and they all had a giggle.

There was a small pause when finally Avery could take it no longer. "So, what's the deal with the bomb? I thought we had either killed or imprisoned all of the Dainian Rogues."

"Apparently not." Jafria always had to state the obvious too.

Avery scoffed, "I realize that. What I meant was, where did they come from, and how did those stinky Rogues get in anyway? I thought your dad would have better security for your party."

Some of the girls rolled their eyes. It wasn't that they didn't like Avery, but she could come off as a little too grown-up and a know-it-all for their taste. They didn't blame her, though. She had always had to be a little more responsible in her family because of her father's absence. Her mother was usually busy taking care of the kingdom's affairs, which caused Avery to have to step in to a mother role of sorts. Especially for Layla, but also for Jaccob, as he only just recently assumed more kingly responsibilities. Plus, his being away for so long affected Avery more than she'd care to admit. So, most of girls just ignored her haughty comments, knowing while she meant well, she just had a hard time communicating it sometimes.

"I'm sure Henry and my dad will take care of it," Lillian said, reassuring her friend. "My dad has already started a list of who to interrogate. He just didn't want it to ruin my party, so he's not acting like it's a big deal. But believe me, King Charming can be very, um, let's just say persuasive when it comes to protecting his family and kingdom." Lillian had only overheard her dad lose his temper once, and that was a few days after the victory over Zoldaine. She was in the secret passage when she had heard shouting. He had been questioning a prisoner about the hidden faction of Dainian Rogues who had infiltrated the Valanti Kingdom. Their sole purpose was to burn the kingdom to the ground to honor their lord who would someday return. The voice of her father and the whimpering of the captive was enough to make her continue on her way. She had never seen that side of her dad before. Part of it scared her. The other part made her feel safe, like he would do anything to protect his family and stand up for what he believed in.

The party resumed without any further interruptions and as the sun began its decent, the crowd thinned, quite a few of them leaving just hoping to remember where they lived. The king and queen always offered their abode to Queen Aurora and her family as well as the Charmings. But both declined. Aurora had an important council meeting to get back to, and the Charmings always enjoyed traveling under the stars. They had been night owls since the whole midnight thing.

Everyone said good-bye as the servants started the great undertaking of cleaning up. Lillian was eager to see their guests off so she could go talk to Alondra about everything that had happened in the forest. She *would* find out what that "ghost" really was and who had shot that silver arrow. She owed him her life.

CHAPTER 4: A Friend?
May 18

After four days Lillian hadn't seen even a wisp of the ghost. She went back out the very next day after her fall to examine the arrow and rope again but there was nothing. A single mark in the tree was the only evidence anything had been there at all. That and the missing plank. Since then, she had gone out during all hours of the day and night, not really even looking but mostly just sitting and hoping to see it again.

She had just finished a filling breakfast of scrambled goose eggs, fresh apple juice, and coconut toast with thackleberry jam. Andrew had somehow managed to get jam on his fresh shirt and was already getting a lecture from his mom about wasting the launderers' time with his carelessness. It was bad enough they practically had to hire another seamstress just to keep up with his boyish play outside with Ethan. So, that just left Lillian and her father at the table. He was reading the latest issue of the kingdom's newspaper, the *Valanti Valor*. There were a few news distributors for the kingdom, but the *Valor* was the most reliable periodical and was published bimonthly by a local family, the Kretchers. It had most of the up-to-date information on what was going on, not only in the Valanti Kingdom but the other two realms as well. Douglas Kretcher

Sr. sent his two sons, Douglas Jr. and Stephen, across the continent on a weekly basis to get the newest scoops on important information. They had the fastest horses on the whole continent. *The Valor* had a small gossip column as well, which was usually the king's favorite part, though he would never admit it. The "who's who" of the kingdom, if you will, and "what's posh or wash." Lillian had to tell him that the advice didn't always apply to him though. One time the column said feathers were in and felt was out. The king walked around for half a day looking like a peacock before she finally saw him and gave him a lecture of her own. Since then, he'd enjoyed reading it but always asked her for her opinion first before doing anything drastic. She actually enjoyed the new hairstyle he picked out a couple of months ago. It fit his age a little better as well as his personality.

Lillian was about to get up when her father asked her a question from behind his paper. "Where are you off to so early, m'dear?"

Lillian was a little taken aback. Did he know? Had he sent someone to spy on her? No, that was ridiculous. Her dad had always been forthright before now. He was not one to keep secrets, nor would he want them kept from him. It was part of what made him such a good king and father.

"What do you mean?" Lillian asked as nonchalantly as possible.

"I mean, you've just seemed a little preoccupied. Miss Cecilia said you've been distant in your studies the last few days. I just want to make sure everything's okay."

Lillian hated lying to her dad, but she really didn't feel like it was lying since she hadn't discovered anything yet. She had eventually come forth about her fall at the bridge because there was no way to explain her tattered dress, but she made no mention of the mysterious figure she saw. "Yeah, Dad, everything's fine. I've just been going out behind the castle. Since the weather's been so nice, I've been thinking about it a lot. I'm sorry, I'll try to focus more with Miss Cecilia."

King Harry stood up to come over and give his daughter a kiss on the forehead. "That's fine, sweetie. I just wanted to make sure there wasn't anything you needed to talk about. Just because you're eighteen doesn't mean you're not still my little girl."

"I know, Dad." She stood up and gave him a kiss on the cheek. "I promise, if there's anything I need to talk to you about, you'll be the first to know."

Lillian started to walk away when her father stopped her once more. "By the way, how's the dating, or whatever you guys call it nowadays, going with Richard? You guys have another outing soon, right? You and your friends?"

That was another reason her dad was a good king, but sometimes an irritating father. Nothing ever got past him. She had almost completely forgotten about the date; her mind had been so preoccupied lately with the ghost.

"Um, yeah, we do. Uh, things are going okay, I guess. I haven't really gotten a chance to know him too much yet because we're usually with a bunch of other people. This is only our fifth date, and yes, we still call them dates, Dad."

"Okay, well, if you ever need some help..." the king gave his classic wink. A wink that meant he was kidding, but not if you didn't think so.

"No, Dad, I'm fine on my own, thank you." The first date Lillian went on was a complete disaster because her father had sent about twenty "undercover" chaperones along with her. Her date had started to put his coat around her because it was cold, but some of the chaperones jumped to conclusions and pounced on him thinking he was trying to cover her up for a kidnapping. Lillian didn't get another suitor for three months after that.

She went upstairs to her room to change into more appropriate attire for going out into the forest. Her mother had a fit about her dress. She had been "grounded" to spend a week with Ophelia the seamstress and help her make another one. Lillian could definitely think of worse punishments, so she politely obliged and didn't complain.

After changing, she went out the west-wing exit. She only used the secret passage when it was necessary and she didn't want anyone to know where she was. She hadn't been secretive about where she was going really, just why she was going there. Her outings weren't hard to explain since it was spring and perfectly logical to go outdoors. Even a castle could feel small when you're pretty much stuck there during a harsh winter.

Going out the west wing to get to the backside of the castle meant passing through the stables. Lillian didn't mind that much. The smell of manure could be a little overwhelming at times, but even that reminded her of the outdoors and riding across her kingdom. Her kingdom. It was an interesting thought that she tried not to think of much, but the truth was, once her parents passed away or got too old, it would become hers to rule. That's why she had been courting different men over the last few years. Finding a respectable "king" was hard.

"Hello, Your Highness," a burley yet handsome young man offered with a smile and a bow as Lillian walked through.

"Quit it, Seth," Lillian replied with a punch to his arm. "You know I don't like it when you call me that."

"I know, I just like teasin' ya 'sall," Seth said as he rubbed his arm as if it hurt. He was basically all muscle from the chores he did around the castle. His main job was taking care of the horses, but he was also a crafter of any cloth: stable boy, wall repairer, baker, furniture mover, tapestry hanger. If there was a chore to be done around the castle, he'd probably done it. But the task of stable boy, or stable hand, as he liked to be called, to the fifty royal horses usually kept him pretty busy.

"Well, stop it. I have enough on my mind without you harassing me."

"What's going on now? You goin' back out to the woods again?"

"Yeah."

"What's out there anyways? You find that ghost or something?"

"Something like that."

"For real? You've finally seen the ghost?"

"No, Seth, I haven't seen the ghost." Lillian still wasn't convinced. "I'm just going to pick more thackleberries for Pierre. Mom wants a pie for dessert tomorrow for some dinner party she's having."

"All right then. Oh, your dad said that he wanted me to go out and fix that plank on the bridge that you fell through, so next time you're going out there, let me know and you can show me where it is."

"Okay, I will." Lillian had had a brief discussion with her dad about the bridge. He wanted to have it taken down all together to prevent something worse from happening. But it didn't take long for her to bat her beautiful hazel eyes and call up a couple of tears for the king to realize that wasn't going to happen. So, they compromised by having Seth and maybe the dwarves help reinforce the wooden bridge. She was okay with that as long as it still swayed in the wind.

Lillian continued on through the stables to get to the castle gate. She said hello to the two guardsmen as they opened the passage for her. Usually, there was only one and not even all the time, but her father and his head of security, Sir Alger, had both agreed that the feeble attack the other day was only a warning of more to come.

There hadn't been a lot of disruption over the last three to five years. During the first few years of the Dainian

Revolution, there were several uprisings in all of the kingdoms, as well as others trying to take Drod for themselves. Rogue citizens planted by Zoldaine. Sleeper agents that went insane after his death. But most disturbances were small and ill planned. There hadn't been any real threats until now. This one was different. The king was taking this one very personally. There had not been an attack during a major gathering of the royal families in many years, let alone *inside* the castle. Lillian did not envy the guards on duty that day.

She continued on around to the back of the castle when an interesting aroma wafted past her nose. She had smelled it before from the kitchen, but that was on the other side of the castle and the wind was blowing the wrong direction. There was also something unusual about this familiar bouquet. Pleasant, she thought, but different. She followed the scent toward the creek and finally saw what she expected to see but in a very unexpected place. There on "her" rock was a fresh loaf of thackleberry bread. She looked around, trying to find any indication as to who could be out there having a picnic and why they would leave such a temptation to the animals.

As she got closer, she realized there was a note lying underneath the bread.

Could that be for me? Who would know I was even coming? Seth knew I was coming. So did Father. But they're both back at the castle, right? What does it say? Should I pick it up? What if it's not for me?

All of these thoughts spun through her head in the last remaining steps it took her to get within arms' reach of the bread. She finally resolved her thinking.

"Hello?" she called out to no one. "Hello?" This time louder. "Is anyone there?" All she could hear was the babbling of the brook. She looked down at the rock. It had to be for her, she thought. This was *her* rock. She carefully slipped the note out from under the bread and opened it up.

A Friend?

Princess, I hope you are well.
A friend

She looked around again. Still no one. She picked up the loaf of bread and sat down on the rock. It was warm from the midmorning sun, which made it feel like it was fresh out of the oven. Even though she had just eaten breakfast, the aroma made her mouth water. It smelled delicious, but she still couldn't place the slightly unusual scent. She was very much like her mother in that she always tried to see the best in people and never truly understood how malicious they could be. A blessing and a curse, it was this quality that had landed Snow White in her eternal slumber. She had been lucky to have been rescued so soon by true love's kiss. But Lillian also had her dad's sense, and what with the incident at her party, ultimately decided against trying any of the bread. She set it back down on the rock.

A strong male voice came from behind her. "It's not poisoned, if that's what you're thinking."

Lillian froze.

CHAPTER 5: A Date

She wasn't exactly sure how or when the person behind her got there, but he was there now. She hadn't heard a thing. *Who is that? Do I recognize the voice? Should I run? Fight? Scream? Play nonchalant? What does he want? How does he know me? How quick could I make it to the castle?* All of these thoughts raced across her mind in the course of only a couple of seconds, but it felt like an eternity. Was he even still there?

"I'm not going to hurt you, you know."

Yep, still there. Okay, she decided, and started to turn slowly on the rock to face her would-be benefactor.

He wasn't too close. Not as close as he felt. He stood about five feet away. He was tall, over six feet with hair like the darkest chocolate brown that rippled to his shoulders. On his back was what she expected, a bow and quiver full of arrows, a few of them silver blue. The "ghost" was a white cotton tunic, hanging from the wide expanse of his shoulders. And from his neck hung some sort of rock or crystal winking a bright blood red in the morning sun. He was lean and muscular, not bulky, but he bore the signs of strength and agility like one might see in a hunter. His hands were large and tan like the rest of him. His bronze skin shone in the sunlight—her very own statue. But his eyes. His eyes were what captured her breath. They were the palest shade of gray—like storm clouds across the mountains. They were unsettling. Not only surprising in color but also because she sensed they saw too much.

Lillian realized she had been holding her breath and quickly let it out.

"I didn't mean to startle you." His voice had a rich timbre.

Trying to recover from the shock of being surprised and the insane handsomeness standing before her, she blurted out, "You didn't scare me. I was just seeing what kind of person would leave the princess a strange loaf of bread and expect her to eat it." *That wasn't too bad.* It was better than what she had been thinking, which was a breathy, *where did you come from?*

"I'm sorry, I thought you would like it. You seemed to enjoy those thackleberries the other day fine enough," he said through a slight smirk.

"I did. I mean, were you spying on me?" Lillian asked indignantly, a little more mad than worried someone had been watching her. The forest was her sanctuary, and he had invaded it without permission.

"I wouldn't say spying necessarily, just observing you from afar is all."

"Well, some people would call that spying. Who are you anyway? I don't think I've ever seen you before and certainly not in the forest."

"I'm sorry. My name is Alexander, and you are, of course, Lillian."

"Princess Lillian." Her title never usually mattered to her, but so far this Alexander seemed to have the upper hand and she wanted to gain some ground.

"My apologies, Princess Lillian," he replied with a respectful bow.

Lillian felt bad. "That's not really necessary. I'm sorry, it's just, well, this is all rather odd, wouldn't you say? I mean, I've never even seen you before today, and then you just show up with bread and a smile." *Albeit a gorgeous smile.* "If anything, I should be giving *you* a token of my thanks. You did save my life after all."

"Your gratitude is all I need. That and your opinion of my bread. Here, I'll eat a piece first to show you there's nothing wrong with it."

Alexander stepped closer. He smelled of the outdoors and green growing things. Like the forest. He reached down past Lillian, plucked off a piece of bread and tossed it in his mouth. "See, no poison."

"I never said I thought it was poisoned," Lillian stated defensively.

"Then why didn't you eat any?" Alexander was playing with her.

"I was full from breakfast," she said matter-of-factly.

"I see. Well, if I were Snow White's daughter, I'd be leery of food left by a stranger, so I don't blame you. But now you know it's not, and I know you like thackleberries. By the way, sorry for picking all the good ones."

"I knew it was you," she said, picking off a piece of bread. "Well, not *you*, but someone because the animals usually can't get close to the thorns." She popped the bread in her mouth. It was amazing and not just because it was thackleberry bread. There was a hidden ingredient she couldn't quite place but had memory of it from before. A realization came across her face. "You *were* spying on me."

"It does look bad, I'll hand you, but I promise I wasn't spying. I was merely taking advantage of your birthday party capturing most of the kingdom's attention. I usually don't come up this way until it is dark so that I'm not seen, but thackleberries are hard enough to pick during the day, let alone in the dark of night."

Lillian picked off another piece. "Well, I've got news for you, you have been seen. Kind of hard to miss in that white tunic and necklace." She was getting a better look at his necklace now that he was closer. It was a very interesting stone, no bigger than a gold coin and a rich shade of scarlet that almost seemed to give off light even without the sun hitting it.

Alexander allowed himself a smile. "Ah, yes, the 'ghost' in the woods. It was really quite by accident at first, but when I realized it would keep people away from this area while I hunted, I took advantage of it."

Lillian's eyes widened. "Hunted? You mean you kill the animals up here in the forest?"

"I'm sorry to say, Princess, but yes, I do. I have a family to feed."

Lillian's heart sank a little. He was married. She was being silly, why was she sad? She had just met him. It was ridiculous. "Oh," she managed. "How many children do you have?"

"Children?" he thought for a moment. "Oh no, no, I don't have children. I'm not married."

Her heart skipped at this.

"I just mean my parents and our animals. I live on a farm in the southern part of Valanti, close to Thaosbane River. It's about a day's ride at most from here on a good horse."

Lillian looked around and didn't see any horse. Alexander practically read her thoughts. "He's closer to the wall, with the rest of my stuff. I usually set up there when I hunt for an extended period of time. It's a good spot because no one comes around, and it's quiet, like home."

She chewed on that for a moment. "So, you plan on being around for a few days, then?" The thought of meeting up with him again made her heart flutter.

"For a while, yes. Now that spring is here, the animals and vegetation are ripe."

She still didn't enjoy the idea of Alexander putting one of his arrows into one of the...well, she'd just rather not think about it. He probably just takes the ones north of the wall anyway. The ones she doesn't see or know. She needed to change the subject. "So, is that one of the arrows that saved me the other day?"

Alexander brought his quiver around and sat down beside her. "Actually, yes," he said as he pulled out an arrow. "It was this one right here." He handed the smooth blue-silver shaft to her as if it were a delicate flower. It was lighter than she expected and cold to the touch, even in the sun. The feathers were black and at its tip was a smooth, shiny arrowhead, but with small holes around the edges.

"How do you know it was this one?" she asked.

"See those holes?"

She nodded.

"That's a special arrow I use for anchoring. It's a broad head tip, which helps." He pressed the notch and tiny spikes popped out of the arrowhead, which made Lillian jump a little. "It's the impact that engages the spikes. Once it sticks in a piece of wood, there's only one way to get it out. You have to twist the notch like this," he explained as the notch popped back out and the spikes went back into the arrowhead, "and it releases. That's how I knew it would hold you." He handed it back to her to look at.

"This is amazing. I've only seen the dwarves make stuff like this."

"Thanks."

"But, I mean, why all the mystery? Why didn't you approach me then?"

Alexander took a deep breath. "The truth is, I'm not exactly supposed to be talking to you. You or anyone for that matter. My parents said that I was…different, and if people found out about me, they wouldn't understand."

Lillian leaned away just a little. "What do you mean, 'different'?"

Alexander noticed her movement. "I'm not sure exactly, but it's not like I have a disease or anything."

Lillian felt embarrassed. "No, I'm not—I mean, I'm sorry, I just, well, it's interesting is all. And they've never told you why you couldn't see people?"

"No. I've asked them several times, but they always say they'll tell me when the time is right."

Lillian processed this for a moment. "So then, why now, why me?"

"I don't know really. I guess more than anything, I was lonely. I don't have any friends, and I kind of figured you owed me since I saved your life and all," he said with a wink.

"Owed you?" Lillian asked.

He became serious. "You can't tell anyone about me, okay? Not your parents. Not your friends. No one. That's the trade-off. Your life for my secret one." Alexander paused and his gray eyes pierced hers. "And being my friend, if that's not too much to ask."

Lillian felt hypnotized. She couldn't have said no, even if she had wanted to. Which she didn't.

She looked down at the arrow still in her hand. Lillian hadn't told anyone but Alondra, and even she didn't know that the ghost was a person. Keeping him a secret was going to be tough, but for now, she could do what he asked. If nothing more than just to see him again.

"Okay," she said as she smiled. "I think I can handle that, on one condition."

He smiled back. "What?"

She handed the arrow back to him. "Teach me to shoot like you."

"Done." He put the arrow back in his quiver.

"Great, so when do I get to see you again? I mean, when do we start, you know, the lessons...as friends?" Lillian was blushing.

Alexander just smiled. "Well, I'm set up here for a few days, so...how about later tonight?"

Tonight? Ugh, Lillian had forgotten all about her friends sleeping over. They'd know something was up. She'd have to come up with something to tell them without breaking her promise.

"I can't tonight. I have…I have plans."

"Ah, I see. Well, how about tomorrow then, around lunch? I'll have something to go with the thackleberry bread. Meet me by the bridge. Does that work?"

"I don't think that should be a problem."

"All right, then, it's a date."

"A date?" Not that Lillian minded, but he was moving faster than she was used to.

"Yeah, like a meeting, you know, one friend teaching another how to shoot an arrow kind of date."

"Oh, yeah, right, right. Of course."

"Why, what did you think I meant?"

"Nothing, never mind. Look, I'd better get back. I still have sewing lessons for what happened to my dress." Lillian got up. "So, I'll see you tomorrow by the bridge then?"

"I look forward to it," he said with a wink.

"Me too." She blushed again.

She grabbed the bread and wrapped it up, slipped the note into her pocket, and said good-bye. He waved a good-bye too and walked back into the forest. She could see now why people would mistake him for some hovering apparition, especially at night. His trousers blended perfectly with the foliage around him, almost magically, leaving just his white tunic and necklace visible.

Lillian felt elated. She couldn't explain exactly why, but she liked Alexander. He was very comfortable to be around. Relaxing. She smiled all the way back to the castle. She had a date tomorrow…with a ghost. But first she had to get through tonight.

CHAPTER 6: Girlfriends

"All right, Jafria, truth or dare?" Lizzy prodded.

"Truth." Jafria was very sure of herself. Lizzy produced a wicked smile.

"Besides Barrett, who would you most want to kiss?" This brought a giggle from the other girls attending. Along with Sophie, Jafria, and Lizzy were their other friends Gwendolyn, Carissa, Hannah, and Camellia. The sleepover was the queen's idea, as she and the king were holding a dinner party downstairs. Usually, Lillian would attend them, but with all the ceremonies and social gatherings of late, the queen thought it would benefit Lillian to just have a small get-together with her friends.

"Hmmm," said Jafria, "well, to be honest, I've thought about it before…Seth."

This brought a look of astonishment from Lillian.

"Seth, as in my stable boy, Seth?"

"Come on, Lil, you can't tell me you haven't given him a second glance," piped in Camellia.

"Yeah, especially when he takes his shirt off while forking hay. And the sun glistens off the sweat rolling down his arms." Hannah was all but staring at him in her mind now.

"Ew, gross," Lillian gasped.

"Come on, ladies, you can't expect her to notice him. He's practically a brother." Sophie defended her friend.

"Thank you, Sophie."

"Although a really hot brother." Laughter spread through the group, and Lillian just rolled her eyes.

"All right, all right," Jafria calmed them down. "My turn. Gwendolyn, truth or dare?"

Gwendolyn looked nervous. She knew how devious Jafria could be. You could never be safe either way with her.

"Um, dare?" she said hesitantly.

"Are you sure?" Jafria goaded.

Gwendolyn thought for a second. The last time she picked "truth" with Jafria, they had all discovered Gwendolyn had a secret crush on Barrett. Not that it was a big deal, but the girls did tease her about it for a while.

"Yes, dare," she said, more assured.

Jafria couldn't contain her nefarious smile. "Okay, Gwendolyn, I dare you to go up to Sir Laurel and tell him how nice his hair looks."

Gwendolyn, like Lizzy, had a crush on Sir Laurel and immediately started to blush and change her mind.

"Truth, truth, I want truth."

"Ah, too late now." Jafria winked at the rest of the girls.

"Come on, Jafria, he's downstairs with everyone else," Gwendolyn pleaded, looking around at her friends.

"Sorry, Gwenny, you know the rules," Carissa reminded her.

"Yep, if you back down, you have to wear The Clencher on our next outing," said Lizzy. The Clencher was something the girls had found at Carissa's attic one time. It was single handedly the most uncomfortable undergarment known throughout the kingdom. Well at least for the eight of them. It itched. You couldn't breath with it on. And it smelled like old feet. Lizzy had backed out of a Jafria dare one time and wearing The Clencher almost cost her a lifetime of ridicule from a group of boys in town.

Girlfriends

"Ugh, fine," Gwendolyn said with a frustrated resolve. She got up and checked herself over once in the vanity, pulling her hair back in a ponytail. The rest of the girls smiled and got ready to follow her so they could all watch the scene from the balcony.

The girls waited until Gwendolyn was down the stairs before they rushed to the railing. Some noses rested just over the banister, while other eyes peeked through its columns.

Sir Laurel, thankfully for Gwendolyn's sake, wasn't with a large group of guests. She made her way slowly over to him, occasionally looking back up to those peering eyes in the balcony with a pair of pleading ones of her own. But there was no mercy in her friends' faces. Only foolish encouragement saying *Go on, go on.*

The conversation must have ended, because a few of the guests wandered off, leaving Sir Laurel with only a couple of other men Gwendolyn didn't recognize. *Thank the faeries.* His back was to her as she approached. She tapped his shoulder.

"Sir Laurel?"

He turned around. His coat tails and hair waving back as he moved. He had a drink in his hand and from the look on his face, it was definitely not his first.

"Can I help you, m'lady?" his breath wreaked of wine.

Gwendolyn took a breath and mustered up some confidence. She decided to give the girls something to talk about. She drew close to him, putting her hand on his chest and twirling her hair with the other.

"I just love your hair. Can I touch it?" she asked with a flirtatious smile.

Sir Laurel had no clue she was toying with him. He was arrogant that way. Probably even thought he would get something out of it.

"But, of course, m'lady, Sir Laurel would never want to disappoint such a beautiful creature." He leaned forward for her, his hair falling down over his shoulder. Gwendolyn reached out and stroked it.

"Oh, it's so soft, m'lord. However do you keep it so?" Gwendolyn was trying hard not to laugh at this point. It was even too much for her, but Sir Laurel seemed oblivious.

"I can show you if you'd care to join me in my quarters later on," he invited, leaning down even closer.

That was all she could take. A small snicker came out. "Excuse me, m'lord, but I must be going." She hurried away holding back laughter all the way.

It wasn't until she made it back to the room with the others in close pursuit that she fell on the bed, rolling with laughter.

"Oh my gosh, Gwenny, that was awesome!" Lizzy joined her on the bed along with the others. Even Jafria had to give her respect.

"All hail, Gwenny! Queen of truth or dare," Jafria proclaimed.

Just then over the laughter they could hear the orchestra starting up again. Lillian jumped up immediately and curtsied in front of Jafria. And in her most proper princess voice, Lillian asked, "May I have this dance, m'lady?"

Jafria, just as proper with a curtsy of her own, said, "It would be my pleasure, m'lady."

They began to dance and swirl and laugh all about the room with the other girls joining them. It wasn't long, however, before they broke out of the traditional dance style and began to shake and shimmy freestyle. There was a new move called the Goblin everyone was doing. Not appropriate for dinner parties, but perfectly acceptable for sleepovers.

Once the party downstairs started to die down, the girls did too. Lizzy, however, had one more item on her agenda.

"All right ladies, time to play one more game..." She looked around ominously, making sure she had everyone's attention. "Lady of the Night."

This brought a mixture of excitement and trepidation.

"No. No way." Gwen was always a little superstitious.

"Oh, come on, Gwenny, it's just a game," Jafria encouraged.

"Look, we'll all go in together," Hannah reassured her as they all started to get up and make their way to the large mirror in Lillian's washroom.

The myth behind the Lady of the Night had come from the former residents of Drod. Apparently, there was a lady who walked around in the moonlight and wore a dark cloak. She snuck into houses of young girls and stole their beautiful essence to keep her vibrant and attractive, leaving the girls withered and old. No one knew her actual age, but the legend had been around for decades. She was eventually killed by a young husband-to-be whose fiancée had been an unfortunate victim on the eve of their wedding. He hunted the Lady of the Night down and ended her life swiftly. However, even though the Lady's life had ceased to exist, her malevolent soul had not. To this day, one could summon her in a mirror by reciting a chant and then naming her next victim.

Of course it was just superstition, and no one believed the myth to be true, and even less in the ability to conjure her old spirit. Nevertheless, not many ventured to test the myth's validity, with people still blaming the unfortunate passing of a young girl on the Lady.

However, Lillian's trepidation for playing the silly game went deeper. Every time Lillian heard the story, she couldn't help but think of her mom's stepmother, a woman vain to the point of insanity, who had a mirror as well. A magic mirror that was almost the harbinger of her mother's death. Even though Lillian had never actually seen The Mirror or its ghostly image, from time to time, in other mirrors, she swore she could catch a hollow face peering back at her. But she knew The Mirror had been destroyed by the faeries and dwarves shortly after the former queen's demise. Yet, the

51

idea of looking into a mirror and calling upon a spirit still unsettled her.

Despite their foot-dragging, all the girls managed to get in the washroom and shut the door. The room was close to pitch black, and once the initial scares and grabs were over, Lizzy got them settled down.

"All right, all right, time to focus. Everyone look at the mirror."

As everyone got focused, their eyes adjusted to the slight amount of moonlight coming in, and their own ghostly images began to stare back at them.

"Ok, now, you all know the chant. Don't goof around." The room was silent.

Lady of the Night, who walks by moonlight
Stealing young girls whole

About this time, the girls noticed the room was getting brighter, but the light was coming from behind them. Soon, a dark figure emerged out of the light.

"Don't stop," Lizzy urged them on. "It's working." However, some of the girls did stop and started to move toward the mirror, away from the figure.

Bring justice for us, wrong or right
And take this young girl's soul!

At the last instant before they could mention a name, the figure threw open its arms and screamed at the girls.

Sophie was first to throw the door open and bolt into the bedroom, but she was quickly followed by the rest of them. All it took was one foot stepping on another for them to become a hysterical pile on the floor. All of them except for two. Lizzy was standing in the doorway laughing uncontrollably with Carissa, who was standing next to her, wearing a dark cloak.

"You...you...you should see yourselves." Lizzy managed to say through her laughter, tears welling up in her eyes.

It was so dark in the washroom at first no one had noticed Carissa slipping behind them and wrapping up in the dark cloak Lizzy had stashed in the corner. A quick light of the candle Carissa held had given her more than the presence she needed to frighten the girls into a frenzy.

"That's not funny," Gwen stated defiantly as she threw a pillow off the bed at Lizzy. "I think I peed myself."

That brought on more bursts of laughter and pretty soon, they were all laughing in a pile on the floor, even Gwen. As Lizzy and Carissa joined the group, everyone was engrossed in recounting their own version of what had happened and who was more scared. Too engrossed to notice the dark, cloaked figure in the mirror, staring in the direction of the bedroom.

CHAPTER 7: A Sleepless Night

aving done the prerequisite sleepover rituals, the rest of the night wasn't nearly as eventful, but still fun.

Andrew and Ethan shot off a few fizzle-snaps into the room, after which a chase of eight girls after two boys ensued. Unfortunately for the boys, the girls were just getting ready to use Hair Hues, a faery-based color dye. *Andrew always did look good in blue.* Lillian smirked as the girls left the befuddled pranksters looking at their reflections in disbelief.

Back in the room, the girls took turns dying strips of their hair different colors with the magic ink. Shimmer pink was decidedly the favorite color.

Alondra brought up some beverages and snacks for the girls. Hot chocolate with Dragonfire Drops was always a favorite. This prompted the traditional "who could last" challenge, but the twist was when Gwen burped at the end with her fire breath. The contest that followed wasn't anything proper ladies should engage in, but they didn't care. Some of them could have given their boyfriends a run for their money. Ultimately, Lizzy was adorned with a paper crown and blanket cloak, deeming her "Greatest Belcher in All the Land," and would decidedly represent them should a cross-kingdom contest ever occur.

The girls continued to talk about so and so and this and that when suddenly Jafria blurted out, "Okay, Lil, who is he?"

The rest of the girls looked almost as shocked as Lillian. They all knew she was dating Richard, so who was Jafria talking about? Lillian tried to play it off, but she could already feel her cheeks flushing.

"Who is who?" she volleyed back, trying not to sound too defensive.

Jafria looked squarely at her friend. "I don't know who, that's why I'm asking you." Jafria got up and walked around the room, looking around coyly at the other girls as if she were putting Lillian on trial, but in a playful way. "You've been quiet all night. At least, quieter than normal. You haven't even mentioned Richard once—not that that's a big loss, but…" she paused before continuing, "you also haven't really joined in any of the other conversations of the night."

"It's true, Lil, you have been awful quiet," chimed in Lizzy.

Jafria raised up her finger as if the point had been clearly made and circled close to Lillian, stopping right by her. "So, I ask again, oh friend of mine, whom I have shared every secret with since we could talk…who is he?"

Lillian felt her face betray her as she grew bright red. "He's no one…" *Flerb.* "I mean, there's no one, there's no one." Too late. The other girls gathered closer and started bombarding her with questions.

"What's he like?"

"Where'd you meet him?"

"Have you kissed yet?"

"What does he look like?"

"How old is he?"

Lillian backed up. "Guys, guys, guys, listen." They hung on her every word. "It's nothing. *He's* nothing. There's nothing to say because there's nothing going on." *But there was something, wasn't there?* "I've only seen him once and that's it." *Except I see him every time I close my eyes.* "Story's over. He doesn't even live around here, so drop it, okay?" The tone of her voice said it all. Yes, there was somebody, but no, she did not want to talk about it. Lillian was afraid of word getting out that she was seeing someone while supposedly dating Richard. But she was more afraid of breaking her promise to Alexander. And the truth was there was sadly nothing to tell. She and her friends had crushes all the time, and it was no big deal. Yet, for some reason, Lillian felt like this was more than a crush, and if anything were to happen, she couldn't start it out by breaking his trust.

Jafria could see the resolve in her friend's eyes. "Hey, Lil, I didn't mean...I mean, you know I didn't realize that he was serious. I'm sorry. Really."

Lillian realized she had probably reacted too harshly. "It's okay, I...honestly, I don't know what it is." *But I know what I'd like it to be.* "It's...complicated. Especially with me dating Richard, not to mention having the entire kingdom judging the princess and her behavior. So, for now, please trust me when I say it's nothing and don't say anything to anyone. Don't even talk about it amongst yourselves. You know my dad has ears everywhere."

The rest of the girls could attest to her last comment. Because of their affiliation with the princess, at one point in time or another, all of them had been questioned about some rumor or another, and it was never a pleasant ordeal. Amiable as the king or queen could be, they were very protective of their family.

Lillian smiled. "But I promise whenever there is something to tell, you guys will be the first to know."

The girls all promised, knowing Lillian was obviously troubled about the situation. And they all understood, being in similar situations themselves, but knowing hers was even more troublesome having suitors brought to her versus having a regular dating life. They all envied their friend and the life she had, but there were definitely some aspects that weren't as appealing.

After that, things started to die down. The party downstairs had seen out the last of its guests, with a few staying the night. The king and queen jumped in to tell the girls good night and give them some late night leftovers.

The girls had picked through the goodies and started snacking when the king popped his head back around the corner.

"So, Sir Laurel said he had an interesting young lady approach him tonight." Gwen stopped eating mid-bite, the other girls getting wide-eyed with apprehension. Lillian was the only one brave enough to poke for more information.

"Really?" she tossed out as if she had no true interest. "Who was it?" All eyes turned to Gwen.

"He wasn't entirely sure. I think he had had a little too much wine, to be honest. But he did mention her infatuation with his hair." He perused the room then looked back at his daughter. "You wouldn't know anything about that would you, sweetheart?" The rest of the girls tried to continue eating as inconspicuously as possible. Gwen began to chew again.

"Nope, sorry, Dad," Lillian shrugged, not minding the white lie but also realizing her dad probably already knew everything; otherwise, he wouldn't have brought it up. He did like to tease. "We were upstairs all night."

"Hmmm, well, whoever it was must have been a fair maiden because he couldn't talk of much else for the rest of the night." He paused for a moment. Everyone just chewed slowly. "G'night, girls," he smiled and left, which was a good thing because Gwen's bright red face would have given her away. That and the small amount of snickers that rippled through the room.

Everyone got ready for bed, some of them still a little leery to look in the mirror, and settled in. There were comfortable pallets of bedding and pillows for most of the girls. Lillian, Jafria, and Sophie shared the bed, as it was more than big enough for the three of them. Silly noises and good nights thinned out as the girls fell asleep one by one. Lillian was the last to go. Her thoughts were happy but troubled. She couldn't get Alexander out of her mind, but she also couldn't forget her duty as a princess and how things were done. *Alexander probably doesn't even like me, or if he does, it's only because I'm the princess. But it didn't seem that way. He seemed to genuinely be interested in me and not Princess Lillian. Of course, I would be too if I didn't have any friends.* But she felt it was more than that. The way his eyes looked at hers. The way he made her feel nervous and excited at the same time. Her thoughts bounced back and forth for a while on the subject. The "what ifs" and "how would I..." and how it would feel to have his arms around her, until the veil of slumber finally found her as well.

She may have drifted off peacefully, but her dreams were anything but. At first, they seemed to be nothing more than flashes of the night's events; however, they quickly turned malicious. Lillian found herself alone in the dark washroom facing the mirror. She called out to her friends, but no one answered back. Then the chant began.

Lady of the Night, who walks by moonlight
Stealing young girls whole

Even though it was just a dream, it felt real to Lillian, and so did her fear. "Stop. Stop! Please." A dark, hooded apparition began to appear in the mirror. Lillian flipped around, hoping against hope, but there was no Carissa. Back around, the figure became clearer with red eyes peering from under the hood. The chanting continued.

A Sleepless Night

Bring justice for us, wrong or right

The dark figure moved right past Lillian's reflection, getting closer to the surface of the mirror. Lillian could now make out a small red crystal hanging around the neck of the dark figure.

And take this young girl's soul!

Silence. The dark figure was as close to the mirror as it could get. Any closer and it would be in her world. Her feet were frozen. She couldn't scream. She heard the soft whisper of the name of the girl the Lady of the Night would take.

Lillian...

The hooded figure lunged through the mirror, grabbing at Lillian's throat. The instant its hands touched her neck, the hood flew back. It was Alexander.

LILLIAN!

CHAPTER 8: Lessons
May 19

Outfits were strewn about Lillian's bed as she had spent the better half of the morning trying on a variety of clothing. There wasn't really a protocol for what one wears to a secret rendezvous with a mysterious stranger with eyes like a brewing storm. The only thing she had settled on was her favorite pair of leather boots, which were the ones she wore anytime she went into the forest. Seth had even made a small pocket inside them to carry her shears for flower cutting—after losing her fourth pair in a month.

Eventually, she opted for practicality. She wanted Alexander to believe she was taking this seriously and didn't want to convey royalty. He didn't seem caught up in such matters, and she wanted to keep it that way.

As Lillian walked to the bridge to meet Alexander, she couldn't get the image of him reaching out for her from the mirror out of her head. She barely knew him but didn't get a negative vibe from him. Her intuition was something she had inherited from her father.

The king had an uncanny feel for people, which was partly why he was such a good king. He had made some of his better advisors look foolish more than once. Not on purpose, but they had allowed certain "trusted" individuals to have an audience with the king, only to have them rechecked and searched by order of his majesty. He had probably thwarted more assassination attempts on his own life than his guard detail had. A poison vial, a hidden dagger, a secret pouch of powder. All meant to end the king's life by those still loyal to Zoldaine, but none ever got the chance.

Lillian could understand why her dad was so furious about the castle incident. He was partly mad at the Rogues' audacity, but he was angrier with his family being put in danger and him feeling helpless. This was another reason why he was so forceful with any rogue agent the guards managed to capture. Of course, the Valanti Kingdom was not alone in its seemingly ongoing battle with a beaten regime. Both Tapera and Caldera had had their share of run-ins with these self-proclaimed vigilantes.

Lillian's task at hand returned when she caught a whiff of thackleberry bread. As she broke through the clearing that opened up to the bridge, she saw Alexander on the ground with a few other delicacies, and whatever disturbing images lingered in her mind melted away when he smiled at her.

"I didn't realize we were having a picnic," she said, smiling back. "Otherwise, I would have brought something."

"I didn't really plan it, but I thought it would be a nice surprise." He gestured for her to sit next to him. "Plus, believe it or not, archery takes up more energy than you'd expect."

She sat down next to him, breathing in the scents of cheese, bread, and fruit. Alexander also had a pleasant scent to him. Fresh air and sun-warmed skin.

"Here," he said, handing her a piece of thackleberry bread with some cheese. "I've found that Frivoly cheese really complements the flavor."

"Frivoly cheese?" She looked confused. *But you can only get that from the Tapera Kingdom.* She took a bite. Delicious. "And it's still fresh. How'd you manage that?"

"I have a few secrets still left to keep, Princess." He winked at her and took a bite of bread and cheese.

"Please call me Lillian. My friends call me Lillian."

"Well, Lillian, are you ready for your lesson?"

She popped the last bite in her mouth. "Mmm, hmm. You do realize that I'm not completely incompetent when it comes to this, right? I mean, I'm by no means close to your skill, of course—I imagine not many are—but I'm not too bad."

"Well, that's what we're going to find out. Come on." Alexander stood up and offered a hand to help her up.

Handsome and polite. Oh my.

They walked for a minute or so until they came upon Alexander's bow and arrows. About ten paces away, Lillian could see a target he had set up on a tree.

"Okay, first lesson to learn is anybody can shoot how I shoot."

Lillian gave him an incredulous look. "I can tell you're a modest type of person, but let me assure you, there are maybe five people on the entire continent of Azshura who can shoot like you."

"Right now, yes, but I'm hoping to add one more to that number." He nodded to her. "I realize that's hard to believe without thinking about years of practice. But I've found that archery is more about how it feels and flows through you versus the technical aspect. Don't get me wrong—practicing and form are important, but when you relax and visualize hitting the target versus thinking about what you have to do to hit it, the arrow tends to always find its mark."

"So, the other day, when you shot that arrow inches from my head, you weren't thinking about it, you just felt it?"

"Yeah, for the most part."

"You could've killed me. Are you crazy? That arrow was this close to my head." She held her fingers barely apart.

"I felt the breeze past my face." She couldn't believe it and slapped his arm.

"Ow, sorry. And it wasn't that close. But the truth is I saved your life, and had I actually had time to *think* about it, you would have taken a one-way trip down the gorge."

Lillian wasn't really mad because she knew he was right. With the way the wind was blowing, she wouldn't have made it. "Hmmm, well, I guess you did help out a little."

He smiled back. "Thank you for allowing me to assist you."

She headed over to his bow. "All right, so what do you want me to do?" Truth be told, she wasn't quite as skilled as she let on and was a little nervous about embarrassing herself. Being royalty, she didn't get put in too many positions where she lacked confidence about a task or people would have to do it for her.

"Just hit the target. I'll step back and watch your form, and we'll go from there."

"Sounds easy enough." She picked up his bow and nocked an arrow. She noticed his bow was surprisingly light. *I wonder what type of wood this is*. She pulled back what she could, but his bow was tighter than she was used to. She checked her target then released. *Flerb*. The arrow flew far enough but landed past the right side of the tree. She could feel her face redden. She didn't even turn to look at Alexander and what his face said, she just got another arrow and adjusted accordingly. *By the faeries*. This time to the left. Lillian quickly grabbed another arrow, determined not to miss all three.

Thonk.

Well, at least this time I hit the tree.

"I promise I'm better than this," she proclaimed.

"Don't worry about it. I've kind of put you on the spot. First of all, this isn't your bow. An archer's bow is like another appendage. Secondly, you're nervous, which is understandable. But that's what I'm trying to get rid of. If you don't think about it, you don't have time to be nervous." He walked over to some supplies and pulled out another bow. "Let's try this one."

Lillian recognized this wood. A type of yew that was common in her kingdom. It was a little smaller and definitely easier to pull back.

Thonk.

Yes! This time she hit the target.

"See. But I can tell you're still thinking too much about the shot."

She was visibly frustrated. "Ok then, what do I do, Mr. Archer?"

He chuckled. "My friends call me Alexander." She smiled and relaxed a little. "And this still isn't a bow you're used to at all, which makes a big difference and we'll take care of later. But most importantly, just breathe and relax. It's just us." *That doesn't help.* "No contest. No one to impress. Just two friends practicing together. Okay?"

"Yeah, okay." *Okay, if all friends are devastatingly handsome and already expert marksmen.*

"All right. First off, you have good form. It's just not as consistent as it needs to be." He walked up to her. "You see that little red ribbon on the string?" She nodded. She had noticed it before but hadn't really thought anything of it. "That's called the kisser." *Are you serious right now?* She prayed she wasn't blushing. "That is the most important part of this whole process. When you find a comfortable spot, that's the place on the string that you pull back to the corner of your lips every time. Consistency. So, what I want you to do now is just fire off several arrows in a row as fast as you can. Don't worry about the target. Your target right now is speed."

"Okay." She didn't really understand.

"Just trust me."

She did as he asked. A few hit the target, but most went around. *Why is he just standing there like a judgmental parent?* When she was done, he didn't say anything for a moment. *Oh, Fae. He's realizing he's made a mistake. He doesn't want to waste his time with me.*

"Well?" she finally managed.

"Oh, sorry, I was just taking it all in."

"That bad, huh? Look, it's okay if you don't want…"

"What? No, it's not that. I was studying your form. Whoever taught you at least gave you a good foundation."

"Well, I should hope so. We have the best archers in all of Azshura in our guard," she assured him.

"Oh, I meant no offense. It's just a matter of different training is all. They're trained for defense and more slowly moving targets."

"And what have you trained for?" She probably was a little more snide than needed, but he had basically just insulted her family.

"Survival."

Geez, Lillian, you are such an idiot. "I'm sorry, I didn't mean you… it's just…"

"It's okay. Really. I shouldn't have insinuated your royal guard wasn't trained properly." Alexander came over and put a hand on her shoulder. All the awkwardness melted away. "Honestly, don't worry about it."

"Thanks. I know you didn't mean anything by it. You are really good. So, who taught you?"

"My dad mostly. He said I had a natural knack for it, 'Must have fae blood in ya' boy.' But he was really good. He won a lot of tournaments back in his day. Even some of the royal ones."

"What was his name?"

"Berchum."

"Elwood? As in 'Split the Elm' Elwood?"

Alexander chuckled. "Yep, that's him."

65

Lillian had just a few memories of the royal tournaments she attended, but she remembered that name. Alexander's dad hadn't just won some of them, he had won all the ones he had entered. He had earned the nickname Split the Elm Elwood because he, on more than one occasion, had actually split the shafts of his opponents' arrows in the target. He was the only one that could consistently beat Sir Alger, who was now head of the royal security. Alexander's dad wasn't just good. He was the best.

"Was he the one who taught you to shoot inches past my head?" she inquired with a smile.

"Kind of. Like I said, you can only teach so much before it becomes feel. And that you can't teach."

"Do you think I'll ever be able to shoot like that?"

"Let's find out."

What came next surprised Lillian. He came directly up behind her. She could feel his chest on her back, the warmth of his skin radiating against her. Then he put his arms in front of her. He moved his head up to hers, his cheek brushing her ear. *Oh. My. Starlight.* She let out a fluttery breath. Well, if she wasn't nervous before, she was now. The scent of warm sunshine and fresh earth filled her nose. His scent. She felt as if her heart would beat out of her chest. *Just breathe. Breathe.*

"Now, close your eyes."

"What?" She almost turned to question him but quickly realized that would have put her mouth dangerously close to his and that made her heart beat faster.

"Just close your eyes, and visualize the target and only the target."

She closed her eyes.

"Take away the grass, the flowers, the trees, the ground," he murmured. "See the target, hanging there in the middle of nothing. Feel the wind around you, and the target is the only thing you see."

Lillian could picture it. The target hanging in midair. A slight breeze blowing her hair to the left.

His voice was distant now. "Pull in a deep breath, hold it." *Breathe.* "When I say, open your eyes and release." *Hold it. Hold it.* A mere whisper. "Now."

Open.

Release.

Bull's-eye.

CHAPTER 9: Figures in the Forest
June 7

Unwaveringly, Lillian practiced every day. It had been almost three weeks since their first lesson. Alexander had told her he had to go home for a while to take back his game and help his parents out, but he gave her a strict regimen of skills to practice in his absence. She had managed to without fail, juggling her princess obligations where she could. She might have had a little crush, which was part of her motivation, but not all. She was truly enjoying her new hobby and for the first time in a while, she was taking pride in what she was doing. Most of her skills were honed because of royal status. She was well versed in history, poetry, conversation, and which curtsey to use for whom. But she rarely got the opportunity to engage in something she chose. Her parents could see how dedicated she was and how cheerful it made her. Thus far, it had not compromised her duties to her kingdom, so they were encouraging. With that, she took advantage of a lull in her royal responsibilities and grabbed this troll by the tail, so to speak.

Lillian was sore by the second day of practice. But Grayson happily made up balms for the blisters and tense muscles. Eventually, the soreness and blisters turned to strength and callouses. She was bound and determined to impress her new teacher once he got back.

Her interest in archery wasn't too hard to justify, but her new set of equipment was. Lillian couldn't very well explain where she had gotten the new bow and, for sure, not the Calderan steel arrows. Therefore, she carried out a set from the armory, but then always retrieved her new bow and arrows from their hiding spot out in the forest. Unsure of Alexander's return, she got ready for another day of practice. As she headed out to the forest, she let her mind wander back to the day he left.

"Like I said, the key is to not think about it, and the faster you force yourself to go, the less time you have to think versus just react."

He showed her a method to grab her arrow from the quiver and nock it while pulling back in one fluid, fast motion. He demonstrated for her and got off three arrows before the first one had even hit its mark. That and they had each hit the bull's-eye on the target, one of them splitting her own. *Yep, Split the Elm Elwood.*

"Hey, that was my bull's-eye," she sounded disappointed. "What if I wanted to keep that arrow?"

"A good archer is not known by his arrows, Lillian, but his aim. If your aim is true, you'll hit your target."

She smiled and bowed a little. "Yes, oh wise teacher."

He smiled back. "Good, I'm glad we got that cleared up."

She retorted, "Maybe I just wanted a token to remember the day by." *Did I just say that?*

"Well, hopefully, there will be plenty of other days and bull's-eyes to remember."

Did HE just say that? She blushed and looked quickly away before he could notice.

He watched her practice for a bit and came over to correct her posture and form a few times until she seemed to be getting consistent.

"Good. Now, I want you to do this as a warm-up a hundred times before you fire."

"One hundred times?"

"Yep, twice a day."

"Twice a…you really must think a princess has nothing better to do."

"On the contrary. If you didn't, I'd say two hundred times four times a day."

"That's ridiculous."

"That's practice. Surely you understand the importance. All the rituals and routines you've had to go through for dinners and meeting dignitaries?"

No kidding. She recalled a particular guest her father had from the Tardilian Lands. There were so many things to do and not do so as to not embarrass her family or insult the ambassador. For two weeks straight, she and Andrew had had to endure etiquette courses. She knew they were important to her father, so she suffered through them. But Fae be true, she was pretty sure her father was glad to see his guest go after a few days. He spent the next three lounging around the castle in his robe and slippers.

"All right, I'll do what I can."

"Try to make a cadence of sorts."

"A cadence?"

"Yeah, like a rhythm. It'll help with the consistency. When I first started, my dad taught me 'Shoes, shoulders, sight, select, slide, sigh, shoot.' Basically, it helps you remember the essentials. Shoes and shoulders, make sure your feet and body are lined up. Sight, find your target. Select, grab your arrow and nock. Slide the string back, let your breath out, and release."

"You go through all that before you shoot?"

"Well, no, not anymore. I mean, I guess I do but just subconsciously. But yeah, when I started, it was slow and steady. The form is the foundation for everything. Without it, you won't hit the fat side of a bear's rear end." Lillian laughed along with Alexander.

That memory brought a smile to her face as she practiced. *Shoes, shoulders, sight, select, slide, sigh, shoot. 58.* He had made an adjustment with the smaller bow and left it with her, along with a couple of Calderan arrows to practice. "But don't rush it. Better not taught than ill taught. Trust me."

Shoes, shoulders, sight, select, slide, sigh, shoot. 59.

When she asked what that meant, all she got was "You'll see," and a wink.

She had to admit she was getting faster. She wasn't sure how well she would hit a target, but she had to look intimidating, which counted for something, right? Now she was just shooting to gauge distance as per instruction. *Shoes, shoulders, sight, select, slide, sigh, shoot. 60.* She had to admit Alexander's methods seemed a little unorthodox, but after the second week, she could see results. She was able to cluster her arrows within about a one-foot circle at a short, medium, and long range, which in the beginning was only about thirty paces, but had since increased to fifty. *Shoes, shoulders, sight, select, slide, sigh, shoot. 61. Yeah, think again, Rogues. Princess Lillian's not just another pretty face. She's...*

Snap.

Lillian spun around drawing an arrow immediately in one fluid motion. A small rabbit came out from under a thackleberry bush. Even though she knew she probably wouldn't have hit it, Lillian quickly lowered the bow. A moment passed. The rabbit gave her an inquisitive look and then hopped away. Her hands were shaking. Her whole body was shaking. But then she took it all in. The pure motion she had. Not thinking about it. Simply acting. *Alexander is a better teacher than I thought.* She took a couple of breaths and then allowed herself a smile. *So, that's what he's talking about.*

She had finished her set and had taken a pause for some water when some movement caught the corner of her eye. As she turned to look, she saw it was no animal this time but a person. And not just a person but people. Two men, to be exact, about 150 paces out. Lillian was fairly certain they had not noticed her. *What are they doing all the way out here beyond the castle?* She decided to find out.

Lillian was able to keep her distance well enough while still keeping the two figures in sight. She concluded they hadn't seen her because they had not bothered to lower their voices. The wind was blowing toward her from their direction. She couldn't quite make out what they were saying, but they were definitely arguing.

The taller one was really letting the shorter one have it. Lillian usually wasn't one to be the mouse in the walls, but the entire situation intrigued her. She never saw anyone this far north of the castle, let alone two people having a heated conversation. She had to get closer.

Once again her familiarity with the area proved beneficial. She moved with ease, barely making a disturbance. She had closed about half the distance when they stopped.

"Everything…place. There's…no…" The taller man was very animated.

"…I…" the other man cowered. Lillian couldn't tell if he was intimidated because of his lack of comparative height or if it was just his demeanor. The wind whipped words toward her, but only enough to weave together bits of phrases.

I have to get closer.

She stood up to move but met resistance.

Someone had grabbed her from behind.

She turned to face her foe, but the assailant had her across the chest. She dug her feet in and twisted harder.

Crack!

A large branch snapped away from the tree she was next to, having caught on her bow. *Thank the Fae.* She had gotten so focused on the two men, she had forgotten about the extra appendage strapped around her back.

Heart racing, she tried to conceal herself from the two figures.

They had to have heard that. What if they find me?

She waited a moment and listened.

"… don't care…"

"I'm not… fault if…"

She readjusted her bow, more mindful of it now, and moved on. The strangers moved on as well. *Where could they possibly be going? There's nothing out here.*

A few moments later, the men stopped again by an outcropping of boulders that joined up with the Kraneth Mountains a few leagues away. Lillian moved to within fifteen paces. Close enough to hear their conversation and then some. Apparently, the ruffians did not get the opportunity to bathe on a frequent basis. Lillian stifled a cough and strained her ears. She wasn't used to hearing common tongue much, but she could make out most of it.

"I told you it's the best chance we'll get," the taller man insisted in a now-obvious Dainian accent.

Peering through a bush, Lillian could now get a little more detail about her visitors. They were both dressed in similar garb—brown trousers, dirty tunics, and leather boots. The tall one had a rope tied around his waist. Definitely for keeping his pants up versus decoration. Lillian thought Slim was an apt nickname, though "emaciated" might have been a better description. He may have been six feet tall but no more than 120 pounds. *And that's if his clothes were soaked.* Unshaven, dark, oily hair and dirt smudges abounded.

"But it's in the middle of town. It'll be crowded. We'll get nicked for sure," the short one answered back.

Pork, Lillian decided to call him, was a good deal shorter and maybe 100 pounds heavier. But it wasn't just because of his portly nature Lillian chose "Pork." His nose turned up just enough to resemble that of a pig, and she swore every time he spoke she caught a whiff of burnt bacon.

"That's why it's called a plan, dragon dung." Slim hit Pork upside the head. "Besides, no one is gonna see you, you just 'ave to make sure the tunnel is clear." Slim reassured his portly friend.

Pork nodded in agreement. "I know. I know. It's just the king has really stepped up the security. And if we get caught, he'll…"

"We won't get caught. And security is the whole reason why it 'as to be now or never. Don't you fink 'e 'asn't fought this frough?"

He. He who? Whatever they were talking about didn't sound just like a simple, well, whatever they were talking about.

"'E's got eyes and ears everywhere, my friend," Slim continued. "Trust me. Trust 'im. 'E's been waiting a long time for this."

"But why did we have to alert them at the castle? It doesn't make any sense to put them on their guard." Pork still seemed unsure.

Slim leaned in close to Pork. "Misdirection, my friend. All great magicians use it, and this is just the opening act. Come on, let's go join the others for a game of tumbler. It'll take your mind off things."

The two started to walk off again around the bend of some boulders. Lillian did not like the sound of any of this. *Others? Magicians? What are they talking about?*

She crept out of hiding when she was sure they were out of sight around the corner. She got to the boulders and listened for them. Nothing. She decided to peek around the corner. No one. *What? But where did they go?*

The two had pulled off their own magic trick. They were nowhere to be seen, and there was nowhere to have gone. There was solid rock on one side and open field on the other. They had simply disappeared.

Lillian searched for a good half hour before finally giving up. She knew there had to be some sort of secret passage with a hidden latch or button somewhere, but for now, it eluded her. More time had passed than she had realized as her shadow stretched before her. She decided to head back to the castle and would continue practicing tomorrow.

Lillian's mind wandered on what the two men had been discussing. And what would she tell her father? *I should tell him. This is probably important, right? Or is it really? I mean, what do I truly have to tell him? They sound like they're just planning on stealing something from somewhere in town. That kind of stuff doesn't happen often, but it does happen. That's really not something to bother him with. What would he do? Close off the forest? That would mean no more lessons. No, I'll tell Sir Alger. He can handle it. It's really his job after all. No reason to bother Father with this.*

Even though Lillian had come to a logical conclusion about today's events, there was still something in the back of her mind that didn't sit right. She couldn't quite place it, but until she did, she'd just have to trust Sir Alger would take care of it.

She was so lost in her thoughts that she barely noticed the buck that had been following her. He was a good size, ten point if Lillian saw right. He was only about thirty paces behind her. As she turned to get a good look at him, he stopped. She didn't recognize him, which was odd. A deer that big had to have been around for a while, and Lillian was almost sure she had never seen him, especially when he started trotting again, getting closer. He had a strange black marking on his chest. And his eyes. *Are his eyes...?* But Lillian never got a chance to finish her thought. The massive, unfamiliar buck started to charge right for her.

CHAPTER 10: Motherly Advice

She couldn't move. The buck covered half the distance before Lillian's brain fully registered what was happening. He advanced another ten paces before her body responded. She felt a point from the antler nick her tunic as she dove out of the way.

The buck reared around and came back for a second attack.

Heart pounding, lungs heaving, Lillian got up and ran. Which direction she was unsure. She hoped toward the castle, but at the moment, she really didn't care as long as it was away from the rampaging animal. She was now sure she had never seen it in her forest before.

She ran as fast as she could, but the buck was gaining ground fast. Lillian tried to weave in between the trees, but her maneuvers were useless. She did the only thing she could think to do—climb. The first decent tree she saw, she scrambled up. It wasn't big, but the branches were thick and close enough she could climb up quickly. She made it about seven feet before the raging animal rammed its head into the trunk. It hit the trunk with such amazing power the blow almost knocked Lillian completely out of the tree. She climbed a few more feet and secured herself before the buck struck again.

WHAM!

Incredibly, the beast hit the tree with even more force than the first time. The creature backed up again to deliver another blow. Lillian braced herself.

WHAM!

The tree started to lean.

This is crazy! What could she do? She couldn't climb back down. But if she stayed there, the tree would fall with her in it. There was only one other option, and Lillian could hardly stomach it. But with time quickly running out, she was left with no other choice.

She pulled the bow from behind her back and secured herself as tight as she could with her legs wrapped around the branches and her back up against the tree.

WHAM!

The tree would fall on the next hit. It was now or never.

She quickly pulled an arrow back and aimed. The buck stopped for a moment and looked up at her, daring her, and started to charge. Lillian pulled her breath in, held it, and released.

Her shot was true.

The arrow hit the buck between the antlers. Its momentum carried it forward to the base of the tree, which was now leaning at a decent angle.

Lillian waited for what seemed an eternity before climbing down. She stayed clear of the buck. She wanted to look it over but changed her mind now that she was back on the ground. The adrenaline rush had worn off, and she was shaking now. She just wanted to get back to the castle.

She would come to regret it later, not examining the beast, because it would haunt her dreams. *Those eyes.* She would never be sure now, but before the creature charged her, those eyes pierced her soul. Burning red eyes.

Lillian managed to get back to the castle but how, she couldn't remember. One moment she was in the forest, and the next, she was back at the castle.

The last sliver of sun was just slipping behind the horizon. Dinner would be getting underway, but she didn't feel like eating with everyone. She didn't feel like anything. She was numb, not just physically but mentally. The adrenaline rush had left her body spent and exhausted. She mindlessly walked to the kitchen and let one of Pierre's assistants know she wouldn't be joining the rest of the family tonight. She mumbled something about being tired and that she'd grab something later.

Lillian made it back to her room somehow. It was then she finally broke down, collapsing to her knees. Tears welled up in her eyes. *What had happened?* The day's events ran through her mind like a gushing waterfall. Now more than ever, Lillian needed someone to talk to, but she couldn't go back downstairs like this. She thought about Alondra and how she might come bring her dinner, but who Lillian really wanted to talk to was…

"Sweetie? Are you okay?"

Lillian turned with tears trickling down her face. Snow White shut the door just in time to receive a running embrace from her daughter. Now, in the comfort of her mother's arms, Lillian's emotions poured out. Tears cascaded down her cheeks. Through uncontrolled sobs, she managed to get out pieces: "In forest… (sniff)… two men… I killed it… (cough)… there was nothing I could do…" Even pieces she didn't mean to share: "I don't want to marry Richard." Lillian pulled back and looked at her mom through watery eyes. "I don't want to marry Richard, Mom. I don't love him." She put her head back onto her mother's chest. "I don't love him."

"Shhhh, shhh. It's okay, sweetie. It's okay, Lillian. No one's marrying anyone." Snow White led her daughter to the bed. "Here, honey, just sit down for a moment. It's okay. Let it out. It's okay." Snow White stroked Lillian's hair while they just sat for a moment.

Lillian took a few deep breaths and wiped her face off. "Thanks, Mom." Lillian sat up. "But how did you know?"

"I ran into Anabell while she was setting the table, and your place was empty. She told me you had come into the kitchen."

"But I didn't look like this then." Lillian allowed a small chuckle as she caught her reflection in the vanity.

Snow White smiled at her daughter. "Sometimes, a mother just knows. You'll understand someday."

Lillian was quickly recalling what she had blurted out during her breakdown. *Oh no.* "Mom, about what I said. I didn't mean…"

"It's okay, Lillian. I only caught some things, but you might want to clear it up for me. It sounded like you killed two men in the forest."

"What? No, no." *Did I mention the men?*

"Well, I figured that," her mom said with a knowing look. "Why don't you just take a deep breath and tell me what's on your mind."

Lillian took her time, choosing her words carefully. She didn't want to lie to her mom, but once again, she was afraid she wouldn't be allowed back into the forest if her parents knew about the two men she had seen disappear. She disguised that truth by saying it was just a play on her mind. A couple of trees and bushes that reflected weirdly in the light. She didn't, however, leave out the part about the crazed buck that had attacked her, which brought on another bout of tears and sobs. Snow White held her daughter again and consoled her.

"It was just so… so… I don't know. There was something about its eyes. I've never seen anything like it,

Mom. I know these animals. You know these animals. I'd never seen it before."

"It does sound very strange." Snow White had a distant look on her face. "But it's not completely unheard of."

Lillian looked surprised. "What do you mean?"

"Well, it's been a very long time, almost since you were born. But when Zoldaine was still in power, there were stories of animals that came from the other side. Animals that didn't act ... right." The queen took a deep breath. "I'll have Sir Alger look into it. In the meantime, I want you to stay closer to the castle."

What?

"No! I mean, sure, but... like you said, it's been a really long time. I'm sure it'll be fine. I just wandered too close to the wall is all." Lillian was hoping that would be enough to convince her mom to change her mind.

Snow White looked at her daughter. "Lillian," *Oh no, what?* "What's really going on, sweetie? Just because I rule a kingdom doesn't mean I don't notice what's going on with my own family. You've been going to the forest a lot lately. I know you've been practicing your archery, which is fine, but why the sudden interest? You can practice here at the castle just as easily as you can out there."

Lillian was afraid of this. Her mom, although naïve at times, was very insightful.

"Oh, Mom," Lillian said, tears welling up again. "I don't know what to do."

"What, sweetie? I promise you can tell me. Right now, you're just my daughter, and I'm just your mother. No titles here. So, please just tell me. I won't judge."

Lillian wiped a tear from her cheek. "You never do, Mom." Lillian took a deep breath. "I met someone."

"Met someone? At the party? What happened to Richard? You are still dating Richard, right?"

"Yes, Mom, yes. Richard and I are still dating, but ..."
How could she put this?

"But you don't have any feelings for him," said her mom. *Naïve but insightful.*

"Yes," Lillian said, her eyes welling up with fresh tears. "Yes."

"And you're not sure what to do about it."

"Yes." She should have known to talk to her mom about this a long time ago.

"Sweetie. I know I didn't have to go through all this. But I do understand more than you might think. I'm always battling the responsibilities of my kingdom versus the ones to my family. Why do you think I make sure to bake your cakes personally?"

Lillian smiled.

Snow White pulled her daughter up next to her and smiled. "Now, I know they don't always turn out the best." Lillian snickered "But it's my way of showing you kids how much I love you."

"I know, Mom, and we really do appreciate it. They've definitely made for some interesting anecdotes during parties."

"Ah." Snow White playfully pushed her daughter down into the pillows. "Well, I'm just glad this year's didn't chase you around."

They both had a good laugh at that.

"But seriously, Lillian, I just want you to be happy. And if you're not happy with Richard, then don't date him. No one said you had to marry him."

"Really?" Lillian couldn't begin to tell her mom how good it felt to hear her say that.

"Of course."

"I just thought, now that I'm eighteen..."

"What? That your father and I couldn't wait to get the castle to ourselves and have you married off?"

"Well, not like that, but…"

"Sweetie. I want you to enjoy your life. I want you to have choices and experiences. But I never want you to feel pressured that you have to live a life you don't want or that I expect you to be me."

"But I do, Mom. I do want this life. I'm sorry, I didn't mean… I guess I never realized how much you lost. How much you didn't get to experience. Oh, Mom, I don't want to leave. I mean, someday but not right now."

"Well, I don't want you to leave right now either," the queen reassured her daughter as she kissed her on the forehead. "And please know that I don't regret any experience I had or didn't have. That's not what I meant. I love the life I have with your father and how it happened. Because it all led to right here, where I have a wonderful life and a beautiful family. Have there been rough times? Sure. Nobody's life is perfect. Especially for royalty. But that's the interesting part about it all. You never know where choices or experiences are going to lead you. All you can do is make the right choice in that moment. If you're true to yourself, then you'll never have to look back with regret because you were the best person you could be at the time." Lillian had forgotten how much she enjoyed talking to her mom.

"I tell you what, let's have a day together. It's been too long for us girls to just get out and shop. How does tomorrow work? I have some things to do, but I'm sure your father can handle them."

"I'd like that." Lillian was going to practice again, but she didn't think she could after today.

"Then it's settled. After breakfast, we'll head out and have a little mother-daughter bonding." She gave Lillian one last big hug. "And Lil', no pressure, but whenever you want to tell me who he is, I'm here to listen."

"Ok, Mom, I will. In the meantime, will you do me a favor?"

"Sure, sweetie, what is it?"

"Don't tell Dad about any of it. He's got enough on his plate right now, and there's no need to worry about me."

"It'll stay between us girls," the queen said with a wink. "Get some rest. I'll have Anabell bring up something to eat."

"Thanks, Mom."

Lillian never found out what Anabell brought up. She had fallen asleep, hoping not to be haunted by red eyes.

CHAPTER 11: A Trip to Town
June 8

ven though Pierre had prepared yet another delicious spread, the ladies had a light breakfast. Just some fruit and a croissant to tide them over. They hadn't discussed it, but both of them knew they'd be eating at Madame LeMarc's for lunch. The lunch menu was good, but it was the pastries they were saving room for. Pierre was an excellent chef, and Snow White and the entire royal company had praised him plenty for his immaculate delicacies. But even he was impressed by Madame's tortes, tarts, and soufflés—recipes that had been in the LeMarc family for generations, passed down from mother to daughter.

Lillian and Snow White usually dressed in regular clothes for the village. Today Lillian donned one of her favorite sundresses she had actually made with Ophelia's help, of course. It was a beautiful fabric of cornflower blue with a print of white daisies. Her mom wore a flowing skirt of sunshine yellow and green with a flattering sleeveless white top. They would naturally garner some attention from the locals, but they didn't seclude themselves in the castle like the previous queen did. The villagers were used to seeing their royal family as one of their own. King Harry was often a favorite to win the pie-eating contest during the Dawning

Festival, the yearly celebration of Zoldaine's defeat. Seeing the king's face covered in thackleberries was not a sight one easily forgets.

By the time the ladies made it to the stables, Seth already had the horses saddled up. Lillian was glad it was such a nice day. She preferred riding out in the open on Patches over the carriage any day. She had talked to Grayson earlier that morning about the weather, and he had said the stars showed no sign of rain for a few days. Snow White rode Mercury, an almost-silver horse that was as fast as the wind. Not faster than the Kretchers', of course, but a close second.

"You two ladies stay out of trouble, now," Seth winked as he assisted the queen.

"We make no promises, Seth," said the Queen, winking back.

Seth walked over to Lillian. "Hey Lil', would you bring me back something from LeMarc's? I've been craving one of her fruit tarts lately."

"And what makes you think we're going to LeMarc's?" Lillian asked defensively.

Seth just grinned. "C'mon, you've got strawberry chocolate petit four written all over your face."

Lillian had to return the smile. Seth knew her too well. "We'll see, Mr. Hamilton."

The ride into town was a short one but gorgeous indeed. Soon after her marriage to Harry Charming, Snow White had redecorated the castle from top to bottom, including the path to town. She had wanted no reminder of her evil stepmother lingering anywhere. Now the trail was adorned with a variety of foliage. Everything was in bloom. The air was sweet with the blossoming flowers. The Valanti Kingdom was known for its agriculture. The Menari River, which began in Drod and forked at the Kraneth Mountains, had more tributaries in Valanti than in any of the other kingdoms, which made for rich farming. One of the kingdom's top exports was thackleberries, which were pretty much indigenous to Valanti. The others being diamonds and other precious gems mined from the Cuanaic Range on the Valanti side of Kraneth Mountains, thanks to the dwarves.

As they approached the gate entrance the structured brick pathway slowly turned to cobblestone. Just beyond the gate was a different world. People of all types wandered around shopping, selling, or simply enjoying the day. Trees were replaced by simple wooden stands of local farmers peddling their wares. Anything from flower bouquets to homemade treats to wooden carved toys. Lillian and her mother always stopped here for a minute because one never knew what could be found. Snow White found an interesting wooden puzzle for Andrew, and after perusing some colorful embroidered shawls, Lillian found two that would complement their outfits. And Snow White insisted a couple of pieces of honey fudge wouldn't spoil their appetite as she popped one in her mouth.

Valanti Village wasn't always a sight to behold. During the evil queen's reign, there was little development and few prosperous shops. Trade increased after her death, but the real boom came after Zoldaine's defeat as the population of each kingdom increased from the thousands of Dainian refugees. Over the last ten years, the village had tripled in size. It was Henry, Alondra's husband, who had come up with breaking the village into various boroughs. The idea was brilliant, as most of the residents had already begun to associate different areas with their particular offerings. There was Old Towne, the original village; New Towne, the nicer and more-developed residences; The Arts, with shops and entertainers; Cuisine Quarter, which was food central; and a place now colloquially called The Trenches, which was a bit rougher part of town. These boroughs formed a semicircle down from the castle. The arrangement could be a little disorienting if you weren't a local but a giant fountain in the middle made it easy to find your way. Falloren Fountain was a collaborative design by the faeries and dwarves—an amazing structure that magically shot bursts of water 100 feet high on every hour. The dwarves had diverted part of the Falloren Tributary underground so the fountain stayed full year-round. However, the dwarves weren't satisfied with just one attraction. Next to the fountain, several complex pedaling devices were designed to allow anyone, children mostly, to pump water from the underground river through a network of tubes that sprayed out into a dazzling display. Except for the makeshift bikes, all of the mechanics were underground, leaving the surface flat. This gave the illusion of the water magically coming from the ground, enticing young and old to play in the dancing water on a nice day.

Today was just such a day. As the ladies made their way through town, children of various ages took turns pedaling as they played a game of chicken with which spout would squirt next. Soon, the aromas of Cuisine Quarter wafted through the air.

"Mmmm, smells like Galen's in full swing today," Snow White took in a deep breath.

The castle's chefs prepared some of the best delicacies on the continent, but there were shops and eateries in the village holding on to trade secrets that couldn't be matched. Galen's Smoke Shop was one of those places. The actual proprietor was Galen IV. Not only had the family's secret recipe for smoked meat been handed down, but the namesake as well. Most of the business was from people bringing in their own meat. But the real treat was Galen's own personal batch. Even the location of where the family hunted was kept a secret.

Galen's smoky scents soon melded with others. Newly baked bread from Flanagan's, succulent fruits and vegetables from up the road at Thackleberry Fresh Juices. Lillian's mouth was already watering, and she hadn't even caught a whiff of LeMarc's sweet temptations.

The beginning of the Cuisine Quarter was marked by the Three Roosters, Valanti's famous inn. While modest back in the day, after the boom it flourished into a must-stay for visitors. The amenities were adequate enough for most, but it was Madame and Monsieur Gosnell's good food and pleasant nature that brought back repeat customers. Their simple meals and excellent ale were praised so much they eventually expanded the lower level to accommodate even more customers.

The ladies took their horses to the stables across from the Three Roosters to be boarded for the day and headed to LeMarc's. It was a few buildings down on the left. The modest store was painted a faded green and pink. A couple of tables and chairs were outside for customers to enjoy the day along with their treat. Inside were several shelves adorned with various packaged goodies and the owner standing behind a counter with a glass display featuring several cakes and pies to buy by the slice.

There was a moderate line but it moved quickly.

"Your Majesties, so good to see you again." Adelade LeMarc's accent was as endearing as her smile.

"The pleasure is always ours, Adelade."

"Well, I hate to mix business with pleasure, but has there been any more on the uninvited guests?"

Snow White had been dealing with this question a lot lately. Luckily her husband was very diplomatic, and over the years, that diplomacy had rubbed off on her.

"The investigation is wrapping up. Consensus is, it was simply some pranksters. Albeit ones with unpleasant taste. We're just thankful no one was seriously hurt."

"Fae be praised. So, what will satisfy the royal taste buds today?"

"Adelade, you never make it easy. I think today we'll have the croquet croissant with ham, two fruit sides, and—what's the dessert special?"

"Oooh, today is the chocolate mousse soufflé with just a drizzle of raspberry sauce."

Snow White turned to ask Lillian if that was okay, but the look in her daughter's eyes said it all.

"We'll take two," said Snow White, smiling back.

"And a couple of fruit tarts," Lillian added

"Will that be all?" Adelade asked in her knowing way. Lillian couldn't resist. "And a couple of strawberry chocolate petit fours if you have them." *Curse you, Seth.*

"I might just have a couple left," Adelade winked and left to make up their meal.

"Mom, I'm gonna go grab some juices from Thackleberry and be right back."

"Okay, sweetie."

Lillian went down to the next corner for the juice. She was almost there when someone hurried out of the alley with full arms. The collision was unavoidable. Both parties went to the ground, and various packages went in all directions.

"Oh my goodness, I am so sorry. I'm such a klutz. Born with troll feet, my momma said." About the time the stranger looked up to see exactly *who* he had bumped into, Lillian smelled the familiar aroma of bacon.

Pork.

"I, I, I, Your Highness, I, I'm terrible sorry. I should have been more careful. It's just I couldn't see where I was going, but that's no excuse. I should have been more careful." Pork avoided eye contact at all costs and hurriedly started to gather up his belongings.

Lillian managed to hide her surprise at who she just ran into. "It's okay, really. Here, let me help."

She grabbed a few of the things strewn farther away. It was an interesting array of fabrics, some types of paint, and a large purple cloth.

Pork quickly took them from her. "Thank you, I can get it, thank you. Really, it was my fault. I'll get it."

Lillian noticed he was hurt. Regardless of what he was involved in, she had to help. "Your hand is bleeding. Let me get a cloth."

"That's really not necessary, Your Highness. It's just a scratch, honest. I'll be okay." And for the first time, Pork looked directly at her. His eyes were sad, almost apologetic. "Thank you for being so kind. I really must be going, though. I..." Lillian could tell he wanted to say something, but he glanced up and something else stopped him. "I have to go." He shuffled off with his things in tow, eager to be somewhere.

That somewhere turned out to be another alley just a few blocks down, Lillian found out. He was just standing looking around, as if he were waiting on someone. Lillian moved toward him nonchalantly. Sure enough, only a few seconds later, Pork was joined by a petite girl and Slim. The girl was dressed in some kind of uniform Lillian recognized but couldn't place. Slim said something angrily to Pork, hit him upside the head, and the trio hastily darted between the buildings into the alleyway. Lillian quickened her pace to follow. She rounded the corner just in time to see them duck around to the left. Almost jogging, she made it to the end of the alley and turned left.

Nothing.

They had disappeared again! Lillian couldn't risk searching this time. Her mom would be wondering where she was, and she didn't feel very comfortable being in the back alleys, even during the daylight. She made a note of the surrounding buildings. *Maybe Seth would come back with me.* She wasn't sure why, but she had a feeling the trio was somehow connected to the "prank" at the party. The king had discussed with her what to say, much like her mom's response, should someone ask, but he had also explained his concern.

"It may be nothing," he had told her, "but I feel something…lurking." Lillian hadn't said anything at the time, but she agreed with her father's suspicion. "So, stay sharp, Lily Flower. You're my eyes and ears." He used to say that when she was little and she wanted to help protect the family. Well, now she had something to report. Twice she had run into these characters. And twice they were secretive and shady. The rest of the day was rather uneventful comparatively. Lillian kept an eye out for the trio all day but never saw them again. Eventually, she talked to her mom about Richard and what she should do. Snow White took a moment. "Well, I never really had to go through this, but I'd say be gentle. It can't be easy being turned down by any girl, let alone the princess. You guys have your big date tomorrow night, right?"

"Yeah, with Jafria, Sophie, and Lizzy."

"I'd say after that. Have a good time. Don't worry about it. I know that's easy to say, but it'll all work out. It usually does."

"Thanks, Mom."

Snow White reached a hand out to her daughter's. "Anytime, sweetie. I know I'm busy being queen most of the time, but I'm your mother first, and I always have time for you."

Lillian thought about mentioning Alexander but decided she'd deal with Richard first. She wasn't even sure when she'd see Alexander again anyway.

That question was answered once she got home. Looking out her bedroom window, she spotted a white *A* on their rock.

CHAPTER 12: Target Practice
June 9

Alexander was back, and it was all Lillian could do to sleep, let alone not inhale her food at breakfast like a starved animal. But somehow she managed both and headed out to meet him.

She all but jogged to where their first lesson took place. She was eager to show off her new skill and talk to him about the buck. But mostly she was eager just to see him.

She kept telling herself that her excitement was just the newness of it all. *But it's more than that.* He treated her with respect but not like a princess. It was refreshing. She barely knew him, but she felt that she'd known him much longer. She felt comfortable with him. With other guys she had dated, she always knew there was an underlying motive of marrying a princess. She couldn't fault them for it, though. Power and prestige attracted many people. Usually the wrong people. Richard wasn't like that, she knew, but she didn't have a connection with him. There was something about Alexander. *He likes me for me.*

The smell of thackleberry bread greeted her nose as she drew near. As she came into the clearing, she saw Alexander sitting and messing with some of his arrows. *Does he know how gorgeous he is?*

"Good morning," Lillian said, slowing down and trying not to seem so eager.

"Lillian," said Alexander. He smiled. "I wasn't sure when you'd show up. Bread?"

"Yes, please." Just like before, it had something in it she couldn't quite place, but it was still delicious. "No cheese this time?" she teased.

Alexander reached into his pack, pulling out a wedge of cheese. "Is this what you're looking for?" he said with a wink.

He cut a slice and handed it to her. It was ripened just like before.

"Okay," she said between bites. "You have to tell me how you have good Frivoly cheese. And what exactly is in your thackleberry bread?"

"So inquisitive. I tell you what. I'll answer one question if you show me your skills."

"Deal," she said as she flipped the last piece of bread in her mouth.

She was surprised at how nervous she was. She'd only done this for the past three weeks; now it should be routine.

She got her bow and quiver and headed over to the spot she'd been shooting from. She took a deep breath and went through her cadence. *Shoes, shoulders, sight, select, slide, sigh, shoot.* She did this three times for each distance, each time she got a little faster and smoother. And not a word from Alexander. *I knew it, I'm doing it wrong. Troll dung.*

Lillian released the last arrow, placing it in her cluster. She stood there for what seemed like forever, unsure of herself, but still heard nothing from Alexander. She finally turned around to make sure he was even watching.

"So…" Lillian expected something.

Alexander shook his head a little as if waking from a trance. "Oh, sorry. Sorry. I was just taking it all in."

"If we're going to keep doing this, we're going to have to break you of this silence habit."

Alexander walked over to her. "I know, I know, my mom says the same thing. I'm sorry. I was just..."

She cut him off. "Taking it all in, yeah, yeah, I heard." It came out curter than she meant and she instantly regretted it. She tried to give a look conveying she was only half-kidding.

He put his hand on her shoulder, and that same shiver of pleasure went down her spine. "What I was going to say is, I was just so impressed I didn't know what to say."

Her heartbeat picked up.

"Really? I mean, *really* really? You're not just saying that because—"

"—because you're the princess?" His eyebrow raised, then he smiled. "No, Lillian, I'm not. I wish now I would have given you more to do. What you've accomplished with your clusters is remarkable. I know archers who have shot for years who couldn't make clusters like that."

Now she was blushing. "It's not that big a deal. I'm not even hitting a target."

"Well, I hope to change that today. I take it the bow's working out. I adjusted the strength a little higher to give you some more distance. Looks like it worked." He started walking to retrieve her arrows and she followed.

"Yeah, it was a little stiff at first, but I've probably added a good twenty paces since you left," she bragged a little. "So, I believe you owe me an answer."

"Most definitely, after that display. So, which is it, the secret recipe or the perfectly aged Frivoly?"

Lillian was pretty sure she'd get the bread eventually, but how he managed to keep the cheese from spoiling was really stumping her. "I'm going to have to go with the cheese."

It wasn't that it was impossible to have fresh Frivoly cheese. It was just rare because of where it came from and the distance it had to travel. It was made from the Frivoly goats of the Tapera Kingdom that resided by Tocarin Lake. It was aged in casks one year to the day and lasted about five days after that. Anytime a shop or Pierre managed to get some, they made sure it was advertised and bought quickly. The journey from Tapera took about three days, and the cheese only lasted a day, maybe two, after that if it had been properly cared for in transit. And last time Lillian looked, Alexander wasn't carrying around a snow box.

He picked up her small-distance cluster. "I know I said it, but I am really proud of you. I'm kind of excited to see how good you'll do on the next part."

He handed the arrows to her and she put them back in her quiver. "Thank you. But don't try to change the subject, Mr. Teacher. Cheese."

"Hehe, I wasn't trying to change the subject. It's just funny because it's like a magic trick. Right now, I have you wrapped up in mystery. Once I tell you the secret, you'll just see me as a regular guy."

They arrived at the medium cluster and started collecting.

"First off, you do not have me wrapped up in mystery." She looked at him coyly. "And secondly, you're not like any other 'regular' guy I've ever met."

"Well, you're not like any other princess I've ever met."
"So, there are other princesses, hmmm?"

He played along. "I've met a few," he said as he handed her more arrows. "But you are the one I like spending time with the most." He smiled at her. An awkward pause descended as they both just looked at each other. Lillian could feel her face getting red and quickly turned away.

"Cheese, please."

"Okay, okay. So, I'm assuming you know the delicate nature of the cheese and where it's made. Otherwise, you wouldn't be asking."

She nodded and continued on to the long-distance arrows.

"Well, there are two parts. The first part will seem simple. As I'm coming back from Tapera through the mountains, I keep it in an airtight goatskin pouch. I've found the less air it's exposed to, the longer it lasts. Then I usually keep it in the river as much as I can on my way back. The river's mostly snow-fed so it keeps the cheese cold. By the time I get here, it's still good for about two to three days."

Lillian just looked at him. "That's it? You keep it cold. Like a snow box?"

Alexander gestured. "Ta-dah."

Lillian punched him in the arm. "That doesn't count. I want another question."

"Ow, hey! I tried to tell you the magic would disappear. Oh, but there is one thing I left out."

She eyeballed him suspiciously.

"I take a secret passage."

"A secret passage? In the mountains?"

"Yeah."

"Why haven't I heard of this secret passage?"

"I don't know. It doesn't look like it's been used very much, though. I just kinda found it one day. Probably shaves half a day, maybe more, off the travel time."

Mental note: Ask the dwarves about secret passages in the mountains.

"Well, that's a little better. Can you show me one day?"

"Um, I suppose." It was his turn to look away. "But for right now, let's focus on archery," he said as he picked up the remaining arrows.

Did he just blush? Lillian couldn't be sure, but Alexander looked flustered for the first time since she'd met him. Whatever it was he hid it quickly as they walked back.

"So, what's on the agenda today?" she asked.

"Well, first thing I want to do is see how fast you can actually shoot. See how you feel the shot. Your cadence was really good. I could tell you just let it flow as you kept shooting. More reflex than thought."

She thought about the rabbit a few days ago and then the buck.

"Can I talk to you about something?"

"Of course. Always."

"The day before yesterday, there was this buck. But it wasn't a buck. I mean it, was but there was something about it." *Its eyes were like your necklace.* "I... I had to kill it," she shuddered. She tried to hold back the tears but couldn't. Alexander didn't hesitate to hold her.

She fit.

"Shh, it's okay. It's okay." She just let him hold her for a minute. His arms comforted her. He was a warm fire on a crisp day. He was safe. Her problems faded away like ripples in a pond. She gathered herself and explained what happened as they walked back.

"I thought you might have seen something since you, well, you know," she said, still not crazy about the idea, "hunt here."

"I've come across some stubborn animals but nothing like that. That's a bit troublesome. I'll keep my eye out, okay? Here, I have something that'll make you feel better." He reached into his pack, pulled out a small wax-wrapped package and handed it to her.

Lillian unwrapped the paper to find a piece of chocolate. "Chocolate?"

"Not just any chocolate. An Elwood family recipe. My mom makes me a batch for my trips. She says it's to make sure I come home to get more," he said fondly.

Lillian took a small bite. It was exquisite. She had never tasted chocolate like this before. "By the Fae." She took another bite. "This is amazing."

"Trust me, I know. It's all I can do not to go through the whole batch before I'm out of sight of the farm." He laughed.

Lillian placed the rest in her mouth. Actually, she did feel better. "Thank you. That helped."

"My pleasure. So, you ready to tackle today's lesson?"

"Yes."

"All right then, it's time to teach you to be the bow."

Alexander explained the process.

"The place we want you to get to is feeling as if the bow is just another appendage, another arm or leg." He reached down, grabbed a small rock, and tossed it at her head without warning. Lillian quickly reacted, catching it before it hit her.

"Hey, what was that for?" she asked indignantly.

"For understanding. How did you catch the rock?"

"What?"

"Did you think about it? Did you think of all the things you needed to do before catching it? Lift your arm? Open your hand? Move to intersect the rock? Close your fingers to catch it?"

"Well, of course not."

"Exactly. You just did it. It was a reflex. Just like how I saved you on the bridge."

"Yeah, but that's different. Everyone knows how to catch. Shooting an arrow is—"

"—is a skill, just like catching. You weren't born knowing how to catch. Someone taught you. Just like someone taught you the basics on how to shoot." He came up to her and handed her some different arrows. "Just like I'm going to teach you how to shoot without thinking. It just takes practice."

Watch out, Lil', don't fall too hard. Problem was, she felt like she already had. He had his own gravity, and she couldn't help but be drawn in. She was definitely smitten with Alexander. How much she wasn't sure, but she liked him.

Now that she could get a better look at the arrows, they seemed familiar. A very lightweight bluish metal. *They look like…*

"Calderan steel," Alexander finished her thought. "I make them myself. It's good for consistency for the really important shots."

"Like saving falling princesses off a bridge?" she joked.

"Like saving falling princesses off a bridge. I usually carry about ten, the rest are just regular arrows. Their strength and weight makes them extremely versatile. I want you to practice with both. But don't go falling in love now."

Lillian started to blush. "Excuse me?"

"The arrows, don't go falling in love with them."

"Oh, yeah, sure. I knew that." *Geez, Lillian, get a hold of yourself.*

"But if you're really nice, I'll make you a set when I go to Caldera."

Lillian panicked. "You're not leaving again, are you?"

Alexander teased her. "You didn't miss me, now, did you?"

She recomposed herself. "No," *Flerb, that was curt.* "I mean yes, I mean, I missed practicing with someone is all."

"It's okay, Lillian. I missed you too. I don't have many friends, remember?" he said with a smile that didn't quite reach his eyes.

Friends. Right.

"It's just nice to step out of the princess role is all," she explained. "Everyone knows me. Everyone knows Princess Lillian. Even my friends treat me different sometimes. With you, I'm allowed to be me. I'm allowed to relax."

"Well, I'm glad you feel comfortable around me. I've enjoyed teaching you. And so far, you've been an excellent student."

"So far?"

"I've got a surprise for you." He winked and grabbed her hand. "C'mon. Let's see what ya got."

He didn't let go as he led her to a grove of trees with a nice opening in the middle.

"I call it the Forge."

"Well, that sounds menacing." Lillian glanced around but didn't see anything out of the ordinary. "What is it?"

"It's a practice area I designed about a year ago. I have one set up back home but needed something to pass the time while I'm up here hunt—providing for my family." He walked over to a tree. "Watch this."

Lillian heard some sort of click and then from nowhere a target about head high dropped down from one of the trees in front of her.

"I have three different settings, which release them at different times. Come look, I'll show you how it works."

Lillian went over to the tree to find an elaborate contraption of levers, knobs, pulleys, and ropes going out in all directions from the tree. A bag released sand, triggering the various targets. He showed her how to start it and reset it so she could practice whenever she wanted. *The dwarves would be impressed with this.*

"So you ready?" he asked. He was adorable. She wasn't sure if he was more excited to see her skills or show off his toy.

"I guess." She walked into the opening.

"You're gonna have to use your ears and your eyes. Remember, right now I'm interested in speed, not accuracy. Reflex. Response. As long as you're shooting in the general direction, you don't have to hit the target."

"Sounds like a challenge," she tossed back playfully.

He parried with a smirk. "Impress me."

She took her stance. The anticipation was killing her. *Breathe, just breathe.*

The first target dropped to her one o'clock about shoulder height. *Shoes, shoulders, sight, select, slide, sigh, shoot.* She missed a foot to the left.

"Faster," she heard from behind her. "Don't think about it, just react."

Easy for you to say. You're already impressive.

The next target came back to her left, knee height. *Shoesshoulderssightselectslidesighshoot.* She was closer this time.

"Is that bett—" she stopped abruptly as the next target dropped again to the left.

Shoesshoulderssight... Another target dropped to the right. *Shoot.* Way off. She turned to the new target and another one dropped. She stopped and closed her eyes. She was flustered. She knew what Alexander was trying to do. She was thinking too much. She just had to react. Just like the other day when she spun around on the rabbit. *The rabbit.* She opened her eyes and shot. She nicked the target. Flipped around to the next one. *Shoshousiseslshoot.* The arrow stuck in the corner. Target. Turn. Shoot. Target. Turn. Shoot. The targets were dropping so fast now she didn't even have time to notice where her arrows were going.

There was a slight pause when a twig snapped behind her. She turned and shot without hesitation.

Her arrow was headed straight toward Alexander.

CHAPTER 13: Closer

o! Lillian could only stare in horror as her arrow seemed to travel in slow motion at Alexander. Just before the scream escaped her mouth, the arrow stopped. In mid-air.

Alexander had caught it just before it hit his shoulder. "Nice shot."

Lillian freaked and ran toward him. "Ohmygosh, ohmygosh! Are you okay? I am so sorry. Are you okay? I didn't mean to... I just heard a twig and I thought... Oh, the Fae, are you hurt?" She grabbed him and checked his shoulder.

"Lillian, Lillian, I'm okay." He grabbed her attention. "I'm okay, really." He looked in her panic-stricken eyes. "Lillian, I'm okay. Look." He stepped back and did a little twirl around. "See, I'm okay. I caught it." He lifted up the arrow.

Her heart was still beating fast, but her breathing was starting to slow. "But I... I didn't see you. I just... it was so fast, I just reacted. I'm so sorry."

"Lillian, it's okay. Look, I'm the one that should be sorry. I should've said something. You did exactly what I asked you to do."

"I know, but it was all too fast. How did you do that?"

Alexander just shrugged his shoulders. "Reflex."

"Like catching a ball?" She eyed him.

"Yep, like catching a ball," he said. She was not happy with that answer. "C'mon, let's check out the targets."

On top of her almost killing him, she couldn't bear the embarrassment of how she did. She closed her eyes as he led her back to the middle of the grove.

Her eyes were still closed. "Okay, be honest. How bad did I do?"

"Open your eyes and find out."

She didn't want to but knew he wasn't going to tell her. Slowly she glanced around. Twenty targets in all. She had hit the last twelve solid. The last four were inches from the bull's-eye. She turned around to see Alexander just smiling at her.

"Impressed."

Yes!

They took a break to calm Lillian's nerves and eat lunch. Alexander had prepared more than just cheese and chocolate. He had an array of fruits and meats along with a loaf of bread.

"Where did you get all this?" Lillian asked as she fished the items out of the saddlebags.

Alexander had a strong-looking horse named Winston who reminded her of one of the Kretchers' newspaper horses, but bigger. He had a beautiful charcoal coat and a matching tail, and didn't seem to mind a stranger grabbing the provisions. As she closed the saddlebag, a blanket shifted and revealed the hilt of a sword. *I wonder if he's as good with that as he is with arrows.*

She brought the food back to a blanket he had laid out under a tree. He walked back from the creek with a bottle in his hand.

"What's that?"

"Some thackleberry juice to go with our meal. The creek keeps it cool."

They ate in relative silence. Lillian was hungrier than she thought.

"You really are full of surprises, Mr. Elwood," she managed to say between bites.

"Well, I'm glad I keep you entertained, Ms. Charming," he replied as he lobbed a bit of cheese into his mouth.

When she was done, she laid back against the tree. The day was beautiful with a light breeze, and the shade was the perfect temperature for a nap. She wasn't sure how long she had dozed off, but she awoke to Alexander gently shaking her.

"Ready for round two?" he asked as he helped her up.

She yawned, taking his hand. "Mmm, how long was I out for?"

"Not long. You just looked so peaceful snoring under the tree."

Lillian hit him playfully. "Princesses *do not* snore."

"Ow. You know we really need to find a different way for you to express yourself," he teased as he rubbed his arm.

They walked over to the equipment.

"More target practice?"

"Kind of. Now that you have a way to practice your speed, I need to show you how to do small targets to help your aim."

"That bad, huh?"

"Not at all. But let's just say I wouldn't want you saving me from falling off a bridge quite yet." He gave her a teasing smile and handed her some more Calderan steel arrows.

They walked out to the other side of the creek where the grass tickled Lillian's knees. A few paces in, Alexander stopped.

"Okay, now I want you to understand what I can do and what I'm teaching you I've been doing for most of my life. So, I don't want you to get discouraged if you don't hit anything. Think of it like painting. You know some brush strokes. You've got a good picture going, but now we're gonna focus on the details—and some painters can take years to figure out how to do the details. Okay?"

"Yeah, but it sounds like I should already be preparing myself to fail."

"Not at all, but you said you wanted to shoot like me— like only five people on the entire continent. I just don't want you to be upset if it takes you a while to become the sixth." He squeezed her shoulder.

"You really think I can be as good as you?"

"After what you've done in the last few weeks and in the grove just now… yeah." He mimicked his father's voice. "'You must have some fae blood in ya, boy.'"

She laughed.

"All right then, I already set the targets up while you were snore—sleeping," he teased.

She looked out. "I don't see anything."

He got up next to her and pointed. She inhaled the sun-warmed skin and clean scent of him. *By the Fae, he smells inviting.* "Look out about twenty paces…see that red dot?" She squinted a little and could barely make out a small red point just above the grass line. It matched the color of his necklace.

"You mean that freckle?" she asked incredulously.

"Yep, there's another about forty-five degrees to the right about ten more paces out, then another to the left even farther out."

Sure enough, there was one that stuck out against the darkness of the mountains and another out toward the coastline. Based on the distance and size, Lillian figured the targets couldn't be bigger than a tea saucer if that.

This is going to be impossible. "You expect me to hit those?" Lillian could only imagine how long she would have to practice to hit those targets at all, let alone consistently.

"Eventually, well… yes, I do." His gray eyes peered into hers. "I believe in you."

She lost her breath for a moment.

"So, you ready for your next lesson?" he said, breaking the moment.

Breathe. "Yeah."

"All right now, hitting small targets is a little different. Usually you're not acting on reflex, so you have time to aim. But there's a lot more variables to factor in. Distance being the first and wind being a close second. Hopefully being able to see the grass waving will help with the wind. What arrow you're shooting with can also come into play, so that's why I try to only use the steel ones if I can."

"But I thought you said an archer is known by his aim, not his arrows," she said with a smirk.

"Ahh, so you have been listening. The student becomes the teacher, eh? Well, why don't you tell me what you remember about our first lesson?"

"Um, it's more about feeling than thinking?"

"Very good. Now realize these targets are smaller and farther out than the first time, but the concept is still the same. But this time, don't close your eyes. Try to fade out everything else. Visualize the target by itself. Feel the wind. Breathe out on release. And here, follow-through is just as important as the setup. Hold your form, let the arrow do the flying. I know it sounds like a lot to think about, but it's just like shooting fast. Simply put, practice."

"Give it a spell, and you'll do well," Lillian quoted the old saying.

"Exactly. So, I'm gonna give you some time while I go scout out our lesson for tomorrow. If you need anything, just ask Winston."

"Okay, I will," she laughed.

"No, I'm serious. He's a really smart horse. Okay, I won't be gone long, maybe enough for you to go through a set for each target."

Alexander walked away, leaving Lillian to her task.

The first target wasn't bad. She never hit it but got close a couple of times. The other two targets were more elusive. She either misjudged the distance or the wind. Both of which Alexander mentioned were the biggest factors, so she didn't feel too bad.

He still hadn't made it back yet, and the mid-afternoon sun had made Lillian thirsty. She went back to the picnic area and hunted around for some water or at least a cup for the creek. Nothing.

"Okay, Winston," she said as she stroked his mane, "let's see how smart you are. Does Alexander have a cup or something for water?"

Winston looked at her for a second and then trotted over to the creek.

Great, I mention water, and he goes to get a drink.

He lowered his head down to the water, but then came up with a rope in his mouth. At the end of the rope was a bottle filled with water. He walked back over to Lillian.

"Wow, you really are a smart horse." She took a nice gulp.

Winston let out a small whinny then bent his head back to the bag. When Lillian didn't respond right away, he did it again.

"What is it, Winston?"

Once again he nudged the bag. Lillian decided to investigate and found a small pouch of sugar cubes.

"Oh, is this what you want?" she teased.

Winston neighed, raising his head up and down.

"Okay, boy, here ya go."

"I see he coaxed you into a treat," Alexander said, walking up.

"Well, he did get me water."

"Told ya he was smart."

"I stand corrected."

"Like I said, I don't have many friends and Winston's a good conversationalist. He doesn't argue with me too much." He motioned to the field. "So, how did you do?"

"Ask again in three weeks."

"That bad, huh? Well, don't worry. You'll get better. Plus, it's not like you're trying to pierce the heart of a dragon."

"Well, not anytime soon, let's hope."

Not anytime ever, as far as Lillian knew. King Phillip was the last person she knew who had had an encounter with a dragon, and it was believed to be the last.

The setting sun indicated Lillian needed to go.

"I should probably head home. I've really enjoyed today, though."

"Me too. It's nice having a friend."

Just a friend, right.

"So, what's on the agenda tomorrow?" Lillian asked.

"I was thinking about trying moving targets, but I don't want to overwhelm you with everything."

"I'm good. I know I need practice in the other areas still, but this will give me variety so I don't get bored."

"Makes sense."

"Hopefully a certain someone isn't gone for three weeks again."

"Yeah, sorry about that, had some things to help out with at home."

"I know. I'm just giving you a hard time, but I was getting worried."

"You were worried about me?"

"Well, yeah. It's what friends do."

They both smiled but then fell into an uncomfortable silence. Winston helped out with a neigh.

Lillian seized the opportunity to clear the awkwardness.

"So, I should get going. Same time tomorrow?"

"Yep."

"Okay. See you then." She was already anxious and excited.

"Looking forward to it."

She turned to walk off before he could see her blush.

"Oh, and Lillian," Alexander called out. She turned around. "Wear something you don't mind getting wet."

She gave him an inquisitive look, and he just smiled as she watched him stroll away.

You are full of surprises, Mr. Elwood.

She knew she'd have trouble sleeping again tonight.

CHAPTER 14: Closer Still
June 10

ownstairs, the king was already at the table with his morning tea, perusing the recent edition of the *Valanti Valor* when Lillian joined him for breakfast.

"Morning, Dad," she said as she kissed him on the cheek.

"Morning, Lily Pad," he said, lowering his paper to give her a smile. "You're up early this morning. Going out to practice again?"

Oh the Fae, does he know about Alexander?

She tried to play it off. "What do you mean?"

"I mean someone must be planning on giving Sir Alger a run for his money in the archery contest this year. I know I may seem busy, but don't think I haven't noticed. Any particular reason for your sudden interest?"

A gorgeous instructor.

"Not really. Just thought I'd do something more with my time than gossip and gander." *That sounded believable.*

Her belief was supported when the king raised his paper back up.

"I suppose I can't argue with that logic."

She grabbed a couple of cinnamon-sugar pastries and some bacon. "Anything interesting going on?" She figured the best way to keep from slipping up was to change the subject.

"Oh nothing much. The Calderan Knight tournament is coming up. Sir Finley usually takes it being captain of the guard, but every year he gets older and his competition gets younger. Sir Laurel and a few others are leaving this morning to partake and represent Valanti."

"Sir Laurel? Really?" Lillian asked incredulously.

"I know, but believe it or not he's swift with a sword, sober or not. He stands a good chance to win. I also heard Princess Avery might enter the sword contest this year. She's really taken it up since Jaccob left."

"Yeah, she was showing us some of her skills when they were here for my party."

"Let's see, The Tapera Tricks & Trades is going on at the end of the month still. I wonder what prank my brother will discover to pull on me this year."

For years, King Harry's older brother Louis had always found some trick at the Tricks & Trades show to make his younger brother the brunt of a joke. Last year's prank had been frog elixir that Louis had put in Harry's wine that caused him to croak like a frog anytime he tried to speak. However, the joke lasted well beyond the elixir's one-hour effect, as the king was constantly teased by his family and friends for weeks afterward.

"Speaking of Tapera," the king recalled, "so you know the 'ghost' that lives in the forest behind the castle?"

Careful.

"Yeah, I guess."

"Well, apparently a similar apparition has been seen near the Tocarin Falls area in Tapera. Usually around a full moon. Spooky, huh?"

"Really?" Lillian wasn't sure what to think about that. Alexander had said he had gone home. Surely it couldn't have been him. *But then again he did have new Frivoly cheese.* "What was similar?" She did her best to feign interest.

"Mmmm, let me see." The king flipped through the pages. "Ah, here it is. 'Reports have been made by several Tapera residents of seeing a "ghost-like figure with a red eye" roaming the mountainside and even "floating over the river."' But if you ask me, my older brother was jealous of our little folklore and is probably dressing up over there himself."

"I wouldn't put it past Uncle Louis." Lillian laughed along with her dad.

King Harry turned a page. "Oh, says here that puffed shoulders are making a comeback."

"No, Dad. No."

"But I'm sure I still have some in…"

Lillian readied a spoonful of jelly for catapulting. "Don't make me do it, Dad."

The king raised his hands in surrender. "Okay, okay. You know you should really write this column."

"And give up all this? Nah. Besides that's really Jafria's deal."

Snow White made her way to the table with a groggy Andrew in tow.

"Going back out to practice again today, Lil'?" she asked making up a plate for her son.

"Yeah, right after I change."

"Well, be careful out there."

Lillian couldn't tell if her mom was talking about Alexander or wild animals.

"I will, Mom."

Lillian finished up her breakfast and headed up to change, thinking about what Alexander had said. *"Wear something you don't mind getting wet."*

Just what do you have in store for me today, Mr. Elwood? She smiled at the mystery.

Alexander was right where she left him.

"Hey, Winston. I got a treat for you." Lillian produced an apple from her pocket, which Winston was all too eager to munch on.

"Are you trying to woo my horse?"

"He's the real reason I'm here. I'm just using you to get to Winston. Isn't that right, boy?" She patted Winston on the nose as he whinnied in agreement.

"The truth finally comes out." Alexander walked over. "So, what do you say, Winston? You like Miss Lillian here?" Another agreeing neigh. "You're right, she is very pretty." Alexander looked right at her. Lillian could feel the blood rushing to her face. "Even if she is dressed like a swamp rat." Lillian didn't think she'd ever heard a horse laugh before.

She punched Alexander. "You told me to dress this way!"

"Ow! Again with the violence. All I said was dress to get wet. I don't recall mentioning that you had to throw fashion out the window."

She punched him again.

"Ow, okay, okay. I'm kidding, I'm kidding. You look fine."

She gave him a scrutinizing look.

"I promise. I didn't want to embarrass you, but you actually look pretty cute."

She started to blush again and turned away. "All right, apology accepted. So, what are we doing today?"

"Moving target practice. We're counting on you for lunch today."

Lillian felt ill. "Alexander, I can't ki… shoot anything. That buck was an exception. I had no other choice."

"Lillian, I know that. And I would never have you do anything you weren't comfortable with. Have you ever been fishing?"

She was confused. "Well, yeah, a few times."

"I bet it wasn't with a bow and arrow, though." He winked at her. "C'mon, let me show you and if you don't want to do it, I'll think of something else, okay?"

She thought for a second. "Okay."

"All right, let me get Winston ready. It's a bit of a hike otherwise."

Alexander tossed some satchels over Winston and climbed up. Alexander offered his hand to help her up in front of him.

The ride to the lesson site wasn't nearly long enough for Lillian. He had his arms wrapped around her as he worked the reigns. Even though she was in front, she desperately hoped he wouldn't feel her heart about to beat out of her chest. She was getting more relaxed in his company, but her attraction was becoming more than just a crush. Ironically, this situation made it even more uncomfortable to be near him. Especially this close. She leaned her head back against his chest, taking in his scent, enjoying his warmth against her in the cool morning air.

"All right, everybody off who's shooting fish."

She hopped down and glanced around. She didn't recognize the area. There was a decent-sized pond fed by a creek coming in from the east. It was surrounded by various plants and flowers, some Lillian had never seen before. She'd have to get a cutting of some to take back and show her mother. The water pooled up and then ran on to the coast, she assumed. Several large rocks were spaced around a quarter of the pond where someone might enjoy bouldering. One outcropping in particular hung out over the water just far enough for someone to make a decent jump for showing off.

Further north, there was a solid black line just on the horizon that ran from east to west.

"Where are we?"

"About an hour's good ride from the wall. Have you never been here?"

"Not this close to the wall, no." Lillian's father had reassured her and her brothers there was nothing to worry about, but he still cautioned them from venturing too close.

"Oh, you've been missing out. I discovered it about a year ago. The creek is the same one that runs under your bridge a couple of leagues away. But the pond has a secret."

And with that, Alexander began to take off his "ghost" tunic. *Oh my starlight.* She tried not to gape. As he finished removing his tunic, she noticed an interesting mark over his heart. A circle with a strange twisted triangle in the middle. Not so much a scar as some sort of tattoo or marking, from what Lillian could catch in a glance. Then he turned and headed toward the pond. His back rippled with muscles, lean and taut beneath his tanned skin. *Is he crazy? That pond has to be freezing!*

"Come on," he said grinning widely. "I promise you'll like the surprise!" he yelled as he dove into water.

Lillian was still skeptical.

Alexander came back up. "I thought princesses were supposed to be tough." He splashed water her direction.

That did it. She wasn't as bad as Princess Avery at being called out, but she wasn't about to look like one of those prissy girls she'd met from other kingdoms. She kicked off her shoes and steeled herself for the icy water coming from the mountains. She walked over and dipped her toes in preparation for the artic onslaught. But instead of cringing at the frigid water, she gasped in surprise at the lukewarm sensation that caressed her foot.

"Surprise!" Alexander said.

"How is this possible?" she asked, stepping into the water up to her knees.

"There are several heat vents at the bottom. It's like a dragon's den down there, but up here, with the river water, it's perfect."

"Mmmhmm." Lillian sighed as she sank blissfully into the water.

"C'mon, I want to show you something," he said, grinning.

Alexander made his way across to the other side where the outcropping of rocks were. Lillian followed leisurely, enjoying the warm water. By the time she made it to the shore, he had already clambered on top of the rock overlooking the water.

"Stay there for a minute," Alexander called out, disappearing behind the rock.

Lillian sat up on the sandy bank and leaned back against the grass. Suddenly, Alexander leapt off, executing a spinning flip, but landing awkwardly in the water with a definitive smack. The ripples settled down until he broke through the surface, closer to the shore where she was sitting.

"Woo hoo!"

"Didn't that hurt?" Lillian asked noticing the left part of his chest was a little redder than a minute ago.

"Meh, a little but it was totally worth it." He climbed up to the shore and sat down next to her.

Lillian tried her best not to stare as the rivulets of water slid down his bronze skin.

"Okay, your turn."

She looked at him. "Are you crazy? I can't do that."

"You don't have to flip or anything. Just go jump."

"I don't know…"

"Why were you on the bridge that day?"

"Huh? What do you mean?" Lillian asked, confused by the change in topic.

"I saw you. Standing there with your eyes closed. Arms spread out. I've done it too. It feels like you're flying. Well, this doesn't last as long, but here there's really nothing but you and the air. You don't have to do anything special, just jump. Surely you've jumped from the rocks at Twin Falls, right?"

"Yeah, I mean, it's been a while, but never from that high though."

"I promise I'll be right here if anything happens. I haven't steered you wrong yet, have I?"

"Okay." Lillian wasn't too sure about it, but she got up, anxious at a chance to impress Alexander.

Once she made it to the rock, she peered over the edge and got a little dizzy.

"Are you sure this is the same rock? It looks higher."

"Hehe. Yeah, it's the same. I know it always looks higher from up top, but I assure you the rock didn't grow on your way up."

"Are you sure it's deep enough?"

"I'm sure. You'll probably feel the grass weed growing up from the bottom, but you won't hit anything. It's a good twenty feet down."

She looked down again to make sure her perch hadn't gotten even higher. A large black shadow passed over the surface of the pond. She looked up expecting to see a bird flying by, but there was nothing there. One more look down convinced her it must have been a cloud or her imagination.

Lillian had done crazier things when she was a kid, like traversing the walls of the castle thirty feet up. But time had passed and made her unsure of herself. She took a few steps back, took several deep breaths, jogged forward—and jumped.

She was flying.

Perhaps not really, but she felt like she was flying for a brief moment, and then she hit the water. Lillian felt exhilarated, eager to go again.

Sure enough, she felt the grass weed tickle her feet and legs as she sank a little more. She could also feel the temperature get warmer as she went down. She thrust her arms down and began to kick her legs, finally breaking through the surface. She looked over to Alexander.

He started clapping. "Bravo, well done." He got up. "Wait there for a second."

I'll stay here for as long as you like. She floated lazily and watched the clouds overhead.

"Lillian, up here!" he called out to her back on top of the rock. "Watch this."

She saw him take a couple of steps back and then leap off the rock, arms spread wide in a beautiful dragon dive. It was flawless. He brought his arms together and slipped beneath the surface.

Lillian slowly treaded water over to where he should have come up. She waited. The ripples calmed down. And she waited. Except for her own movement, the pond was still.

"Alexander?" she called out. She began looking around the pond, frantically searching for any signs of him. There were no bubbles, no disturbance.

Alexander was not coming up.

CHAPTER 15: Anticipation

She called out, "Alexander!"

Lillian's brain went into overdrive. *What if he hit a rock? Or got tangled up in the grass weed?* She began to dive down to look for him when—

"D'ya miss me?"

Lillian screamed and whipped around to face Alexander, who had snuck up silently behind her.

"Geez, sorry Lil'. I didn't mean to..." he began as he took in her terror-stricken face.

"Are you out of your mind?" She splashed him and swam to shore. He followed.

"Lillian, wait. I'm sorry."

She didn't stop until she got to shore, and even then she kept walking toward Winston. Alexander quickly caught up to her.

"Lillian, stop. Wait. Will you please just wait a second?" She crossed her arms and turned to face him. He stopped short, surprised.

"Well?" she asked crossly.

"Well, I, I'm sorry. I didn't mean to scare you popping up behind you like that. I just thought..." Alexander hung his head down. "I was just playing around is all."

Lillian realized she may have reacted a little too harshly. She calmed her voice. "It wasn't that you came up behind me. I thought something had happened to you."

He looked up to meet her gaze. "Like what?"

"I don't know. I thought maybe you'd hit a rock or gotten tangled up or something. I'm not sure, I just started to panic when you didn't come up right away, and then you snuck up behind me... It just scared me is all." She couldn't explain it but tears started to form in her eyes.

"Hey, hey, it's okay. I'm okay. I'm really sorry." He walked up and embraced her, holding her against his chest still slick from the pond. His warmth radiated through her wet clothes. She relaxed against him, reveling in the feeling of his arms around her.

"I know. I'm sorry, I shouldn't have gotten so upset. I was just afraid. I just had a bad feeling."

"Well, I forget you haven't known me that long."

She pulled back, sniffed her nose, and looked up at him, his damp locks dripping water onto her cheeks. "What does that mean?"

"Nothing really. It's just that I don't get hurt."

She raised an eyebrow. "You don't get hurt?"

"No. I mean I've gotten scratches from time to time, but I've never broken a bone or gotten sick or anything. My dad says I must have the best faery godmother in all of Azshura watching over me."

"That must be nice." Lillian reflected on the time she had broken her leg on one of those traversing the castle wall trips and was laid up for six weeks.

"I suppose. I can stay underwater for quite a bit too. That's why I wasn't really thinking about it."

"It's okay." *I just really like you is all*. She stepped back, trying to play it off. "I wasn't really worried about you as much as I was thinking about who was going to keep teaching me."

"Ah-ha, so the truth finally comes out. You're just using me for my skills with the arrow then."

"Well, what else are you good for?" she teased.

"I'll have you know I'm a man of many talents."

"Well then, maybe I'll just have to stick around and find out what else you're good at." *Oh my gosh. Please don't let that sound as bad as I thought.*

"Um…" *Is he turning red?* "How about we *dive* into those lessons?" he joked, trying to lighten the moment.

"Ha, ha. Now you're a comedian?"

He shrugged. "Like I said, many talents."

They picked up their equipment and then strolled over to where the pond turned back into a creek. There were several fish swimming around, even jumping out of the water to catch an elusive glitter bug. On a day like today, the bugs were easy to see as the sun reflected off their golden wings.

Alexander held his hand up for a moment, and Lillian stopped. He pulled his bow out in front of him, carefully watching the symphony of movement in the creek. Suddenly, Lillian heard the sound of an arrow flying through the air, catching a fish mid-jump right before its own catch. It thudded and stuck into the bank on the other side.

"You just couldn't resist showing off, could you?" she asked.

"What? No, I… well, okay, yeah. But I don't get to shoot with anybody unless it's my dad. It's just nice to be able to share with someone else is all. That and it'd be nice to have something other than bread, fruit, and cheese for dinner tonight."

"I'm just pulling your tail, Alexander. It's okay for you to show off. I like watching you shoot. It encourages me toward something to work for, even if I'll only be the second best," she said as she wrinkled her nose at him.

"In that case, remind me to show you what I can do with the Forge," he said slyly. "But in the meantime, let's focus on the task at hand. Eventually we'll work on combining your speed with today's lesson, but for now we take it one step at a time."

Anticipation

He motioned for her to come closer to the water.

"Now, when you're shooting moving targets, it's all about the anticipation of where they're going to be, not where they are. I know that sounds elementary, but there's more to factor in than just how they're moving. You have to open up and let everything in to help predict where they're going to be. The reason we're practicing on fish is because they are some of the most sporadic animals as far as movement. Any change in their environment—a breeze causing a ripple, a bubble from under a rock, a sneaking predator—will alter their path. I call these the outside influences, but you still have to account for them."

"So, what you're saying is that if I can learn to shoot a fish, I can shoot anything."

"Pretty much."

"And that's how you just shot that fish?"

"Yep. I was paying close attention to the glitter bug's pattern and how its wings were catching the sun. I noticed it catch the fish's attention and watched the fish preparing for its jump. Then as soon as the glitter bug flew back into the pattern and the fish was circled around, I knew he'd jump and voilà, smoked fish for dinner."

"You saw a pattern in how the bug was flying? I don't know if I'm up for this."

"It's okay. We're just going to focus on shooting fish in the water for now."

Lillian still wasn't sure about the whole shooting animals thing, but she had been fishing before several times and she reconciled this wasn't that different.

"I'm just going to stand on the other side and take it all in…" he said.

Lillian giggled at his little catch phrase. Alexander gave her a dirty look and continued.

"Once you go through a quiver's worth, we'll make adjustments."

Lillian didn't do too badly. She didn't hit anything, but she got close several times.

"Sorry," she apologized when she missed her last target. "Guess you'll have to settle for bread and cheese tonight."

"I have faith in you. And I have a good feeling you'll get something after lunch. You hungry?"

Lillian hadn't really been thinking about it, but now that he mentioned food, her stomach rumbled. Once again, Alexander had prepared an array of delicacies.

"How in the Fae do you always manage to put together such a wonderful variety of food while you're teaching a fumbling student like me?"

"I have some magic up my sleeve. And for the record, you're not fumbling. If anything, you're striding ahead."

"Well, I will make a toast to that, then," she said as she raised her cup of juice.

"Here, here." Alexander raised his too. "To Princess Lillian, the soon-second-best archer in all of Azshura."

She scoffed. "You mean soon-to-be-the-best archer in Azshura."

"Let's just keep focus on the task at hand, shall we?" he teased back, and they both took a sip

Alexander got quiet and sat back just looking at Lillian.

"Taking it all in again?" she joked.

"Heh, no. I was just thinking."

"What's on your mind?"

"Well, I didn't want to be too forward or suggest something you wouldn't be comfortable with, but…" He was still hesitant.

"Out with it already. I'll decide what is and is not appropriate for a princess, thank you very much," she stated matter-of-factly.

"I was going to say, I do have one more lesson to teach you."

"I'm not following."

"You could come night shooting with me tonight."

Spend the night with you?

Alexander sensed he had crossed the line. "Never mind. I was being too forward, just forget I said anything."

Lillian realized she had given him the wrong impression. "No, no, it's not that. I'd love to spend the night with you."

FLERB!

Now she was the one backtracking. "No, I mean, yes. I'd like to go night shooting. I didn't mean spend the night like, you know 'spend the night.' I just meant—oh, by the Fae."

Alexander was laughing. "It's okay. I know what you meant."

The thought of seeing Alexander by firelight made her heart speed up. *I wonder if he'd hold me if I got cold? Lillian Charming, you shouldn't be thinking about that. You're with Richard.* But she couldn't help thinking about it.

"It's a different adventure worth experiencing. You have to use your other senses more. Really feel the target rather than see it. So, I'm not sure how easy it will be for you to get out of the castle at night, and I don't want to get you in trouble, but we wouldn't be going out until after dusk, so…"

Going out. Lillian just remembered. Her heart sank.

"Oh no. Alexander, I'm so sorry. I forgot I'm going out with some friends tonight."

The outing had been planned for a while now. She and Richard and some other couples were all going to Talula's Tapas. It was a fairly new restaurant featuring a magic act that was supposed to be phenomenal. Her parents had been invited to the opening and talked about it for a week afterwards. She had been there once with her dad.

Alexander looked disappointed. "Oh, well, that's okay. I mean, I'll be around for another couple of days, so maybe we can do it then."

"Yes, of course." She tried to sound more upbeat. "I'd really like that."

Alexander started to pick up the lunch items. "So, what are you guys doing?"

"Some of us couples," *Flerb.* "I mean, Alexander, look I know we're just friends," *Are we* just *friends?* "and it shouldn't matter, but I don't want you to think I am ever being dishonest or hiding something from you."

He stopped and looked at her.

"I'm kind of in a relationship right now."

His face said it all. He tried to cover it up, though. "Oh, well, yeah, I mean, why wouldn't you be? You're the princess. But besides that, you're a great catch. You're smart, ambitious, beautiful. It only makes sense. You probably have suitors lined up all the time." He continued picking up.

She could tell he was hurt. She should have told him sooner, but she was about to break up with Richard and that had to count for something, right?

"Look, Alexander, I'm sorry. I didn't mean to…"

He looked at her, sincerity in his bright, gray eyes. "Lillian, you don't have to apologize for anything, really. Like you said, we're just friends, and I'm just glad to have that." He carried stuff back to Winston.

Friends. She had regretted saying it as soon as it had come out of her mouth and almost winced when he had said it back. *Well, if he was thinking of us as more than friends, he definitely won't say anything now. Flerb!*

The rest of the afternoon was awkward to say the least. Alexander was less playful. Lillian tried to lighten the mood with a couple of jokes, but he only returned a smile.

Needless to say, she didn't manage to help Alexander with his fish dinner that night.

CHAPTER 16: Misdirection

"**M**'lady, you sure are quiet," Alondra said as she braided Lillian's hair.

Lillian was plucked from her daze where she'd been reflecting on this morning's events. "Hmm? Oh yeah, sorry, Alondra. I guess I'm just thinking about tonight."

"I see. What are you guys doing tonight?"

"Jafria got us reservations at Talula's Tapas."

"Oh, that should be fun. Isn't that the new place where a magician comes out and does tricks with the audience?"

"Yeah."

The last time Lillian had gone was with her dad on a sort of father-daughter date. They dressed in regular clothes and disguised themselves. A jester picked her dad for a trick that ended with a pie in her dad's face. When the king started to wipe off the pie, his disguise came off too. Lillian thought the jester was going to faint as his faced turned white as cream. She thought her dad was mad too because he just scowled at the jester, but sneakily he'd grabbed some mashed potatoes from a diner's plate and mashed it in the jester's face, saying "You can't have dessert before you finish your veggies." Everyone laughed, even the jester, once he realized the king wasn't mad. That's another reason why her father was a good king—he had a sense of humor, thanks in part to his older brother's relentless pranks.

Lillian finished getting ready. She was wearing a flowing gown of olive satin that left her shoulders bare. Its bodice and hem were embroidered with bits of cream lace and gold thread, which glinted in the candlelight. Her hair was braided to the side and accentuated with sprigs of greenery. The dress and floral touches really brought out the green in her hazel eyes.

Her dad had graciously allowed her and her friends to use the extended carriage so they could all ride together. The group would be her and Richard, Jafria and Barrett, Sophie and Gage, then Lizzy and Brock. All of them had started their courtship around the same time except for Sophie and Gage. They had been courting for about six months now. For everyone else, this was their fourth or fifth outing. And this one was their first evening without chaperones. King Harry had agreed to it awhile back before the party incident, and he was not happy about keeping his word. But a promise was a promise. He had just kissed Lillian good-bye, telling her to be careful.

"Especially of pie-wielding jesters," he said with a wink.

Seth was just finishing up the hitches to the carriage when Lillian walked up.

"Your carriage awaits, Your Highness. But I must say its beauty and eloquence pales in comparison with you." He gave her a nice bow as she approached.

"Oh, stop it, Seth." She punched him in the arm.

"Ow, geez, you don't have to be so touchy. All that arrow shootin' has muscled you up. I actually felt that one." He rubbed his arm. "But seriously Lil', you look great. I hope Richard knows how lucky he is."

You mean how lucky he was.

"Well, thank you."

"You guys are going to Talula's, right?"

"Yep." *Though I wish I were going somewhere else...*

He helped her up into the carriage, then he did his best King Harry impression. "You kids have a good time now, and don't stay out too late."

Lillian played along. "Yes, 'Dad'."

"And you make sure those boys mind their manners. They only have one thing on their mind and that's…"

"Seth!" Lillian started to blush. He just laughed and shut the carriage door.

Lillian hadn't ridden in the carriage since the dwarves adjusted the wheels and axels. It was almost like riding on a cloud. She could barely feel any bumps at all. She'd have to remember to let the dwarves know how well their new system worked. She was always impressed with their inventions, and they were always tinkering with something since they didn't have to mine diamonds all the time.

It was just before dusk. One of Lillian's favorite times of day. She lay back in the plush seats of the carriage and just relaxed—something a princess doesn't get to do very often. She couldn't help but let her thoughts wander back again to this morning and Alexander. His disappointed face when she mentioned Richard. She wanted to mention she was breaking up with him, but she figured it would seem she was doing that because of Alexander, indicating she wanted to be more than friends. Which she thought she did, but she wasn't sure if she was ready for him to know or if she was ready to jump into another relationship before she'd barely ended this one. She hoped tonight's outing would provide enough distraction for her not to worry about it for now.

The carriage made its way through town. Most of the shops had closed up for the night, except for the taverns and late-night eateries. Candles illuminated the people inside as they sat down for dinner, read stories to children before bed, or just enjoyed a good ale and pipe before the fire.

Finally, the carriage pulled up to Jafria's house, where Barrett, Jafria, and Richard were all waiting outside. The footman helped Jafria in first. She was dressed in a beautiful spring gown swirled in light pinks and blues. Her black hair was swept up into a bun held together with two twisted silver hair pins.

"Hey, Jafria, you look stunning." Lillian was always amazed at her friend's sense of fashion. Jafria was generally a trendsetter and even if what she did was totally "over the wall" (a phrase the younger generation termed from the Drod wall for being crazy), she owned it to the point where other people thought they were crazy for not dressing like her. She had even started to dabble in designing her own clothes and was thinking of opening up a little shop. It would be a little while before that happened, but all of her friends had already agreed to be her fashion models when needed.

"Thanks, you do too. Wait 'til Richard sees you. But, ugh, you should see what Barrett's wearing. I swear that boy must have eyes like a bat."

Before Lillian could ask, Barrett stepped in wearing a very nicely tailored suit, but its fabric looked like dragon droppings. A lot of brown with some jeweled colors mixed in.

"Hey, Lil'," Barrett greeted her. Most of Lillian's friends didn't worry about her title except during formal affairs, which is how she wanted it.

"Good evening, Barrett."

Richard came in after him. He looked as attractive as ever, donning a modest dark-blue ensemble with a vibrant-red vest underneath.

Richard took Lillian's hand and kissed it. "Good evening, Lillian. You look more stunning every time I see you. I'm sorry you have to be in the company of such ill taste," he said, gesturing toward Barrett. "Can you believe he actually gave someone coins for that?" he said with a wink.

Barrett scowled back. "I was assured it was the height of fashion." He looked down at his coat. "It's not that bad. Jafria, tell them this is the latest style."

"Sweetie, the only style it is, is the one going out."

The group chuckled at Barrett's expense as the carriage door shut and they traveled on to pick up the rest of their friends.

Shortly after the sun had set, the eight companions emptied out of the carriage in front of Talula's. As they walked in, they were greeted by the hostess, Talula.

"Greetings, Your Highness and guests. We 'ave your table right zis way." Talula liked to be right up front and interact with her patrons. Many of them were beginning to become regulars and enjoyed the personal touch she took to make them feel comfortable. Her restaurant was unique to Valanti as it didn't serve a traditional-course meal. *Tapas* meant "pre-meal" or "hors d'oeuvres." So, the menu was comprised solely of appetizers that were meant to be shared, which made it perfect for this evening's company.

"Are we celebrating anything special tonight or ees it just an evening out for zee young couples?"

"Nothing special really. Just a chance to get Lillian out of the castle and spend time with friends is all," Jafria replied as Barrett pulled her chair out.

"Well, as always, I am honored to 'ave you, Princess and your friends, so should you need anything, please let my staff know."

"Thank you, Talula. I'm sure we'll be fine." Lillian responded.

"Some of your friends, zis ees zeir first time 'ere, ees it not? I'll 'ave the chef make up zee special first-visit sampler dessert tray for later. Ees fantastique!" she exclaimed, kissing her fingertips.

Lillian never looked for special treatment, but before she could interject, Talula was off to the kitchen.

The jester was skipping around, pulling silly pranks on unsuspecting patrons. When they weren't looking, he would switch their plate with another that was empty and toddle away behind another table, waiting to see the reaction. Lillian couldn't be sure, but she felt the jester seemed familiar. More familiar than just seeing him the last time, but she couldn't quite place him. His face was painted and his clothes were a hodge-podge of fabrics, which made it all the more difficult. She couldn't give him any more thought though, as she had yet to figure out how to end her courtship with Richard, and let her mind focus on figuring out the best course to take.

The food was fabulous. So far, they had sampled seven different plates with a variety of textures and flavors to tempt the palate. They even had Frivoly cheese. *Not as fresh as Alexander's though.*

One dish, called Dragon Tarts, was a combination of meats in a roll with a touch of Dragonfire. The surprise came at the end when it prompted the eater to burp a small ball of fire, much to their friends' enjoyment. Especially when Barrett's coat got singed by Jafria, who swore it was an accident but winked at the rest of the table when he left to clean up.

"Now he *smells* like dragon droppings," Sophie joked, making her friends chuckle.

"Ah, well, he can't be good at everything; I wouldn't have anything to tease him about," Jafria replied fondly.

Lillian's favorite, and perhaps the whole tables', was the house special, Wizard Wonderfall. It was an amazing delicacy that actually changed flavors in their mouth. A small flaky pastry of sweet chili that surrounded a blend of chocolate in its center. Yet as the chocolate melted, it became a savory caramel-flavored crème that even cooled as it traveled down once it was swallowed. They all had at least two.

The evening was awkward for Lillian. Richard was a complete gentleman, but when he reached over to hold her hand, she withdrew. She quickly smiled at him and gave the excuse of her fingers being sore from practicing so much, hoping he would accept her apology. She had concluded her best approach would be to talk to him when the carriage dropped them off. That way, there wouldn't be any long discussion of the matter and she wouldn't have to see him again for a while. Her thoughts were interrupted by a sudden announcement.

"Ladies and gentlemen." Their attention was drawn to a colorful announcer in the center of the room. "Allow me to direct your gaze to a most courageous conjurer. A most stunning and daring performance you won't believe but will talk about for days. It is my pleasure to introduce the marvelous, majestic Bim Zala Zands!"

A round of applause went up as a loud crack and flash of smoke produced a tall, thin man in a hooded cloak of patches. His head was bowed and he stood perfectly still as the applause died down and stilled. Right about the time people started to look around, he whipped back his head and flung out his arms, producing a dazzling array of colored lights that revealed his visage and changed his cloak to a solid vibrant purple. His dark black beard covered most of his face. His age was hard to guess, but his salt-peppered black hair gave some indication. His skin was a deep brown and held few wrinkles. A large necklace with medallion dangled from his neck, and his left index finger bore a ring with a rather large green stone.

"Greetings and welcome, my friends. I am the fantastic Bim Zala Zands."

Another round of applause greeted him with some cheers.

"It is my pleasure to perform for you tonight. So, please sit back…"

A small cough came from Talula.

"…keep eating," this drew a few laughs from the crowd, "and, of course, enjoy the show."

Bim Zala Zands was an entertainer to say the least. He had witty banter to go along with his tricks for the eyes. He was well versed in close-up illusions, making patrons' plates disappear right from under their nose, only to have it reappear beneath a napkin fully loaded with a sample of tapas.

"Zat's coming out of your payment," Talula yelled jokingly, bringing laughs from the crowd.

Zands replied by having coins drop from under the seat of another patron in the group. "I believe this should cover it."

He continued his act by bringing two patrons up to the makeshift stage, one male and one female. He had them sit in chairs and covered them completely, except for their heads. He waved his hands, chanted in a foreign language, and whipped the covers off. Well, the stories were right about the audience talking for days about his tricks. Somehow he had swapped the clothes of the patrons! The crowd roared with laughter as the gentleman attempted to walk off wearing the lady's raised heels, and she almost tripped over the pants of her baggy suit. One of the waitresses took them around a corner to change back presumably.

Lillian only caught a glimpse of the waitress, but she recognized the girl she had seen a few days ago with Slim and Pork.

So, this is where she was going that day. But why was she hanging around the other two? Lillian's attention was soon directed back to Zands, where the wine he had just drunk was now pouring out of his ear. He offered the wine back to the gentleman he took it from, who respectfully declined, much to the audience's amusement.

Zands walked to the middle of the room and waved his arms in a grand sweeping motion. All the torches grew dim, creating an eerie ambiance in the room.

"And now, ladies and gentlemen, I will perform tonight's final illusion," he said as his gaze moved around the room. "The tricks you have seen tonight, no doubt, have dazzled your eyes and tickled your mind. The next feat, however, shall leave you questioning the very fabric of reality. I will, of course, need a volunteer to assist me in this grand quest."

Several hands shot up, but Zands' eyes landed squarely on Lillian's table.

He walked slowly toward her group. "I appreciate the eagerness, but to add to the authenticity of the illusion, I shall need a special volunteer." He stopped in front of Lillian and reached out his hand. "Your Highness, would you do me the honor?"

Lillian looked around hesitantly. A vague warning pinged in her mind from something she couldn't quite place. Her friends gave her looks of *Go on.*

"Some encouragement for the princess." He motioned for the crowd to applaud.

She held out her hand, and as the applause continued, she followed him to the stage where he indicated a waiting chair. Once she was seated, he motioned for silence.

"Now, Princess, we have not set this up in advance, correct?"

"No, we haven't. I've only just seen you tonight when you appeared."

"Thank you. This is one of the reasons I have chosen you—that, and your status among the people, I believe, will lend more credibility to what I'm about to do." He turned to face the audience. "Ladies and gentlemen, before your very eyes, I am going to make Princess Lillian disappear."

Murmurs rippled throughout the crowd.

"Now, Princess, I just need you to relax and let your body sink into the chair. Just listen to the sound of my voice and relax. I'm going to place a fabric over you, but you'll still be able to see." Zands manifested a large, thin purple cloth, seemingly a layer from his own cloak, and draped it gently over Lillian, covering her entirely. From her perspective, everything in the room now had a slight purple hue. Lillian found herself growing tired. The chair was very comfortable. She felt like she could sleep right there.

"May I have silence, please, as I speak the ancient words of my ancestors."

The entire room sat in anticipation as Zands whispered words of an older tongue.

"Audite sermones meos dominum meum. Da mihi virtutem. Tolle eam, de hoc mundo, o antiquus animus. Da mihi virtutem. Nunc accipe eam!"

On his final statement, Zands pulled the cloth down to reveal an empty chair where Lillian was sitting mere seconds before. The silent room broke into wild applause as Zands took plenty of bows. Lillian's friends cheered along with the rest of the audience and looked around to see where Lillian would reappear from.

Somewhere nearby, Lillian was fighting the grogginess from Zand's hypnotic trance. She came to abruptly as she realized she was being gagged and her hands bound behind her back.

CHAPTER 17: Kidnapped

All around her came the sound of echoing voices. The lighting was very dim. She could see only silhouettes of a few figures around her. She thought she must be somewhere underground, considering how the chair bottom had dropped out and she had fallen through the stage's false bottom. That and the stagnant air was dank with an odor of mold.

"Will you hurry up? It won't be long 'fore someone starts wondering why she's not coming back." It was the waitress.

"You don't want her to get loose, do you? Feel free to come tie these yourself." A man.

"Just get it done," she barked.

Lillian started to look around when another man put a bag over her head. "Ah ah ah, Princess. Can't 'ave you seeing 'ho we are now, can we?"

Lillian didn't need to see the man to recognize him. She had heard his voice recently.

The jester.

But there was something else. She hadn't heard him only in the restaurant. She knew his voice from somewhere else.

As she tried to recall, she was hoisted up and forced to move forward.

"Careful. He said she's not to be harmed," instructed the girl.

"Trust me. I know what I'm doing," snipped the jester.

Trust me. Trust him.

It was the exact phrase she had heard before, but from where? *Slim!*

A few days earlier, she had overheard him say that to Pork. Now that she made the connection, she felt stupid for not recognizing him earlier, as his identity was quite apparent to her now.

Someone else came running up to join the others. Someone who smelled like bacon. *Pork!*

"Where 'ave you been?" Slim yelled at him.

"I'm sorry, Dax, I had trouble with the door, and I—" His response was cut short by a definitive slap.

"Shut up, you idiot! No names, remember, no names!"

So, Slim's name was Dax.

"I'm sorry, I'm sorry. I just . . . I just don't like this. He's not gonna hurt her, is he?" Pork sounded very nervous.

"That's not your concern. Go make sure we're not being followed. You fink you can 'andle that?"

Lillian heard Pork shuffle away.

She felt like she was dreaming.

Am I really being kidnapped? This can't be real.

She stumbled momentarily and hit a rocky wall.

Ow.

No, this was no dream. Her mind quickly went into survival mode. She tried to yell out, but the gag kept her cries to a minimum. She also received a quick jerk and verbal reprimand after that to remind her she was not in control. She may not be in control, but she was not going to go easily. She began to work on removing that gag.

They traveled in silence after that, through what Lillian guessed was a tunnel, for about three minutes and then they stopped.

"All right, I'll go through first and make sure it's clear," said the waitress.

Lillian heard something that sounded like running water for a brief second and then silence. A few seconds went by, and then she heard it again.

"Okay, send her through."

Send me through? Send me through where?

She didn't have time to argue, even if she could. She was being pushed forward. She suddenly felt a cool wave of what felt like water go over her body and then she was back in the tunnel. It was an odd sensation because she wasn't wet.

She heard two more "splashes" and was rejoined by Dax and Mystery Man. They walked another few minutes when they stopped again. She heard the metal clinking of a lock and latch followed by the creaking of a door. She immediately felt a breeze of the cool night air rush into the tunnel. This was her chance. She had successfully maneuvered the gag out of her mouth. She didn't know where they were taking her, but she still had to be relatively close to town. If anyone was going to hear her, it had to be now. She waited until she was sure she was outside.

"Help! Someone, help me!"

The bag was ripped off her head, and she found herself face to face with Dax, whose smeared makeup cast a sinister face on the already traumatic ordeal. The moon's light only amplified the effect.

He grinned, showing a mouth of rotting teeth, some already having taken a permanent leave. "Go a'ead, Princess. Scream your little 'ead off. Ain't no one gonna 'ear you out 'ere."

Lillian was allowed to look around this time. She recognized the area—it was where Dax and Pork had eluded her the other day. Dax was right. No one would hear her way out here.

"Look, we're not in the clear yet," the waitress pointed out. "We still need to get past the wall."

The wall? They're taking me to Drod!

Now Lillian panicked. "Help! Help! They're kidnapping me!"

"Will you shut her up?" growled the waitress.

Dax moved back around her.

"And put that bag back over her head. We don't need..."

Lillian heard a thump come from the vicinity of the waitress. Lillian turned her head to see the waitress slump down, an arrow protruding from her chest.

Alexander?

Another thud swiftly to her right and Mystery Man's back arched as he fell forward with sudden finality. This time, Lillian could see the arrow more clearly in the moonlight. It was blue.

Alexander was here.

Alexander!

Dax unfroze from his surprise and took a defensive position behind Lillian.

"'Ooever you are, you're making a big mistake!" Dax yelled trying to sound brave. He started backing his way toward the door they had just come from, dragging Lillian in front of him. "You wouldn't want to shoot the princess, now."

Oh, he won't hit me, Dax.

No sooner had she thought it, she felt the whoosh of an arrow. Dax screamed out in pain, Alexander's arrow now skewering Dax's calf.

"Aaaaaaah!" Dax continued to shuffle backwards, making it to the door.

From the darkness came, "Release her or the next one *will* shut your mouth for good."

Lillian couldn't see Alexander but knew he could make good on his threat.

"I'd do what he says, snake. Or should I call you Dax?" Lillian's voice was full of spite now.

Dax yanked her head back so close she could feel his putrid breath on her ear, and whispered, "You got lucky this time, Princess, but 'e won't give up. 'E will 'ave you and destroy your family before your eyes."

He shoved her away and backed into the tunnel.

Lillian stumbled forward, landing on her knees, her hands still bound behind her. She looked back, but the door had already disappeared and turned back into rock.

Alexander came running up to her.

"Lillian! Are you okay? Are you hurt?" he asked, desperation and fear in his voice. He glanced over at his two lifeless targets as he cut the rope off her hands.

She was surprisingly calm. "I…I don't think so. A bump here or there, but otherwise, I think I'm okay." She peered down at her dress. "Can't say my dress fared very well though." It was torn in several places and smeared with dirt and muck.

"Lillian, what happened?" He held onto her shoulders, studying her face. "How did you get all the way out here?"

"I'm not sure. I was at Talula's with everyone and the magician picked me for a trick. He put a cloak over me…" *The cloak. It did smell weird.* "It must have had some sort of elixir on it because I got really tired. He said some words in the old tongue, I think, then as he pulled the cloak off, the bottom of the chair dropped out and I fell."

I fell into the dark.

"Are you sure you're okay?" His gray eyes searched hers. His hands were warm.

"I'm fine. Really."

The castle bells started clanging their alarm sequence.

"We should get you back." His voice resumed its calm control.

Alexander whistled for Winston.

"What about these two?" She pointed to the motionless captors.

Alexander thought for a moment. "I'm not sure. Your father needs to know about them, but he can't know about me. I'll have to change out the arrows. Mine are too unique. They would raise too many questions."

"What will I say about all this? How will I explain my rescue?"

"Just say it was too dark to see your protector, if you saw anyone at all. The less I'm part of this, the better."

"Alexander, I'm sure my father will be grateful for whomever saved me. I'm sure he'd understand."

"No, I'm sorry it's...it's too complicated. I can't explain why now. You'll just have to trust me."

Winston trotted up and nudged Lillian with concern.

"Hey, Winston, I'm okay."

Alexander got on and then helped Lillian up.

They galloped back toward the castle. Once the village lights came into view, Alexander slowed Winston to a trot and stopped.

"I'm sorry, but I can't risk getting any closer. There may already be search parties looking for you."

"Of course, I understand," she said as she climbed down. "Alexander?"

"Yes?"

"Thank you."

"If any harm came to you, Lillian, I..." Alexander said, his calm demeanor cracking. He stopped. When he spoke again, his control had returned. "Well, I would hate to lose my only friend."

Her mind was racing. She had so many questions and theories. She needed to talk them out with someone who would understand.

Well, it's now or never, Lillian.

"Will you meet me later tonight?" Lillian asked tentatively.

"Assuming your family lets you out of their sight, yes," he said wryly. "Why?"

"I don't think I'll be able to sleep, and I think we could both use a friend."

"I'd like that very much, Lillian."

The alarm started pealing again, and this time they could hear voices approaching in the distance.

"Tonight. Our spot," she said.

Our spot.

As he swung Winston around, he said, "Dress warmly. It gets chilly in the forest at night."

And with a flick of the reins, he disappeared into the inky darkness.

Lillian thought of the article her dad had spoken of from Tapera. If she didn't know better, Alexander would look like a ghostly figure moving swiftly through the air.

Talula's was crawling with troops who were questioning everyone. Lillian walked in and was instantly bombarded with hugs and sobs from her friends who reached her first, only slightly ahead of Snow White, who nearly tackled Lillian to the ground.

"Oh, thank the Fae! My sweet Lillian, are you okay? Where have you been?" she cried as she checked Lillian all over for damage.

King Harry was now pushing his way through the troops to get to Lillian himself. It was apparent tears had recently been running down his cheeks.

"Lillian! Thank the Fae you're okay. You *are* okay, aren't you?" He noticed the blood and dirt on her dress now, and before she could reply, "Alondra, come quick. Lillian's been hurt!"

"I'm fine, Dad, I'm fine. It's not mine. I just got a little bruised is all."

Alondra came running, rags and water in hand.

"Where are you hurt, Lillian?"

"Nowhere, I'm fine, really. More mentally exhausted than anything."

"Lillian, sweetie, what happened?" Snow White asked, not letting go of her daughter.

Lillian explained everything she could, leaving Alexander out.

Jafria interjected a couple of times to fill in any blanks for the king and queen. "We were all looking around, waiting for Lillian to pop out from a corner or something. But then Zands bowed and gave the audience his thanks and left. We started to get worried. I flagged Talula down, but she looked just as surprised. 'Ee 'asn't ever done zhat trick before,' she said. Then she said she would go find him, but when she came back, she was pale. She immediately started ordering her staff to find him."

"So, where is he?" Lillian interjected.

King Harry, even with a tear-streaked face, now sounded more angry than panicked. "We don't know. I have half the guards searching every residence, store, and room in the village. Henry!"

The king's advisor marched over. "Yes, Your Majesty?"

"Anything on this Zands character?"

"Not yet, Your Majesty. The guards have cleared the Cuisine and Arts boroughs. They're working their way through New Towne and Old Towne, saving The Trenches for last. The hope is to box him in if he's moving."

"The instant you hear anything, you find me."

"Of course, Sire."

"And Henry, tell the men to be careful. This 'Zands', if that's even his name, is to be considered extremely dangerous."

"I'll let them know."

"Also, send a group about half a league northwest, to an outcrop of boulders. Lillian said two of her assailants were taken down, apparently, by an anonymous hero."

"Is that all, sir?"

The king looked at his daughter to see if she had any more information to divulge.

He knows I'm keeping something.

But she said nothing.

"Yes, that'll be all. For now."

Things began to settle down as patrons were released to go home and there were no more questions to be asked. Talula gave the names of Lillian's captors: the waitress, whose name was Abigayle Landon, and Eustace Cooke, who Lillian knew as Mystery Man (both dead now); and the jester, Daxon Windwater, who Lillian told her father had been wounded and was probably hiding out in The Trenches.

Lillian saw Richard waiting stoically and managed to pull him aside so she could to talk to him.

Richard embraced her. "I'm so glad you're okay. I wanted to go out looking for you, but Jafria forced me to wait for the King's Guard, and then they wouldn't let me accompany them."

"I understand, really. I know it was hard for you." She paused for a moment. "Look, Richard…"

He cut her off. "Lillian, you don't have to do this."

"I'm sorry?"

"What I mean is, you don't have to do this now. You've been through a lot, and I'm just not sure if you should be making any important decisions at the moment."

"And what decision is that?" she asked curtly.

"Well, I'm assuming you're getting ready to call off our courtship."

Oh.

She was surprised he had that much foresight. "Well, yeah, I was. I am. It's nothing against you. I just…"

He put his hands on her shoulders. "Don't do this now. You're upset. You're not thinking rationally."

She took his hands off her shoulders. "I'm fine," she said firmly. "And I had made this decision before tonight. I will admit, I was a little unsure, but thanks for making it easier."

"Lillian, I'm sorry. I didn't mean…"

But she was already walking off. She had no more patience to deal with any further drama tonight.

Back at the castle, Lillian was getting ready for bed, but not really, when her father knocked on her door.

"Mind if I come in for a minute, Lily Pad?"

"Of course not, Dad."

King Harry looked tired for the first time in Lillian couldn't remember when. He sat down on her bed and gave a pat next to him, requesting her to join. She walked from the vanity and sat next to her father. He took her hands in his much larger ones.

"Lillian. Are you sure you're okay? Because I know I'm not. Besides going to face Zoldaine, this night was the scariest of my life. I was ready to tear the kingdom apart. The whole continent if necessary."

"I'm fine, Dad, really. It's all so surreal right now. I'm sure I'll have a hard time sleeping, and it will all hit me tomorrow, but for right now, it's like a dream."

"Well, if you remember anything at all, no matter how small, you let me know."

"I will."

The king took a deep breath. "Lillian, your mother and I have discussed this at length tonight. She argued with me for the better part of an hour insisting it was important that you should have freedom to leave the castle but…"

No, don't say it.

"In light of the infiltration at the party and especially after tonight, I am asking you to stay within the castle walls until we get this sorted out."

"Dad, you can't…"

The king lifted his hand to stop her, his voice sliding from her father's to the king's. "I have already gone 'round this issue with your mother, and I am too tired to do it again with you. I know you have taken to the country lately to practice your archery, but you can do that for the time being here." His next words rang with the full weight of the crown behind them. "My decision is final."

He stood to leave.

"But, Dad, I…"

He cut her off. "Lillian, there's more to this than you know. This was no random act. They had a plan and there's nothing saying they won't try again. We… I got lucky tonight. Whoever saved you tonight, I owe them my life." He bent over and kissed her forehead. "You're my life. You, Andrew, your mother. If anything were to happen to any of you because I didn't take this threat seriously, I would never forgive myself." His voice now that of her father again. He walked to the door. "You'll understand someday when you have children. I know you're eighteen and more adult than child now, but you'll always be my little girl. Sleep tight, Lily Pad. I promise you, I *will* get to the bottom of this. They will answer to the *king*."

And with that, Lillian was alone again with her thoughts. She had never known her father to be this upset and outwardly protective.

"There's more to this than you know." What did he mean? What's he not telling me?

Only more questions to add to her list. Lillian would have to do a little more investigating on her own. She went to her vanity, pulled out some parchment, and began writing a letter.

I hope you can help me with this.

Once done, she sealed it in an envelope and took it to be delivered. The castle was fairly quiet as most of the guard was still searching for Zands and now Dax as well.

Why didn't you tell them about Pork?

Well, for one, she had kind of forgotten he was there since he had remained behind. And two, she didn't know his real name.

Oh yeah, and there was this other guy, kind of short and smelled like bacon.

She wasn't sure that'd be helpful as that description could account for a decent portion of the population. Plus, she couldn't be sure, but Pork didn't seem dangerous. She almost felt sorry for him, in a way.

As she expected, no one was in the correspondence room sorting letters. It was late, and most everyone was in bed. She placed the letter in between a few others to be sent out, hoping it would not arouse suspicion. If anything came of it, she'd tell her father, but for now, he had enough on his crown.

She casually strolled by some of the exits that led outside the castle. All of them had at least two guards. She would have to use her secret passage then.

The cool night air made her skin ripple as she pulled open the secret outside wall. She did feel some remorse about disobeying her father, but she *needed* this right now and hoped he would understand.

Hopefully he won't find out.

She snuck off into the moonlit night, her excitement of seeing Alexander overtaking her fear of being discovered.

CHAPTER 18: Midnight Rendezvous

Late was the hour, as the moon had slid a good distance across the sky since her ordeal. But it was full and shed more than enough light for her to recognize Alexander in the distance, sparring against an imaginary opponent, his blade flashing in the moonlight.

So he is *a swordsman as well.* Lillian recalled seeing the hilt wrapped up in his pack on Winston.

Alexander's form was fluid. With the moon behind him, his smooth, rhythmic motions were all but hypnotic. Lillian found herself slowing down so she could watch him for a little longer. On certain moves, his necklace would catch the moonbeams, flashing blood-red brilliance against the dark horizon. He finished with a final move Lillian had never seen before, then looked her direction.

"You can come over, you know." Alexander waved at her.

Did he know I was watching him? Lillian was thankful for the darkness, which hid her flushing cheeks.

"I didn't know you knew the sword as well."

"I dabble a little."

"Uh huh, like you dabble in archery?"

"Something like that." She was close enough to see his lips upturn.

Oh. That smile could melt the caps off the Kraneths.

He walked over to Winston, wrapping his sword as he went.

"How are you doing?" he asked as he put away his sword.

"I'm okay, I guess. Still seems like a dream. I suppose I owe you another thank-you for saving my life...again."

Alexander tugged a strap and turned around. He prowled toward her, his gray eyes like roiling storm clouds, anger flashed across his face. Lillian's heart sped up. He looked downright predatory. He closed his eyes at his last step and took a deep breath. When he opened them again, they were still hooded, but the fury they held had passed.

Gulp.

"Lillian, I thank the Fae I was there to save you," he said, his voice husky with emotion. "Who knows where they would have taken you..."

Lillian shuddered at the thought.

"We still need to get past the wall." That's what the waitress had said. But why *was the real question. Who was orchestrating the plan? Zands? It seemed unlikely, as she had never met him before as far as she could remember.*

Alexander shook his head as if to clear it. "Let's not make a pattern of this, hmm?"

"Deal."

Lillian didn't think it could hurt to ask, "Have you ever been into Drod before?"

"I've been past the wall, but not really that far in. Why?"

"That's where they were taking me, past the wall. I didn't think anyone lived there anymore."

"Not that I know of, but I just cross over to hunt sometimes. I've never really explored. It is a pretty big place, though, so who knows? Let's not think on this anymore right now. How about a little treat?"

Lillian nodded with a smile.

"C'mon," he said and grabbed her hand, pulling her along.

He's holding my hand! Calm down, Lillian, it's so you won't fall in the dark.

He led her to a small fire where some tasty-looking items rested atop a log nearby. Lillian could hardly wait to try the morsels Alexander had prepared. Each treat was some type of squishy sugar ball and his mom's chocolate, sandwiched between two sweet crackers. The log was close enough to the fire to warm the treat perfectly, toasting the sugar ball and softening the chocolate. The result was a gooey mess of glorious deliciousness. She had three.

As she licked her fingers clean, she had to know. "Where did you come up with this? It's *amazing*."

"Really? I couldn't tell after you inhaled three of them." He laughed.

"I did not," she argued, but a resounding burp betrayed her. He let out a deep belly laugh, his chest shaking with mirth. As he did, she noticed his necklace again. The beautiful gem, a ripe cherry-red in the moonlight.

"Your necklace," she pointed. "It almost seems to glow."

"Oh, yeah." He moved closer to her so she could see. "The closer it gets to the full moon, the brighter it gets."

Oh, he's serious.

He moved closer and held the stone up to the full moon. "Like tonight."

"It's beautiful." She reached out, taking it in her hand, moving it back and forth between the light and shadows.

"That's why most of the 'sightings' happen around the full moon, because it's so bright," said Alexander.

"And you don't remember where it came from?"

"No. I asked my parents, but they just said it was part of me."

"Part of you?"

"Yeah, guess they tried to take it off me when they found me, but they said I cried something awful and only stopped when they put it back on."

"Wait, found you? What are you talking about?"

"Did I not mention it? Sorry. I'm adopted, I suppose you'd say. My parents found me on the river when I was just a baby."

"What? Seriously?"

"Yeah. I thought I had said something, but it must have slipped my mind. I don't really think about it that much. They've just always been my parents, so… is that weird?" He suddenly seemed insecure.

"What?" Lillian realized she sounded a little judgmental. "No! No. I'm sorry, you're fine, I mean it's fine, I mean, you're not an it, of course you're not, I just—oh, flerb!"

His warm laugh eased her mind. "It's okay, Lillian. I know what you mean. Don't worry about it."

"So, is that why they don't want you to have friends? Are they afraid that whoever let you go will want you back?"

"I guess. I've asked them about it a couple of times, and they're pretty insistent that we don't talk about that part. They just assure me they have good reason, and they've never really given me any cause to doubt them. So, I don't push it."

"Well, tell your parents that the princess is very impressed with how they've raised their son and they shouldn't worry. And that he makes delicious treats," she added.

"I'll tell my mom you liked them. It's a family recipe. Say, want to get in a little practice tonight? Night shooting? Assuming you can still shoot, sticky fingers."

"Lead the way," she responded, gesturing him ahead of her, and covertly licked a stubborn sticky spot off her thumb.

They went back to the grove. For a moment Lillian thought he was going to make her run through the Forge at night, but he led them a little deeper into the forest where the moonlight was slowly disappearing.

"Are you trying to kidnap me, too?" Lillian poked him in the side.

He jumped a little. "Hey now, you better be nice to me, or I might let you find your own way home."

Lillian had to admit she was a little disoriented in the deep darkness, and she couldn't get her bearings. She gave her best whiney voice. "Are we there yet?"

Alexander stopped and looked around. "Actually... yeah."

"How can you see anything let alone tell where we are?"

"Set your stuff down."

Lillian did as asked and then stood there. "Okay, now what?"

"Close your eyes."

Lillian closed her eyes for all the good it did. She hadn't been able to see anything but occasional slivers of light slicing through the foliage. Then she felt his hands come up from behind and rest on her shoulders. A tingling went down her spine.

"What do you see?" he said softly, his lips inches from her ear.

What do I see? My eyes are closed. I don't see anything.

"I don't understand."

"Relax." His hands were so warm. "Take a deep breath in...and let it out. Try and calm your mind. Stop thinking about seeing with your *eyes* and accept what your *other* senses are telling you." He began slowly caressing her neck in methodical strokes. She felt the day's tension ebbing. "Don't focus on anything."

You're making that impossible.

"Let it all in. Breathe." The strokes continued, moving out to her shoulders. And in spite of his hands on her body, Lillian began to notice things, her senses sharpening. The closest sensation she could liken it to was when your ears pop as you come down from the mountains and everything suddenly gets loud, though you hadn't even noticed before that things were dampened.

The rustling of dry leaves to her right. Scratching on a tree before her. She felt a soft breeze across the fine hairs of her skin as it wove its way through this timber sanctuary. The faint puff of a moth fluttering past her cheek. The strong aroma of various plants laced with the sweet scent of decomposing leaves. And then there was him. Familiar to her with scents of warm sun and fresh air, but now she could detect something like pine underneath it. And something darker. Darker but tempting.

Ever so softly, Alexander's hands slid down her arms...to her hands...and trailed tantalizingly off her fingertips.

A whisper that sounded leagues away. "Now, what do you see?"

And suddenly, the sun seemed to have risen early and was now shining brightly overhead. Her eyes were still closed but she could see everything. Hear everything. Feel *everything*. She was wary of moving, not knowing if it would break this enchanted spell, but she couldn't resist. She turned her head, keeping her eyes closed, and the newly lit world followed. She smiled. It was amazing. She continued turning in a circle until she faced Alexander. He was smiling too.

That's impossible. How could I possibly know he's smiling?

Lillian had to know for sure. She opened her eyes. The world grew dark again, but she was still aware. Alexander was grinning.

"How did you *do* that?" Lillian was infatuated with him before, but now she was in awe.

"I didn't do anything but give you a little nudge. To be honest, I wasn't entirely sure you could gleam but I had a feeling."

"Gleam? What kind of weird thing is that?"

"Well, it's easier than saying 'seeing in the dark without opening my eyes.' But sometimes it's more than just seeing. Sometimes I can *sense* things. I didn't want to freak you out earlier, but that's why I was already so close when you got kidnapped. I just felt you were in trouble and headed in that direction. It didn't make any sense to me because I knew you were in town, but I've grown to trust this feeling, and it's never been wrong."

"Grayson talked about something like that before. He said most magic folk have it. But he calls it the third eye."

"Third eye? Now *that's* weird. C'mon, let's shoot some arrows."

Night shooting turned out to be an interesting adventure. He had set up a few targets, which, of course, she couldn't see.

This, apparently, was where "gleaming" came in. It was very hard for her without Alexander's help. She could barely get a "glimmer," let alone a full gleam. And trying to do that and concentrate on shooting made it nearly impossible for her to hit anything. She finally threw down her bow in frustration.

"This isn't working. I can't do it." She started walking nowhere in particular.

Alexander chased after her. "Wait, Lillian. Wait up." She stopped but did not turn to face him. He ran around in front of her. "Hey, don't be so hard on yourself. You've learned more in two days than most archers learn in two *years*. It's going to take time and…"

She didn't let him finish. "I know, I know—practice. I just…it's hard, you know. I feel like I'm finally doing something I enjoy and I just want to be good at it."

"You *are* good at it. You also have to remember you've been through a lot today. We both have." His voice tinged with sadness.

She felt guilty. She hadn't been a good friend. What he had done for her…

"Look. You're here in the dark, chilly night shooting arrows when you should really be home getting rest. So, your resolve isn't in question."

"I know. But I have to be better." She started to cry. "I have to be better." She fell to her knees.

Alexander sank down beside her and gathered her against his chest, enfolding her into his arms.

"I was so scared, Alexander," she sobbed. And all the emotions she had been holding back suddenly came pouring out of her. Her kidnapping. Her breakup with Richard. Her feelings for Alexander. All of them, along with her frustration, were spilling out like the tears down her cheeks. "I was afraid. There was nothing *I* could do. Why do they want me? Why are they trying to hurt my family? I have to get better so I can protect myself. Protect my family," she cried angrily.

"Shhh, Lillian, shhh. You're safe now. It's all okay."

"I just don't understand! First at my party, but it just seemed like a prank. But after tonight, why? Why am I so important? Why *now*?"

Alexander thought about trying to answer, but realized it would do little good. She needed to let everything out. The shock of it all was finally catching up to her. He just held her and let her cry.

After a while, her sobs subsided and her breathing slowed. Alexander judged it safe to talk. "You know I'll help you any way I can, right?"

She sniffed and wiped her nose. "I know."

He lowered his head to look down at her.

"Don't look at me. I look like a troll," she moaned.

"Nonsense. Here." He handed her a small cloth from his pocket.

She took it begrudgingly and wiped her eyes before blowing her nose.

"Well, I was going to want that back, but now I think you can keep it."

She punched him in the arm. "That's not funny."

But he smiled anyway. "That's my girl, back to physical violence."

She laughed despite everything. *My girl.* She liked the sound of that. "Thanks." She peered up into his gray eyes, wrought silver in the moonlight. "How do you know?"

"Know what?"

"Just what to say, what to do to make me feel better."

Alexander shrugged. "I don't know. I didn't think about it really. Probably the gleam again."

No, it's just who you are. Which is why I'm falling for you so hard.

"We should probably head back," he said as he unfolded his legs and stood, offering a hand to help her up. "I think that's enough for tonight."

She thought about arguing but realized how drained she was after her emotional outpouring and changed her mind. She was exhausted.

Still, her mind raced as they headed back. *Who was this Zands magician? Could he be Zoldaine? Was the party a warning? Why are they after me? What isn't Dad telling me? What should I do about Pork? What should I do about*

Alexander? I have feelings for him, but the situation is hardly manageable now. I got out tonight, but it's going to be increasingly difficult to disappear, especially during the day. Dad is going to start posting guards around the perimeter.

A cool breeze brought her back to the present. The night's shooting had caused her to work up a light sweat, but now that she was cooling down, the night air made her shiver. Lillian wanted to ask Alexander to hold her, not just because of how he made her feel but because she was legitimately cold.

She was reluctant to get close to him, however. She had just gotten out of a relationship, if she could call it that, a few hours ago, and now was all but plunging into another one with a guy she had only known a month. But she *felt* as if she'd known him for much longer. She'd felt that rare familiarity she had experienced with only a few people before, as if she had known them over many lifetimes. She had that with Alondra, and Jafria, but never a guy. That emotion, coupled with a lack of peering eyes or chaperones, had her heart racing as they walked into camp.

She shivered again.

"Here, let me get a blanket for you." Alexander walked over to Winston. "I didn't realize how chilly it must be for you. I've grown accustomed to it." He unfurled the blanket and wrapped her up. "Let's sit down over here out of the wind."

They both sat, sheltered behind a tree that blocked most of the breeze.

The silence grew heavy and awkward.

Does he want to hold me?

Lillian couldn't tell, but could feel his unease.

He's just chivalrous, Lillian. He knows you're dating someone. Well, were dating. Just tell him already! But tell him what? "Alexander, I broke up with Richard tonight so I could be with you. Because I think I'm falling for you, but that's silly because I barely know you, but do you feel the same way?" FLERB!

Even with the blanket, she was beginning to hurt, she was so cold.

"Lillian, I don't mind holding you," he said as she fought back a shiver. "I just didn't want to overstep, because you're dating someone."

Always the gentleman.

"I don't think he'd mind in this case." She moved closer to him as he lifted his arm. "Besides, it's just one friend keeping another friend warm, right?"

Lillian hoped against hope he'd say something to indicate more. But all he replied was, "Right. One friend to another."

She laid her head on his chest and he put his left arm down against her side. His words said *friend* but his heartbeat was saying something else. He was so warm she stopped shivering almost instantly and felt her body slowly start to unclench. She had to tell him. She knew she was making him uncomfortable for no reason.

"Alexander, I need to tell you something."

"Okay?"

"But before I tell you, you have to understand it had nothing to do with you. I had already decided before I'd even met you this was the right decision."

He paused. "Okaaay. Should I be worried?"

She just blurted it out. "I broke up with Richard."

She waited for a reply, but Alexander didn't say a word. He just put his other arm around her and held her tighter.

June 11

The warmth of the sun's rays hit Lillian's face and slowly brought her from her slumber in Alexander's arms. At first she was confused where she was, but soon her memories of the last twenty-four hours hit her like a wave. Her friends. The dinner. Zands. The kidnapping. Richard. Her dad. Alexander.

Alexander!

She peeked up at him and found him looking back at her. "G'morning. Did you sleep well?"

She stretched. "Mmmmm, yeah, actually." Then reality hit her.

Oh. Oh, oh, no. No, no, no, no! No!

"By the Fae!" She shot up, looking around frantically.

Alexander jumped up too. "What? What is it?"

"I have to get back. I have to get back *NOW*. If my dad finds out I'm missing, he's going to go full dragon-fury. He'll ground me 'til I'm eighty."

And he'll be so scared! All of her family would be. To do this to them a second time by being thoughtless!

Alexander whistled for Winston, who cantered over briskly, sensing the urgency.

"It would be best if I went alone," Lillian said. "If someone were to see you, they might shoot you on sight, after last night."

"I understand. Go."

Lillian hopped up on Winston.

"Thank you! I'm so sorry I have to leave like this. Last night was…" She just looked at him.

Alexander took her hand. "I know. Me too…Now GO, before I never get to see you again!"

With that, he slapped Winston's hindquarters and the pair bolted toward the castle.

Lillian turned to see Alexander slowly disappearing against the horizon.

She stopped Winston just short of the open terrain and dismounted. She didn't need anyone seeing her riding a strange horse to start asking questions. There were already too many after last night.

"Thanks, Winston. Give this to Alexander for me." She leaned over and gave Winston a kiss on the cheek. Winston neighed and galloped back toward the deeper forest.

Lillian surveyed the back of the castle. There wasn't anyone on ground level, but there were two sentinels patrolling just this section of the wall.

Dad wasn't kidding.

She'd have to time her return almost perfectly to sneak back in.

Three... two... one. A quick dash, the secret button, a push, and she was in. She headed up the stairs, listening at the top for anyone who might be walking the halls. It was still early. The only ones awake would likely be down in the kitchen preparing breakfast. In the morning stillness, the usually quiet door seemed to grind across the floor like a battle axe against a boulder. Lillian cringed, but it brought no inquisitors.

I can't believe I made it. She slipped down the hall and ducked into her bedroom.

"I hope it was worth it," came an ominous voice from behind her.

Lillian recognized her father's voice at once.

CHAPTER 19: Grounded
June 13

*L*ight rain from an overcast sky mirrored the imprisoned princess's mood. Lillian just stared out of her bedroom window dejectedly, watching the drizzle slowly melt the *A* from the rock face where Alexander had put it just a few days earlier. It seemed like forever ago.

Her thoughts swung erratically. She knew she didn't really have any right to be mad at her dad. He was just trying to protect her. But the way he had talked to her made her feel like such a child. That she was some little girl who was just being selfish and silly.

She thought about Alexander. The way he smelled, the feel of his hands, how his warm arms had held her only nights before.

Sigh.

She replayed her kidnapping, hoping to recall some detail of what her captors had said to put any meaning to all of this. If she had that, her imprisonment would at least be significant, worth the fight she had had with her dad.

The king hadn't been back. She hadn't really expected that he would. He was busy and knew she was safe—for sure, now—so he needn't worry. All entrances and exits to the castle were guarded, including the secret ones, which (depressingly) he had known about all along.

Both her mother and Alondra had made attempts to talk with her through the door but to no avail. The only person she wanted to talk to right now, she couldn't. She jumped to her window at every foreign sound that came from below, hoping Alexander would risk it. Risk being seen just to see her again. Risk being discovered to talk sense to her father, to ask for his blessing to take Lillian away and hide her. Protect her. But the sounds were never him. The wind and animals were always to blame.

Her empty stomach had gnawed all morning and could no longer be ignored. She got up from her chair and was halfway across the room when someone knocked on her door. She listened for her mother's voice, but the one who spoke was quite unexpected. Andrew.

Lillian and Andrew weren't the closest brother and sister. Most of that had to do with their age difference.

"He'll grow out of it, dear. He's still just a boy." Snow White had tried to defend her son numerous times, unintentionally leaving Lillian feeling even more frustrated and alone.

But it was her annoying, pestering, pranking little brother who was about to give her a swell of hope in her moment of despair.

Andrew had been told—no, warned—not to go near his sister. But he had an idea of how bad things were. He'd never heard Lillian or his dad yell at each other as much as they had the morning Lillian had snuck back in. The argument had ended in a slamming door and the king marching off.

Lillian had not come out of her room once since, and the king had not attempted to reconcile. The queen knocked on Lillian's door a couple of times but was met with nothing but silence. Food was brought and left outside her door. Some of it looked disturbed occasionally, but not often and not much.

Andrew had approached her door cautiously, as if the door alone could deliver the wrath that lay cooped up behind it. He carefully held the package he hoped would break Lillian from her spell.

Knock. Knock. Knock.

The noise had startled Lillian because she hadn't heard anyone approach, and neither her mom nor Alondra knocked like that.

"Who is it?"

"It's me." Andrew's voice was timid and muffled. She barely heard him.

She opened the door a little, seeing Andrew standing beside the food left for her lunch.

"What do you want?" she asked. Andrew winced slightly at her tone.

Lillian knew it wasn't his fault she was grounded. If anything, it was her fault that he was held captive as well, because it was her "they" were after for some reason.

"I'm sorry, I didn't mean to snap at you."

"I know." Andrew looked down at her food and then at the envelope in his hand. "I'm really sorry you got grounded, Lillian."

"It's not your fault, little brother. This one is on me. And I probably made it even worse for you."

"Meh, it's okay. Mom's been real nice to me. She didn't even get onto me for walking the wall the last couple of days."

"Well, I'm glad they haven't come down too hard on you." She noticed Andrew fidgeting with an envelope and card. "Do you have something for me?"

"Yeah, a couple of things." He handed her a decorated card. "Mom wanted you to sign it for Jaccob's birthday.

Even though he's away, she wanted Queen Aurora to know we were still thinking about him and praying for the Fae's blessing on his and Marcus's safe return."

Lillian took the card. "You said there were a couple."

He looked down at his hands again. "Yeah, well, I think so. See, I was walking the castle wall yesterday and I happened to look over toward the forest when all of a sudden I see this arrow hit a tree and it has this paper attached to it and I kind of waited for someone to go up and retrieve it but no one did and then I thought maybe, I don't know, that maybe someone meant it for me, but I don't know why I just kind of had this feeling." Her brother's story tumbling out in a single breath.

Lillian kept listening, her heart leaping. She knew it was from Alexander.

Can the gleam work two ways? Did he influence Andrew?

"Now, I know Dad told us not to leave, and I didn't want to get grounded like you," Andrew's speech slowed after his initial exhale as he continued, "because at least right now I can have friends over, but I went to Seth and told *him* about it, so he went out to the tree and got the letter, or whatever this is." Andrew finally handed Lillian the folded-up letter with a hole in it.

On the outside was a simple "To: L From: A" Lillian took it and started pouring over the lines inside.

"So, I kind of figured it was for you since you're really the only one I know with a name that starts with *L*, but I couldn't figure out who *A* was." Andrew's voice was rising louder than Lillian wanted out in the hallway. "I mean, obviously, the first name that popped into my head was Andrew, but I know I didn't leave it for you, that would be silly. My next guess was Alondra, but then I thought, *Why would Alondra be shooting a message to my sister?* So, that didn't make sense. Do you know someone else named *A*, Lillian? Is that who you went to see the other night?"

Lillian couldn't risk anyone overhearing, so she tugged Andrew inside, nearly upsetting the whole tray of food. "Will you shut *up* and get in here? I don't think our neighbors in Tapera heard you!"

Andrew stumbled into the room, and Lillian quickly shut the door.

"I'm sorry, Lil', I didn't mean to…"

"I know, it's fine. I'm not mad at you."

She padded over to her bed and made a spot for him. "Come on over."

Andrew walked forward timidly.

"Andrew, I promise, I'm not mad at you. If anything, you should be mad at me."

He wasn't quite sure what to think but still sat down.

"I haven't been a very good big sister lately, and I'm sorry. I've been caught up in my own world recently, and I haven't paid you much attention—which I have a feeling is why you've been such a little troll lately." She ruffled his hair.

"I'm sorry, Lil'. It really was all Ethan's idea to put cream in your hair. I promise."

"Don't worry, Andrew, really. Besides, I think you've made up a lot with this." She held up the letter.

"What is it? Who is *A*?"

She looked at her little brother and realized he needed a big sister. Someone to conspire with, someone who placed their trust in him.

"Andrew, what I'm about to tell you is a *really* big secret, okay? Not even Mom or Dad or Alondra knows what I'm about to tell you."

His eyes got big at the thought of possessing such a secret.

"I'm serious, you can't tell *anyone*."

"Not even Ethan?"

"Not even Ethan. This is really important to me."

"Okay."

"Here we go." Lillian drew a breath to prepare for what she was about to do. "The reason I've been leaving the castle a lot and why I snuck out last night is because... well, because of a guy."

"A guy?"

"Yeah."

"So, that letter's from him?"

"Yeah, his name is Alexander. Want to read it?"

Andrew's eyes lit up like she'd given him a puppy. "Yeah!" He scooted over as she opened it.

Lillian, I saw your brother walking the castle wall and figured he would get this to you. I'm sorry I can't come see you, as I have a feeling you really can't come see me. I hope you understand. I have to go away for a while, but I'll be back. Look for the sign. Keep practicing. Impress me. —A

For awhile? What did that mean? Last time he was gone for almost a month.

But, then again, she wasn't going anywhere anyway, so maybe it was better if he *was* gone.

"What did he mean by 'keep practicing'?" Andrew was reading over the letter again.

"He's been teaching me how to shoot." She realized she hadn't practiced at all since the other night. She couldn't just sit and mope about like a goblin with no gold. And while the castle didn't have nearly the elaborate setup like Alexander did with the Forge, she could make do. "Remember, Andrew, you can't tell *anyone*."

"Right."

"Promise?"

"Well…"

"Andrew, you *have* to."

"I promise, only if…" His face held a playful look.

"Yes?" Lillian would play along.

"I promise, if you'll play hide 'n' seek again with me," he said, grinning, "like we used to."

She stuck out her hand. "Deal."

They shook hands and then she gave him a big hug. Maybe this grounding thing wouldn't be so bad after all.

Andrew pulled away quickly. "You count first!" he shouted, as he ran out of the room.

CHAPTER 20: Vendetta
June 20

Along with trying to figure out Alexander's thackleberry recipe, Lillian had passed the time by practicing her archery, and playing games like "Pigs or Pearls" and "Don't Touch the Mountain Fire" with Andrew, but mostly it was hide 'n' seek. They had played in the east wing, the expansive courtyard with its vast shrubbery, and the servants' quarters. Today featured the west-wing bedroom area along with the foyer.

Andrew was currently counting at the base of the stairs while Lillian was lurking around in her bedroom hallway, looking for a new place to hide. She could hear her brother's voice echoing off the walls.

"Thirty-four, thirty-five..."

There were two guards coming toward her from down the hall at a quicker-than-normal pace. Her interest was piqued, which wasn't hard considering she'd been playing hide 'n' seek with an eleven-year-old in her spare time.

"What's the hurry, gentlemen? Troll got your tail?"

"Pardon, Your Highness, but we have urgent business with your father." One of the guards shifted to move around her.

"Yeah, they caught one of the men involved in your kidnapping." The other looked excited and got a quick dragon eye from the other.

"What part of *discretion* do you not understand?" the first guard asked.

"But she's the princess, surely—" The second guard was cut off.

"—surely nothing. He said no one. Now, come on before you get us in more trouble with that flapping mouth of yours."

"Wait!" Lillian called out as they hurried off. "Who did they catch? Was it Zands? What did he look like?"

Over his shoulder but not stopping, the first guard called back, "My apologies, Your Highness, but your father's orders are clear. Please forget what you've heard." And they both disappeared around the corner.

"Sixty-seven, sixty-eight…"

She and her brother had both agreed no secret passages or hidden hideaways, otherwise they'd be searching for hours. Lillian didn't want to cheat, but she knew there was a good chance her dad would be interrogating whoever it was next to her secret passage. She had to know who it was and what was going on.

Making sure no one saw her, she slipped into the wall and started down the stairs. She was about halfway down when she could hear voices and knew her hunch had paid off. They were still too muffled and the echo in the passage didn't help. She'd have to get closer.

As she approached, the voices became clearer.

"It doesn't…you just…" It was her father.

"You 'ave no idea…more of us than you know." It was Dax.

"We can be lenient with your sentence, traitor," said Sir Alger. "The punishment is up to you."

Lillian got closer to the wall. It had been a long time since she had examined it, but it now had a small crack, making part of the room visible from this side. Lillian could see Dax tied up in a chair with her father, Sir Alger, and Henry all standing around him.

"Spoken like a true loyal dog. I remember when you used to 'ave bite to that bark. Your words are as useless as your sword, old man," Dax jeered at Sir Alger.

"You're lucky the king is present, you troll; otherwise, your tongue would find out how useless my sword really is."

"Enough, Sir Alger," the king interjected. "I will not have us pulled into a madman's twisted game. Henry, bring them in."

Lillian saw Henry leave and her father address Dax again.

"This is your last chance, Mr. Windwater. I assure you what is about to happen will not be pleasant. Why are you after my daughter? Who is orchestrating these attacks? Where is this Zands character?"

"You 'ave no idea, do you?" Dax was arrogant. "The mighty king who can't protect 'is family. Especially 'is sweet daughter. 'E doesn't even know 'oo she goes off to see every day in the woods."

Lillian was shocked. *How long have they been watching me?* The passage suddenly felt arctic as chills crept up Lillian's spine.

Dax continued, realizing he was getting to the king. "You should 'ave 'eard 'er begging me to release 'er. Calling for 'er daddy, who was 'elpless. Clueless."

Lillian saw something she never thought possible from her father. He punched Dax across the jaw.

"Your Majesty, please," Sir Alger pleaded.

For the second time, Lillian heard the protective voice of her father.

"You listen to me very carefully, you worm. Whatever you think you may know of me and who I am is nothing compared to what I am capable of. I *will* find out who's behind this. And when I do—they and anyone else involved will have wished for death before I found them."

Dax was not phased as blood ran down his mouth. "That's good, Your Majesty. That's good. Make sure you keep that fire. Let it burn deep inside you. Let it consume you. It'll be that much sweeter when 'e snuffs it out. Right after you watch 'elplessly as your family is extinguished one by one before you."

Lillian heard the door open again, which was probably good for Dax. She had never heard her father burn with such intensity before; like low-burning coal, its silent blue flame licking close, burning hotter than a roaring blaze, rendering any who misjudged it to ash before they even recognized the heat.

"You called for us, Your Majesty." *Faeries?*

"Switwick. Nyssa. Thank you for coming. Has Henry informed you of the situation?"

"Yes, Sire." Switwick was a woodland sprite. He always had a chipper disposition, but today he sounded grave.

"I regret having to put you in such a compromising situation, but I'm afraid I have no other recourse to take."

Nyssa was quick to relieve the king. "No need for apologies, Your Majesty. The magic realm is just as much at risk as the kingdoms, if the rumors are true, which we pray to the Fae, are not."

"Nevertheless, I am in your debt."

"Shall we proceed?" Switwick seemed eager to be done with this task.

"You fink your overgrown swamp flies will be of any 'elp?" Dax drawled.

"Quiet, toad. The only words that will come from your mouth are the truth," Nyssa lashed. This surprised Lillian as well. Nyssa was usually the shy, timid one.

Lillian watched Switwick mumble some spell while Nyssa circled around Dax's head, then silence.

"Okay, Your Majesty, he's ready."

"What is your name?"

"Daxon Windwater." His voice sounded as if he was in a trance.

"Who is behind the attacks on the royal family?"

Dax struggled to answer.

"Answer me, traitor," the king said low and menacingly.

"You know 'oo. It is 'e who controls the dark. 'E who supplies your nightmares."

"Give me a name."

Silence.

"Why attack now? Who is your target?"

"Revenge."

"Who? Who wants revenge? For what?"

Dax struggled again, writhing as if in pain.

Switwick interjected, "Your Highness, I feel an opposing force at work."

"Can you tell who?"

"No, but it is strong. And dark. I'm not sure how much longer we can…"

A painful groan built from Dax's lungs and he screamed, "You will not stop 'im! You will pay for what you've done! All of you will *PAY*!"

"Who? Tell me who!"

Lillian had never heard such agonizing sounds come from a man before.

And with a long, final, bloodcurdling shriek, "*ZOLDAINE LIVES!*"

Lillian saw a blackness flash out of Dax; it filled the room and exploded into the passage, knocking Lillian to the ground.

It was only for a split second, but Lillian had never felt such darkness and soul-sucking despair. Every bad memory, every moment of weakness, the worst moments that haunted her dreams, her kidnapping, all of them flowed through her head. Stygian emotions of misery, anguish, torment, and fury welled up inside her and pressed against the inside of her skull. She prayed for death.

Then, it was gone. Over. And the weight lifted.

"Your Majesty." Sir Alger was the first to recover. "Your Majesty, are you hurt?"

"Besides the flash of rage and feeling as if I had no reason to live—I'm fine," he said darkly, "though I'm not sure we can say the same for our prisoner."

Lillian noticed that she had heard moans from everyone except Dax. She stood gingerly and peered back into the room and immediately wished she hadn't. Dax's body hung limp in the chair, only held upright by the ropes that once restrained him. But where his eyes should have been...lay only ruined, hollow holes. Sunken points of inky darkness.

"Switwick, what *was* that?" her father asked.

"A very old and powerful spell. I'm sorry, Sire, there was nothing we could do. It was set in motion the instant we put our spell on him. Whoever placed it didn't want him speaking. They must be very well versed in the darkest of magic. And very powerful to have laid an underlying spell of such strength as to kill a man."

"What we have seen, what we have heard, does not leave this room. Understood?"

A uniform response resounded from the room, "Yes, Your Majesty."

"Henry, go find my daughter. It's time we talked."

Then her father looked directly where she stood behind the wall.

CHAPTER 21: A Friendly Informant
June 23

Still haunted by what she had seen from the passageway, but even more so from what her father had discussed with her afterward, Lillian mulled over all that had transpired within the last few days.

"There have been other attacks."

Apparently, similar instances had been happening in the other kingdoms, though he didn't go into detail. And he was not going to.

"Well, what happened? Are Avery and Olivia okay? Was Zands involved?" She pleaded with him for more, worried and weeping.

"I'm not at liberty to say right now," he replied, unmoved.

She turned to anger. "Not at liberty? You're the king! You make the rules! I need to know. I have a *right* to know."

What came next, Lillian was unprepared for.

King Harry Charming, her father, for the first time since she was a child, raised his voice towards her. "You are *lucky* you have the right to leave your *ROOM*! *Every* turn you get, you've crossed my words, defied my authority. And for *what*? Some *crush* who's teaching you archery? Your latest love interest?"

Immediately, she could sense her father resented his outburst, most likely for letting her know that he knew about Alexander and because he wasn't ready to divulge that information quite yet, regardless of what Daxon had said. Her insolence. The safety of his family. These things were clearly affecting him in ways she had never seen. But that still didn't make her feel better.

He composed himself, seeing the tears in her eyes. "Lillian, I'm sorry. I didn't mean to lash out at you. This is not your fault."

"Don't," she said as her tears spilled out, "just go."

"Lillian, please just let me…" Now he was pleading.

"Get out!" She was a myriad of emotions, but anger was the one that could find its voice.

Her father didn't say anything further. He pulled the door closed behind him on his way out, and when it clicked closed, the floodgates for Lillian's emotions broke open.

She buried her face in her pillows, soaking them with her tears, and eventually cried herself to sleep.

She was better the next day but hadn't seen her dad since their fight. Part of her wished he'd come back to talk, but the other part was glad he didn't because he respected her space. She hadn't really come out of her room much since their shouting match, either. She didn't really feel like seeing anyone. Most of the time she gazed aimlessly out her window, hoping to see some sign of Alexander's return, but there never was any.

A light knocking on her door caught her attention.

"Sweetie, it's Mom. I have a surprise for you."

Snow White had been trying to pull her daughter from her melancholy ever since her grounding, but with renewed vigor since Lillian's clash with her father.

Lillian shuffled to the door, planning to humor her mother but decline, once again, whatever idea or food she was proposing.

She cracked the door open. "Mom, I really appreciate you trying to cheer me up, but…"

"Surprise!" Jafria jumped in front of Lillian.

"Jafria? What're you doing here?" Lillian looked at her Mom. "I thought I was grounded?"

"Well, you are, but Jafria's not. You just can't leave the castle, but that doesn't mean someone can't come in."

Lillian wrapped Jafria in a full hug. "I missed you too. We were all really worried about you. Even Richard. None of us really got a chance to talk to you and then you went and got grounded."

"I know. I'm sorry. There's just a lot that's been going on. I've been a bad friend."

"Well, lucky for you, you have the rest of the day and all night to make it up to me." Jafria said, picking up her bag and strolling into the bedroom like it was her own.

"Thanks, Mom. I really needed this." Lillian sniffled and hugged her mom.

"Don't thank me, sweetie. It was your father's idea."

Lillian was taken aback. "Dad…Dad suggested this?"

"Lillian, honey, you have to realize what your dad has done, and is doing, is because he loves you. Because he loves all of us. It's *his job* to protect us. And not since Zoldaine was in power has there been a threat like this to our family, to our kingdom. He just let his protective emotions get the better of him after the…the interrogation. He felt really awful about how you two left things."

"I know, I just wish he wouldn't keep things from us. Especially when it's about me," Lillian said sadly. "But I guess I understand. I should go apologize. And tell him thanks for letting Jafria come over."

"He's not here right now. He left early this morning for Tapera to meet with King Louis and Sir Aaron from Caldera to discuss what actions need to be taken. Lillian, you have to understand something is going on across all of the kingdoms. Someone is targeting the royal families. And if it's not Zoldaine, then it's your father's job to figure out who and why. He's not even telling *me* everything, and you know we've had *discussions* about that."

Lillian did know. She had heard raised voices from both her parents more frequently since her kidnapping.

"So, even though I know you think your father is being unreasonable, his greatest fear is losing you or any of us, and he will do whatever is in his power to keep that from happening."

"Thanks, Mom. I'm sorry for the way I've been acting. I know it's been a little childish. Please let me know when Dad gets back, okay?"

"I will." Snow White leaned her head inside the room. "You make sure she stays out of trouble, Jafria, or I'll ground you too," she said with a wink.

"Yes, ma'am."

The second the door shut, Jafria assaulted Lillian with questions.

"Why'd you break up with Richard? I mean, I know why, but why now? Is it because of that guy? What's his name? Who tried to kidnap you? Have you seen him since you've been grounded? Is that why you're grounded?"

"Whoa! Slow down, slow down." Lillian grabbed her friend by the shoulders. "I'm fine, thanks for asking."

"Sorry, sorry. It's just been a circle of gossiping *imps* out there, and I've been in the center. I promised them I'd come back with *something*."

"It's okay. I can only imagine. I've been going crazy in here not knowing anything that's going on out there, too."

"But let's start with you. Richard." Jafria said pointedly, her slender brow arched inquisitively.

Lillian took a deep breath, trying to figure out how much she wanted to divulge to her friend. "Okay, you know Richard and I weren't exactly a perfect match and I was planning on calling it off soon. Well, the kidnapping and," *Well, she already knows there's someone.* "yes, another guy. Well, it just bumped the timetable up."

"Oooo, I *knew* this other guy was involved!"

"It's not like that, Jafria. I mean, yeah, I like him, but we're just friends." *Well, maybe not so much anymore.* "He's teaching me how to shoot, but, like, expertly. Not just your basic stuff."

"I bet it's *not* your basic stuff," Jafria teased.

"Okay, okay, enough. My turn. What happened to Zands?"

"Mmmm, that's a tough one. The only thing I know is that he disappeared just like you after the show. Some people are saying he's hiding out in The Trenches. Others say he's back in Drod, where he came from."

"Drod?"

"Yep. There's even a rumor going around that he was Zoldaine himself. Is that true, Lillian? Is Zoldaine back?"

"No. Well…I don't know."

"Lillian, there are a lot of people scared right now, so anything you can give me would help."

"I wish I could, Jafria, but I've got nothing."

I want to tell you about Dax and what happened, but I can't.

Lillian looked despondent.

Jafria noted this and kindly changed subjects. "Hey, you'll never guess what happened to Barrett that night."

As much as Jafria wanted to talk about the kidnapping and this mysterious guy Lillian was seeing, she let it go and caught her friend up on the latest gossip. She started with how Barrett had tried to rally a bunch of guys together to search The Trenches right after Lillian had showed back up. Apparently, it was dark and as he turned to charge forward, he slipped and fell into a pile of pig manure. So, the suit that looked like dragon dung ended up smelling like it too. This image pulled a chuckle from Lillian.

"I don't know what he was *thinking*. The King's Guard was there and they weren't about to let him and a bunch of hooligans march off to The Trenches to stir up more trouble. But that's why I like him, I guess. Brave and headstrong, noble to a fault. That's my Barrett. Oh, and not to bring you back down, but Hannah and Richard have kind of started spending a lot more time together. I just wanted you to know before you found out some other way."

Lillian looked indifferent. "It's okay, really. Hannah's always had a little crush on him. Didn't take Richard long though, huh?"

"Yeah, I told Barrett he wasn't allowed to hang out with him anymore. Pig."

"Hey, well, my ex-boyfriend is a pig and yours smells like one!"

That brought both of them to tears of laughter.

"Speaking of smells, I have something that your new guy might like." Jafria went over to her bag, pulled out a small bottle, and walked back over.

"What is that?"

"Only the newest fragrance from Tapera," she said airily, wagging it between her fingers.

Tapera was known for its range of perfumes. The kingdom's floral variety was immense and contributed to some of the most unique and alluring aromas. Tapera's perfumes were one of their greatest exports, not only within the other two kingdoms, but also to other continents.

Jafria removed the glass stopper and waved it in front of Lillian's nose.

I know that smell. It's in Alexander's bread!

"Mmm, that smells heavenly. What is it called?"

"Dewdrop Delight. It's a combination of the six different Dewdrop Daisy flowers that grow there. Isn't it amazing?"

Oh! Dewdrop, of course!

Lillian had to test out her theory. She jumped up. "Come on!" she said and grabbed Jafria.

"Where are we going?"

"To the kitchen." Lillian was excited. It was the first time she'd felt close to Alexander since the last night she saw him. She hurried off with Jafria in tow.

CHAPTER 22: Secrets Discovered

h ha!
Lillian would have to thank Chef Pierre next time she saw him. The culinary master did not disappoint with his surplus of cooking ingredients. He had sweetly humored Lillian in her cooking endeavors since her grounding and made sure the cupboards were well stocked, including a variety of dried, powdered Dewdrop Daisy petal varieties. Lillian tasted a few samples and was finally satisfied with the one she thought was close. She threw it in a traditional thackleberry batter, tossed it in the oven, and soon the delicious aroma wafted from the open oven as Lillian lifted out a loaf.

Jafria was impressed. "This is amazing! How did you come up with this recipe?" she mumbled as she popped another bite into her mouth.

"I didn't. It's Alexander's," Lillian said softly. "He made it…"

Flerb!

She had been so excited she found the secret ingredient that she had let his name slip.

Jafria immediately latched on. "Alexander, huh? So, the archery instructor does have a name after all." She wagged her eyebrows at Lillian.

"Jafria, *please*, you can't tell *anyone*," Lillian pleaded.

"I don't know…inquiring minds want to know."

Jafria was teasing, but Lillian was still worried. She put her hand on Jafria's shoulder. "Jafria, you have to promise me. *NO one.* It's really important."

"Geez, Lil', I was just pulling your tail. I promise, no one will hear it from me. But...you *have* to promise to tell me more about him than just his name, later tonight."

"Okay, I promise." Lillian relented, somewhat relieved.

Lillian was almost glad Jafria wasn't giving her a choice. She really wanted to tell someone about Alexander. Besides Andrew. Someone who could really grasp how she felt around him, someone her own age who could understand that feeling, that rush of something new. *Of falling for someone.* That was so hard for her to even think about. But the feelings she had for Alexander were different, and she couldn't explain them any other way. Maybe Jafria could help sort them out.

The girls decided to go share Lillian's new-found secret thackleberry recipe with the castle. It was well received. *I'll have to let Alexander know.*

They were headed back to Lillian's room when Jafria spotted Sir Laurel.

"Oh, Lillian, let's go ask Sir Laurel if he knows anything."

"I don't know, Jafria. My father has issued a silence ordinance on the entire castle, especially the knights and guards."

"Yeah, but it's *Sir Laurel.* You know he can't resist a pretty girl flirting with him. Plus, we know his weakness...his hair." Jafria just smiled and pulled Lillian along, not waiting for a rebuttal.

Sir Laurel was dressed in regular clothes, which meant he wasn't currently on duty. Which meant Lillian wasn't surprised to see a goblet of wine in his hand. *Could he make it any easier for Jafria?* Lillian wasn't too keen on trying to sneak information out of someone and possibly get them in trouble. But her father hadn't really left her any choice, and she didn't care much for Sir Laurel, which made it easier.

It never ceased to amaze Lillian at how forward Jafria could be. If she didn't know her, Lillian would probably peg her as some stuck-up spoiled brat. But that was only a ruse, a defense mechanism for Jafria to know who her true friends were, and to use in times of need, like this one. Truthfully, Jafria was one of the most caring, selfless people Lillian knew. Jafria would do anything for a friend and did a lot for the Valanti Kingdom's more needy refugees from Drod. But she would never own up to it. Ironically, she didn't want the attention.

Jafria strolled casually up to Sir Laurel, smiling flirtatiously. "Well, Sir Laurel," her voice dripped with sweetness, "where in the Fae have you been? We've been searching the entire castle for you."

Sir Laurel turned to face the girls with a look that clearly indicated the cup of wine in his hand was not his first. "Well, hello, ladies," he said, and as he recognized Lillian, he gave a partial bow, and a partly tipsy, "Your Highness. So sorry to have kept you waiting for me. To what do I owe the pleasure?"

Jafria took a bit of bread from Lillian. "Well, we wanted to see what you thought of our new recipe. It has a secret ingredient." Jafria said conspiratorially. Sir Laurel held out his hand but instead Jafria put it directly in his mouth.

Oh, she's good.

"Oh my, that is very good. Do you have anything else for me to taste?" he said a little wolfishly.

Oh, the Fae! He is such a troll! How did my dad ever knight him?

Lillian knew the answer of course. Sir Laurel had been the first Drod native to be knighted. It was only a couple of years after the battle. Sir Laurel, or just Laurel as he was back then, had been a young refugee. At only sixteen, he had shown great promise. Soon, uprisings began, demanding equal rights for all the refugees who came from Drod. It was a difficult time for all the kingdoms, as most people were willing to take in these poor, tortured souls, but there was a good handful of citizens who distrusted the newcomers, and the refugees were beginning to feel they would never be truly welcome. It was then that her father made a difficult choice. Even though many of his own people disagreed with him, he invited select Drodic citizens to join ranks and positions across the kingdom. Laurel was the first official Drod immigrant to be part of that group, and he was knighted and joined the King's Royal Guard. One of only a few decisions she had ever seen her father regret. Once Laurel was knighted, he became lazy and took advantage of his position to "enjoy certain *ladies'* company," was how her mom put it. A position that Jafria was taking full advantage at the moment.

"Well, that depends on what you have for me," Jafria teased.

Sir Laurel stepped in closer, "I have a lot I can offer a pretty girl like yourself. You want to come see the trophy from the knight tournament in my quarters?"

Ugh! Jafria, hurry up so we can get out of here.

Lillian cleared her throat.

"Well," Jafria said, twirling his hair around her finger, "I was wondering what you know about the investigation on the kidnapping. You see, I'm trying to help my friend not worry so much. Would you happen to know anything at all that might help put the princess's mind at ease?"

Sir Laurel's pose became more alert, as if becoming aware of the ruse being played. But his lingering gaze on Jafria clearly betrayed his thoughts—the possibility of having her would be worth the risk of whatever consequence might lie ahead for him.

"Well, I'm not supposed to talk about this, but," he paused for a glance at Lillian, as if looking for assurance he wouldn't get in trouble, "apparently, there have been sightings of Zands meeting with some unscrupulous fellows in The Trenches." It was all Sir Laurel could do not to slur the last word.

Jafria played it off. "Everyone without goblin hair stuffed in their ears knows that. If you want another bite of something tasty, you'll have to give something tasty."

What would Barrett say if he could see you now?

Jafria was really putting on a show.

Sir Laurel leaned in closer, though he was incapable of whispering in his condition. "Lillian's not the only one they're after."

Now, this did interest Lillian. "What do you mean I'm not the only one they're after? Who else are they trying to get? Do they want Andrew too? The whole family?"

Sir Laurel shook his head. "No, no, no. Apparently, they're only interested in the princesses. There have been other attacks."

Her father's words echoed again in her head.

"What other attacks? Was anyone hurt?"

"I don't know. That's one of the reasons the king left. To collaborate with the other kingdoms," he slurred. "Gather up all the information on what's going on. He took one of the Kretcher boys with him too. The Kretchers have informants across all the kingdoms for their paper, which makes them valuable associates."

Mom didn't tell me that.

Now, Jafria interjected. "If that's true, then why haven't I read anything in the *Valor*? Who else has the power to censor the paper?"

Sir Laurel had forgotten about the quid pro quo part of their deal, and was giving whatever information he had in order to keep Jafria's attention.

"He couldn't cover up the incident at your party and even your kidnapping entirely because there were too many witnesses." Sir Laurel was on a roll now, his frequent partaking loosening his lips. "But he put out any fires, or at least contained them. Anything that would stir up angst and make his people think he wasn't in control. This isn't the first time the Rogues have tried something. A few years ago, one of them actually made it into young Andrew's bedroom with a knife. Rumor was they were looking for you." He looked at Lillian again.

Lillian put her hands on either side of Sir Laurel's face and positioned it into her gaze. "Who are they? Who is leading them to do this?"

Her grasp unfortunately had sobered Sir Laurel up. "I...I don't know. No one knows for sure. But they seem to be everywhere. And as far as their leader goes, the only name ever mentioned is—"

Lillian cut him off. "Don't. Don't say it. I've heard enough." She brushed past him angrily, and Jafria had to trot after her to catch up.

"Please! Don't tell your dad I said anything!" Sir Laurel called out. "It's all just rumors. I really don't know anything." His voice faded as Lillian covered ground. Jafria's steps got louder as she struggled to catch up.

"Lillian! Lillian, wait *up*."

Lillian stopped but didn't turn around. She tried to stop her tears, but couldn't. They came spilling down, unbidden, in angry streams.

Jafria came around to face her. "Hey, hey. It's okay. He was just saying stuff to impress us, well, me, but still."

Lillian just shook her head. "No. No, he wasn't. You don't understand, Jafria. There's something going on. There's someone trying to..."

"Trying to what?"

"I don't know." She wiped her eyes. "I don't know, that's the point. But it's not good. And if he's right, if there have been attacks on the other princesses, then this is way bigger than a random prank at my party."

"Come on, let's get you upstairs." They started back to Lillian's bedroom. "I was supposed to come here to cheer you up. So, for the rest of the night, no more talk about that stuff. We're just going to stay up late talking about boys, eating junk food, and putting on a fashion show with all the new clothes I brought with me."

"Deal," Lillian said, brightening at the thought of some normality.

"Are you sure you thought this one through before you made it? A person is supposed to wear this, right? It's not like some horse blanket or anything?" It was the fourth outfit Lillian had tried on. The first three were decent. They definitely had Jafria's flare, but Lillian could see people wearing them. The one she was wearing now she wouldn't buy for a horse.

"Oh, will you stop? It can't be that bad." Jafria had promised this was the last one. She had been adjusting the ones Lillian came out in and making notes about what colors would be good, where to hem, and what accessories would go well with them.

Lillian had come out looking like a cross between a jester wearing a troll's overcoat, paired with pants for a dwarf. "Now, tell me this is what you were going for with a straight face, and I promise to be quiet."

Jafria examined Lillian's attire slowly from top to bottom, but when she got to the pants, she burst out laughing. "Oh, take it off, take it off. I just couldn't help it. Of course, it's hideous. I was going to see if you'd wear it around the castle, but I just can't."

Lillian pulled off the giant coat and threw it at her friend. "You dragon turd. I was trying really hard not to hurt your feelings."

"But I want you to, not hurt my feelings, I mean, but be honest. How else will I know what's good? I have great taste, but it can be a little eccentric for the masses." Jafria put another piece of thackleberry bread in her mouth. Both girls had decided they needed to make another batch just to make sure the secret ingredient hadn't been a mistake. At least that's how they justified it. "So…"

Lillian grabbed a piece and plopped down on her bed. "So what?"

"You know *what*. You promised." Jafria hopped up on the bed with her. "Come on, Lil', I told you I wouldn't tell a soul, I swear. I mean, have you told anyone at all?"

"Andrew knows, but…"

"You told your little *brother* before me?" Jafria hit her with a pillow.

"I had to. He brought me a letter and wouldn't shut up about it."

"Alexander sent you a letter? Okay, back it up. Start from the beginning."

So Lillian did. She told her about the bridge during her party, the archery, the kidnapping, and their final night before her grounding. She even told her about the nightmare. Jafria didn't say a single word the whole time.

"Well?" Lillian asked, having just bared her soul.

"Wow. Lil', I had no idea. Why didn't you say anything before?"

"I don't know. There was never really a good time. Alexander told me it was important no one knew about him. I still don't know why, but I trust him."

"Girl, you more than trust him." Jafria nudged her with a wink.

"I do not." Lillian didn't sound as convincing as she wanted.

Jafria just smiled "Yeah, you do, but from what you've said, I'm pretty sure he's falling for you too."

Lillian blushed three shades of red, each darker than the first.

"He can't. I can't. We barely know each other."

"Your parents didn't know each other at all."

Oh. Well...

Her parents. Was she getting the story she'd always wanted?

"I know, but..."

"But what?" Jafria challenged her.

"There's still something he's hiding from me. He says he goes home, but I know he's been in Tapera. Not just because of the bread and cheese, but he's been seen there. Not seen-seen, but people have reported a ghost on Tocarin Lake. Same white tunic and 'red eye.' He's not being completely honest with me, and I don't know why."

"Is it possible he goes home and then to Tapera before coming back here? I mean, he was gone for a while. Did you ever ask him?"

"Well, no. And I guess he could do both. He just said his family lives in the southern part of Valanti." Lillian hadn't received a response back from her letter yet, and she was hoping it would piece everything together, but she supposed what Jafria was suggesting could be possible as well.

"See? So, stop looking for the bad, and just enjoy it."

"It's just really hard when my life being in jeopardy on a regular basis keeps interrupting things."

"Yeah, bad timing for sure. But do you think about him all the time? Do you imagine what your life will be like in the future? Do you feel like you're missing something when you're not around him, like you're not quite complete?"

Lillian was starting to tear up again. "Yes. Yes, I do. I miss him *so* much. And I don't know when he's coming back."

Jafria held her friend and let her cry. "I know you miss him. And I'm sure he misses you. That's how I know he'll be back," Jafria said softly. "I don't know when, but hopefully, it's not until after you're ungrounded. I've missed you too, you know. I don't need you sneaking out again and getting grounded until you're queen."

This made Lillian laugh. "I've missed you too. I'm so glad you came."

"Well, it's only because you're the princess. I can't really say 'no,' can I?" Jafria teased.

"Thank you."

"For what? All I've done is make you cry. Come on, let's finish off this bread and go scare your brother."

Jafria made sure Lillian enjoyed the rest of her night. And for the first time in weeks, Lillian had good dreams, even about Alexander.

CHAPTER 23: Past Life
June 27

Maybe it was just having someone her own age to talk to, but Jafria's visit had picked up Lillian's spirits considerably. Though Lillian was still down about being grounded, and there was still no sign that Alexander was back, the cloud of gloom that had surrounded her had lifted. While she wasn't happy that her friends' lives were also in jeopardy, the fact that she wasn't alone in this, that there were other attacks going on in the neighboring kingdoms, made her feel better.

She had even incorporated Andrew into helping her practice. He would toss apples randomly up in the air and she would try to hit them. They weren't quite as unpredictable as fish, but Andrew tried his best to keep her guessing.

She was hoping her father would be back soon so she could speak with him. She wasn't sure how to bring up the things she had learned without incriminating someone or upsetting him, but it was important she be involved in the decisions concerning her life and not secluded from them.

A special knock on her door let her know Andrew was back. She hated to disappoint him, but she really didn't feel like playing any games right now.

She opened the door. "Hey, Andrew, I really don't…"

"Look, Lillian! Look what I brought you!" Andrew held out a bag full of fresh thackleberries.

"What? How did you get these?" Lillian managed to get out.

"Mom let me go out, with an escort, of course. I think I was driving her spiral, and she told me if I didn't go outside and get rid of some energy, she'd make me live with Grayson until this was all over. But I did just like you said and didn't get a scratch. Look at 'em all." He handed her the bag excitedly.

The bag made a crinkly sound as she took it from Andrew. Opening it up a little more, she found a berry-stained note. She quickly removed the note and rushed over to her bedroom window. She hadn't seen the *A* on the rock, but maybe she just missed it.

Andrew followed her in, licking his sticky, stained fingers. "It's not from Alexander."

Lillian still looked out her window.

"It's from Seth."

From Seth? Why would he send me a letter? He can just talk to me.

She saw it was addressed: "For the princess." It was in handwriting she didn't recognize. The same handwriting was inside.

Princess Lillian, I have vital information regarding your kidnapping and upcoming events. It is imperative I meet with you. Dragon's Wrath. Wear a disguise. Two weeks from tonight. Tell no one. Ears are everywhere.

She turned it over.

No signature. Two weeks from tonight at the Dragon's Wrath?

Lillian counted out the days. It was the night of the big dinner party. That couldn't be a coincidence.

———————➤

Lillian couldn't possibly imagine who would have sent the letter. But she needed to know. And she needed to know who could wield such powerful magic. Dark magic. Dax had named the source of this evil, and his confession had cost him his life. But no one, especially the king, was willing to believe him. Her father had seen Zoldaine die by King Phillip's sword with his own eyes. Someone was hiding behind Zoldaine's name to strike fear into the kingdom. And to King Harry's dismay, it was working. Rumors were surging through Valanti that Zoldaine was back and that he had actually been in town. Zands was the first suspect, as he was still yet to be found, but the king believed differently.

Lillian needed a plan. She already figured on asking if Jafria could come over again. She just had to talk to a couple of people inside the castle to help her out. To think like the enemy, she had to know the enemy—and there were only two people she could think of who might know a lot about the Rogues. Mostly because they had been Drod citizens themselves. But between the two, there was only one she thought worth talking to. And perhaps the only one who would have the answer to who sent the letter.

"Hey, Seth."

"Oh, hey, Lil'. I didn't hear you come up." Seth was tinkering in the workshop.

"What are you working on?"

"Oh, this?" He started to cover it up. "This is something you can't see. It's a surprise Grayson's got me working on for the Dawning Festival."

"If we still have one."

"Your father still thinking about cancelling it, huh?"

"Yeah."

"Man, that's a tough call. I'd understand, though. He's always got the citizens in his best interest. Especially ones he's related to."

"Yeah, I know."

"How much longer are you grounded for?"

"Not sure. It was a month, but he's extended it indefinitely." *Because Zoldaine may be back and a prisoner died in interrogation* is what she wanted to say but knew better. "Maybe until all this is over, if he has his way."

"Still looking for that Zands guy?"

"Yep."

"Well, may the Fae's luck shine upon us all then, and he'll pop up. It would be a shame to cancel the festival," said Seth.

"To be honest, that's kind of what I came to talk to you about." She pulled out the letter. "That and this. Is there anyone else around?"

"Not that I know of. What's going on, Lil'?"

"I was hoping you could tell me. Who gave you this?"

"I have no idea. It was lying here on my workbench this morning. I caught Andrew coming back in from getting thackleberries for you and gave it to him to take back. It doesn't say who it's from?"

"Nope, that's why I came to ask you."

"I wish I could be more help. What did it say?"

Tell no one.

Lillian had to think fast. "Um, it was just something about the festival. A personal request, but they didn't leave their name so…"

"Huh, that's weird. Well, maybe they'll leave another note with a 'P.S. By the way, here's my name.'"

"Yeah, hopefully," she said.

Silence hung between them.

"So, was there something else?" Seth asked.

"Yeah, um, I'm trying to figure out how to ask."

"You know I'd do anything for ya, Lil'. What's up?"

"I want to go into town and see what I can find out about all this. Specifically Dragon's Wrath."

"Are you over the wall? That's a death sentence, Lillian! Dragon's Wrath is in The Trenches."

"Thank you, Seth, I know where it is."

"But doesn't your dad have people out hunting down information?"

"Yes. That's the problem. Everyone knows they're his people. And no one's volunteering anything. Everyone's afraid that Zoldaine has returned. I can't just sit here, Seth, and wait for something to happen. It's driving me insane."

"So, why are you telling me?"

"I need your help getting out."

"What? Oh, no! You're not getting me tangled up in this. Your dad's wrath on you may have been bad, but what do you think he'd do to someone not related to him for helping you?"

"Come on, Seth," Lillian pleaded. "I promise he will never find out. Andrew has already agreed he'll cover for me."

She hadn't talked to Andrew yet, but Seth didn't need to know that. She was sure Andrew would help, so it was only a small lie.

"Yeah, well, he's your brother. I'm nobody. Your father would tie me to one of my horses and have me dragged through town."

"I promise, Seth. Seriously, he will never find out. And if—*if*— he does, I'll tell him I threatened you."

"You? Threatened me? Yeah, he'll believe that," Seth said derisively.

"Hey! I can be threatening." She reached out and grabbed a chisel. "You better help me or else."

"Oh, yes, well, now I can see it."

"Just think about it, okay?"

"I'll think about it. I'm assuming you have a plan?"

"Mostly. A lot of it really depends on if you'll help or not."

"Oh, so no pressure. And when, do tell, are you wanting to do all this?"

"During the dinner party coming up."

"The one in a couple of weeks?"

"Yes. I figure with all the people coming and going, it will be easier for me to slip out unnoticed. So?"

"So, I'll think about it. How do you plan to go unrecognized?"

"I've got a few tricks up my sleeve as well." *I hope.*

"If you say so." Lillian just stood there for a minute, unsure of how to ask the next question, but Seth helped her out. "I get the feeling you're still not done."

"Yeah, well, I just, I don't want to overstep our friendship, but I don't know of anyone else to ask."

Seth sat down. "It's okay, Lil', you won't offend me."

"I just know you don't like to talk about it, but I think it will really help me understand what's going on."

"Go ahead." Seth exhaled, knowing what Lillian was about to ask.

"What was it like living in Drod?"

He took a deep breath. It wasn't a fact many knew about him, and of those who did, there were very few he was willing to talk to about it. Seth was a Drod refugee. His family had lived in Drod during the attack, and unfortunately, his parents had been a casualty. He was found wandering around the castle a few days later. He was taken in, like so many others who had eventually found families to live with around the different kingdoms. Seth's knack for fixing things at the young age of ten impressed the castle staff, and they all adopted him as their own. Ever since, he had been fixing things, building new trinkets, and taking care of the stables.

"Mind if I ask why the sudden interest?" he said.

"No, it makes sense." It was Lillian's turn to pause. "Well, these people are after me, Seth, and I don't know why. I don't understand why they continue to worship a man who was so awful and heinous to them. I'm just trying to find out what they want and why they want me."

"I'm not sure I can answer that, Lil'."

"I know. But I just, I don't know, maybe if I have some information about how they think or act, then it might help." Lillian could see the pain on Seth's face. "Never mind, I shouldn't have asked. I'm sorry."

"No, it's okay." He took her hand. "Really. I just haven't thought about that time in my life for a while now, but I want to help. As far as what they want and why you, I couldn't say, specifically. What I do know is if it's you they want, for whatever reason, they won't stop until they accomplish it— or die trying."

Especially, if they've been spelled to die for their cause.

Dax's haunting screams had woken Lillian up on more than one occasion since the interrogation.

"But Zoldaine is dead, right? I mean, who could possibly be orchestrating this? Zands?"

"Once again, I'm not sure. Zoldaine was a very powerful, very old warlock. Rumor was, he was older than the dwarves. And the same spell his sister used on your mother, taking tears of others, was what maintained his youth. He came to rule in the age of the dragons, which was a high magic time. So, who's to know if he's truly dead?"

"My dad and the other kings and guards saw him die. They buried his body with the faeries' help."

"I'm sure they did. I'm just saying, from what I've heard and seen him do, personally, I wouldn't be completely surprised if he were back. If, and once again, it's a strong "if," but if it *is* Zoldaine, the reason he would be doing all of this is simple—revenge."

"I guess that makes sense, but what about his followers? My dad freed them from his terrible wrath. Why in the Fae would they still be taking orders from him?" Lillian said.

"I'll do my best to try and explain it, but I'm not sure it will make sense. People in general are resistant to change—whether for good or for bad."

"But why would people not want change that was good for them?" Lillian asked, baffled at the notion.

"Just bear with me. People don't like change because it's unfamiliar. Growing up in Drod was horrible, but believe it or not, predictable. Zoldaine punished without mercy, but in a weird sense, he was fair. The same crime was punished the same way every time. And every year, ironically around the time of the Dawning Festival, he would make us suffer some plague or disaster. Some say it was the anniversary of his wife's death."

Lillian looked shocked.

I never heard he was married...

"Oh, yes, for a time Zoldaine was married," Seth said in answer to her unspoken question. "Way before my time, of course, but she was his villainous female counterpart. Beautiful as she was evil. There are many tales of how she died, but no one really knows. But the point is, life was miserable but people understood it. And for some, there was twisted hope."

"Hope? How could anyone have hope in such a dismal existence?"

"Well, much like the rulers of the other kingdoms, Zoldaine had his hierarchy of help. Not much, mind you, because he trusted no one. But he had a few families in various districts who maintained his rule. I'm sure you've heard the story of his servant who betrayed him, causing Zoldaine to attack on the day of your brother's christening?"

"Yeah, basically after the great battle, they found the servant dying slowly in excruciating pain. Zoldaine had put some curse on him. But I heard the man didn't regret what he had done, even though Zoldaine tortured his family before his eyes—he felt he had done the right thing," said Lillian.

"Well, not everyone saw it that way. There's a saying that goes 'Better to rule a pile of troll dung than not rule at all.' In other words, these families had power in Drod, regardless of the price they paid or little amount of power they actually had. They saw the servant as a traitor. And when the other kingdoms attacked Drod, they knew their time of power was over. As was their predictable life."

"But what about the people who didn't have any power? Why would they not stand up and fight for themselves or demand change if it was so bad?" Lillian asked, the logic eluding her.

"That's the thing. Zoldaine controlled everything that came in or out of Drod. So, we didn't even realize it was bad. It was just life."

"That's absurd. How could anyone ever think that type of existence is normal?"

Seth thought for a moment. "Well, this is a poor analogy, but I think it'll do. What if, since the day you were born, you were only ever fed porridge for every meal, every day? And porridge was the only food anybody ever said existed. Now, imagine that for *generations*. All your parents, grandparents, great-grandparents ate and knew about was porridge. You'd have no reason to ask or believe there was anything *but* porridge. That's how it was in Drod, just on a much wider scale."

Lillian's face wrinkled in aversion.

"That's how the circle of torment and abuse happens. It's hard to understand if you've never been in that situation, but you can't break the cycle if you don't realize the cycle is wrong or even there to begin with."

Lillian sat, mulling his words over in her mind.

"Like I said, it doesn't make sense. But that's the best I can do. I can only surmise some of the old families stayed in Drod, and whether they're under Zoldaine's influence or not, they still feel it their duty to exact revenge in Zoldaine's honor. Then, if or when he does come back, they will be rewarded. I guess when you've grown up knowing only pain and suffering and have been rewarded for mistreating others, any other way of life seems wrong. It's a vicious circle that's hard to break and escape. Some do. Most don't."

"I guess...I just never knew how bad life was there. No one ever talks about it," she said.

"Now you see why."

"I'm sorry, really. I didn't mean to make you go through all that again. I had no idea."

"It's fine, Lillian. I have a better life now. Sure, I miss my parents, but I have a new family now."

"Well, I hate the circumstances that brought you here, but I'm sure glad you are." She gave him a big hug. "I've always wanted an older brother—my younger one is kind of a pain." They both laughed. "So, I have one more question if that's okay."

"Shoot."

"On the night I was kidnapped, they tried to take me back over the wall. Why do you think that was? As far as I know, Drod is deserted."

"Far as I know, it is. But if you think about it, what better place to kidnap someone and start a revolt than somewhere no one wants to go."

The thought of rogue Dainians plotting against her and her family was troubling enough. But the thought of them starting a revolt in Drod, only a few leagues away from

where she slept, was sure to keep her restless for nights to
come.

CHAPTER 24: The Talk
June 30

Over the last week Lillian had practiced every chance she got. Her draw was becoming more automatic, more fluid. She wasn't thinking so much and her clusters were getting more consistent. Her muscles were growing stronger and she was tiring less, allowing her to continue longer.

After a couple hours today, she was famished and decided to head to the kitchen.

It was only a little past lunchtime, so there were still several servants milling about cleaning and taking various meals to those unable to attend the usual buffet.

Lillian was greeted in passing by the staff, but a special welcome always came from the chef.

"Ah, Mademoiselle Lillian, you 'ave been practicing again, I zee." Pierre gave her the usual kiss on each cheek. Even though he had been in Valanti for more than twenty years, his native accent had never surrendered.

Lillian brushed some sweat-matted hair back behind her ears. "Yeah, just came in to grab a quick snack."

"And maybe make zome more of that *délicieux pain*?"

"I *was* thinking about it." She put her arm around him. "Would you like me to make an extra loaf for you again?" she teased, already knowing the answer.

"Well, if zat wouldn't be too much trouble?" he asked genially.

"Of course not."

"Well, zen, I leave you to it."

Pierre gave a few other instructions to his staff then headed out.

Lillian had become very familiar with the kitchen since her grounding. She grabbed the ingredients to bake with and set to work. She figured she would get the bread going so it would be done by the time she'd finished eating. Once she poured the batter in the loaf pans, she gently slid them into the oven.

While she waited, she grabbed some leftover turkey and rolls from lunch, a few pieces of fruit, and a mug of honey-mead juice and plopped herself on the counter out of the way of the staff. There were only a few people left now, bustling to clean up and start the preparations for dinner. Preparers Hayden and Finley were busy chopping, and stewards Anabell, Micah, and Blaine were cleaning up the pots and pans. It was the latter that caught Lillian's attention.

Blaine was looking around furtively. After confirming no one else was around, he launched into the sure-to-be taboo conversation. "Have either of you talked to Foster lately?"

Both girls shook their heads.

Anyone in the castle knew the kitchen was the catchall of any gossip going on around the kingdom, and Blaine was the king of them all. Most of what he said was greatly exaggerated, but there were always nuggets of truth to be found if one listened close enough. And Lillian was listening.

Blaine glanced behind him, building the suspense as if it were imperative no one could hear what he was about to say except them. He hadn't even registered Lillian's proximity, or her identity, as she munched nonchalantly on her midday snack from an out-of-the-way corner of the kitchen.

"Well," Blaine continued cautiously, "Foster said his brother-in-law was with a hunting party the other day and they were up by the wall." Blaine gave a dramatic pause and the girls leaned in. "He says that one of them saw a troll lurking around and when the troll saw them, he didn't even try to hide. Just stared back at them, glaring, then slowly turned back and walked away."

Micah hit Blaine in the arm. "A troll? This close to the castle? Are you serious?"

"That's what he said." Blaine held his hand up as if to swear to the Fae and glanced in Lillian's direction. Lillian quickly feigned picking up something off the floor to hide her face.

"I thought they were all taken care of during the war," Anabell said.

Before he could answer, Micah interjected. "That's what they want you to think, but there were hundreds of trolls who retreated and hid so they wouldn't get killed or imprisoned. I overheard my dad talking with one of the dwarves, the really cranky one, and he said they see goblins all the time in the mountain caves."

Something else I might ask them about at the dinner party.

"The goblins don't really do anything but steal scraps of food, I guess, but still—I mean, goblins just roaming about like that? Rogues, trolls, and goblins. What's this kingdom coming to?"

Blaine tried to refocus the conversation back to himself. "Well, I don't know about all that, but I *do* know that there's something going on in Drod. I heard there was a faction of Rogues who used to be in power there, and they've just been waiting to take revenge on all the kingdoms. You know there've been attacks in the other kingdoms, right?"

I know that, but how do you *know that?*

"Now, I can't tell you exactly who was involved," said Blaine. *Ah, that's because you* don't *know.* "But those families who had power in Drod are the ones behind all these attacks, not Zoldaine. They were left to rot in Drod, and now they're hell-bent on getting *revenge.*"

Lillian wasn't sure how much truth there was to what Blaine said, but his story did at least match up with what Seth had said the other day.

"Well," Micah chimed in, "I still think Zoldaine is behind it somehow. I mean, how could a guy live for so long and just get killed all of a sudden? He was really powerful. I don't think King Phillip could have killed him with just a regular sword." Micah quickly looked around to make sure she hadn't been overheard.

Lillian didn't like how the servants were talking.

No wonder the kingdom is in disarray if people in the castle *don't feel safe.*

Anabell scolded Micah, "You better watch it or someone might hear you and think you're a Rogue."

Micah retorted, "Don't say that! You know that's not what I meant. I'm just saying it's possible he could still be alive is all."

Blaine supported Anabell. "And what we're saying is those thoughts need to stay in your head."

The trio quieted down a bit, none wanting to say anything that might get taken out of context now. But the silence didn't last long as Micah felt the need to redeem herself.

"Did you hear what happened in The Trenches?" she blurted out, eager to be remembered for something else.

Anabell was first to reply. "Gage told me that his girlfriend, Carissa, has a cousin who lives in Old Towne, and apparently, yesterday one of the guards started asking questions about Zands and," she lowered her voice, "other people in The Trenches—there was an uprising at the

Dragon's Wrath. The residents are mad the guards keep focusing their search in The Trenches and Old Towne, like it was already concluded anyone who lives there is guilty."

Micah piped back in, "I know my boyfriend's house was having some roof work done, and he told me the carpenter was from Old Towne and did nothing but complain about the interrogations while he was there. He supposedly went on and on about 'why weren't they questioning people in New Towne or the Arts,' and how it was all a conspiracy to relocate them somewhere else so they can remodel the area."

Blaine couldn't wait to pitch in his tidbit. "They *actually* started throwing rocks, and some even took up sticks to the guards. The king is going to go *ballistic* when he gets back."

"And just what will I go ballistic about?" King Harry entered the kitchen.

The king's entrance startled Lillian mid-sip and she spluttered into her mug. If she was startled, the trio was all but bowled over.

Blaine's jaw dropped along with the pot he had been cleaning, and he started stuttering apologies while picking it up, "N, nothing, Sire. My apologies, Your Majesty. We were just, I was just…I'm sorry, Your Majesty."

King Harry looked pointedly at the trio. "I'll meet with you three later regarding the rumors of my kingdom, but right now, I'd like to talk to my daughter, alone," and his gaze swept to Lillian's corner. Realization hit Blaine first, as the identity of the feminine form in the corner suddenly became clear. The king looked back at the trio, then glanced to Hayden and Finley, including them in the dismissal.

Once the room was clear, the king walked over to his daughter and took her up in a rib-cracking hug. "Do you know how much I love you?"

Lillian was a little taken aback. She and her father hadn't exactly been on good terms lately. "I love you too, Dad," she wheezed. "What's going on?"

As the king pulled back, she could see tears in his eyes. "Dad, what's wrong?"

"Oh, Lily Pad, I wish I could tell you, I really do."

"Dad, you have to stop treating me like a child. You have to start including me. Including Mom. You don't have to do this alone. I know you're trying to protect us, but you can't carry this burden by yourself. If you tell us what's going on, we can help you. If it's me they're after, then I have a right to know."

"Your mother told me the same thing right before I left." The king took a deep breath. "I suppose you're right. You *do* have a right to know. Before I left, I told you there had been other attacks. And now it seems the other princesses have been the targets too." He leaned up against the counter across from her. "I was meeting with your uncle and Sir Aaron to exchange information of what's been going on. Whomever is behind these assaults is well organized, but we don't know who it is yet. There seems to be no connection to them other than the fact that they're centered around you, Olivia, and Avery. And the attacks aren't at random. They seem to have intel. Your kidnapping was proof of that. The attackers knew you were going to be at Talula's at that time, on that day. Similar instances have happened in the other kingdoms."

"Are Avery and Olivia okay?" Lillian pressed. "What happened?"

"Yes, they're fine—and it's not because I don't trust you or want you to know—but the less who know about specifics, the fewer people I have to worry about. I'm even contemplating not telling your mother, and I'm not looking forward to that conversation."

"It's okay, Dad, I understand. So what *can* you tell me?"

"There's something going on in Drod. We've sent a party up from Tapera to investigate. And to be honest, we're not exactly sure what they'll find. Originally, when we set out to take out Zoldaine, it was more chaotic than people realized. Our troops were spread out, and there were so many repressed citizens, there was no way to keep track of everyone."

Lillian could hear the strain in her dad's voice. "It's okay, Dad, you don't have to get into this now."

"Yes. Yes, I do. I should have had this conversation with you a long time ago," the king said, shaking his head. "You just have no idea, Lil', how bad things were up there. So *much* suffering. The living conditions were deplorable. But the people, they wanted to stay. We couldn't understand it, but what were we going to do? Make them leave? We never thought they would be a problem afterward, though. The entire kingdom was disorganized and imploding on itself. We left some troops to try and help restore order. Some were up there for nearly five years."

"Does Mom know about all this?" Lillian was stunned both at how open her father was being and at the information he was giving her.

"Most of it, yes. But as for everyone else involved, we debriefed the soldiers and requested they not talk about what they saw. But I'm afraid now that things have stirred up again, so have old memories."

Lillian could see the old memories flickering behind her father's eyes. They held pain and sorrow. "I'm sorry, Dad, I never realized…"

"Oh, I know, sweetie, and that's why your mom and I, and the rest of the royal council, decided not to talk about it if at all possible. However, the unknown is always more dangerous. Which is why this knowledge needs to be heard once again. Not to intimidate people, but to make them aware of what dangers truly lie out there." Her father paused momentarily. "Speaking of unknown dangers, why don't you tell me about your new friend."

Flerb.

The Talk

Lillian was dreading this. She knew they would have to have this conversation eventually. She just wasn't ready for it now.

"Well, what would you like to know?" She was playing coy, hoping to buy time.

"How about a name, for starters?"

She looked at her father. She wanted to tell him, she owed it to him after he'd been so forthright with her. But she had made a promise to Alexander. *"You can't tell anyone about me, okay? Not your parents. Not your friends. No one. That's the trade-off. Your life for my secret one."* She had already broken that promise twice. Not on purpose, but still two more than he had wanted.

"I can't, Dad. I want to, I really do, but I made a promise. I'm probably breaking it just by admitting he exists."

"Okay, I can respect that."

That surprised Lillian. She was expecting a bit more of a dispute.

As if sensing Lillian's perplexity, the king continued. "A man's, or in this case, a woman's word should be a sacred bond. Not something to take lightly," he said wisely. "How about this? What if I tell you everything *I* know about this mystery friend and *you* can tell me if I'm right or wrong? Fair?"

She thought it over for a moment.

If Dad already knows certain things about Alexander, then it's not like I told him. If anything, it'd be better I clear any misconceptions up with Dad so he trusts Alexander and me more.

"Okay, I think I can do that."

"Well, let's start with the fact he's a guy, which can I say, as a father, puts me on *high* protective alert from the go."

"Yeah, but Dad, he…"

The king held up his hand. "But I also know that if he hadn't been treating you well, you wouldn't keep going against your father's wishes to see him."

Lillian sighed. She really did feel bad. "I know, Dad. And …about that night, especially, I'm so sorry. I just needed to feel safe after all that happened. It's complicated, I…you don't understand."

"Well, help me, Lily Pad, because your mother and I have had long conversations about your newest interest. First off, we can both tell he's more than a friend."

Lillian cheeks blushed scarlet.

"We also know he's an excellent marksman, just by how much *you've* improved. But we're also worried at how much time you're spending with him. We don't know much about him, and besides being our daughter, you *are* the princess, which makes vetting strangers even more vital. I hope you can see our side of this."

"I do, Dad. I do understand. I have my reasons though."

"Well, you should know my scouts have informed me they believe he's from Drod; he hunts near our side of the wall and then just disappears for weeks on end. We also know he goes to Tapera. He's the 'ghost,' isn't he?"

"Yes, but Dad, he's not from Drod. He actually lives…" she stopped, biting her lip, not wanting to divulge too much.

"Where, Lillian? Tell me anything you can to help ease my mind, because, frankly, with the attacks and you having a new boyfriend—of whom I know nothing about—your mother pointed out the increase of grays even through my blond hair."

Lillian just sat there in silence, wavering for a bit on just what to say in return. "You know how you've always just kind of had a third eye when it comes to people? How you've just *known* about the assassination attempts or who to trust? I *trust* him. And not just because I like him," she said. *I more than like him.* "But because I can feel it. I promise you, I was cautious, but the more time I spend with him—the more I actually get to know him, I can tell he's different. He doesn't care that I'm a princess. He likes me for *me*. And you can't imagine how good that feels. And you don't have to worry about him kidnapping me or hurting me. He's already saved my life twice. He rescued me from the kidnappers."

"*He's* the one? How did he know?" he asked, questions and concern flashing across his features.

Lillian could tell her dad was wondering if Alexander was somehow involved with what was going on.

"It's kind of hard to explain. He calls it the gleaming."

"The gleaming?" Her dad seemed both curious and a bit skeptical.

"Yeah, it's kind of like the third-eye thing. He said he could just *feel* me in trouble, and followed that feeling till he found me."

"So, where is he now?"

"I…I don't know. He hasn't been around since I was grounded."

"Ah, about that, I still need to talk to your mother, but I think there might be something we can work out. Not roaming around on your own, mind you, but at least being able to leave the castle." The king took his daughter's hands. "And about this guy, as much as I may not like the situation, I trust you. And so does your mother. And she has been your ambassador more than anyone in this whole situation. We've both tried to raise you right—not just tell you what's right and wrong, but hopefully teach you how to make those decisions on your own." Her father sighed. "That's the hardest part for any parent, I think. Letting go and trusting your child. I know you're not a child anymore, I truly do, but you will *always* be my little girl." Unshed tears welled in his eyes and she let him drag her into the perfect hug only a father can give.

He finally released her. "And to prove I trust you," he said, producing a letter from his waistcoat, "I believe this is for you. I didn't even open it." He gave her a wink.

Lillian reached out and took the letter. She couldn't be certain but was fairly sure it was the response she'd been waiting for.

"Thanks, Dad. This means a lot to me."

Right about then, the king caught a whiff of her special bread. "What is that heavenly smell?"

"Oh! That'd be the bread, just a minute." Lillian grabbed the pot holders and took the two loaves out of the oven.

"A new recipe?"

"Yep." She cut slices of the still-steaming bread. "Here, try it. This other loaf is for Pierre."

The king took a bite. "Wow! This is delicious. It's thackleberry bread, but there's something different in it. But I suppose this will be another one of your secrets?"

"Well, I'll let you think about it just for a little bit, first."

"At least tell me how you came by this recipe, so I can thank them."

Lillian just smiled.

"Really? It's your archer friend, isn't it?"

Lillian's smile turned into a grin.

"By the Fae. Saving my daughter, producing," he smelled the bread again, "an amazing new treat. I'm finding it harder and harder to not like him."

Lillian put her hand on her hip. "You'd better not be displeased with him if you want any more bread."

The two each finished another slice each and chatted about less serious affairs.

"Well, I should probably go find your mother. I'm sure word of my return has gotten to her by now."

Lillian stared in horror. "You didn't tell *Mom* you were back *yet*? She's gonna throw you in the dungeons! You better take her a slice."

"That, dear daughter, is a very good idea. I knew I kept you around for a reason." He grabbed two pieces. "Just in case I lose one on the way up," he teased.

As he headed out, he turned around. "Lily Pad, I want you to know, I really do trust you. And I hope if there's anything, or anyone, you want to talk to me about, you know you can trust me too. I love you."

"I love you too, Dad."

Lillian was left alone in the kitchen. She took the letter out. She recognized the wax seal. It was authentic and indeed unbroken. She broke it and read the response. Twice.

She hadn't been able to figure out how her kidnapping party had gotten so far from the village so fast. She had her suspicions before, but now they were confirmed. The mysterious "water" she had walked through in the tunnel somehow transported her across a distance that would normally have taken hours.

There were magic pathways in the mountains and throughout her kingdom. And perhaps, from what the letter said, the whole continent.

CHAPTER 25: An Old Rival
July 4

ncharacteristic light filtered into the bedroom as Lillian woke up to a breathtakingly sunny day. She could finally go outside to the courtyard and practice again. The last several days had been rainy, which had kept her not only from practicing but also from developing part of her plan.

Ever since she had convinced Seth to help, she was steadily procuring various parts of her escape plan. Seth would work on the device to help her escape, while she would take care of her disguise and "body double."

Going out to practice served a two-fold purpose. First, she got to hone her skill in the hopes of impressing Alexander once he came back, and second, it afforded her the chance to steal hay from the targets in order to create a dummy, so should anyone check on her after the party, "Lillian" would be lying there. Andrew had agreed to tell anyone who asked that Lillian had fallen ill and gone to bed.

After a round of target practice, she grabbed several handfuls of hay, storing them in the pocket of her knapsack that held her archery essentials.

"I haven't seen shooting like that in years."

Gah!

Lillian hadn't heard anyone behind her; she quickly assumed an inconspicuous position and turned to face Sir Alger, who stood with his archery set.

"My apologies, Sir Alger, I didn't realize you'd be practicing today. I'll come back later."

"On the contrary, Your Highness. I was hoping you might indulge me in a friendly competition. And please call me Braelyn. Only my knights and your father call me 'Sir.'"

"Sir, ah, Braelyn, you flatter me, but I am nowhere near your skill."

Am I?

"Well, I am a bit out of practice, but from what I've seen over the last fortnight or two, you could take a bit of coin from an old man. What do you say? Best of two rounds?"

"We're not actually betting money, are we?"

Sir Alger laughed. "No, no, of course not, just castle bragging rights. I'm afraid your father doesn't pay enough for me to gamble." He winked.

"Okay then, bragging rights. Uh, how exactly does this work? I've never been in a duel before."

"Well, usually the two rounds consist of distance and speed. The first is usually set about thirty paces, best of five. The second is at fifteen paces with ten arrows, but you only have ten seconds to get them off."

"Sounds fair enough." Lillian could see a few of the staff starting to peek into the courtyard to see what was going on and could already feel her nerves start to creep up.

She had only recently begun to feel comfortable shooting around Alexander, and now she was up against a well-known marksman, with an audience no less.

Fae, please don't let me make a fool of myself.

Sir Alger took the honor of going first. His first arrow was off target, but the next four found a nice cluster just a few inches to the left of the bull's-eye.

Lillian stepped up and noticed several more staff observing the impromptu duel. She was definitely nervous. Her first arrow barely hit the target and her second was not much better.

"Hey now, don't let them make you nervous." Sir Alger put a hand on her shoulder. "I've seen enough to know you've got the skills. Just right now you've also got the nerves. Try and relax. Take your time." He backed up. "Just focus on your target."

Sir Alger's vote of confidence did help Lillian feel a bit better. She took a deep breath.

Shoes, shoulders, sight, select, slide...sigh...shoot.
Ah!

Back on target. Her next three arrows mingled with Sir Alger's.

Applause came from around them as the two strolled over to the target.

"Must have been out-of-practice for longer than I thought," he remarked as he retrieved his arrows. "There was a time these would have been a couple inches to the right and several more of them."

"I remember those times. And it wasn't *that* long ago, Sir Alger. Don't let those guys make you nervous," she returned jovially, which was rewarded with a deep laugh from Sir Alger.

"All right, Miss Lillian, ready for the speed round?"

"I think so. Leaders go first, right?"

"I can do you that honor, I suppose. Though I'd step aside. Taking aim is one thing; I can't guarantee where these go flying in the heat of the moment."

Lillian knew he was kidding but gave him his space.

Ten arrows. Ten seconds.

He took a miniature hourglass from his pocket, unclipping it from its chain and handed it to Lillian.

"When I grab my first arrow, flip this. If any arrows haven't left my bow once it's done, they won't count."

Sir Alger took a last look at the target, then dropped his head, took a deep breath, and let loose.

Flip. One, top left. Two, lower left. Three, outer ring. Four, closer. Five, inner ring. Six, almost. Seven, bull's-eye. Eight, bull's-eye. Nine …

"Time," Lillian said reluctantly. He had only gotten off eight.

"Now, I *know* I was away too long." Sir Alger still got an enthusiastic round of applause as he stepped aside for Lillian.

"Try not to embarrass me too much, my ego might not recover," he said with a smirk.

He grabbed the dial. "Whenever you're ready, m'lady."

Lillian looked at the target and Sir Alger's progression of arrows.

Come on, Lillian. You've done this a million times now. Just concentrate.

She took her stance.

Just focus on the target.

She closed her eyes.

Ready. Steady…now!

Flip.

One—missed target. Two—missed target. Three—top right. Four ……

Later on, when Lillian thought back, she couldn't remember how it had happened, just that it had.

Without meaning to, she slipped into a gleam. Everything except the target dulled around her. Colors grayed. Sounds muffled. Her senses heightened. She could feel the grain of the shaft, hear the pitch of the string as it vibrated, the whistle of her arrows as they hurtled forward, and the crunch of the hay…as each and every one found the bull's-eye.

The glass dropped the last of its remaining grains a moment later.

Lillian just stood there. The world was still muffled, but she could make out the servants' voices around her.

She comprehended a few approving gasps and several outbursts she processed as being positive.

"Can you believe that?"

"That was amazing!"

"Did *you* know she was that good?"

Lillian was pulled back when Sir Alger clasped his hand on her shoulder, calling out, "How about a round of applause for the princess?"

There was an uproar as servants clapped and whistled enthusiastically at Lillian's victory. Lillian looked around a little, the familiar light and sounds crashing over her, and the gleam left her. She looked up to Sir Alger, the realization of the matter fully connecting. "I'm so sorry, I...I didn't mean to do that well. I mean, I was trying, but you said not to embarrass you and I think did, but it just happened. I didn't..."

"Your Highness," Sir Alger stopped her, his face gentle and warm, "you have nothing to be sorry about."

"But I feel awful. I've never shot like that before," Lillian stuttered.

"My dear, it was my pleasure watching such a performance. I haven't seen something like that in a very long time."

Lillian gave a wan smile in return.

"Would you do an old man the honor of taking a walk," he glanced around and smiled, "ah, away from your adoring fans?"

Lillian blushed from her scalp to her toes and went to retrieve her arrows.

They walked away, striding in silence for a while. Once they were out of range of the onlookers, Sir Alger broke the silence. "May I ask who taught you how to shoot like that? Might it be the new friend you've been going to see?"

By the Fae! Does everyone already know about Alexander?

But Lillian didn't break stride. "What makes you think someone taught me?"

"All due respect, Your Highness, but who was it do you think informed your father?" He gave her a genial but knowing look.

Lillian returned it, not breaking the eye contact. They both stopped, and he continued to hold the gaze.

"Lillian, it is my job as head of security to protect this kingdom and all of its citizens. There's nary a mouse that scurries 'cross the floor I don't know about, especially when it comes to the royal family. Lately, however, I seemed to be lacking some knowledge when it came to you."

"You know that's not true." Lillian felt bad. "This isn't your fault. I don't blame you, you know that, right?"

"Of course. But it doesn't make it any easier for me to deal with. And the way your captor perished, struck down by a foul curse for telling the truth. I'll admit, this old man is feeling out of his league." He looked down, pensive. "I'm glad someone has been teaching you how to defend yourself. The way you shoot is quite impressive. I, myself, have only seen that style of shooting from one other person in my life— and since I haven't met your friend, I'm assuming he learned from him."

Uh. Flerb.

This conversation was headed down a dangerous path, and fast.

There was no helping it, though. Lillian was pretty sure the elf was out of the knapsack. And although she knew what the answer would be, she still had to ask. "Who was it?"

"Berchum Elwood."

The lack of surprise on Lillian's face sealed it.

"My old rival." But Sir Alger's face crinkled into a smile as he looked out over the grounds. "Yes, yes. He was the only one who could consistently best me. The world lost an amazing skill when he passed," he said, his smile ebbing slightly. "Ah, well, what I thought was lost has apparently been found." He turned his face to hers with a chuckle.

"When he passed?" Lillian was confused.

Alexander didn't say anything about his father being dead.

"Oh, about five years hence. He left behind a wife and a son, Alex, I think it was, or Lex, maybe. Met the lad when Berchum was here for his last tournament. Such a polite boy. Showed a lot of promise even at ten."

Ten? That can't be Alexander, then. But he never mentioned having a brother…

Lillian was beginning to realize just how much she didn't know about Alexander.

"If I remember right, he won his division that week. But once Berchum died, I never saw the boy again. I suppose Berchum must have had an older apprentice he never mentioned, though. Whoever he is, he knows his stuff, if your shooting is any basis. You've only been doing this for a couple of months, and you're already besting one of the best." Sir Alger winked.

A blush crept up Lillian's cheeks, along with a growing sense of pride.

"Lillian, your stance and shooting, you seem to have a cadence. I remember Berchum having a mantra of sorts back then, and I bet you're using the same—if I recall, it goes something like, *shoes, shoulders, sight…select…*ah…"

"Slide, sigh, shoot," Lillian finished.

"Yes, yes. I knew it!" He tossed his head back and laughed. "I can't believe my old nemesis actually figured out a way to beat me from the grave."

He just shook his head in good-humored incredulity.

"Ah, but they say a carpenter is only as good as the tools he has to work with," Sir Alger said as he nodded toward Lillian.

"Well, thank you."

The pair walked a while longer, Sir Alger talking mostly about his glory days in archery, but Lillian didn't mind. He also talked about Berchum, which Lillian particularly enjoyed. It made her feel closer to Alexander.

As they circled back around the paddock, Lillian excused herself. She needed to meet Ophelia to finish her "common-dress" disguise. Not that Ophelia knew what it was for. Lillian had alluded to it having something to do with Jafria and one of her apparel projects, and no questions were asked.

Once Lillian had finished tying off her last stitch, she strolled down to find Seth. They chatted nonchalantly in the afternoon sun about the weather and the party while Seth covertly signaled that everything was settled. He'd be ready for the party and knew the plan.

Finally, Lillian went up to her room where she moved aside some dresses in her closet to reveal a makeshift scarecrow. She took out the final bundles of hay from her knapsack and filled in the left arm.

It's not pretty, but it'll have to do.

Now all she had to do was wait.

CHAPTER 26: Dinner Party
July 11

ervants in the castle were bustling about, preparing for the guests who would arrive any minute. And with each passing minute, Lillian grew more and more nervous. She double- and triple-checked that her scarecrow and the vial of black Hair Hue were still in place. They were. Just as they were the last time she'd looked.

Lillian had ventured to Seth's workshop once the sun went down to practice hooking up the device. The fourth time Lillian repeated her journey, Seth shooed her off.

"Lillian, I've shown you three times now already. You could hook it up with your eyes closed and hands behind your back if you had to. I promise, it will attach to any undercarriage that comes here. Now go. Relax. You've got an exciting evening ahead of you." Then to emphasize his point, he settled his hands on her shoulders, turned her around, and helped her off with a gentle shove.

Lillian went back to her room and tried to preoccupy her mind by getting ready for the party. Plus, she wanted to be dressed and appointed by the time the dwarves arrived. She was almost finished when Andrew's secret knock was heard at her door.

Lillian opened it to see both Andrew and Ethan dressed in finely tailored outfits, replete with coat, starched shirt, waistcoat, and collar. They would help escort the guests to the pre-dinner gathering for hors d'oeuvres and conversation.

"Oh! Don't you two look debonair? Shouldn't you be downstairs, though? The guests should be arriving."

"Yeah," Andrew answered as he scratched an itch under his layered attire. "We just wanted to say we're not gonna do anything tonight."

"Well, I appreciate you letting me know in advance."

Andrew looked at her as if he had something else to say, but he didn't continue.

Lillian said, "Okay, well, I have to finish getting ready, so I'll see you down there in a minute."

Ethan turned and walked away, but Andrew paused, then leaned in and gave Lillian a hug. "I'm really glad to have a big sister again."

The act surprised her, but she easily returned his affection. "And I'm glad to have such a sweet little brother." She bent down and checked to make sure Ethan was out of hearing distance. "You know what to do tonight, right?"

"Yep. Keep an eye on your door and if anyone asks, you went to bed and asked not to be disturbed. You weren't feeling well."

"That's right. And in return, I'll tell Grayson to let you and Ethan help him with the light show for the Dawning Festival."

Andrew smiled but then bit his lower lip. "You're not gonna get in trouble again are you, Lillian? Dad's finally getting in a better mood."

"Not if I don't get caught. Which I won't, all thanks to you, right?"

Andrew stood straight up and saluted. "Yes, ma'am. You can count on me."

"All right. Now, off with you before you send Mom in a spiral."

Andrew ran off to catch up to Ethan, leaving a smile on Lillian's face as she returned to her vanity to finish putting on her jewelry.

Lillian could hear the mingling of the guests' conversations as she descended the sweeping staircase. Ophelia had really outdone herself this time. Lillian's dress was a flowing gown of rich, dark-green silk, stitched with gold thread. The top of the bodice was heavily embroidered with the gold thread, but as the dress swept downward, the stitches diminished little by little, revealing a pattern of tiny stars, which gently fell down the fabric, as if they were being poured from some celestial cup.

When her slippered feet reached the marbled floor, a steward escorted her to the threshold, where the doorman announced her presence.

"Introducing Her Royal Highness, the Princess Lillian of Valanti."

The guests all turned to applaud her entrance, and as her eyes swept the room, she found her mother and father already present, and they waved to her from across the room.

The hall was set up much like it had been at her birthday party, though clearly for a formal meal this evening and for much fewer people. The food was an array of local appetizers and tapas Chef Pierre had collected over the years to happily tide the guests over until the full meal that was to come later. Resplendent decorations draped the hall. Guests in their finest milled about, making introductions and catching up. Several of the King's Guard did their best to mingle without making anyone uncomfortable, and several more were stationed at every entrance. Her father was taking no chances tonight.

Lillian slowly walked through the small clusters, stopping briefly for polite formalities, but she was hunting for someone in particular. A rousing outburst of laughter pointed her in the right direction.

She eventually worked her way over to her target. Behind the throng of other guests, this group stood out from the crowd (and always did, but they preferred it that way). Unlike most of the guests, who were dressed in gowns and suits to impress the other people in attendance, these guests were simply not interested in impressing anyone at their great age. In a passing glance, they might seem to be covered in something like castoffs and junk. Perhaps work clothes (though Lillian had actually seen their work clothes, which were far beyond cleaning).

Each had their own style, just like their personality. When her mother had met them so many years ago, she had named them based on their quirky characteristics. They allowed Snow White to call them by her self-appointed nomenclatures, even though most everyone else called them by their actual names. But one alias had been in place even before Snow White had given them affectionate nicknames. He was the wisest and oldest of the dwarves.

"Doc!" Lillian stooped to give her rugged, though still quite handsome, friend a hug.

His outfit consisted of browns and blacks topped with a checkered coat with tails that hung to his knees. His best leather boots were buckled with bits and pieces of old polished mining equipment, which matched his belt buckle. The buttons on his shirt were small gears, most likely from old contraptions he had built, which had since run their course. Though from what Lillian could tell, the gears of his mind never stopped turning. Doc was the mastermind behind Falloren Fountain and many other feats of machinery around the village.

"Lillian, m'dear. 'Ow are ya, lass?" He returned her hug and kissed her cheek. "I 'aven't seen much of you lately. I 'ear you've been reprimanded foor seeing some lad." He gave her a sly smile.

I really need to explain to Mom what discretion *means.*

"There's, ah, a little more to it than that, but I guess that sums it up. I've missed you, old friend."

"Ta, I am not so old."

"Doc, you're exactly one-hundred-and-eighty-five years old," she said.

"Aye. But not so old for a dwarf."

They were distracted by another dwarf who harbored a permanent scowl.

"Hey, what's the deal here? Did'aya give your only hug to an old man?"

"Of course not, Byme." Lillian gave him a warm hug in proof.

Byme, with his curmudgeonly charm, had been one of many unfortunate souls who suffered before Snow White under the evil queen's wrath. During a drought of gems, the evil queen had scarred his face, and with it, his demeanor. Though by his friends' accounts, he's been markedly merrier since the moment of her demise.

"Right, right. Let's not make a show o' it." Byme pulled away, attempting to feign dislike of the attention.

In contrast, the next dwarf to reach Lillian bore a grin from ear to ear. "Oh, don't listen to that ould sour dragon. He loves it and 'e knows it. How'r'ya doing, m'dear?"

"I'm well, Ferrell," she said, smiling at his infectious cheerfulness.

Hugs and greetings continued all around. Casen was of course reluctant, and Erwyn reached to get another hug, which Lillian was happy to give. They talked of mining and mechanics and other things that amounted to small talk for them, 'til Lillian saw an opportunity to take Doc aside. She led him to a couple of chairs, out of earshot of the other guests.

"Aye, what's on yoor mind, darlin'?" Doc could always tell when something was amiss.

How do I start this without giving away Alexander?

"Well, you know about the boy that I've been seeing?"

"I 'ad 'eard a smidge or two about it," he said impishly.

"And by the way, he's teaching me archery, so that's why I haven't been around lately," Lillian hastily added, as she knew it'd been nearly two months since she'd visited them.

"Ah, it's more than archery, dearie. I can see that in yoor eyes," he said shrewdly, "but go on."

Lillian thought about how to proceed. "He's been telling me stories, stories about passages in the mountains. Special passages that might be magic, but I'm not sure if he's telling the truth."

"Well, what 'as 'e told you about these supposed magic passages?"

Lillian recounted what Alexander had shared with her, as well as what she had seen and experienced herself. Doc sat patiently, listening and nodding his head as she spoke.

At the last of it, she said, "Well, that's pretty much it. And I just figured if anyone would know, it would be you. Is it anything you can help me with?" Lillian waited, edging forward in anticipation. She could tell he knew something, but whether or not he'd share was another story.

"Aye. There are many secret things to be found in the mountains," he said sagely.

Annnndddd?

"Weel, I've come across several in my lifetime. Magic ones, that is. But in truth, our mountains, the Kraneths, are much like ant 'ills. There are regular tunnels that lead in all directions. Back in my youth, I'd travel 'cross the continent using them."

"The *continent*?" Lillian repeated.

She knew it was a possibility from what her letter and Alexander had said, but the affirmation was still a shock.

"Aye, to be sure of it. I could get from 'ere to Caldera in a day easy as blinkin' with the right passage. Trouble was, if ya took a new one, you never could tell where you might pop out. And not all of them lead to the good kingdoms."

Oh.

Doc thought for a second and continued. "That's how Byme and I met. 'E was actually in the process of mapping out the dern things, but one of the evil buggers took 'im across—or under—the wall, 'owever you want to look at it. He ran into some nasty goblins that stole 'is map. I found him woonderin' around tryin' to find 'is way out. Some of those passages take ya to dead ends, and some to places yoo're likely to end up dead. We tried to mark the ones we knew went to Drod. But most of them are 'armless and do what they were intended to do."

"So, why is it that no one knows about these or uses them anymore?"

"Weel, most of the magic ones 'ave faded away. We went to use one to get back from a field in Tapera one day an' it was just gone."

"Gone?"

"Aye, lass. At first we thought maybe our brains were addled and we'd come back to the wrong spoot, but there's none too many bare rock caverns in the middle of a field. *That* was a fun trip back to Valanti, I'll tell ya. Ol' Byme really lived up to yer mom's nickname. Gripe, gripe, gripe."

Lillian smirked at the thought of the odd pair's road trip.

"But a lot of them 'ave oolso been lost to cave-ins. I can't imagine there being too many left that are accessible, and those that are could be unstable unless…" Doc hesitated.

Lillian prodded, "Unless what?"

"Unless, o' course someone is keeping them up fer some reason. That's why we figure the others disappeared, because whoever created them 'ad passed on or 'ad no more use fer them."

"So, it's possible someone *could* be using them?"

"Sure, I guess. But they'd 'ave to be well versed in the art. It's not just any regular magic, the way I understand. Someone would 'ave 'ad to 'ave taught them. You might be better off asking one of the godmothers. They'd probably be able to tell ya more."

"Well, could this person make *more*? New ones, maybe?"

Doc looked at Lillian. "Yoo've seen one, 'aven't you? One o' the portals? Maybe even been through one, aye?"

Lillian didn't know what to say.

"It's a'right. You don't 'ave to tell me. And I won't mention anything to your mum. Just promise me yoo'll be careful. Thing about ant 'ills is they attract lizards. Lizards with sticky tongues, if ya get me. An' we've been seeing a few more beady eyes staring back from the dark recently."

So there are *goblins.*

"I will, Doc, I promise." Lillian wanted to ask about Alexander's gem. Find out more about the way it glowed in moonlight. Or why he couldn't be separated from it.

"I can 'ear those gears turning, Miss Lillian. And now yoo've lit the fuse of my curiosity, so go on."

"My friend also told me about a gem. A red one that glows in moonlight…and it supposedly has a connection with its wearer."

"Gems. Now there's something I know a little about. Red that glows in the moonlight, eh? You wouldn't be talkin' about that ghoost that's been roaming around now, would ya?"

Lillian's silence was all the confirmation he needed.

Doc nodded. "Right, right. I get it. Hmmm, red gems that glow at night under the moon. Now, that is an interesting toopic." He leaned back in his chair, getting comfortable. "I've only known o' three, and I only ever seen one." Doc looked Lillian straight in the eye. "An' evil surrounded them all."

Lillian held her breath, trying to process this new piece of information.

No one would know more about gems than Doc.

"Do you mean the gems were evil or that they were used for evil?"

"I can't say I know for sure what they were to start with, but I do know they were used for evil. One was possessed by the sorceress that tried to kill Lady Aurora. The dwarves in Caldera swore it changed color by firelight and 'elped 'er alter 'er form. I probably wouldn't 'ave believed them, 'cept I 'ad seen a similar gem do the same thing—the one we found in Valanti—the one we gave to the evil queen."

"You *gave* her the magic evil gem?" Lillian couldn't believe it.

"Weel, we didn't know it was magic or evil at the time. With the queen 'aving eyes everywhere, we really didn't 'ave a choice either. She knew we were bringing it to 'er before we'd even arrived or said anything about it."

Lillian was flooded with embarrassment. "I'm sorry, I didn't mean to accuse you of...I mean, I know you wouldn't have done it intentionally," Lillian stammered.

"Think nothing of it, m'dear. I knew what ya meant. Trust me, 'ad I known, I would 'ave eaten the bloody thing to keep it out of 'er 'ands. But in giving it to 'er, we realized it was kin to the sorceress's gem. Howd'ya think she changed into an old 'ag to fool your mum?"

"So, what happened to the gems after, well, you know, after the queen and the sorceress died?"

"Wish I could say. Neither body was ever found nor were the stones. But Lillian," Doc asked, his tone getting serious, "'Ave you seen one? Does yer friend have one? Because if 'e does, I'm not saying 'e's evil, but in the stones' short awakening, they've done naught but. I'd be very careful if I were you. And if they truly do 'elp its bearer change shape, there's no telling who 'e really could be."

Lillian's heart sank. She hoped to find solace in getting answers, not more questions. She dreaded the thought of Alexander being someone else, let alone thinking he was out to harm her in some way.

But he's had plenty of opportunities to let me die or kill me outright.

No. This was something she was not ready to even consider.

"You said there were three such stones but only mentioned two. Who has the other one?"

Doc blanched at her question.

"Please, Doc, it's important."

He drew in a deep breath. "The owner of the last gem was Zoldaine 'imself."

CHAPTER 27: The Escape

Every conversation Lillian had for the rest of the night was a haze. Doc had given her enough to think about for weeks to come. She was polite, of course, but only half of her was ever engaged, which, admittedly, made her come across like a half-witted faery. Nevertheless, she made it through the night without arousing any suspicion that her boyfriend was possibly evil with a capital *E*, or that she would be sneaking away once the night was over.

The four-course dinner was a chore to get through, which was a shame because Pierre had compiled an amazing array of delicacies Lillian normally would have savored. But she was anxious and worried—what if she got caught or Seth's contraption didn't hold and...

Easy, Lillian. You're just flustered right now. Remember what's at stake.

She managed to smile prettily and eat politely, when all she wanted to do was devour everything and move on. When dinner was officially over, everyone was invited to the library for petit fours and a new frozen cream treat Pierre had developed with a little assistance from Grayson. As much as she wanted to try the new concoction, Lillian knew this was the best time to excuse herself to get ready before the guests started to leave. She said something about not feeling well and was just going to turn in early.

The Escape

"Are you sure you don't want Grayson to make you anything? At least to help you sleep? I don't mind bringing it up to you, sweetheart," her mother said. Even with a room full of guests, Snow White put her children first.

"I'll be fine, Mom. I really just think I need some rest. I'm just going to go clean up for bed and lay down. You stay here and enjoy yourself, please. I'll be fine." Lillian gave her mom a kiss for good measure. "I promise."

Lillian said good-bye to a few of the other guests and headed to the stairs. Her adrenaline climbed along with every step.

Am I really doing this?

When she reached her room, she went to her closet and shoved her clothes aside, retrieving the "Lillian" scarecrow she had created over the course of the past few weeks. She changed into her new but old-looking outfit she had been making with Ophelia and put on her outdoor boots. Then she set the scarecrow in her bed, checking it from all angles.

Well, if no one brings in a light to check on me, I should look asleep.

The last touch was Hair Hue to dye her hair black. It would last about twelve hours, which would give her enough time to investigate but would wear off by the morning. After that, she used some kohl to darken her eyes, a trick Jafria had taught her to look mysterious, though Lillian wasn't using it for that purpose tonight. She let her newly darkened locks down to cover her face as much as possible. That completed, she gave herself one last look in the mirror.

Let's hope this works. Fae be with me.

She took the long way to Seth, hoping to avoid anyone that might recognize her.

So far so good.

She could still hear guests in the library as she snuck by, but no unexpected encounters occurred.

As she slipped into the stables, she walked up behind Seth.

He turned around and looked right at her. "I'm sorry, miss, but the horses are put up for the evening and...Lillian?"

"You really didn't recognize me?" Lillian was impressed with herself.

"No, I didn't, I mean, I do now, but that's only because I know. Wow. I mean, if I didn't know any better, I would have thought a faery godmother put a spell on you."

"Come on, I don't look that different. You're just trying to make me feel good."

"No, I'm serious. The outfit, the hair...I'm impressed."

"All right, enough flattery. Let's get me rigged up. The guests will be leaving soon."

"Before that," he said, pulling out a letter, "I'm pretty sure this is for you."

Lillian took it, recognizing the mysterious handwriting from before. "Where did this come from?"

"Same as last time; I have no idea." Seth thought for a moment. "Actually that's not entirely true. This time I saw someone leaving."

"Really? Who?"

"He can't be involved though. There's no way."

"Who, Seth?"

"I was just coming back from the kitchen, and I bumped into Sir Laurel coming the other way."

"Sir Laurel?"

"He may not have been coming from the stables, though...but I'm not sure where he *would* have been coming from."

Lillian processed this. Sir Laurel was from Drod, but his involvement was either an amazing coincidence or he was the best actor Lillian had ever seen.

She opened the letter.

Red hood.

Once again, no signature.

"Lillian, be honest with me. This letter and the last one are both about tonight, aren't they?"

Lillian hesitated.

"C'mon, Lillian," Seth urged. "I'm in this just as deep as you now, and Fae forbid, but *if* you don't come back or something should happen—someone needs to know."

"Tell no one," it had said. She chewed her bottom lip.

"Lillian, this isn't some secret boyfriend rendezvous we're talking about here, this is The Trenches—at night, alone. Give me *something* so I don't go spiral while you're gone."

Lillian sighed. "All right, I'm supposed to be meeting someone at the Wrath. Someone who has information about what's been going on, including my kidnapping."

"Someone? There's still no name?"

"Nope." Lillian showed him the letter.

"Uh, I don't know about this, Lillian. I mean, whoever left these letters *has* to be from here inside the castle. And I can't believe it was Mr. Perfect Hair. I was only gone for a bit tonight grabbing something to eat, and the letter was here when I got back, just like last time. And I guarantee no one snuck onto the grounds with this party going on tonight. Your dad has it clamped down tighter than a dragon's claw around a gold coin."

"I'm sneaking out, though," she pointed out.

"Well, yeah, but that's different."

"How so?"

Seth just smirked. "Because it's me who's helping you, that's how so. So, the Wrath, huh?" Seth walked over to his tool bench, grabbed something, and came back. "Here." He handed her a small sheathed knife. "Take this."

"A knife? Seth, I can't take this. I wouldn't even know how to use it."

"Just take it. Just in case. It'll make *me* feel better. Please?"

Lillian took the knife. "And where am I supposed to put this?"

"Slip it into your boot pouch. It can hold more than just shears, you know. That way if someone checks you, more than likely they won't find it."

Lillian dropped the knife into her pouch. "Feel better?"

"Much. Come on, we better get you situated."

Seth strode to an empty stable, retreating into it momentarily, then backing out as he produced his creation. He brought it over to Lillian and helped her secure it to her torso.

"And you're sure this will hold me the whole time?" Lillian asked. She still questioned the contraption's seemingly fragile nature.

"The metal is all reinforced. The clasps are made from a special interlocking system of my own design, which I've used during climbing for an entire day. So, yes, I'm sure it will hold you the whole time. It would hold ten of you, trust me."

"Okay. Sorry, just a bit nervous. So, which carriage is going to get me closest to The Trenches?"

"I've already picked the one. Come with me." Seth escorted her to the rows of carriages from the visiting guests. "This one belongs to Archibald Conway. Should take you right there."

"How do you know that?"

"I've got a friend who works at Wizard Wagers, the gambling spot. She says he frequents it often. Like clockwork after any soirée he attends."

"*She*, huh?" Lillian teased.

"Just a friend. You know I've only got eyes for you," he said in mock reverence. "Okay, let's get you hooked up before anyone comes out."

Lillian crawled beneath the carriage.

"See the front and rear axles? Just hook the clasps," he said, reaching under and pointing, "here and over there. Then place your feet right there."

Lillian did what he said but was nonetheless reluctant to let go with her hands.

"Relax. Just let it cradle you; that's what it's designed for. If you try and hold yourself up all night, your arms will be like rag dolls."

She slowly loosened her grip and relaxed, easing into the harness.

"Hey, it's actually pretty comfortable."

"Told you. Now, when it stops, just make sure you put your feet down first, unhook, and you should be good to go. And I'll be here waiting to sneak you back in."

"Thanks, Seth. I really can't thank you enough."

"Just find out what's going on so we can have the Dawning Festival."

"Thanks for keeping things in perspective, dragon dung." She scowled at him.

He quickly added, "And of course, so nothing else happens to you. Your safety is what's most important here. But seriously though, be careful. Trust your dad's instincts you've got inside you, and if anything feels wrong, you get out of there. Right then."

"I will."

"Promise?"

"I will, Seth, I promise. Now, get out of here before someone sees you."

Seth turned his head toward the door. Lillian heard it too. Guests were starting to leave the party. "Perfect timing. All right then, good luck, Lil'." He headed off, then looked back as if to say something else, but a pair of servants emerged through the door before he could.

Lillian waited and watched as the servants retrieved various carriages, pulling them around to pick up their passengers. Even though she knew she couldn't be seen, she still got nervous every time someone approached.

Finally, after what seemed like eons had passed, she heard, "Mr. Conway is ready to leave. I'm getting his carriage now."

About a minute passed and the carriage lurched forward for its short trip to the circle drive. It stopped near the entryway and she saw a pair of portly legs come down the steps as the doorman opened the carriage's door.

"Heading home tonight, Mr. Conway?"

"Home? Why, the evening's still early and my pockets are full. What say we go risk a little coin at Wizard's."

Thank you, Seth's friend.

As Conway got in, Lillian sank a little closer to the ground.

Good thing there's not a Mrs. Conway or I might be dragging the whole way.

The carriage door clicked closed, and the horses trotted forward, their stowaway tucked neatly beneath. Lillian couldn't see the usual references at this level, but she could still mostly make out where she was. They passed through the main gate and headed into town. They went by Falloren Fountain and took a left into The Arts, where buildings reflected the various artists' talents and their wares through ornamentation or color. Lillian could make out Valanti Valor from its print-covered door and Trixie's Pixie Paints from the pink glitter covering the front bricks. After a bit, the carriage rolled into the residence quarter of Old Towne. She knew this place for sure because of all the work being done. Her father was really putting in some effort to reconstruct the living quarters. Not that they were unlivable, but they were some of the first houses and shops to be built in the kingdom, and they suffered greatly during the evil queen's reign. So, he and Snow White decided to refurbish them with new material and add in some of the dwarves' upgrades.

Finally, the carriage neared The Trenches. When the evil queen reigned, this was where most of the more malicious deeds were done. The king had done his best to rid the area of any negative influence. And while he had mostly succeeded, some vices remained. Guards patrolled the area regularly, but unless things got out of hand, they usually turned a blind eye to the often-shady deals that took place down its alleyways. The king himself would drop by occasionally, in an attempt to keep things in check, but evil will always find a foothold somehow, no matter how noble the attempts.

Though Seth had exaggerated when he said going to The Trenches was a death sentence. No one had actually died here for years. Well, at least none that were made known. A lot of Drod natives settled here and in Old Towne after the war simply because they had no money to afford finer accommodations. While the monarchy did what it could, poverty was still an issue, which is why the king was making it one of his top priorities to rebuild not only the buildings but also the people.

The carriage turned a corner and began slowing until it stopped in front of what Lillian could only assume was Wizard Wagers.

Her heart raced as she mentally prepared herself. *You can do this.* The carriage lifted as Mr. Conway stepped off and headed into the establishment. Seth's contraption released easily, and Lillian gently lowered herself to the ground. She did a quick check for any oncoming carriages or horses and then rolled out from under the carriage and stood up. Several passersby gave her an odd look, but apparently they had seen stranger. They looked away and let it go.

Lillian paused to try and get her bearings. She had been to The Trenches a few times in the past, but it was usually during the daytime. It was a different beast altogether at night.

Wagers is on this side, so that must be north...which means the Rusty Nail would be over...yes! Now, that means the Wrath is behind me, over...

As she turned to look, she saw the wooden sign depicting a dragon's head breathing fire. As she made her way to the Dragon's Wrath, she caught sight of people in the alleyways. All manner of goods and services were being traded in their shadows.

These were the sorts of goings-on Lillian had heard the knights swapping stories about but never thought she would actually witness.

Or be a part of.

Lillian pondered that as she went to meet with the mysterious red-hooded figure.

The pungent aroma of ale, tobacco, and sweat filtered out from the doorway before Lillian had even grasped the handle. The smell only magnified when she wrenched open the door. Lillian turned her head and sucked in one last bit of fresh air before venturing into the lively tavern.

Though it was after dark, the merrymaking was just getting underway and didn't look like it would die down for quite some time. Lillian had never seen the inside of a tavern before. A perpetual haze of smoke hung in the air from various pipes and their owners. The pub guests were busy eating, drinking, laughing, and a few even danced. Waitresses carried various trays of meats, breads, cheeses, and ales. Lillian could tell they earned their tips by performing fantastic acts of balance while weaving through the crowd and avoiding wandering hands.

A bard sat in the corner with a small mandolin, plucking away some favorite tune, and most of the patrons were singing along. When the chorus came back around, everyone hoisted their mugs high in the air with renewed enthusiasm. A couple of overly gregarious guests bumped into a waitress, spilling some drink on her attire, apologized, and stumbled on their way to a bench in the corner.

As Lillian's gaze followed them, something caught her attention. A red hood. She couldn't see who was under it, so she began slowly skirting the room to get a better look. Her father's voice of reason lectured her the entire time.

What if this is another ploy, Lillian? You are totally out of your element here. This is way bigger than you. It's happening in every kingdom.

But then her voice of reason would argue back.

But no one is finding out anything. It's my life, and I can't stay barricaded in the castle for the rest of my life. If something's going to happen to me, it's going to happen on my *terms, not theirs. Besides, it's not like I'm in Drod, surrounded by a bunch of goblins. These are my subjects.*

His parried back.

Are they? Most of them came from Drod. Subjects? Spies? You don't know.

Well, that's what I'm here to find out.

Lillian felt more certain of her mission as she squeezed past a burly, and rather robust-smelling customer, which finally gave her a closer view of the hooded figure.

They seemed relatively alone, their face turned away, searching the crowd.

Ah, they haven't seen me yet.

Lillian took the opportunity to find a better vantage point from which to scrutinize the mysterious Red Hood for a bit before walking up blindly.

Well, any more than you already are.

At that moment, Red Hood turned back.

Lillian sucked in an involuntary breath.

Hayden?

Lillian kept examining the hooded face in disbelief, but there was no denying it was the castle's kitchen servant. Lillian knew her from all the time she spent in and out of the kitchen as of late, but they never exchanged too many words. Hayden was exceedingly shy, and other than performing her duties in the kitchen or serving at events, Lillian wasn't sure she had ever seen the girl outside her quarters.

Lillian thought it made her an unlikely candidate to know "vital information."

Maybe she's only the messenger for someone else?

But so many unusual things had been happening lately. Perhaps what she didn't know about Hayden was what made her the ideal possessor of critical knowledge.

Well, the dragon's not going to just give you its gold.

Lillian began snaking her way around bodies, tables, and chairs until about halfway there, when Hayden looked up directly at her. Lillian stopped.

Does she recognize me?

But Hayden stood up and started working her way through the crowd in the opposite direction from Lillian. She didn't seem to be in a hurry, though. Lillian watched her retreat before Hayden stopped and swung around with a look that said, *Are you coming or not?*

Hayden didn't wait for a response. Lillian remembered the prior warning, *"ears are everywhere,"* and hurried to catch up, the undulating crowd hampering her progress. The servant only paused once more to see if Lillian was indeed following, then disappeared through a door in the back. No one even glanced at her.

Sure, let's go out the back door into a dark alley in The Trenches. What could go wrong?

According to the guards' stories, though, that's where all the good information was passed. And she couldn't think of any better information to be had right now.

Lillian reached the door, cast a glance behind her to see if anyone was watching, or Fae forbid, following. No one was.

Lillian pushed open the door. She was not, however, met with a wave of cool night air and a moonlit alleyway; what lay before her instead made her insides twist.

Stairs.

And they went down.

CHAPTER 28: Into the Lion's Den

own? Really?

Her father's reason began all but shouting.

There's something wrong here and you know it. Seth only knows you're at the Dragon, and there's no telling where this will take you. Please, I beg you.

Lillian stood there looking down the dimly lit stairwell. Memories of her kidnapping resurfaced, and Lillian fought down the fear trying to strangle her.

She closed her eyes. *No. I will not live my life in fear. I will not have my life dictated by others. I'm sorry, Dad. But I have to.*

Her father's final plea faded as she descended. At the bottom, she could see torches staggered the length of tunnel, which ran in both directions, their flames providing alternating moments of safety from the visceral fear of what lie in wait outside their light. Lillian saw Hayden standing a few paces away, looking down the tunnel to their right where light eventually stopped, the darkness absolute and all-consuming beyond it.

Lillian slowly approached the girl, who still hadn't said anything.

"It's Hayden, right?"

Hayden held up a finger. She reached into her cloak and produced a small black orb.

Lillian backed up. "Wait! What are you…"

Hayden threw the sphere to the ground where it smashed and burst into a large sphere, immediately enveloping both girls. Any residual sound Lillian had heard was now muffled as if she had stuffed wool in her ears. Memory flickered as she realized what the sphere was. Her dad had even used them on occasion during confidential council meetings before his forces conquered Drod. They were called secret spheres or hush balls.

"By the Fae! What are you doing?" Lillian yelled, but the aptly named secret spheres muffled it to barely a loud whisper.

"I'm sorry, but I had to be sure no one hears us," Hayden apologized.

Lillian looked around the tunnel. "Who could possibly hear us down here, over the ruckus up there?"

"Humans aren't the only creatures with ears, Your Highness." Hayden motioned at a couple of mice that scurried past.

"You can't be serious," Lillian said incredulously.

Hayden was impatient. "You know about Cinderella's animal friends being turned into horses and footmen. Well, the same can be done in reverse. I realize Tapera is known to be the more magical kingdom, but it doesn't mean traces of it don't linger here. Your hair, for instance."

Lillian reached her hand up to touch the inky locks; she had forgotten about her appearance. She did not miss the curtness in Hayden's response and realized the girl's shy personality must be a ruse.

"And I'll never get through this if I have to keep explaining everything to you. So, may I continue?"

Lillian nodded, still unsettled by the abrupt change in perceived personality.

"As I was saying," Hayden continued, "there's a reason why I needed you to come here. I wasn't sure if you'd get the notes or not, since I had to trust someone else with the task. The castle isn't safe anymore. At least for talking."

"Wait. It wasn't you who left the notes?"

"No, of course not. I couldn't risk getting caught and jeopardizing this meeting."

"Why aren't you telling my father these things?"

"If a lowly kitchen servant suddenly starts asking for an audience with the king multiple times, it would raise suspicion, and the wrong heads would turn."

"But why now? I was kidnapped over a month ago."

"There have been new developments accelerating faster than we had anticipated. Your kidnapping was one of them."

"I'm sorry, 'we'?"

"There are several of us, ever since Drod's liberation, who have kept a watchful eye on things. Some believe Zoldaine has returned, others aren't certain. Either way, *something* has been brewing in Drod—and it's centered around you and the other princesses."

"But why? Why now? Why me or us?"

"That's what we're trying to find out," Hayden answered.

"Not to poison your potion, but you haven't really told me anything I don't already know."

"Tell me, what about Zands? We know he's here, in The Trenches. And we know the reason no one can find him is that he changes his appearance. And I'm not just talking about Hair Hue. So far, we've discovered three different personas. The one you saw, although dressed as a magician, we call his true form, then there is a middle-aged woman and an old man. The woman appears to be in her fifties or sixties. Grayish brown hair, creamy skin, dark eyes, about my height, and she always seems to have a purple scarf. That and a red ring." *Zands had the purple cloak.* "The man is tall with darker skin, appears ancient, and wears a purple tunic. The only reason we spotted him for certain is that he also wears the red ring."

Lillian thought back. His ring was green when she'd seen it at Talula's.

"There could be more identities, but we're not sure yet. Your kidnapping rescue was a hitch in this circle's plan to be sure. There's been a low buzz amongst them ever since."

"Them? How many 'them'?"

"We're guessing one to two hundred here in the kingdom, more in the others, and untold numbers in Drod."

Lillian felt her mouth gaping. How was all this possible? Drod was supposed to *deserted* for Fae's sake, but the more people she talked to, the more it sounded like it was the breeding pool for a rebellion.

Hayden said, "Look, I realize this all might be a little shocking to hear. But you had to know."

Lillian felt so naïve. So sheltered from reality. She knew there were problems and issues but not like *this*. Not to this scale. No wonder her father was being overly protective. He probably knows all about this and has just been trying to protect his little girl.

"Is there anything else?"

"Actually, yes. We think Zands is planning something—big. And soon. Like I said, you were supposed to be out of the way a month ago, and whoever *is* in charge does not have patience for failure."

"But how could anything of that nature happen with my father's increased security? You should have seen what I had to do to get out of there tonight."

"That's what we don't get. Why would they be planning for something unless…"

At that moment, the sphere around them throbbed a translucent red. A built-in warning system for prying ears and unwelcome guests.

Hayden yanked off her red cloak. "Here, put this on now," She thrust it into Lillian's hands.

"Wait, what? I don't understand."

"Just *do* it! Someone is coming. We can't let them see you. Finding me is one thing—finding you is their end game.

Lillian swallowed down the bile that threatened to come up and did as she was told, the sphere growing ever brighter.

Soon, she heard the sound of men tromping down the stairs.

"Crouch against the wall," Hayden whispered and did the same, although to Lillian, it appeared neither of them would be very well hidden. Hayden whispered something else, and both the sphere and nearby torches suddenly went out.

Three men reached the bottom of the stairs, laughing about something, and headed in their direction. One grabbed a torch from another wall to carry with them.

Oh no!

Lillian's heart beat a frantic rhythm. She was trying to keep her breath steady, but all she managed was strangled gasps, which to her sounded about as quiet as a troll with a cold. She had never been so scared in her life.

The circle of light that held the men was steadily getting closer. They were sure to see two females hunkering along the wall. Lillian looked over to Hayden, who had seemingly disappeared.

But Hayden was there; she somehow simply blended into the wall of muddled rock. Lillian wasn't even sure she would have spotted Hayden if she hadn't known where she was. And she had already produced some knowledge of magic, so there was reason to believe she had more.

But for Lillian, Hayden's red cloak may hide *who* she was, but not *where* she was....

Of course! That's why no one seemed to pay Hayden any attention in the tavern; her red cloak must be enchanted to make the wearer invisible! But how could I see her plain as day?

Lillian would be the first to admit she didn't know much about the magical realm. That was more Olivia's strong point. Lillian made a note to converse more with her cousin about magic if she ever got out of this mess.

The men were nearly on top of them, and Lillian held her breath, hoping their disguises would work. "So, how are things coming?" the torchbearer asked.

"He's taking his time, this go 'round. There can't be any more mistakes," the bald one answered.

"There better not be, or we'll all end up like Dax. Have we heard anything else from the inside?"

The torch's light was just passing over Lillian.

The bald one piped up again. "No, and we probably won't until it's closer. They've had to lay low since the kidnapping. The king's got eyes and ears everywhere and he's got a sneaky intuition that's caused problems in the past. The only reason we've been able to stay one step ahead of him so far is the arrogance he and the other royal families have about their kingdoms. Right now, they're all focused on Zands. Which is exactly where *he* wants it to be."

The trio had made it past, and Lillian began to take in slow, shallow breaths to her burning lungs. That's when she smelled bacon.

Pork!

He would have been the shy one who hadn't spoken.

What is he doing here?

She looked back to Hayden, who was deftly repositioning herself so she could watch the men's moves.

Then Lillian heard something that made her stomach drop out from under her.

A rock had dislodged from where Hayden was hiding.

The men paused mid-step.

"Lemme see that." The bald guy grabbed the torch and headed straight toward Hayden.

Lillian's heart raced.

No, no, no. Fae, hide her, please.

But it was too late, and Hayden knew it. She sprang up and darted toward the stairs, but the man caught one of her sleeves. Hayden struggled and managed to wrest herself free of it, but by then the original torchbearer had joined him and grabbed her. Pork stood by, watching anxiously.

"Please! Please, let me go. I'm just a simple bar maid, I didn't hear anything. I'm new and got lost. Please, I beg you." Hayden's performance was convincing. Even Lillian was buying it, and she knew better. But Hayden stared right at Lillian, widened her eyes, and inconspicuously shook her head.

"Finding you is their end game."

"What do you think, Garrick?" the bald guy asked the form who held Hayden.

"I think," Garrick said as he jerked Hayden's arms, "what I think, Digby, is it's not my call. She can come with us. He'll know what to do with her. She might be one of those squealers."

"No, please, I don't know what you're talking about." Hayden struggled, but to no avail.

"We'll know soon enough. He'll be able to tell. He always gets the truth out. Doesn't he, boys?" Garrick snorted and laughed, Digby joining in.

Lillian watched helplessly as Hayden continued to protest and struggle as the men dragged her off down the tunnel. Lillian's mind struggled with what to do, reason and worry arguing their sides.

I can't just let them take her!

But what can you do? You can't fight them off.

I can at least follow them.

And what good will that do? What if they see you?

They won't. That's why she gave me the cloak. They won't see me. I have to try.

Just before the receding torchlight disappeared around a corner, Lillian hopped up and followed, as sneakily as possible, after them. She didn't have to travel far before the party slowed up ahead of her, and she saw why. There was a shimmering vertical pool of water.

"All right, I'll go through first. Give me a second to find someone, then send the girl." Then Garrick walked through. The shimmering portal rippled for a moment then was still once more.

"You're in for a real treat, squealer." Digby smirked. "He likes squealers. You know how we got the name 'squealers'?" He waited as if he actually expected her to answer. "Well, ya see, first he gives you this..."

"Come on, Digby," Pork interrupted. "Just put her through already."

"Oh, Piggy, you never want to have any fun," Digby complained. "Enjoy the trip, sweetheart." And with a quick shove, Digby sent Hayden through.

It seems only one person can go through at a time.

Lillian wasn't sure why, but that fact seemed important to remember. She waited for the other two men to walk through. As they did, the light from the torch went with it, and it was suddenly dark, though there was a soft glow emanating from the pool. Lillian cautiously walked up to it. The last time she went through one of these things, she didn't have a chance to examine it. Plus, she needed to make sure the guys weren't going to be right on the other side—wherever that might be.

It was like a mirror, but she didn't see any reflections. She traced her finger on the surface. It felt cool and wet, but when she pulled it back it was dry. She hoped no one would be looking as she stuck half of her arm through and pulled it back. Same thing. Even her cloak was dry.

The cloak. The cloak will conceal you.

Lillian just prayed it had a longer-lasting enchantment than Hair Hue.

It's now or never.

She took a step forward and felt the cool "liquid" flow over her face and chill her body. It really was like being underwater. Like all her senses were shut off for a moment except the coolness.

Her journey was dark but short. On the opposite side, it took her a moment to orient herself and for her eyes to adjust. She found herself in some sort of natural cavern. She could hear several voices echoing off the walls. Even though she knew the cloak offered some sort of coverage, she wasn't sure exactly how much and still didn't feel comfortable out in the open. She surveyed her immediate surroundings and found several crates stacked up against the wall to hide her.

Those will do nicely.

Even with the small torches around the walls, the cavern was still very dim. As her eyes adjusted, she peered through the crates and got a better sense of where she was. The cavern was larger than she originally thought, at least thirty paces across and about ten high. She counted four different tunnels leading to who-knew-where and however-many tunnels that branched out from them. There were several areas stacked with crates or various tools and supplies. Lillian couldn't quite make out clearly what they were. The only thing that appeared imminently disturbing was, as she could finally see, sitting right next to her.

A number of small barrels, more like kegs, sat stacked close to the portal—each bearing a red skull and crossbones.

She knew she had seen that symbol before but couldn't place where. Whatever it represented, she figured it couldn't be good.

Voices continued to bounce around, making it impossible for Lillian to hear where Hayden might be, let alone what any of the conversations were about. Soon, however, two voices became clearer as Garrick and Digby walked in from one of the tunnels across the way and headed toward Lillian.

Don't worry, they can't see you. Just hold still until they pass through.

But they didn't pass through. They came right up to the crates Lillian was hiding behind. Garrick lifted off the uppermost one.

Digby stepped forward and looked right into Lillian's eyes. "Hello, Princess."

CHAPTER 29: My Hero?

Even if Lillian managed to get out of the ropes that bound her hands, her left leg was shackled to the wall. Nevertheless, she struggled against the bonds that held her in the chair.

Garrick and Digby had taken her to a remote part of their underground labyrinth. She tried to remember the turns and directions they took, but the tunnels all looked too similar, and after the fifth right or left, she gave up. Lillian wondered if Hayden was somewhere like this. The only other things she spotted in the room were two torches and a small table that held several sets of parchment.

Think, Lillian! Think!

She looked around and shuffled her feet awkwardly to turn her chair, when she felt something digging into her calf.

The knife!

Thankfully, it was in the boot that didn't have a manacle locked around it. Lillian wasn't sure how exactly she'd be able to get it up to her hands, but it was more than she'd had a moment ago.

If I can get my boot up to my hands and reach into the pouch...as long as no one comes in and catches me.

No sooner had she finished her thought, than three people walked in. Garrick, Digby, and Hayden.

"Hayden!" Lillian cried. "Oh, thank the Fae you're all right! Did they hurt you?" Lillian now noticed Hayden wasn't tied up. Or being held by anyone.

Hayden walked over, a cruel and calculating smile spread across her face. "See, I told you she'd come after me. Curious little cat. So good and noble like your mother. Such trusting innocence I knew we could count on."

Shock, anger, and then shame flew over Lillian's face. How could she have been so naïve? That part of her father in her had warned her, *pleaded* with her, and she had ignored it.

"Hayden, I...I don't understand. You've been working for my family for years. What happened?"

"What *happened*, Princess? You just said it. *I've* been working for *your* family."

"But your life was, *is* good."

"You really are sheltered, aren't you? You think I'm the only one who feels this way? You think washing pots and pans all day for *your* family and *your* elaborate parties is 'good' for *me*? Doing menial tasks or following that senile old codger, Sir Alger's, orders? Our people are everywhere. In the castle, the kingdom, the continent. Pretty little princess in her pretty little castle with no worries in her pretty little head."

The comment hurt. That anyone would think of Lillian like that was upsetting. Her eyes stung, but she knew crying was not an option. Not now. So, she grabbed onto the only other emotion at her disposal. Anger.

Lillian lashed out. "I'll have you know, people *know* where I am and they *will* come looking for me."

It was an empty threat, and they knew it, which was disheartening. The trio all shared a chuckle at Lillian's outburst.

"By 'people,' you mean Seth?" Hayden laughed again. "Trust me, Princess, even if he did come looking for you, he has no idea where you are, because you're certainly not at the

Dragon. The entire royal army could come looking for you and they wouldn't find you."

Lillian whispered, "The portal."

Hayden slowly clapped her hands. "Good job, princess. There seems to be some gears turning in that head after all. Yes, the portal. They come in quite handy when you want to travel long distances."

Long distances?

"How far away are we?"

Garrick drawled, "Well, that's really not your concern right now, is it? What *I* would be concerned with—is what comes next."

"Why? Why is there a 'next'? Why are you doing all of this? What did I ever do to you?" Lillian eyes brimmed with unshed tears, her flogged emotions betraying her.

Digby mocked her, "*'Why are you doing all of this?'* Woe is me, I'm the poor princess."

"The reason is simple," Hayden interjected. "Revenge."

"Revenge? For what?" Lillian couldn't fathom what she or her family had done.

Her response angered Garrick, and he spat back, "For what? *For what?* You spoiled little brat! Do you have any idea what your family has done? What the royals are responsible for? They *destroyed* a kingdom. His kingdom— *our* kingdom."

Lillian shook her head in confusion. "Are you talking about Zoldaine? He was a monster! Worse than any troll or dragon. He killed his own citizens for fun. Tortured them."

"Only the ones who disobeyed him. Those who were loyal were rewarded."

"By rewarded, you mean not punished?" Lillian couldn't believe what she was hearing. It was warped logic just as Seth had explained.

"You'll watch your tongue when you speak about the master," Garrick erupted, raising his hand as he advanced on her.

Luckily for Lillian, Hayden intervened. "Careful, Garrick," she warned. "You know Zoldaine wants them unharmed. He wouldn't think twice peeling the skin off your bones if even one hair was out of place."

Garrick backed down, reluctantly.

"You see, Princess," Hayden continued knowingly, "he has big plans for you. For all of you. Olivia and Avery included. But for now, you can just sit and relax while…"

Ka-BOOM!

The ground shook so hard it knocked Lillian over. Dust and rocks rained down. But Lillian realized she wasn't the only one on the ground, as all three of her assailants were attempting to rise as well. She couldn't be sure, but the air felt suddenly warmer as well.

Her suspicions were confirmed when someone threw open the door. "Someone's set off the kegs! The whole place is on fire and caving in! You gotta get out of here!" And the harbinger was off as fast as he had come.

Another deep rumble and the sound of cracking rock confirmed his warning.

Hayden shouted orders. "Digby, come with me. Garrick, get the princess loose and bring her along. If anything happens to her, it'll be worse than death for us. Move!"

Hayden and Digby scrambled out of the room that was rapidly filling with smoke. Garrick ran over to Lillian and righted her. "Now don't make this harder than it needs to be, Princess. I *will* knock you out if you fuss. Plus," he chanced a look at the chaos behind him, "I don't think you want to die in here either."

Lillian coughed as more smoke bellowed into the room. Her eyes watered. Garrick pulled a ring of keys from his pocket.

As he bent down to unlock the manacle, Lillian smelled bacon and an unexpected figure loomed behind Garrick— and promptly hit Garrick over the head.

Pork?

Sixpence to pixies, the portly little fellow had knocked Garrick out cold and was in the process of retrieving the keys. He unlocked the cuff around Lillian's leg and she felt the whoosh of blood rush back into her foot.

"Just sit tight, Princess. I'll have these ropes undone in a minute."

The cave rumbled again.

We might not have a minute.

She wasn't sure why Pork was helping her, but present circumstances as they were, she would risk trusting him. "There's a knife in my right boot."

Thank you, Seth!

She realized there weren't any people running past anymore. "Hurry!"

Pork reached inside her boot, pulled out the knife, and began slicing away at the bonds. Once she was free, he helped her up and grabbed her hand. "Come on. I can get you out."

Lillian was reluctant to trust him as her recent choices hadn't proved worthy, but she was out of options. As they headed out, Lillian went past the table that still held the piles of parchment; her running glance showed one was some sort of sketch of a machine, like something Doc would draw up. Still others looked like maps, and there were places marked with the red skulls, just like the kegs. She wanted to examine them further or go back and grab them, but Pork pulled her out of the room—which caved in a second later. They lurched forward, ducking low and running. As soon as they reached the main cavern, everything intensified. The smoke. The heat. The roar of the flames. People were running in all directions shouting at one another, hurtling by Lillian, without so much as a second glance. Pork held her hand like a vice, not wanting to lose her in the confusion. The maze of tunnels and cavernous rooms seemed endless and impossible to navigate, but he deftly wove through them, pulling her right and left.

As they ran farther, they reached a room where a figure was engaged in actually fighting off some of the Rogues. A cloaked figure with a sword. Lillian couldn't make out the person but recognized the moves.

Alexander!

She yanked her hand from Pork's and stopped. "Alexander!" she yelled but knew he couldn't hear her over the chaos. She ran closer, shouting, "Alexander!" The hooded figure turned for a second but was immediately engaged again.

Pork ran over to her, taking her hand again, pulling her away. "Princess, we have to go. Now!" Pork's words were validated as the roof above them started to collapse. He pulled Lillian out and onto the ground in relative safety, while Lillian could only watch in horror as her line of sight to Alexander was filled with tumbling rocks and choking dust, cutting her off completely from him.

"*No!* Alexander!" Lillian reached out, scrambling up and running toward fallen rocks.

Pork grabbed her. "Princess!" Then he twirled her around to look her in the eyes. "Lillian, we have to go. There's nothing you can do for him. There are plenty of tunnels that way. He still has a chance, but we don't."

His eyes were pleading and fearful. He was not trying to trick her.

"Please, Princess." He held out his hand.

Lillian grasped it and fled with her unexpected hero.

Her lungs burned. Her eyes burned. Her legs burned. But finally, they broke into the fresh night air, which had never tasted sweeter. Her eyes worked to see in the cloudy night as Pork (she really would need to call him something more noble after this) continued to drag her through the darkness until he thought they were out of harm's way, and then they both collapsed. For the next few moments, all the mismatched duo did was catch their breath. Pork flopped on the ground and Lillian found a stump. The smoke was bad enough, and Pork was definitely in no shape to run like he just had; Lillian was afraid his efforts to save his own life might have been in vain as he looked as though he would expire right there. But eventually his rattling wheezes softened to only sucking gulps.

"Are you all right?" he gasped.

"I should be asking you the same thing."

"I'll," he puffed, "I'll be fine. Believe it or not, this body," he said, motioning to his prostrate form, "wasn't built for running."

Lillian couldn't help but laugh.

How is this guy mixed up in all this? He doesn't seem bad.

"I'm glad to see you're okay," he said, more seriously.

"Why?"

"Why, what?" he said, seeming genuinely perplexed.

"Why did you save me? Why are we not with the rest of the Zoldaine supporters? Why do you care what happens to me?" Lillian's questions tumbled out.

He closed his eyes, which were smudged with ash and smoke. "I don't know," he said quietly. "It just...it just doesn't seem right what he, what they're doing. You didn't do anything. You're a nice person. It's not your fault what happened years ago. It wasn't your choice. You shouldn't be punished for it."

"So then, why are you with them? Why are you or *were* you helping them?" Lillian asked, trying to understand.

"I dunno. I guess it was what I was born into. It was my life. They were my family. And maybe it sounds like a child's excuse, but I didn't know any better." Pork scrunched his eyes tighter, as though ashamed at what he was saying.

Seth's words echoed in Lillian's head. *"If all you ever know is porridge..."*

"I just," he looked up at her with tears in his eyes, "I just didn't want that life anymore. I won't sit here and lie to you, Princess. Tell you that I never did anything wrong. There's plenty of things I'm ashamed to have done. Things that will haunt me for the rest of my life." His voice grew sadder and heavier.

Lillian wasn't sure what to do. This man, whom she barely knew, was part of a huge plot to kidnap her and the other princesses under direction from one of the worst people history had ever known. And now, here he was, pouring his heart out to her.

"Look, you don't need to hear all this." He wiped his eyes, leaving streaks as the soot came away with his tears. "I should go. Once everything settles down, they'll be looking for me. You should go too, before things 'settle down.' You can take my horse. He's tied to a tree over in that direction."

"Oh, I can't take your horse. I can just walk back to the castle, I'm sure."

"You might want to rethink that." Pork jerked his head in a direction.

Lillian followed his gaze. Off in the distance was her home, glowing softly on the horizon. There was also another glow off to the left that Lillian couldn't place. "How far away *are* we?"

"I'd say about two leagues. Will you be wanting that horse, now?"

"Yes," Lillian said, "I suppose I will."

"His name is Moose. He likes it when you scratch his ears."

Lillian teared up at this for some unknown reason. Perhaps the affectionate way he spoke those simple words, or perhaps she sensed Moose might be his only true friend. She'd have to make sure she returned Moose to him, no matter what happened.

"I don't know how to thank you. I don't even know your name," she sniffed.

"Most of them called me Piggy, but I never really liked that." And for the first time, Lillian saw her unlikely hero stand up straight. "My name is Preston. Preston Miller."

Lillian walked over and stuck out her hand. "It's nice to meet you, Preston Miller. The kingdom of Valanti is in your debt."

He shook her hand.

"And you will forever have the favor of its princess," she said sincerely, leaning over to kiss him on the cheek.

"Thank you, Your Highness. Now, you must go. Before they realize you're missing as well."

But before she could say anything in return, Preston strode off in the direction from which they came. Lillian slogged toward where Preston said Moose was tied. Her legs were like lead weights. The surge of energy from her capture and harrowing escape had left her, and she was drained. She was extremely grateful for any conveyance that meant she didn't have to move.

She found Moose easily enough and quickly realized why his name was Moose. Preston's horse was easily twenty-hands high and as thick as an ox. Lillian wondered how the stout man could even get up on him.

"Hey there, boy," Lillian slowly reached up, way up, to scratch his ears. Moose snorted and pulled away, straining against the rope for a moment, but then he caught a whiff of her and along with her, he smelled his friend and master.

Moose stopped moving and allowed her to reach behind his ears. "Yeah. That's a good fella. He said you'd like that." When she stopped, Moose turned his head back and pulled with his teeth at a leather strap on the saddle. Another folded leather stirrup fell from the first.

So that's *how he gets up. Smart fella. Smart horse.*

She patted Moose again and ran her hand over his cheek. Lillian unhitched the huge horse and carefully climbed up. From so high up, she could get a better layout of where she was. Lillian still couldn't believe it. Apparently, those portals knew no limit.

If someone thought it out, an entire army could pop up from all over the kingdom with virtually no detection, smuggle in anything they wanted. Lillian shuddered.

"Well, boy, I guess we better get going." And with the tiniest of nudges, Moose trotted off, leaving Lillian to ponder everything that had just happened and attempt to wipe the soot off her face. She hoped against hope that no one had noticed her absence back at the castle and prayed to the Fae that Alexander had made it out.

CHAPTER 30: Growing Up
July 12

No one was more thankful than Lillian that it was still dark outside when she arrived at the castle. She dismounted from Moose and came in from the west side, where Seth would leave the signal to come in or not. Sure enough, there was a small blue cloth waving in the breeze off the backside of the stables.

All clear.

As Lillian got closer, Seth actually ran out to meet her partway. "Seth, what are you doing? What if someone sees you?" Lillian hurried her pace to get under cover.

"There's no one to see us, trust me." Seth looked relieved to see her, and then he saw Moose. "Whoa, where did you...you know what? Never mind." Seth reached out and gave her a huge hug. "Thank Fae you're okay. I was going spiral, praying you weren't in there when it happened."

"When what happened? Seth, what has gotten into you?"

"Come on, I'll explain inside," he said, grabbing the reigns to Moose, "and I'll get this big fella something to eat."

Inside the stables, Seth was like a wind spinner, questions and statements whirling. "I can't believe you're all right! Thank the Fae! If anything had happened to you, I don't even want to think of what he would have done to me.

How did you possibly escape? Who was it that was sending the letters? Did you find out anything?"

"Geez, Seth, take a breath already. What are you talking about? What happened? Who would do what to you?"

Seth did take a breath and gathered his thoughts. "There was an explosion of some sort in The Trenches tonight, about three hours after you left. Specifically, at the Dragon's Wrath. The entire guard has been dispatched. It was all I could do not to tell anyone you had gone there. I just prayed to Fae you weren't anywhere near it when it happened."

He must be talking about the explosion in the caves, but how in the Fae did...the portal.

Whether by accident or on purpose, Lillian suspected accident the way the Rogues were caught off guard. The kegs by the portal must have exploded, sending part of the blast back to the Dragon.

Maybe that was Alexander? Oh, Fae, let him be okay...

"Lillian, you weren't there, were you?" Seth then began to register the sooty remains that clung to her. "Oh, Fae! But you weren't hurt, right?"

"No, Seth, I'm fine. A little shaken up and really exhausted. Look, I better get to my room before anyone *does* come check on me. I'll come down tomorrow and tell you everything, okay? Promise. You'll take good care of Moose?"

Seth glanced over at the behemoth that barely cleared the stall's ceiling. "Yeah, sure." He grabbed an apple and walked over to Moose. "We'll be fine. Right, buddy?" Seth lifted the apple and Moose promptly ate it with one bite. "Guess that's a 'yes.'" You're right. Go get some rest. We'll talk tomorrow."

Lillian started to walk away and then remembered, pulling the knife from her boot. "Here's this back. You're right, it did come in handy."

"Then keep it. You never know when you might need it again. Sleep well."

Lillian headed upstairs. Seth hadn't been kidding. There wasn't a soul to be seen or heard. She went to Andrew's room first to let him know she was back. He was sound asleep in his bed. "Andrew. Hey, buddy." She gently shook him.

Andrew rolled over and blinked sleepily. "Mmm, hey, Lil', you're back. Everything okay?"

"Yes, little brother, everything's fine. Anyone ask about me?"

"Um, Mom had me check in on you a little bit after everyone left. I told her you were sleeping."

"Perfect. Thanks, Andrew, I owe you one." She leaned over and kissed his forehead. "Possibly two."

"Just play hide 'n' seek."

She smiled. "I can do that. Now go back to sleep."

Lillian padded a few rooms down to hers and slipped in. She was alone. She checked herself in the vanity. The Hair Hue was wearing off as streaks of brunette were taking over the ebony strands. But her face—her face was filthy with dirt and soot except for streaks where sweat had run down it. You could barely tell she'd tried to wipe it off; she was surprised Seth had even recognized her.

She went and took her body double out of the bed. She could dispose of everything in her fireplace tomorrow morning. Right now, she just wanted to get clean and sleep.

"No hot bath tonight," she said longingly to her body double.

The tepid water still was marvelous. To be clean, after so much grit and grime, was exquisite.

Lillian crawled into bed. As she settled in, she let the events of the night replay through her head.

She had been taken hostage just as before, but this time she wasn't upset. She was angry. Angry at herself for being fooled so easily. But even angrier that she was viewed as some pawn in an insane man's machinations. Hayden's voice rang through Lillian's ears. *"Pretty little princess in her pretty little castle..."* Tonight had opened Lillian's eyes. There were forces at work she may not fully understand yet, but she understood enough to know this was bigger than just her. She would have to tell her father everything she had learned, even if it meant being grounded for life. And she would insist he tell her everything as well. She would have to train even harder with...

ALEXANDER!

She had been so worried, praying for him to have survived unscathed, or just survived—she had forgotten he actually might have! She bolted out of bed and rushed to the window.

It was there.

His *A*.

But her heart shuddered. Because the real question was, did he write it before, or after, she saw him tonight. *Oh, dear Fae, please let him be okay.*

Lillian desperately wanted to go look for him but knew sneaking out a second time tonight wasn't an option. She would have to wait until morning to discuss things with her father and pray he would relinquish her confinement.

Exhausted, she fell back into the bed, the image of him fighting just as the roof collapsed passed through her head a hundred times before the heavy wave of sleep finally washed over her.

Lillian awoke to someone shouting down the hallway outside her door. She sat up groggily. The light gave her room a soft glow indicating the hour was still early. She shambled to her door to discover the reason for such ruckus. She didn't find it, but she did find a plate of breakfast outside her door. She brought it in, set it down on her bed, and started her morning fire herself, eager to dispose of her silent witness. Once the fire was feeding off last night's evidence, she devoured her breakfast. Not only had last night's events left her famished, but she was anxious to talk to her father as soon as possible and then (hopefully) find Alexander.

She could still hear a lot of commotion coming from downstairs but nothing discernable.

Must have been quite a party.

Lillian tossed the last bit of bacon in her mouth and got dressed hastily. While she did, she ran through various ways to tell her dad what she had learned.

"So, you know that fire last night in The Trenches? Dad, I know you're going to be mad at me, but it's important… Dad, you know I love you, right?

None of them sounded right. She'd just have to play off whatever mood he was in.

She found him in his council chambers talking to Sir Alger and Henry. The king looked exhausted. "Morning, Dad."

"Ah, sweetie, good morning," he said, brightening at the sight of her. "I hope you're feeling better. I was just finishing up with these gentlemen."

"Good morning, Your Highness." Sir Alger gave a slight bow.

Henry did the same. "Princess."

"Good morning, Braelyn. Henry," Lillian returned with a curtsy.

Sir Alger turned back to the king. "We should be going. If any new developments occur, I'll let you know immediately, Your Majesty."

They started to walk off when Lillian stopped them. "Wait, what I have to say, you'll want to hear." This statement not only caught their attention, but the king's as well. Lillian took a deep breath.

"Before I begin," she said, addressing her dad, "you have to promise not to interrupt me until I'm done. You're going to have a lot of questions, I'm sure, the least of which will be wondering how I came across this information. But you will have to trust me. Right, Dad? You said you would."

The king looked reluctant. "I'm not sure I like where this is going, Lillian, but yes, I said I would trust you, so I will."

"Well then, the first thing is, I don't think last night was an attack. At least not one they planned."

Sir Alger beat the king to interrupting. No one had mentioned last night, let alone an attack. "How do you...how could you possibly know that? And what do you mean by 'they'?" Sir Alger stammered.

Lillian just looked at him.

"I'm, I'm sorry, Your Highness, continue."

"I understand. As I said, you're just going to have to trust me."

Lillian proceeded to share with them all the information she could, without directly incriminating herself for sneaking out. The notes, the portals, the Dainian Rogues, the marked kegs, Zands' different appearances and misdirection, Hayden's treachery, and even her own suspicions about Sir Laurel. The three men sat silent in confusion and in awe of the delicate princess they had known all their lives, who had suddenly just become their top informant.

When she was finished, the king didn't ask any questions. He simply turned to Sir Alger.

"You heard my daughter. Be careful who you share this information with, Braelyn. Have the men look for those characters in addition to Zands but don't say why. Also, tell Doc I would like to speak with him. We need to discuss these tunnels and what he knows about these explosives. Henry, send for Switwick and Nyssa." The king stood. "Discretion is key, my friends. It appears the walls truly do have ears and until we know whose—nothing is discussed outside this room."

"Understood, Sire."

The men bowed and left Lillian alone with her father.

Lillian stood there, waiting for her father to bombard her with questions. But he just went to the window and looked out. Lillian walked over to join him. "So?"

His gaze didn't waver. "So, what?"

"Aren't you going to ask me? Aren't you curious as to how I got all that information?"

His tired eyes looked into his daughter's. "I *am* very curious. Especially since your information correlates with some we already had. But—you asked me to trust you. So I am."

Lillian returned his gaze in disbelief. "And, and that's it. That's all I had to do, was ask you to trust me?"

The king laughed. "Of course not, sweetie. You had to earn that trust, which I'll admit you haven't been doing a great job of lately, but I believe what you said today. And you have earned that trust over the years. I can see something's changed in you. Something happened to you last night and when you're ready to tell me, I'll be here. But I'm leaving the time up to you." He motioned to the soft leather chairs by the fireplace in his study. "Come sit over here with me for a moment."

The two walked over and sat down by the hearth. This room didn't require a fire this time of year with the warm morning sun coming in.

"Lillian, I'm going to let you in on a secret. One day, you'll share this secret with your own children. It's a day you'll always know is coming, but won't be sure when. And it's a day every parent dreads. For me and your mom, that day is today. I knew it the moment you walked in this morning. I hoped I was wrong, but when you started talking about everything that's been going on, well..."

Lillian's heart lurched in a building panic.

"Dad, you're scaring me. What is it?"

"I'm sorry. I'm probably making it out to be more than it is, but like I said, you'll understand one day." He shook his head, and while Lillian still didn't quite relax, she let loose the breath she hadn't realized she'd been holding.

"The secret is, you're grown up," he stated simply. "And I realize we celebrated your coming-of-age birthday a couple of months ago, but *today* is when you became an adult. Today is when your mother and I have to look at you no longer as our little girl but as a young adult." His final words ended on a grimace. "Oh, your mother, she's not going to take this well...ah, but you let me worry about that."

"Dad, I'm sorry, but I don't understand."

"I know, it's hard to explain. Let me try a different approach. All your life, your mother and I have tried to instill in you the qualities and characteristics of not only a good princess but also a good *person*. Most parents try to teach their children right from wrong by making choices for them. Don't touch that, don't put that in your mouth, get down from there, no, you can't have cookies for breakfast, you need your rest, say thank you, and so forth. You get the idea. We do this all your life until the day when we finally must let go and believe we have done our job. To trust you to make your own decisions. For you, that day is today."

Lillian sat in silence for a minute. "Thank you, I guess?"

The king chuckled. "You're welcome, *I guess*. But just so I'm clear—we do and will trust you, but we will never stop giving you advice or worrying about you. Especially your mother. And regarding this information you've told us today, you can tell whomever you like, but my advice as a father and as the king is that you don't tell anyone. I think whatever happened to you last night opened your eyes a little bit. Maybe for the better, maybe not. I just hope it hasn't affected you too badly. I meant it when I said you can talk to me about it, on your timeline, of course."

"So, what do I do about Mom, then?"

"Don't worry. She's going to be clingy like a goblin to gold, but I'll help with that. I'll have her talk to your aunt. She's already gone through it with Marcus. Be glad he already dug the trenches for the rest of you. Being the oldest out of all the children is the worst. Ella all but shackled him in his bedroom before he and Jaccob went off."

They both laughed.

Lillian was hesitant but decided to test her new grown-up waters, "So, while we're in this new stage of our relationship, my archery friend is back and I was wondering if…"

The king sat back and let out a dramatic sigh.

"What? Dad, you can't keep me locked in the castle forever." She grabbed his hand. "He means a lot to me."

"I wasn't going to keep you locked up forever, just until you were thirty."

"Dad!"

"I'm kidding. Look, I've been thinking about this, quite a bit actually. Your mom and I have had a few discussions as well. Here's what we have decided. You may continue to see this young man…" Lillian squeezed his hand in excitement. "However, you must have an escort and—"

"—an escort? Dad, you don't understand, he—"

The king continued. "*An escort*, and he has to meet your mother and I. Over dinner or lunch, nothing formal, just so we can get to know him."

Lillian started to get upset, doors of possibilities slamming closed again. "Dad, he can't. You don't understand. You said you trusted me."

"I do trust you, Lillian. I *don't* trust him. Not yet. I'm sorry, but those are our stipulations. And the guards won't be so close, just within eyesight. Plus, if this young man plans to court you like a proper gentleman, you should have chaperones and meet the parents. It's still my job to protect you. You may be a young adult now, but you will always be my daughter. I know it's hard, but one day you'll…"

"I know, I know. I'll understand," Lillian groaned. She wondered what Alexander would say.

What if he says no? Then what?

She couldn't think about that now. "I'll have to talk to him. So, if I go out today?"

"I have two men I can pull whenever you need them."

Lillian was worried about what Alexander would do. *"You can't tell anyone about me, okay? Not your parents. Not your friends. No one. That's the trade-off. Your life for my secret one."* The thing was that there were a lot of people who *did* know about him. Not specifically, but enough. And their relationship had evolved since then to say the least. If it was going to progress, he couldn't live in the forest forever. "Okay, Dad. I'll see what he says. I just don't think he's been around people that much, so if he does agree to meet with you, you can't play the overprotective father role like you've done in the past."

"I'm not sure if I know what you're referring to," he said with a sly grin.

"I'm serious, Dad, this one's different. I don't want you to scare him off."

The king held up his right hand. "I promise to be on my best behavior."

"Thank you."

"Now, your mom, on the other hand…"

They both laughed.

She asked, "Do you remember when she tried to fix the meal when Richard came over for the first time?"

"Yes. Thank goodness Pierre found her cooking and as the dinner progressed, he 'happened to have some leftovers.' See, it's not always *me* who scares them off."

Lillian was aching to make sure Alexander was okay, but a familiar feeling assured her he was fine. She could tell her father needed her right now. And if she was honest with herself, she needed him too. For a little longer, they reminisced on the numerous occasions the queen had mommoments in front of Lillian's prior suitors. But more importantly, for the first time in a long time, they forgot their troubles. And instead of king and princess, they were simply father and daughter.

CHAPTER 31: A New Suitor

Sneaking a quick glance behind her reminded Lillian she was not alone on her trip to see Alexander. Two of the King's Guard followed about a hundred paces behind her. She had asked them to stay back farther because she wanted to talk to Alexander before he saw them, but their only response was "Sorry, Your Highness, but your father gave strict orders to keep you in line of sight at a close distance in case something should happen." If she walked faster, they walked faster. She finally gave up and just hoped she could explain it to Alexander fast enough before he saw them. If she saw him…

The image of the cavern collapsing kept trying to resurface, but she wouldn't let it.

He has to be here, I know it.

She did more than just believe it. She felt it, yet the tightness in her chest didn't fully release until she finally saw his outline in the distance.

Thank the Fae.

He was performing a sequence again, like he had with his sword, only this time he was using his bow. It was mesmerizing. He was all leonine grace and control. She almost paused, wanting to see the full routine, to watch from afar, but then remembered her not-so-far-behind escorts. She could hardly believe he was really there, it had been so long since she had seen him last. Her heart hammered in her chest.

And she couldn't help it, she had that nagging little insecurity of wondering if he was as excited to see her as she was to see him.

Alexander finished a final move, looked up, smiled and waved, then walked her way.

She took that moment to memorize every feature. The broad shoulders and the restrained power in his honed form. A balance of strength and agility hewn in the outdoors. His bronzed skin, deeper, since summer had begun, which only further set off the startling combination of gray eyes. Even from here, they were piercing.

She wanted to remember him, in case…

He strode up to her and smiled.

Wow. This is just ridiculous.

"Hey stranger. I wasn't sure you'd make it. I take it you're not grounded anymore?"

"Not exactly." She almost turned around to the escorts but didn't want to tip Alexander off before she had a chance to explain. She talked quickly. "Look, Alexander, I don't know to say this. I'm really sorry, I promise I tried, but it was the only way they'd let me see you, and if you don't want…" Her eyes stung and her heart clenched, preparing for the worst.

"Lillian. Lillian, slow down. It's okay." He reached out and grabbed her hand. "It's okay. I know."

She looked at him, tears threatening to spill over. "You know?"

"Yeah. The two men behind you? I saw them a while ago. It's okay."

"But I thought you'd be mad. You said not to tell anyone, and I promise I didn't, Alexander. Well, just my brother and Jafria, who sort of guessed, but not my dad or anyone else, I *swear*."

He took her other hand, holding them both between his. "Lillian, I believe you."

"And I just...I was so worried after..." She had to pause to fight back the strangling sob that was trying to escape. Curse her emotions for betraying her!

"Come on. I know what will help. Let's have something to eat. We'll get some fresh thackleberry bread and Frivoly cheese in you. That'll make you feel better."

"I don't suppose you have some of your mother's chocolate?" Lillian sniffled a tiny bit.

"As a matter of fact, I do. Only the best for my girl. Right this way."

My girl.

She warmed at those words. Just as before, a smile crept up her face.

He led her over to their usual picnic area where Winston was waiting eagerly for his greeting as well.

The escorts were noticeable, but true to their word, kept their distance, which Lillian was grateful for. She wanted to at least be able to talk to Alexander like they were alone.

The food was wonderful. He didn't disappoint. And he was right, it was starting to make her feel better. But mostly it was him that was making her feel truly comfortable like only he could. His necklace glimmered in the sunlight. And she didn't feel a breath of evil.

This can't be one of those gems.

Alexander didn't seem angry, let alone evil.

"I just don't understand," she asked between bites, "why *aren't* you upset or anything?"

"Lillian, if there's one thing I've come to learn about you is that you are kind-hearted. Tough, but I know you'd never do anything to hurt someone else on purpose. I'm sure there's a story to tell, but...well, if this was the only way for me to see you, I wouldn't mind if the whole kingdom had to see me. It would be worth it." His voice was raw with emotion.

Lillian blushed from head to toe.

"Plus, I can't hide forever, right? Being a ghost is lonely." He winked at her.

Then he hopped up. "Wait here, I got something for you." He walked over to Winston, grabbed a bundle out of his bag, and brought it back to her. It was a slender but long package.

"What is it?"

"It's a gift, silly. You have to open it."

Lillian slowly untied the string wrapped around it and lifted the paper. Inside were six new Calderan steel arrows.

"Your very own set." He smiled.

She touched them as if they were made of glass. "Oh, Alexander, they're beautiful. When did you find time to make them?"

"Well, I have been gone for a month, you know. Here, look," he said, pulling one of the arrows out, "this one here. Notice anything different?"

Now that Lillian was really looking, she could see the tip wasn't the same as the others. "Is this the arrow you saved me with? The one that anchors?"

"Well, no, not *the* arrow, but one just like it. Do you remember how it works?"

"I think so." She pressed the end of the shaft where the notch was and felt the familiar click. Spikes popped out of the arrowhead. Then she twisted the notch, allowing it to pop back out and the spikes retracted. "Alexander, I really don't know what to say."

"Well, a generally accepted response is 'thank you'."

"Thank you," she smiled and wrapped her arms around him in a big hug.

His taut form and familiar sun-warmed smell were comforting.

"Wow. And a hug. I'll have to get you presents more often."

"I wouldn't object to that."

"Well, I currently don't have any at the moment, but would you settle for an archery partner instead?"

"I guess that'll do." She winked at him.

"Then, let's go see how those new arrows fare."

As they walked, Lillian couldn't help but wonder when he was going to bring up the night before.

Maybe he doesn't want me to know he was there. Maybe he doesn't want me to know that he saved me again. Well, kind of saved me. Don't forget Preston.

Lillian hoped *he* was okay. They went across the creek like before and into the grass. A month before, it had reached Lillian's knees; now it was up to her waist. But it still didn't cover up the distant red targets.

Alexander stopped and set his gear down. "All right, now I know you haven't had time to come out here and practice, being *grounded* and all," he said as she gave him a dirty look, "but I think that's for the better, since it will show your true progress. I mean, that is, *if* you practiced?" he teased.

She hit him in the arm. "Of course I practiced."

"Ow, well, you've definitely gotten stronger." He rubbed his bicep. "You know, in an odd way I've missed that." He gestured for her to step up. "Okay, let's see what you got."

She knew she could hit these targets, at least the first one. She still couldn't help but feel nervous, though.

Just breathe, you can do this.

She pulled out one of her new arrows. They felt just like the ones he had left her.

Such precise craftsmanship. I'll have to introduce him to Doc when I get the chance.

She nocked the arrow and pulled back. She noticed the breeze coming in from the coast and adjusted her aim. She took a breath, held it for a second, slowly let out—and released. Lillian watched the arrow slice through the air for what seemed like forever.

Thonk. Nailed it.

Yes!

She moved to the next target with the mountains in the background. The first arrow missed. She pulled out another one. This time she hit the target. The last target proved more elusive. She came close both times, although how close she didn't realize until they were retrieving her arrows.

"Looks like you weren't as far off as you thought." Alexander pointed out the top parts of the target where it had been chipped. "Those weren't there before. You *have* been practicing. I'm impressed."

"I told you." She allowed herself a smile. Even she was impressed. "So, are we going to the grove now?" She was eager to show off her new skills.

He chuckled. "Not yet. I figured we might do that later tonight, if you're allowed to come back. I want to see how you do in the dark. See how your gleaming is coming along."

"About that...can it happen without you really thinking about it?"

"How do you mean?"

She told him about her match with Sir Alger.

"That's amazing!" He was astonished.

"So, that was normal?" She was still a little unsure.

Alexander was excited. "Well, I mean, yeah. It happened without you thinking about it. Obviously you can *will* it to happen, but when you gleam without trying to, just because you need it, that's a whole other level. And you bested Sir Alger, that's just...wow!" Alexander was pacing, running a hand through his hair. "My dad said he was the only other person in the kingdom, possibly the whole continent who could push him to be better, and you *beat* him. I know it probably doesn't mean much, but I'm proud of you. Not like a teacher-student type of thing, but as a," he hesitated, "well, a friend."

She couldn't help herself. "Just a *friend*?"

She wouldn't have believed it possible, but Alexander's burnished skin reddened in a fierce blush. "Well, I mean, yeah, for sure, a friend. But, you know, um, the night before you were grounded, I thought we...I thought there was something else."

Lillian laughed. Finally, he was the one who uncomfortable. "It's okay, Alexander. Of course there was something. Why do you think my parents want to meet you?"

Now, the blood left his face. "Wait. Your parents want to meet me?"

"Did I not mention that earlier? I'm sorry. Yeah, that's one of the stipulations of me being able to keep seeing you. They want to have you for dinner or lunch or something. Nothing formal, but they just want to meet you if we're going to be seeing each other is all."

His typical calm and charm had left him. He was visibly flustered. "Meeting your parents? I don't know, Lillian," he said, raking his hands through his hair again. "My parents . . . I, I'd have to talk to them first for sure. And even then, I'm not sure I'm ready to..."

"Alexander, calm down. I didn't mean to upset you. Honestly, we can take this as slow as you want. It's just with everything going on, they want to know I'm safe. You understand, right?"

Alexander took a deep breath and replied, "I do. I'm sorry, it's just a lot all at once."

It was her turn to take his hand. "I know, and I'm sorry this is all being piled on you. I can't imagine what you must be going through. I'm sorry I'm not some normal girl with normal parents with normal expectations."

"Don't say that." He grabbed her shoulders, gray eyes piercing hers. "I'm not sorry, and you shouldn't be either. This is my thing. I imagine any set of parents would want to meet their daughter's suitor."

She snaked her arms around his waist. "So, you're my suitor now, huh?"

"That is what they call it, right?" he said as his hands slid from her shoulders to behind her back.

"Yes, that's what they call it. It's just nice to know where we stand officially." She beamed.

"Well, I'll still have to talk to my mom first. You understand, of course?"

"Of course. When do you think you could get back?" she asked, not wanting to think about him leaving again.

"I could head out tomorrow, I guess. Be back in a little over a week, just long enough to make sure things are in order. But I still want to practice tonight."

"I should be able to do that—but I don't think I can stay the night this time." She blushed a little.

"Yeah, I kind of figured. Especially now that we're 'official'." Oh, and he was blushing too.

He's cute when he's a bit bashful.

"All right then, I'll tell my parents next Friday?"

"We're really going to do this, huh?" He sounded both hopeful and nervous.

"Oh, come on, it won't be that bad. Besides you're already in my dad's good graces. He knows about how you saved me—both times—and he *loves* your bread."

"Loves my bread? How's that?"

"I figured out your secret recipe, that's how. I can't believe I didn't figure it out earlier, what with the 'ghost' being in Tapera and all. I *knew* I knew that smell from somewhere. Dewdrop Daisy. I have to say even our chef was impressed with the pairing."

Alexander looked confused. "I'll give you the daisy, but what's this about the ghost being in Tapera?"

"Oh, it was a while ago. My dad read about it in the paper. People saw a ghost around Tocarin Lake. I didn't get it until I met Winston. They must have seen you riding him across the lake. 'Floating' over the lake."

"Hmmm." Alexander had a troubled look on his face. "That's interesting."

"What is?"

"It's probably nothing. Don't worry about it. You ready for lunch?"

Lillian hadn't realized how hungry she was. She felt like she had just gotten there, but the sun was definitely higher. "Yeah, actually."

"Good, cause you get to catch it."

CHAPTER 32: Two's Company, Four's a Crowd

ating a roasted fish lunch was thanks to Lillian this time. Shooting fish was a little different than shooting apples, but the practice had helped. She hit three nice-sized trout, and Alexander was no slouch in cooking them up either. He carried many more spices and powders than just dried-up daisies in his pouch.

"Don't tell me you know potions, too?" She had seen a variety of those sorts only in Grayson's alchemy room.

"You never know what you might need out here. Especially on your own. Your stomach doesn't seem to be complaining much." He pointed to her almost-empty dish.

"I'll have to admit, you really are a tailor of all stitches." Lillian scooped up her last bit of fish. "I should get going. I'm sure the escorts need to get back and eat something too." She stood up and grabbed her bow and new set of arrows. "I'll be back tonight, though, to impress you some more."

"Looking forward to it." Alexander started to clean up. "So, how much are you going to tell your parents about me?"

"I don't know. How much do you want me to tell them?"

"Well, it seems they should probably know my name. Sir Alger already knows my dad, so that'd be okay too, I suppose."

"What about your age? You seem to be a little older than me, but I actually don't know."

"You're going to laugh, but to be honest, I actually don't know either."

"You don't know?" Lillian gave him a look. "What do you mean you don't know? How can you not know?"

"My parents never really told me."

"Yeah, but you had, like, birthdays and stuff, right?"

"I mean, it was always just me and them, so no, not really."

"Do you even know when your birthday *is*?"

"No. Remember they *found* me."

"That's so sad. No cake, no presents? That's settled, then. I'm going to bring you a present. Your first birthday present."

"Lillian, you really don't have to…"

"Ah, ah. No arguing. It's done. I'll just tell them you're twenty. My mom is always saying older men are more mature anyway." She looked back at the escorts. "Okay, I really need to go now. They've got to be hot in those outfits. I don't even know if they brought any water." She went over and wrapped her arms around Alexander. "I'll see you tonight," she said, inflecting just a little sultriness into it. She couldn't help it.

He blinked at her a couple of times.

Then she let go, smiled, and walked away.

Yes!

Once back at the castle, Lillian cleaned up and went to find her parents. They were in the study discussing the possibility of having the Dawning Festival that was supposed to be coming up in a few weeks.

"I'm not saying it has to be as big as before," the queen was trying to make a point, "but we could hold something *in* the castle. Surely we could monitor that."

"For the entire kingdom? Sweetie, even if we opened up the courtyard and every single room, there wouldn't be enough space. Besides after what Lillian told me this morning, I'm not sure the castle *is* safe. I talked to Switwick and Nyssa this morning about putting a protection spell around the grounds. They said it's possible, but without more spell casters it wouldn't hold for long. Any spare ones are currently working on the spell in Tapera. The only thing they can do is run a spell individually on every single person, which will take a while. I had them start with the guard so Lillian could have her escorts this morning."

Lillian poked her head in. "Knock, knock."
Snow White vaulted up to hug her daughter. "Oh! There's my baby girl. How are you?"

Lillian looked over her mom's shoulder to eyeball her dad. "You told her didn't you? The whole growing up thing?"

Her dad simply replied with a sheepish grin.

"I'm fine, Mom."

"I know, I know. I just thought I had a couple more years of…well."

"It's not like I'm not your daughter anymore or something."

The king finally decided to rescue his daughter. "How was your archery friend?"

Lillian walked over to sit down. "He's fine, and his name is Alexander, by the way."

"Oh, Alexander. I like that name." Her mom smiled and sat back down.

The king was focused on more important information. "I assume he agreed to the terms?"

"If by *terms,* you mean to meet you and Mom, yes. He said okay. He wasn't as upset as I thought. He's going to leave tomorrow morning. He needs to talk with his mom about some things, but he should be back by Friday."

"I'm so excited to meet this young man." Snow White could barely sit still. "I'll tell Pierre immediately to make something special."

"Mom, promise me you're not going to go overboard. He's nervous enough as it is. He hasn't had that much interaction with people, let alone protective parents."

"I just want to make him feel special. You know me, sweetie."

"Yes, I do. Dad?"

"I promise I will keep an eye on your mom," the king teased, feigning a stern glare at his wife.

"Oh, you two stop it." The queen glowered back. "So, what else can you tell us about this mystery suitor?"

Lillian told them what little she had. Where he lives, his age, who his parents were.

"Well, that explains your increase in skill recently and how you beat Sir Alger," her father stated. "If Berchum was Alexander's father, that would make sense. That man could shave the hairs off a troll's chin from three hundred paces. It's good to know his talent was passed on before he died. If I remember right, his son won the juvenile division for the ten-to eleven-year-olds. Probably could have beaten most adults to be honest."

Lillian looked confused. "Sir Alger said the same thing, but Alexander's never mentioned a brother. Are you sure he wasn't older?"

"Pretty sure, sweetie," the king said, thinking back.

Lillian couldn't understand why Alexander never mentioned having a younger brother, but then again, she had never asked him about siblings. She'd have to ask him tonight. "Anyway, he'd like me to come back tonight. He wants to see how my other ability is coming along. The gleaming."

"It's fine as long as you take escorts again," the king reaffirmed.

"But, Dad, he's coming to dinner. You know who his parents are. He comes from a good family."

"And that's all fine, Lillian, but the point is, pending his marriage to you, it's still *my* job to protect you. And even then, it will be my job. I trust you. I even trust him now, for the most part. However, Zands is still out there and until he and his little fire he has set is extinguished, everyone is under guard."

"Your father's right, dear. Even *he* will have escorts anywhere outside of the castle. Isn't that right, darling?"

"Not that I will be leaving the castle much, but yes, even I will have guards. As many as can be spared once they've been through the screening process Switwick and Nyssa are preparing. The two you had this morning were the first. You'll have two more when you go out tonight."

"Four escorts? Dad, honestly, don't you think…"

The king interjected, "You're spinning with no yarn here, Lillian."

"All right, all right." She stood up. "I'm going to go take care of some things before tonight. I'm probably just going to grab something to eat on my own later and then head out around dusk."

"With the escorts," her dad reminded.

"Yes, Dad, with the escorts," she replied, exasperated.

The afternoon went by at a snail's pace. Lillian thought of everything she could to do to keep herself occupied from her excitement of seeing Alexander again tonight. She went by to talk to Seth but couldn't find him. But Moose was there so she fed him an apple and talked to him some. She bumped into Andrew in the training yard practicing his sword lessons. She helped him for a bit until he had to go to his tutoring. She entertained the idea of listening to Sir Laurel babble on about his exploits when she saw him meandering the hallways, then realized she wasn't that desperate.

She dabbled around in the kitchen, perused some books in the library, helped Ophelia with some stitches, and even tried to take a nap. It was the slowest day in Lillian's life.

Finally, the sun began to kiss the horizon. She grabbed some provisions, her bow and new set of arrows, and swung by to pick up her escorts. There were four new soldiers waiting for her, and she saw several others still going through the faeries' protective spell. Once she and her quartet were all headed out, the sky had turned a brilliant orange trimmed with a deep violet that followed it down. There weren't any clouds to block the sprinkling of stars that slowly emerged overhead. It would be a beautiful night for shooting.

Alexander walked up to meet her, tall and gallant. "I must say, you look just as beautiful by moonlight."

A little shot of pleasure went through her. *My, he can be charismatic.*

He offered his hand and glanced behind her. "Can't say as much for your bodyguards though. Four this time? I take it the talk didn't go as well as you'd hoped."

Lillian accepted Alexander's strong hand. "No, it's not that. Dad's having the whole regiment go through a sort of truth spell. They don't bother you, do they?"

"No, it's all right. Like I said before, I can't stay invisible forever."

They strolled to a fire he'd built, and some familiar treats sat on the log nearby.

"Are those what I think they are?" Lillian's eyes got excited.

"Well, I gathered you seem to like them, after you inhaled so many last time. Though I thought you might be part troll after that…" He braced himself for the impending arm hit that quickly followed his remark.

"Are you saying I'm fat?"

Alexander laughed, which was the wrong response, and got another hit. "Ow, of course not. You just have a healthy appetite is all." This time he managed to dodge her swing, causing Lillian to lose her balance and almost fall, but he grabbed her arm and pulled her to him. "Careful now. I caught you."

His magnetic eyes pulled her in. "Yes, you have," she breathed.

Alexander began to lean down when approaching footsteps interrupted them.

"My apologies, Your Highness. But we'll have to stay a bit closer, being dark and all."

Alexander righted Lillian to stand on her own. The moment was gone.

"Of course you do," Lillian said tersely. "Thank you, Harris."

Alexander busied himself by rubbing his palm against the back of his neck, looking anywhere else.

The guards retreated, and Lillian and Alexander walked up to the log and sat down. Alexander handed one of the sweet, gooey treats to Lillian.

"You'll have to show these to Pierre," she managed to say between sticky bites, "he would go over the wall."

"Sounds like I can win everyone over with food," Alexander joked.

"Why do you think you're my friend?" she teased back.

"Ah, that hurts. And here I thought it was for my amazing diving skills."

"Sorry, I'm just here for the food. Learning archery is a close second. And then I guess, you're okay company."

Even his pout is adorable.

He stood and went to retrieve the final treat that was basking in the fire's warmth. "Well then, I guess I'll just have to toss this last one away."

"Let's not be hasty, I said *you* were okay. Those are delicious." She beamed at him playfully.

"Oh, well, how can I resist those pearls?" Alexander walked up to Lillian with the treat, momentarily blocking out the moon, leaving his form only lit by firelight.

Something caught Lillian's eye. His necklace. It wasn't red anymore.

It was green.

Lillian's mind flew in a downward spiral. Doc's words and Hayden's wrenching at her insides.

"The dwarves in Caldera swore it changed color by firelight and helped her alter her form."

"That and a red ring..."

But Zands' ring was green...in the candlelight of the restaurant. Oh.

"Lillian?"

Alexander was right in front of her. His necklace shining like summer grass.

"Lillian, you okay? You don't have to eat it. I was just kidding."

Lillian pulled her brain back. "Um, yeah, no, I want it. Uh, what's with your necklace?" It was the most casual way she could think to ask.

Alexander handed her the sticky mound and then grabbed his necklace. "What? Oh, you mean the color. Neat, huh?" *Neat* was not the word Lillian was thinking of.

Neat? Surely evil overlords didn't use words like neat.

"I've only seen you really during the day, so I didn't really think about it. Here, watch." He turned his body so at one point the moonlight lit up his necklace and at another angle only the fire. "It changes color depending on what type of light hits it. I've never really figured out how. My mom's never seen anything like it."

But Doc has. And Zands. And Zoldaine with his malicious sisters. "And she's sure she doesn't know where it came from?"

"No, like I said, they found me with it. Lillian, what's wrong?"

Oh, nothing, just the fact that you could be someone completely different because you're wearing an evil color-changing, form-altering gemstone.

"Nothing, it's just I've never seen anything like it either. Doc would be really interested in looking at it if you didn't mind sometime." She reached out to touch it, expecting it to bite her, but it didn't. It felt like any normal jewel or gem. She definitely didn't get an evil vibe. But she'd been fooled before, and all too recently.

"That's your dwarf friend, right? Sure, I'd love to know more about it."

Careful what you ask for, Alexander.

Alexander looked up at the moon. "Well, we better get going. The grove should be almost dark now. Perfect for gleaming."

Or killing me.

It was a flippant thought, Lillian knew. Alexander had done nothing to indicate anything but the truest intentions. Still, the thought that four guards weren't far behind was comforting.

Once they got close to the grove, Lillian explained to the escorts that they could stay outside of the tree line as she and Alexander would just be about fifty paces in. They were reluctant to agree, but she was the princess and they obeyed her orders.

Alexander wasn't wrong. The grove was all but pitch black. Lillian could barely make out the tree line. The last few times they'd been here, the moon had been visible through the opening. Now, it was farther down, heading toward the horizon, barely peeping through the tops of the trees.

"Sorry you didn't get a chance to come out here and practice. But honestly, like I said, we'll get a true measure of how much you have improved. Just as long as you don't try to shoot me this time."

She couldn't see his teasing smile but could hear it.

"So, you ready?" he asked.

Lillian couldn't help it, she felt at ease, not like she was about to get murdered. She allowed herself a small laugh at the errant thought brought on by stories and paranoia.

"Yep. Do you want me to gleam before you start or during?"

"Whatever comes naturally. Remember, it's all about feel."

"Right. Feel," she reassured herself. She got situated. She set her feet, took a deep breath in, and let it out. "Ready."

She had barely gotten the word out when she heard the familiar click of a target drop in front of her. The red painted circle stood out a little against the black backdrop, but not much. She pulled and released. Missed to the left. Another target dropped to her left. She was definitely faster than last time, but still missed. She was getting frustrated. She could barely see the targets at all and one by one she missed them. Lillian heard a click and no more targets fell. Then she heard them retract back into the trees. She turned to see Alexander walking toward her.

"I'm sorry. I don't know what's wrong." She was embarrassed, looking around at all the missed targets.

Alexander came and put his hands on her shoulders. They were warm and instantly calming. His deep voice was soft. "Don't look at them, look at me." He put a hand beneath her chin and gently lifted until her eyes met his pale ones.

"Take a deep breath...and let it out." He breathed with her. Deep and slow. Helping her relax. "Now, keep your eyes on me," he said as he began backing away, "stay with me. Right here." He made his way back to the lever. "Okay, close your eyes now and just listen to my voice. Keep breathing."

Lillian stood there, breathing, eyes closed. Alexander's voice finding her in the darkness. "Feel. Don't think about what you *know* to be there. Feel it. Feel the breeze. Feel the trees, the grass, the animals. Feel the light." Alexander's voice was clear, but she felt it fading with every breath. She could feel the gleam getting stronger. It began to flow through her with each inhale and exhale. The grove around her became alive and clear.

Click. A target dropped behind her. In one fluid motion she spun around, pulled her arrow, set it, drew, and fired.

Bull's-eye.

Another target. And another. And another. They were coming quickly, but this time they didn't seem that way to her. She was reacting without thinking, muscle memory and gleam taking over. She felt the tension throughout the bow. The individual blades of grass shifting beneath her feet. A deep energy within her flowing into each arrow she sent coursing through the night air, finding its mark. It was magnificent and beautiful.

She fired the last arrow, hitting the mark before the target had finished falling.

Then she opened her eyes.

She looked around confirming what she already knew, and finally back to Alexander, who was smiling. "I'm impressed."

"That was...I can't believe...how I did...how did you..." Lillian couldn't hold her elation back any longer and yelled triumphantly. "Woooo!"

But Lillian's celebration was cut short. She heard a rustling. Alexander turned in the direction from where they had come. Several somethings were making their way to them. Fast. Alexander looked to Lillian, eyes wide, "Hide!"

It was all he got out before the first figure emerged right in front him.

CHAPTER 33: A Couple's Quarrel

illian barely registered what was happening before Alexander was fending off four assailants with his bow. He was faster than she had seen him earlier. They all had swords, but they might as well have been feathers. He spun and slid through them like water. Glancing off their blows and delivering his own with either end of his bow, sometimes both. It wasn't until one of the assailant's armor glinted in the light that Lillian realized what was happening.

"Stop! STOP!" Lillian ran toward the scuffle. "Don't hurt him, s*top*!" She managed to find a small break in the struggle and stepped in between them and Alexander.

"Lillian, what are you doing? Get out of here!" Alexander was on high alert, trying to circle to put himself between her and the assailants, which were now keeping their distance.

"Stop it! All of you!"

She turned to Alexander. "Everything's fine, they're my escorts."

She left him open-mouthed and turned to the assumed assailants. "I'm fine. Completely. Please, stand down."

Well, at least three of you.

The guards looked worse for the wear from the encounter. One man was still on his knees from Alexander's last blow. Two had some fairly sizable marks on their heads, which were sure to swell and turn a variety of colors over the next few days. And the final man had a bloody nose.

"But Your Highness, we heard you scream," Bloody Nose explained stuffily. He was holding his head back with his hand on his nose, trying to stem the flow.

"I know. I'm sorry," Lillian said a little sheepishly. "I was excited. That was all. I never thought you…" She motioned at the mess in exasperation. "Are you okay?"

They almost looked affronted, but Head Injury One said politely, "Nothing we haven't experienced in a daily sparring, Your Highness. We'll leave you be now. Sorry for the intrusion."

The men that were still standing gave a small bow, most wincing slightly as they did so, helped up their fourth man, and retreated back into the tree line, though at a gimp pace.

Lillian felt like they were putting on a brave face for her. She had never seen injuries like that from sparring.

They probably don't want to admit they just got their armor handed to them.

She couldn't help but be a bit proud of Alexander's prowess in four-on-one combat.

Alexander piped in, "I'm fine, by the way."

Lillian rolled her eyes at him. "I could see that, you dope. How did you…uh?" She gestured at the tree line. "I've never seen anyone best the King's Guards like that one on one, let alone four on one. Who *are* you? What, was your dad an expert in hand-to-hand combat too?"

"No, I just…" Alexander seemed unsure how to proceed.

"I'm giving you a hard time, Alexander. But seriously, where did you learn how to defend yourself like that? I mean, I saw you doing those exercises and stuff, but tonight, that was intense."

And hot.

He looked at her and gave her a dazzling smile. "I could teach you if you want."

She just laughed. "I'm sure you could, Mr. Elwood. I'm sure you could. But let's take it one thing at a time. Like tonight. How did you get me to gleam?"

They began to walk around the area retrieving Lillian's amazing round while Alexander explained it. "I didn't get you to gleam. I just got you to relax. You did the gleaming on your own. You felt it instead of thought about it."

"Right. Feel it, not think it," she repeated.

"Exactly. When you're tense, you're…maybe the best way I can describe is it's like you're off balance. But internally. You can't flow. Trust me, it used to happen to me all the time when I was around my dad."

Lillian feigned shock. "What? The great Alexander Elwood missing his mark?" she said as she pulled out her last arrow, a perfect bull's-eye.

"I know, I know, it's hard to accept, but alas, I'm not perfect," he apologized with mock sincerity.

Lillian wanted to make sure the guards could relax a little, so they headed back to the fire. Somewhere along the way their hands brushed together, and eventually Alexander grabbed hers. Lillian thought it was so interesting that he could seem so confident but nervous at the same time. She found it endearing.

Most guys Lillian had dated always appeared to be trying to impress her or her father. Alexander wasn't like that. He treated her like a person, not a princess, and she loved it. Ironically, his ability to treat her like a normal girl rather than a title made her feel more special than anytime she'd been treated like a princess by one of the others.

When they got back, the guards had just finished dressing their wounds as best they could until they returned to the castle. Lillian inquired and was assured none were serious, but she insisted the two with head wounds go back to the castle. They didn't even argue too much, as they realized Lillian's new suitor was more than capable of taking care of her. Alexander cordially apologized to them, and they grumbled back an acceptance. Lillian imagined their pride was the thing that was hurt the most.

Once the remaining two withdrew, giving Lillian and Alexander their distance, Alexander invited her to snuggle up against him next to the fire.

"Well, the evening didn't go quite as I had expected, but it was definitely an adventure." He chuckled.

Lillian laid against his chest, pulling his arms around her, which he readily assisted. Her cheek rested against the soft cotton, the only thing separating the solid warmth of him. She breathed in his perfect mix of green and growing things and sunbaked skin. And she felt a peculiar sensation, one she'd never felt before. A sensation of being...*home*, as if this was precisely where she was meant to be.

Alexander's necklace glittered in the firelight next to her, the color of wet spring leaves. She wasn't sure what role it played in his life, but she was certain Alexander didn't have an evil bone in his body. And the way he had defended her in the forest only strengthened the depth of what she felt for him.

"I wish you didn't have to go home tomorrow."

"I know, and I hate to leave you, but I need to make sure my mom is okay and take care of a few things."

Lillian noticed he didn't mention his dad. She raised up and looked at him. "Alexander, I was really sorry to hear about your dad. Sir Alger told me the other day. I would have liked to have met him." Lillian paused gently. "Why didn't you say anything earlier?"

"I don't know," he said, looking pensively into the dark. "I guess it's because I don't really feel like he's gone. He shared so much of his life with me and his skill that every time I shoot an arrow, I feel he's right beside me, still teaching me." Alexander dropped his gaze to Lillian. "He would have liked you. He liked your father. Said he was a good king. The 'people's king.' Obviously, anything was better than the previous queen, but he actually got to meet and talk with your father a couple of times. One of the prizes for the archery tournament was dinner with the king. I actually came with him once, and won," he said, remembering fondly. "But after that, my parents said it was best if I stayed home and let someone else have a chance. Dad said, 'Son, a talent like yours isn't meant to win archery tournaments. A talent like yours is meant for something else. Something great.'" Alexander's voice was deep with memory.

"I believe he's right," Lillian said, caught in the moment. *Gah!*

She recalled the important point here. "Back up. Then you have been around people before. Here in the village? During a tournament?"

"Yeah, I'd kind of forgotten about it, it was so long ago. I do remember my mom actually got really mad at him for taking me because they didn't talk about it. He apologized to her, and then to me, saying he was just so proud of me but had made a mistake. That was the first and last time I ever really left home. He died shortly after that, and I had to go out to make sure we could get by."

"What about your brother? Doesn't he help out?"

"Who are you talking about?"

"Your brother. Sir Alger told me about him too. How he won his division at the tournament. It must have been the same year you did."

Alexander sat up a bit. "Lillian, I don't know what he told you, maybe he's confused. I don't have a brother. I'm an only child. My parents couldn't have any children. That's why they were so happy to find me. I wish I had a brother. I've always wondered what it would be like to have someone to go shooting with or just play around with. I'm actually looking forward to meeting Andrew."

"Trust me, it's not all glamour. You fight, they pick on you and put cream in your hair. Don't get me wrong, I love Andrew, but he can be a real orc wart sometimes."

"Yeah, but if you had a choice, would you rather be an only child?"

Lillian thought about it but knew the answer. "No, probably not. He does have his moments. He actually helped me sneak out the other night."

"Sneak out *again*?"

Ah, now we're getting to it.

She would have to put the mystery of his childhood travels on hold, the crux of that night in the tunnels and his lack of acknowledging it was swiftly taking over her curiosity.

"You probably didn't see me," she said. "There was a lot of smoke. I never really got a chance to talk to you about it because of the escorts, but I saw you in the caves. I didn't even really know if you got out alive until I saw you yesterday…" Emotions Lillian had forgotten she was holding back surged forth. "When I saw the roof caving in where you were fighting, I didn't, I couldn't see you anymore, and I, I had to get out or else I'd be trapped and…then I saw your sign and I was afraid it might have been from before…" Lillian's eyes welled up, and she couldn't stop the tears that streamed down her face. "I didn't—I, I'm just so glad you're—" she choked as a wracking sob overtook her and she buried her head against his chest, one of his arms coming up to stroke her hair.

"Hey, now, no need to get upset. I'm right here. Shhhhh. Shhhh, there. I'm here, I'm here."

Lillian was pulling in shuddering breaths, but her crying had nearly stopped.

"That's it, now." He held her. "But I need you to help me, I'm a little lost. When did you see me fighting? And what roof caved in?" Alexander sounded genuinely perplexed.

Lillian leaned back to study his face. "You're pulling my tail, right? I mean you were there. I *saw* you. You had a cloak on, but they were the same moves I saw you doing with your sword before and your bow tonight."

"I'm sorry, Lillian, but I swear I have no idea what you're talking about."

She was so confused.

I guess I could have been wrong, but I could have sworn...

She said, "Then a lot has happened since you left. Got time for a story?"

So she told him. Everything. Everything since she'd been grounded all the way up to her conversation with her dad that morning. When she was done, he just sat there. He didn't look happy.

"Just taking it all in?" she joked.

He got up abruptly and walked away.

"Alexander?" She went after him. "Alexander, what's wrong? I told you, I'm okay. I'm not hurt."

He turned around quickly to face her. He was furious. "But it's not for your lack of trying, is it?"

Whoa!

She stepped back, visibly stung by his words and tone. "I...I don't understand what you mean. Why are you mad?" Tears threatened again.

"You don't get it, do you? When I left, we..." He raked both his hands through his hair in frustration. "I mean, I know the kidnapping wasn't your fault, but after you know they're targeting you, why, *why* would you risk your life and choose to walk right into their hands?" He stomped off again.

"But I didn't know, Alexander. I thought Hayden was in trouble. I wouldn't have been able to live with myself if something had happened to her." Anger was taking the place of hurt and confusion. "And it is *my life*. But recently, I haven't felt that way. Last night was the first time in a month I felt like I was taking it back. I was in control."

He was fidgeting with his pack. "But you *weren't* in control. You did exactly what they wanted. These people, whoever they are, are smart. They're ruthless. And thank the Fae that someone, not me, was there to rescue you last night or…or who knows where you'd be right now. And the thought of that…" His silvery eyes shone with sudden unshed tears. "Don't you know how important you are to m—to the kingdom?" He turned away.

So he does feel the same…but why did he stop himself?

They hadn't really had a chance to talk about the last night they spent together. It felt like ages ago, but all her feelings were welling back up. She was furious at the events that had taken place and how they were interfering with their relationship. She was so excited to see him. So happy he was even *alive*. He had just become her new suitor. And now it was—it was all *wrong*. There were so many other emotions sloshing around inside her right now. But the ones that were closest to the surface were anger and heartache.

"What were you going to say?" she demanded.

Alexander kept messing with his pack. Winston was becoming restless and uneasy at the situation. "What? Nothing."

"Why is it so hard for you to open up to me? I've never felt so comfortable around someone I know so little about, but I'm starting to feel like I don't know you at all." Grief pulled at her insides.

Alexander whipped around to face her so fast she backed up a little.

"What do you want to know? Ask me," he snarled. His gray eyes stormy and dark.

"I, I don't know, I just meant…"

"You want to know why I have such a hard time opening up to you? You want to know why? I've barely been around people before, Lillian, let alone whatever this is. This relationship. I don't know what to do. I mean, is that what people in a relationship do? Question each other? Accuse each other?"

Lillian was trying not to cry. She wrapped her arms around herself. "No, I just...I don't understand why you didn't tell me about your dad. Or that you had a brother."

Alexander tensed. "We're back to that again? Lillian, I don't *have* a brother. Why don't you believe me?"

"Then who did Sir Alger and *my dad* see at that archery tournament with *your dad*? It couldn't have been you. You'd only be fifteen now."

And you are definitely not *fifteen.*

"I don't know who they saw, you'd have to ask them, but it wasn't my brother because I don't have one." He turned back to his saddle to keep his anger from her. "I told you I won a tournament when I was ten. Maybe they have their years wrong, I don't know. And I wasn't in any caves fighting these Dainian Rogues. I didn't even get over here until around then and was probably here putting my mark on the rock, which is why *I* didn't feel you in trouble this time if you were as far past the wall as you said." Alexander paused for a moment. "Actually, I know when that was because I heard an explosion from town. Besides, you said the figure was cloaked. You're just going off a few moves that you *think* you recognize, through smoke, while you were being pulled away."

"Then who was it?"

"How should *I* know? Maybe your dad was having you followed. He seems to know you pretty well, always sneaking out, putting your life in danger."

The last statement hit her hard. And as much as she tried to stop them, the tears started falling. "I think I should just go."

He didn't even turn around. "Yeah, you probably should."

Lillian bawled all the way home. She didn't even care that the guards were there. Her heart felt like it was being squeezed in a vice. She was bereft.

As she stumbled home, her mind tried to replay everything that had just happened and figure out how it had all spun out of control. She had never seen Alexander angry before, ever, let alone toward her. She recognized it though, she thought. It was similar to how her father reacted the night she snuck out to see Alexander after the kidnapping. They had gotten into a huge fight then too. She later realized that his anger was simply him caring for her so much.

Please let it be that!

She had to remind herself that this was all new to Alexander. She wasn't trying to accuse him of lying, but she couldn't figure out how to explain what she had seen or what her dad and Sir Alger had seen.

"A straight stick looks crooked in water."

She thought about that saying her dad would use when trying to figure out a dispute. He explained it to her when she'd asked its meaning; the same thing can look different based on someone's perspective. And he'd usually resolved the quarrel by pointing out both sides and helping them understand it was a miscommunication by both parties involved. Lillian was hoping that's all this was. A misunderstanding. She couldn't let Alexander leave for over a week like this. She decided to get up early in the morning to meet him, hopefully before he left.

Get up in the morning. If I can ever get to sleep.

CHAPTER 34: A Long Farewell
July 13

I nitially, Lillian laid in bed, but as spent as her emotions were and as exhausted as her crying had left her, Lillian couldn't sleep a wink. For most of the night, she just sat and stared at Alexander's *A* on the rock. It was hard to see the rock, but somehow his mark seemed to glow in the moonlight, just like his necklace. Their rock was how she liked to think of it now. It was the first place she had met him. The memory brought a smile to her face. She never would have thought a strange voice just a few months ago would mean so much to her.

The stars slowly winked out as the night sky began to lighten. She breathed a sigh of relief; Lillian had to wait until at least first light for an escort. She got dressed and knew there was nothing to be done about her swollen eyes and blotchy cheeks. She just wanted to leave the castle before dawn.

Sunrise was always interesting in Valanti because of the Senari Range. The sky would get bright before the sun ever glanced over their jagged peaks. But when it did finally break free, it was glorious. Lillian was hoping that Alexander would wait at least until then; surely he hadn't left already.

Lillian got her answer soon enough when she saw Alexander's silhouette sitting by the fire. The escorts held back as she got closer. Word had spread quickly overnight of Alexander's abilities, and they didn't want any more misunderstandings.

Her stomach did flips as she got closer. She was afraid he wouldn't want to talk to her. The speech she had thought of and memorized slipped from her head. But once again, he surprised her. He got up and walked toward her.

"I was hoping you'd still be here," she managed to get out.

"I was waiting until you came." He gave a weak smile. His eyes appeared as though he didn't get much sleep either. He helped her to sit. "You hungry?"

She hadn't thought about food all night but as soon as he mentioned it, her traitorous stomach grumbled. "Yeah, I guess I am." The wind shifted and she could smell the bacon and bread in the breeze, causing her stomach to start making further demands.

They ate breakfast in relative silence, with one or the other commenting on the weather, when he'd be back, anything to keep from talking about their argument last night. But eventually the sun slid up over the mountain, indicating it was time for Alexander to head home.

He started. "I'm sorry I was cross with you last night, Lillian. I had no right. You were only asking questions. I don't know why I got so defensive."

"It's okay. I'm sorry too. I know it must have sounded like I was all but accusing you of lying. I should have believed you, not questioned. I just started to realize there's a lot I *don't* know about you," she hesitated, but then grabbed his hand, "but I want to."

"And Lillian, I want to get to know *you*. Believe it or not, being the princess doesn't mean too much to me, so I haven't followed your life like others have. I have been sheltered for most of mine. Most of this is new to me. But that isn't an excuse. I think some of it has to do with my mom. I'm used to protecting her. I worry about her when I'm gone, even though I know she can take care of herself. You, on the other hand…" Alexander glowered at her with a fake frown.

"You don't *have* to protect me," she replied contritely.

"I know I don't *have* to. . .but I want to," he finished softly. "And the thought of you being in danger, and me being nowhere near to protect you, to save you," his throat constricted, his voice choking up. "I just don't want to think about it, about what could happen. You have to know that people care about you right, that *I* care about you?"

Her eyes welled up. "I'm so sorry, Alexander. I wasn't thinking about anyone else, I just wanted my life back."

He looked at her and said earnestly, "I get that. I really do. My life has always been a secret. My very existence. And now that I'm finally starting to build one, I just…I don't want to lose it before it even begins." His broad hand reached out, wiping a tear from her eye, before he settled both his hands on her shoulders. "You are important to me. I care for you."

She laughed a little, finally hearing him say it aloud.

He said, "It's true. I've thought about our first night together every day since."

"Me too."

He drew her into his arms. "I'm sorry I got so upset. I'm kind of new to this whole being around people a bunch thing, let alone, well, *being* with someone." He pulled back, strands of his wavy locks catching in the slight breeze, his argent eyes searched hers. "Do you forgive me?"

"Of course! But only if you forgive me for being so reckless. I promise I was only trying to help."

"I know you were. But how about we leave the dangerous heroics to me now, at least for a while anyway?" he joked. He offered his hand to help her up. "Here, if you're done with breakfast, let's go take a walk."

She took his hand, gentle but calloused from use. "You want to practice? Now? Don't you need to leave?"

"I've got time," he said, "especially for you."

Her heart picked up its pace a bit.

"But no, we're not practicing. We're going for a walk. Just to talk. That's what couples do right?"

"We're a couple now, huh?" she teased fondly.

"Would you just come on and stop being a troll's butt?" He smiled, shaking his head in exasperation.

The salty breeze carried from the coast and the rising sun made for a pleasant morning stroll. They walked close enough where their hands grazed each other's until Alexander found his courage again and took her hand. Every now and then, Lillian caught him glancing at her. She was happy. She was with someone who just wanted to be with her. With Alexander, she wasn't *the* princess, she was *his* princess.

"Red," Alexander stated abruptly.

"Huh?" Lillian looked around, trying to figure out what he was talking about.

"My favorite color. It's red. My favorite number is eight. And I don't know when my birthday is but I've always liked the month of March."

"Why are you telling me all of this?" Lillian was amused.

"You said you didn't feel like you knew me, so that's what we're doing. Consider this our first official date. Getting to know each other." Alexander let go of her hand, took a step back, and bowed. "How do you do m'lady? My name is Alexander Elwood. Pleased to make your acquaintance."

Lillian played along and curtsied. "Prin—Lillian Beverly Charming, my good sir. Pleased to meet you as well."

They both snickered at the farce and continued their stroll. They exchanged likes and dislikes. Favorite foods and desserts. Lillian promised to take Alexander to Talula's for the Wizard Wonderfall. He picked some wildflowers for her and put a couple in her hair. She asked about his mom and dad. She told him about growing up in the castle. The responsibilities. The dignitaries she'd met from other countries and some of the silly traditions she'd had to participate in. He told her about growing up on a farm and how all their chickens got out one time. Before she knew it, they had come full circle back to the campsite.

"I have to go soon, if I'm going to get home before dark. My mom doesn't like me coming in after dark. Even though she knows I can take care of myself, she still worries."

"My dad said something similar. That I would understand when we have kids someday."

Flerb! I did not just say that!

"I meant me, I, when I have kids someday. I didn't mean…" Lillian could feel her face flushing and pulsing ever redder.

Alexander let out a rolling belly laugh. "Can we have a wedding first?"

Lillian turned away, her palm over her face. She bent to pick up the stuff from breakfast. "I'm just going to pick up this stuff over here," she said, then under her breath, "before my horse runs off with the wagon."

They both gathered up his things. She folded the blanket they had sat on and she walked over to Winston.

"Don't worry, boy, I'm going to miss you too." She fed him a leftover apple. She lifted the satchel flap to put the blanket away and noticed something at the bottom. Purple fabric. Her heart stopped. She slowly pulled it out to reveal some sort of scarf. She did her best to sound nonchalant but her stomach twisted. "Hey, Alexander, what's this?"

He turned around. "What's what? Oh, that. It's a sash or something my mom made me. I don't wear it very often. Never thought purple was my color, but I didn't have the heart to tell her." He laughed sheepishly.

She went up to him and put it over him. He was right. Purple wasn't his color. "Yeah. But if you wore it, maybe people wouldn't think you were a ghost."

"Well now, where would be the fun in that?" He took it off.

He can't be Zands. He just can't.

And even though she knew it couldn't be true, some part of her deep down wouldn't stop saying, *but what if*?

For most of the morning, Lillian had forgotten all about reality. About how her life was in danger. How there was a deranged lunatic here, in her kingdom, trying to kidnap her, for Fae knows what. And it all came back to her like waves crashing against the cliffs.

"Lillian? Is everything okay?" He brought her back from her spiraling thoughts.

"Yeah, sorry, I…I just wish I could come with you," she managed to compose.

"Well, someday you will. My mom will want to meet the girl who has pulled me from seclusion. She predicted this would happen."

"She did?"

"Yep. She knew that someday I would catch the eye of a girl, although I wasn't sure how, since I never met any, and I would have to bring her home so she could explain why her boy was so special."

"By special, you mean something *besides* the cooking, archery, and saving my life? That I would like to hear."

"Well then, maybe when I come back and meet your parents, you can come back and meet my mom. She's got her roots in the ground, but she still might make a fuss over the princess." He grinned.

"My dad would probably send half the guard for that trip," Lillian joked—sort of.

Alexander took her hands and looked into her eyes. "It's going to be okay. I know it's hard to see right now, but everything that's happening now has a reason. Don't ask me how I know, maybe it's the gleam a little, but I do. It's going to work out just how it's supposed to. You just have to have faith." He collected his thoughts and looked at her, eyes full of questions. "I'm sure you know by now there's more to us than just *us*."

Lillian couldn't deny it. She *had* felt it. Especially last night. "The gleaming?"

"The gleaming," he affirmed. "It's similar to what my father and I shared but different. It's a bond. And it gets stronger the closer we are to each other. Both in distance and…emotionally. That's how I felt you the night you were kidnapped. That's how you *knew* I wasn't dead from cave collapse. And that's how you hit all those targets last night…with your eyes closed. That's how I *know* you'll be okay until I get back." He cupped his hands around her face, leaned in, and placed a gentle kiss on her forehead. "I'll be back before you know it."

She watched him ride off until he disappeared over the horizon. She believed every word he said. That everything was going to be okay. But she also believed in her other feeling. The inherited gift from her father. She hadn't listened to it before, but she was now. Something was wrong. She just didn't know what.

July 19

Days crawled by. Lillian had run out of things to do to keep herself preoccupied. She had helped Pierre in the kitchen and did her best to replicate the fireside goody Alexander had introduced to her. Pierre didn't have everything but was intrigued enough to import some of the white fluff through Caldera's port. She played hide and seek with Andrew and Ethan. She insisted they play at night though. She watched them bump into things and each other as she gleamed in the cover of the shadows. She couldn't help it, feeling somewhat vindicated for all their pranks. Jafria came over a couple of times. Lillian showed off her new archery skills and told her about Alexander, officially. Lillian couldn't decide whether she or Jafria was more excited. Lillian had gone out to the Forge a few times, sometimes during the day, sometimes during the night, but she could never repeat her performance with Alexander. She was getting better at the distance targets too, but the farthest one still eluded her.

But where she spent most of her time was with Ophelia. Lillian had been diligently creating a new tunic for Alexander. A deep royal blue piece. Purple may not have been his color, but Lillian knew blue would be. She used silver thread to match his eyes. She couldn't wait to give it to him in a couple of days.

"Don't forget to double knot ven you finish the hem, Lillian," Ophelia reminded, her thick accent a familiar and warm staple since she could remember. "But the rest of it looks very good. Sehr schön."

"Danke, Ophelia. I'll probably come back tomorrow for finishing touches, but..." Lillian held up what she had accomplished. "What do you think so far?"

"I'm sure he vill love it."

Knock. Knock. Knock.

"Pardon the intrusion, m'dears." Doc stood in the doorway.

"Doc, come on in. I was just finishing up." Lillian put in the last few stitches and double knotted the end. "I'm glad you could make it. Remember those weird rocks I was telling you about? Well, I found some more out at this grove I practice in." Lillian hoped Doc picked up on her hint. She put her things away and headed off to the stables with him. "You don't mind going for a little ride, do you?"

"A ride with the prettiest lass around? Aye, I think I can manage." He winked.

Lillian had invited Doc to talk about Alexander's gem, though she was using the target system as her excuse. It was a good one, however, because she really did want to show him the mechanism that Alexander had made. She was afraid of what Doc might tell her about the gem, so she stalled by letting him examine the special arrow Alexander had made as they rode.

"Fascinating! Simply amazing," he exclaimed, turning it over in his hands, examining it from all angles. "Calderan steel is a tricky enough metal to forge regularly, but this," he said, whistling, "this is truly remarkable. Did 'e mention who 'e studied under? 'Ow 'e learned to do this?"

"Not that I remember."

"Well, if 'e's self-taught, then that boy has some fae blood in him, because this arrow is nearly magical."

Lillian laughed. "His dad said the same thing."

"I knew Berchum too. Smart man, so it must be troo."

Lillian mulled this over. It wasn't unheard of for humans to have a bit of magic in them. Princess Olivia always seemed to be in tune with that realm, so Lillian supposed it was possible for Alexander to be as well. Gleaming had to be magical, and she was getting better at that every day. And she couldn't deny that unexplainable bond, that intangible connection she had with Alexander. Maybe that's what love is. Magic.

The familiar line of trees approached. Lillian would have to revisit these thoughts later. Maybe even talk to Olivia about them. "All right, we're there. The setup might not impress you as much as the arrow but it's pretty elaborate."

Lillian was afraid Doc's gears would come loose as she showed him the way the mechanism worked and the different settings. She heard him mutter words like *impeccable* and *astonishing* and *intricate*. He pulled the lever several times, watching it work in wonder. His eyes glistened with the excitement of a child.

"I mean, I've always thought about something like this. Actually a self-sustaining guard who would have different settings like this to help train real guards or knights. The system of pulleys and gears 'e 'as are just, weel, they've given me some ideas I'd like to get down before they slip out of this old brain. Do ye' mind if we 'ead back?"

Lillian let Doc talk about all the mechanics and intricate workings of the Forge on the way back. But Lillian knew they'd arrive at the castle soon, and she needed to talk to him.

No sooner did she think it than Doc abruptly changed subjects. "So, are you just goona let an old man prattle on, or are you goona tell me why you really brought me out 'ere?"

Doc, no one ever gives you enough credit.

"I saw it change color, Doc. The gem that he wears, it changes color just like you said."

"Ah, lass…"

"But I swear to you, Doc, it can't be the same one. Maybe it takes on the persona of whoever has it. Maybe the gem isn't evil, just the people who had it before."

Doc took a deep breath. Lillian could all but hear the gear teeth clicking in his head. "I'd 'ave to see it to be sure, sweetie. Maybe bring in some 'elp from Tapera; get the faeries involved. I know this fella means a lot to you. You've got that gleam in your eye when you talk about 'im." Lillian smirked at his interesting choice of words. "And from what I understand, 'e'll be meeting your folks in a couple of days. Your father should get a feeling from 'im. 'E was always good at that. But what's important is you. What do *you* feel, deary?"

"He's saved my life twice. Three times if you count the misunderstanding the other night."

Doc chortled. "From what I 'ear, he gave those boys quite the wallop. They've turned more colors than a dragon's scale."

"It wasn't that bad. But let's just say he can take care of himself." She smiled proudly but then paused a moment. "He's nice, Doc. A complete gentleman. A good cook. Smart. He treats me like a normal person. All this royalty stuff doesn't matter to him."

Doc trotted up next to her and halted the horses. "I 'ear what you're saying, darlin', but what do you *feel*?"

Lillian thought about it, but she knew the answer. "I feel safe. I feel nothing but good from him. I feel...I feel like it's where I'm supposed to be."

Doc took her hand. "Then trust that. Trust that feeling, because it's just as real as the gem 'e's wearing."

As they rode up to the stables, Seth was there to take their horses. But there was an obvious commotion going on in the castle.

"Seth, what's going on?" Lillian was concerned.

"It's Sir Laurel," he replied. "They've arrested him for high treason."

CHAPTER 35: Traitor in the Midst

nowing Sir Laurel had been detained didn't surprise Lillian, but she still couldn't believe what she had just heard. "What?"

Seth helped her down. "Yeah. Apparently he didn't pass the faeries truth spell, or whatever it is, and they took him."

Doc hopped down off his horse. "What do you mean they took 'im? Who, where, and why?"

"Sorry," Seth took the horses to the stables. "It's just, things have been a little crazy this afternoon. The faeries were running the knights through their spell. Sir Laurel didn't pass. So, the king ordered to have his quarters searched and they found some kind of plans—a map of tunnels under the Cuisine district, correspondence written in code, drawings of some sort, all hidden in some loose piece of slate under his bed. He denied ever having seen any of it before. Said it was a setup or something; that they weren't his. Of course, he did all this with a glass of wine in his hand."

Lillian was still wrapping her head at how the bumbling knight was seemingly even more involved than she had suspected. "I don't understand. He was always so..."

"Wine glass all-empty?" Seth interjected. "That may have all been an act it seems. The broken spell made them suspicious, but when they found those plans and stuff, they had markings of red skulls on them in different locations, they shackled him up immediately. Word is right now he's being interrogated."

Doc's face whitened. "Powder keegs."

"Yeah, I guess you would know."

"Ah, and I thought oold Byme was just slippin' 'is gears." Doc shook his head. "I need to speak to the king immediately. If you'll excuse me, Your 'ighness. I 'ad a wonderful afternoon. An' doona forget what I said."

"What was all that about?" Seth asked Lillian as Doc headed into the castle.

"I'm not entirely sure, but I think it had something to do with the explosion the other night in The Trenches. When I was in the caves, I saw a bunch of those kegs. I knew I had seen them somewhere before. The dwarves use them all the time for blasting. Look, I'd better go let my parents know that I'm back. I'll catch up with you later though, okay?"

Lillian wasn't worried about her parents knowing she was back. The escorts would report back and they'd know soon enough. What she was more interested in was getting to the passage to see if her father was interrogating Sir Laurel yet. By the time she had made it into the passage without being noticed, they were done with him. Sir Alger, Henry, her father, and the faeries were present once again, along with a couple of guards. Sir Laurel looked like he'd tussled with a troll and lost. He wasn't hurt physically, but Lillian could tell the faeries had spun his mental yarn.

Switwick pleaded with the king. "Sire, we've done all we can do without killing him. I'm sorry."

"He has to know something!" Her father was frustrated and started shaking Sir Laurel.

"Your Majesty," Henry attempted to calm the king down. "Your Majesty!" He grabbed the king's shoulders and pulled him away. "Harry, look at me." Hearing his first name got the king's attention. "We have the correspondence letters and plans. Our best men are working on the code as we speak. Look at him, he doesn't know anything—but if he does, we'll find it." The king looked at Laurel then back at his friend. "We'll find it, Harry, I promise."

Sir Alger motioned for the guards. "Take him back to his cell. Make sure he has food and water."

Once they were gone, Sir Alger turned to the king. "Your Majesty, I take full responsibility for my men, as always, but I have to admit, I'm truly at a loss. I know Sir Laurel has had his shortcomings, but he's no traitor. Something isn't right here."

"Nevertheless, he's all we have at the moment," the king reminded him. Then he addressed the faeries, "Where are we on the protection spell for the other guards?"

Nyssa spoke first. "We should be finished by tonight, at the latest tomorrow morning. But as we've discussed, it's not foolproof. Someone could slip by if they know the counter spell."

"But they'd have to know it *and* be powerful enough to cast it, right?" Sir Alger clarified.

"Correct," Switwick replied. "Even Grayson would have trouble fooling it."

"I think we're done here. Keep me apprised of any new developments and when the rest of the guard has been cleared," her father said.

The company made their way out. Lillian sat on the stairs for a moment. She needed to talk to Sir Laurel herself. She had to know if it was him who left those notes. But she'd need to talk to her father first.

Lillian found her father in his study talking to Doc.

Doc was upset. "I'm sorry, Your Majesty. I should 'ave said something. Even if I thought it was a mistake, I… the other night in The Trenches. Someone coulda been seriously 'urt or killed. Thank the Fae that they weren't, and 'opefully I'm not too late."

"It's okay, my old friend. How would you have known? The important thing is you're telling me now and we know what to look for. It will at least make it more difficult for them to move them around. I'll send out word immediately to check all wagons or carts carrying any type of barrel or keg." The king looked up and saw Lillian. "Come on in, sweetie. Doc and I were just finishing up."

"Hello again, Doc."

"Hello, deary. Thanks again for the ride. I'll be interested in meeting this young lad when 'e gets back."

"I'm sure you guys will have plenty of time to gab gears in the future." She smiled at him.

He gave her a wink and disappeared around the doorway.

"Dad, how is everything?" She walked over and gave him a long hug.

He shook his head. "I don't know what's going on anymore, Lily Pad. This thing with Laurel breaks my heart. I can't believe it, but what choice do I have? He didn't pass the faeries' test and on top of that, their spell revealed his hidden items. I just don't know how I couldn't have seen it or felt it like usual."

"You've been under a lot of stress lately, Dad, it's not your fault. Think of how many other people have been around him and Hayden. People who had been with them every day and didn't see anything or notice anything out of the ordinary. You can't put this all on you."

"But I do, sweetie. This is my responsibility. You, our family, the kingdom. And I'm not alone. I've been in correspondence with my brother and Aurora almost on a daily basis. Kretcher and his sons have been running leagues over the last month to keep information as current as possible. And I have Alger and Henry, your mom. I know you don't see us, but your mom and I talk every night. She may be a little naïve at times, but she knows more than you think. She's my rock. Now, I hate to cut this short, but did you need something or were you coming just to check in on your old man?"

Lillian really didn't want to add more to her dad's plate, but she had to know. "I...I need to talk to Sir Laurel."

"*Talk* to Laurel?" Lillian noticed her father had unceremoniously dropped the "Sir." "Sweetie, I don't know if that's such a good idea. He just..."

"Please, Dad. It's important."

"And I suppose you can't tell me what this is about?"

"Not yet, but I promise you, Dad, if he tells me anything important, I'll come straight to you."

The king took a deep breath and let it out. "All right, but not today. And I can't promise when. There are procedures we need to follow first so it may be a few days." The king could see her look of disappointment. "I'm sorry, sweetie, but it's the best I can do."

It wasn't the exact answer Lillian was hoping for, but she was thankful her dad agreed to it at all. "It's fine, Dad. I really appreciate your trust." She gave him one last hug and left her father to his thoughts. But when she got to the door, she turned around. "Hey, Dad?"

"Yes, Lil'?"

"I love you."

A weary smile lit up his face. "I love you too, Lillian."

July 22

Friday. Finally. Lillian thought it would never come. She still hadn't gotten a chance to talk to no-longer-*Sir* Laurel, but right now that didn't matter because today was Friday and Alexander was coming for dinner.

Lillian started making the rounds a few hours before dinner to be sure everything would be ready for Alexander's arrival. She was both excited and apprehensive for her parents to meet him, which was odd because she never had been before with other suitors. She worried they'd find something wrong, even though she knew there wouldn't be. She fretted that he might feel uncomfortable in new surroundings, engaged in a serious sort of conversation. *What if they don't like him?* The question kept forcing itself to the forefront of her mind and keeping her nerves on end. A question she didn't like thinking about so she set about looking for distractions. She found Andrew first in his bedroom. He was to spend the night with Ethan; her mother's idea.

"Are you sure you have everything? Change of clothes? Your toys? Don't forget your bear. You know you can't sleep without him." Lillian was moving around his room like a goblin searching for gold.

"Yes, geez, Lil', you're worse than Mom. And I can sleep without Mr. Paws," Andrew insisted, even though both of them knew better, "but if you insist, I will pack him." Andrew grabbed his one-eyed bear rather forcefully at first but gently placed him in his carry case. "There. Now, will you please go away?"

"I just want to make sure my little brother has a good time with his friend, is that so wrong?" She grabbed his head, rubbing his hair.

"More like you want to make sure you have a good time with *your friend*. I could have behaved, you know. I'm so happy you've been playing with me again; I wouldn't want you to stop. I'm sorry you got grounded, but I'm really glad you've been spending time with me."

"I've enjoyed hanging around you too, little brother."

"I like us spending time together again. You're not going to start ignoring me again now that Alexander is going to be courting you, are you?"

"No, of course not. But he's different than the others. He'd probably enjoy playing hide 'n' seek with us. He doesn't have brothers or sisters, so he never got to play with anyone. He actually said he was looking forward to meeting you."

"Really? Do you think he'd teach me how to shoot like he's been teaching you?"

"I'll have to ask him, but I don't think he'd mind one bit. I think he'd like having a little brother."

Andrew got excited at the notion of having a partly adopted older brother as well.

Lillian wasn't sure why she said it, but it felt normal. She had never sensed that about the other suitors, but as she had told Andrew, Alexander was different. She felt like he fit better than the others. Like he wanted to be part of a family versus courting the princess.

With Andrew seemingly in hand, she headed off to the kitchen to check in on Pierre. She had given him a menu to follow, but occasionally he would stray off the beaten path and add his own flare. She knew Alexander was adventurous in nature but not as certain about his food. Just a simple three-course meal consisting of tomato soup, pork loin with roasted vegetables, and finished with Pierre's specialty dessert, a chocolate soufflé drizzled with thackleberry syrup.

"How are the dishes coming along?"

"Zey are coming along well, Miss Lillian."

"You're not making any alterations to them, are you?" Lillian raised an eyebrow.

Pierre feigned insult. "Moi? Why, Miss Lillian, when 'ave I ever done zat?" But he couldn't help but smirk.

Pierre knew exactly what she was referring to. He had a tendency to garnish perfectly decent meals with exotic spices—or creatures. Pierre had come from Caldera where the ports brought in a variety of food and people to learn a multitude of culinary tricks. It was one of the reasons why he was such a good chef. But it was also the reason he cooked up wild recipes with which more timid taste buds didn't always agree. Once he added prickle bugs without telling anyone. Most of the guests had gotten through half the dish before one of them commented on the crunchy texture. Seeing how pleased everyone was, he promptly told them the secret ingredient. The evening did not end well and closed on a very firm scolding from the queen. Since then, he usually asked permission or made a separate spread for the more adventurous palates. "Usually" being why Lillian was checking in.

"Pierre?"

"I only tease, Your 'ighness." Pierre bowed. "I promeese on my 'onor as a chef, everything will be perfect for your friend. No 'Pierre experiments' tonight."

Lillian was still leery and tasted the tomato soup just to be sure. It was delicious.

Next stop was Ophelia's to pick up Alexander's new tunic, which Lillian had sewn for him. Ophelia was checking it over to make sure all the stitches were sound.

"Well, Ophelia, how does it look?" Lillian called as she entered. "It's not going to unravel on him, is it?" She looked around for the seamstress. "Ophelia?" Lillian walked past the wall of spools in every color and the labyrinth of fabrics only Ophelia knew how to navigate. Specially designed shelves held several bolts of assorted colors and patterns. Lillian never got used to the sensation of walking through them. It was as if the fabrics swallowed all the sound. "Ophelia?" She called a little louder.

Ophelia poked her head around a pile of fabrics. "Your Highness! Es tut mir leid. I didn't hear you come in. You've come to pick up the tunic, ja? I have it right over here for you." Ophelia made her way back to the front and picked up a wrapped package. "I hope you don't mind. I vent ahead and vrapped it for you. It was excellent vork, Lillian. Gut gemacht. The buttons complement the thread very well. I'm sure he vill be very pleased."

"Danke." Lillian gave a small bow. "And thank you for wrapping it. I can't wait to see what he thinks."

"Vell, you make sure to come back and tell me how it vent."

"I will, Ophelia." Lillian headed out.

"And make sure you bring him by in it for my approval." Ophelia winked at her.

With the package tucked under her arm, Lillian went to her last stop before getting ready herself.

Her parents were in their room. They were just starting to get ready.

"Lillian, sweetie, shouldn't you be getting ready?" Her mom greeted her with a kiss on the cheek.

Lillian returned the sentiment. "I was just heading that way. I wanted to see what you guys were wearing."

Her dad answered first. "I was thinking about wearing my white pressed trousers, red button-up, and my navy coat with the gold buttons and tails." He turned to his wife. "Honey, do you think I could wear the manacle this time?"

Lillian scowled at him. "Dad?"

"Oh, Harry, quit teasing her. Can't you see she's anxious?" Snow White poked her husband.

"I'm just pulling your tail, Lily Pad. We have both chosen what's on the bed. Go see for yourself."

Lillian walked over to where the clothes lay and mused over them. Her dad had actually laid out a pair of brown trousers with a nice sky-blue shirt. Her mom was going to be wearing a simple evening dress of red silk that matched her lips.

The queen went to her daughter and put her arms around Lillian. "Honey, everything's going to be just fine. We can both tell this one's different and we're very excited to meet someone who has made our daughter so happy. Now, don't worry and go get ready."

Lillian kissed both her parents and thanked them for understanding.

Alondra was waiting for her upstairs to help her get ready. "I've laid out a few options for tonight's dinner, Your Highness. And I've been thinking about your hair. Initially I was thinking curls, but since you were wanting simple, I think a braid arranged in a bun, maybe."

"Sounds perfect, Alondra."

The gowns Alondra had laid out were each beautiful. The first was cream linen, trimmed with delicate silver brocade and a fitted bodice and full skirt; the second, a sea-foam green satin Jafria had helped pick out, embroidered with tiny seed pearls along the heart-shaped bodice and shoulders, and also dotted throughout skirt that pleated at the back and would have pooled behind her. She thought it a little too dressy, considering Alexander had only ever seen her in simple cotton ensembles meant for wandering out of doors.

She settled on the third gown. It was left unadorned, but it's cut and fit needed none. It was of luminous emerald satin, with a wide neck that stretched to the shoulders. The sleeves were short but voluminous. It was perfect for a July night. It was just what she was looking for. Simple yet extremely elegant.

Lillian tried to relax as she got dressed and Alondra did her hair. For a time, the two ladies were silent. But Alondra could sense Lillian's tension. "I remember the first time Henry met my parents. I'd had other fellas meet them before, but this time was different. I really cared about Henry. I had already made up my mind that if they didn't approve, I would run away with him wherever he would take me. I was a silly girl."

"So, how did it go?"

"It went okay. But my mom gave him the cold shoulder the whole night. I thought she hated him."

"Is this supposed to make me feel better? What did Henry do? What did you do?"

"I apologized for my mom later on that night when he went home. But Henry, Fae bless him, didn't even really pick up on it. I talked to my mother later that night, but she didn't, no, wouldn't talk to me about it."

"So, what happened? I mean, she must have come around eventually because you got married."

"She warmed up to him later on. He was so polite and helpful, which helped. But I actually didn't find out until years after Henry and I had gotten married." Alondra finished wrapping up Lillian's bun. "How is that?"

Lillian turned her head in the mirror to admire both sides. "It looks wonderful, Alondra. It's funny, but I don't think Alexander has ever seen it except in a ponytail." Lillian turned around to face Alondra, wanting to hear the outcome. "So, what did your mom say?"

"She told me the reason she was so guarded the first night was that she knew. She knew he was the one. That this gentleman sitting in front of her was going to be the one who would take her little girl away. Not in a bad way, mind you. She just wasn't ready to let me go yet and she knew that time was coming soon. But the more time he spent with me and my family, she realized that old adage was coming to pass; she wasn't losing a daughter but gaining a son. And I'm sure your family will feel the same way."

Lillian stood up and gave her friend a big embrace. "How do you always know what to say to make me feel better?"

"I have known you a bit of time. That always helps. Now, step back and let me see."

Lillian did a little twirl, the lustrous silk catching the candlelight.

"Well, I have a notion of how you feel about him. And all I can say is, if he hasn't fallen for you yet, he will tonight."

"Thanks so much for everything, Alondra. I'll find you later tomorrow and tell you all about it."

Lillian could see the light dimming outside as she headed downstairs. Her parents were already in the spare dining room sharing a bottle of wine. This room was used for more intimate seating when the party was twelve or less. The table had already been shortened to accommodate six, as there would only be four this evening. The trio made small talk while they waited for the guest of honor. The sun had completely set when Pierre came to see if they wanted an hors d'oeuvre. The king thought about it, but seeing Lillian, he declined. He was hungry but knew it was rude to start eating without all the guests.

"Thanks, Dad. I don't know where he could be. We didn't really talk about a specific time, but I thought he'd be here by now."

"It's okay, sweetie," her mom encouraged. "I'm sure he's on his way. Does he know where to go to get in?"

Lillian hadn't really given much thought to his arrival. She just assumed he would know. She excused herself briefly to go and talk to the guards around the perimeter and inform them of the situation. None of them had seen anyone suspicious walking around the grounds, as they would have informed Sir Alger or the king immediately. But they reassured her they would keep an extra eye out for her visitor.

Another half hour passed when Pierre came in again. "I'm zorry to intrude, Your Majesties, but if we don't begin zee meal zoon, I will not be held responsible for its appearance or taste."

"Understood, Pierre." Snow White turned to her daughter. "Honey, maybe if we just start with the soup. A watched pot never boils. I'm sure he'll show up as soon as the spoons touch our lips."

Lillian reluctantly agreed. She knew she should be hungry as well, but her nerves were on end worrying what could have possibly happened to Alexander. She kept replaying their discussion in her mind, knowing they had said Friday. She was wishing now she had had the forethought to designate a time or maybe even a place to meet.

Both of her parents tried to lighten the mood, but none of them, especially Lillian, could shake the feeling that something was wrong. Pierre poked his head in once again to see about the roast and inform them the soufflé would have to be eaten immediately after.

Lillian couldn't believe or explain what had happened to Alexander. She was about to excuse herself to go out to where they usually met when one of the knights burst through the doors.

"Many apologies for the intrusion, Your Majesties, but this couldn't wait." He stood there for a second, unsure of what to say next.

"Well," the king insisted, "what is it?"

"It's Zands, Your Majesty."

The trio sat upright, giving their full attention.

"He's been captured."

CHAPTER 36: The Game
July 27

ven though it had been five days since Zands' incarceration, tension still lingered in the air. Lillian's tip of him looking like an old lady had paid off. At this point she hadn't even bothered with seeing Laurel. She was more interested in seeing Zands, but her father said it was out of the question. The guards who had captured Zands had become mysteriously ill, and anyone posted to watch him had been found asleep and unable to be wakened. The king was even advised not to interrogate Zands without the aid of some powerful magical wards, which the faeries were working on. In the meantime, he called for another conference in Tapera to discuss recent developments and, against his better judgment, entertain the idea of still holding the Dawning Festival due to his wife's encouragement. She insisted the kingdom and its people needed it right now.

"Harry, we haven't missed a festival in nine years. The people expect it. They need it," the queen pleaded with her husband.

"I said I'll think about it." He was stern. "But what they need is protection."

Lillian could tell this was not a conversation her father wanted to have right now. Even though the guards had captured several dozen Dainian Rogues over the last few days, her father was still on edge. The immediate danger seemed to be in hand, but the coincidence of Zands being caught ten years to the day of Zoldaine's attack was not lost on the king. Lillian had come to wish her father well before he left. He had really been supportive over the last few days, letting her go out any time of day to look for Alexander. He had even sent a couple of men to find Alexander's farm in the south to see if everything was okay.

"Just be careful on your trip, Dad." She gave him a kiss on the cheek but couldn't help teasing him a little about his yearly festival volunteer duty. "You know how eager the citizens get for a chance to dunk their king."

The king looked at both women. "You two will be the death of me someday, you know that. I'll only be gone a few days, and I promise we will discuss the possibility of holding the festival when I get back. But until then, no jester juggling." Both of the ladies laughed a little. "You're going to start planning as soon as I walk out that door, aren't you?" He just shook his head, not needing an answer.

Snow White walked up and gave her husband a kiss. "I love you, sweetheart."

"Mmhm, I love you too. Are you going back out again, Lillian?"

She gave him a look.

"Sorry, of course you're going out. Are you sure you don't want me to send more men with you to help you look?"

"No, Dad, I'm fine. I kind of enjoy the alone time."

"All right, well, come give me a hug because I'll be gone once you get back."

They embraced warmly. "When will you be back?"

"If everything goes well, I should be back in a few days. Hopefully, in time for this festival your mom is throwing with or without me." The king shot a sidelong glance at his wife. She just smiled sweetly back.

333

It had been five days since Zands was captured and five days that Alexander had been missing. There was no sign of him. No markings. No letters. He just disappeared like a marble in a magic trick. Lillian had been out two or three times a day, every day, to look for even a sign that he had been there. Tracks from Winston. Evidence that the Forge had been used. A crumb of thackleberry bread. But there was nothing. And she refused to believe that Alexander was somehow connected to all of this, let alone *be* Zands. However, the little voice in her head, which she was getting quite tired of, kept saying, *But what if?*

Going out today served two purposes: She was going to look for Alexander, but she was also biding time for her father to leave and her mother to get preoccupied with the planning. Lillian knew she wouldn't get a chance to talk to Zands with her father around. Even she had to agree it was risky. But she knew he and anyone else involved didn't want her dead or they would have killed her either time she was captured. And this time, he was the one who was captured.

She figured she would spend a few hours looking for signs of Alexander and practicing in the grove. She had done that a lot over the last several days. It helped her feel closer to him, even though deep down she knew something was wrong. But not just because of her typical intuition. Her new instincts that had been awakened by the gleaming were telling her a similar story. She hadn't felt this magical connection with Alexander until their last night together, but she could sense him now. Alexander was in trouble. She just didn't know where or what to do about it yet.

The little voice chimed in. *"He's in trouble because he's been captured. He's in your father's dungeon right now."*

No! I refuse to believe that. Alexander is not Zands. He's not. Tears formed in her eyes.

She tried to block the voice out with some practice and release some nervous energy. After a couple of rounds, she had worked up a good sweat and figured enough time had passed to head back. The voice was gone, but her nerves grew more anxious with each step back to the castle.

Once back at the castle she got cleaned up and mentally prepared herself for what was to come. Her father was gone, of course, and her mother had already headed into town as expected to talk to the local shops about the festival. Usually the festival required a month of planning, sometimes two if the queen was really involved. Now she had less than two weeks. The queen would be unavailable to say the least.

Lillian knew she couldn't just walk into the dungeon and question Zands. Guards weren't posted directly outside his cell anymore, but there were three different sets stationed just to get to the dungeon. The king even had Laurel moved to the east wing with the other dissenters, making sure Zands didn't affect him or, worse still, communicate some plan of escape. Laurel was more than happy to move, denying his involvement again all the way. The guards had also refashioned a part of the east wing as a hold-all for the Rogues they'd captured. The only person who saw Zands was Grayson, who brought him food, but even Grayson was escorted by two faeries.

The thing about castles was that with each owner, there were new additions and additions forgotten. The most recent owner had let much of the castle become dilapidated. The renovations were coming along but slowly. The area Lillian was in now hadn't been renovated yet. It was an older part of the castle, probably one of the first to be built, so it needed the most attention and was the least used. For that, Lillian was thankful because she didn't have to explain what she was doing to anyone.

She walked along the moss-covered corridor with its quiet drips of water. There were a few passages that veered left or right that lead to various locations in the castle. But the end of the corridor came out behind the castle on the east side. Lillian could only surmise it had been part of some evacuation plan for the castle residents.

She kept walking along, feeling for where the special spot was, hoping it still worked. She hadn't used it in a long time and even back then the magic felt faded. She wasn't sure who had made it or when or why, but she was using it today to get to Zands. A secret passage into the dungeon. It couldn't be opened from the inside alone, so escape was out of the question unless one had an accomplice. There was no handle or out-of-place rock to aid in its discovery. If she had been asked back then, Lillian wouldn't have been able to explain how she found it. If she was asked now, she wouldn't hesitate in giving all credit to the gleaming.

Come on. I know it's around here somewhere.

She slowed down just enough to get a good feeling, or a good gleaming.

There. On the bottom, toward the left of where she was standing. She placed her hand gently on the rock. For a second, she thought she had the wrong rock or that the magic had faded away, but it wasn't long before she felt the familiar warming sensation and the rock started to glow. It was the oddest sensation, since the rock didn't actually get warm, just her hand. She could still feel its cool dampness. Small lines started to work their way from the rock and maneuver around other stones. Slowly, an outline of a jagged door appeared and opened its way toward Lillian. She looked down at her hand, which was still warm but was now a nice purple color. She'd forgotten the small side effect of the door's magic. Apparently, whoever made the passage wanted some type of sign to mark whomever had used it. She smiled, remembering the first time she had found the door. Lillian had worn gloves to dinner, and all the rest of the night, to keep her purple palm hidden until it finally faded away. Thankfully, her parents thought it was just their little princess trying to be proper, wearing her white formal gloves to dinner. And thankfully its magic stain didn't last any longer than a vial of Hair Hue.

The air was stale and dank. There hadn't been much need for the dungeons since the last queen. Sure, the occasional misbehaviors needed correcting, but that was usually handled with a day or two of labor. The king had made a special exception for Zands. Streaks of light filtered in through the window bars of the cells, giving Lillian just enough to see where she was going. Not that she needed it. Whatever force Zands was emitting, hers was pushing against it.

"I was beginning to think I wasn't going to get any visitors. Especially those of royalty." Zands' voice was just how she remembered but darker. "Hello, Princess."

A couple more steps and he came into view. He didn't look like someone who had been in a dungeon for five days. She noticed where plates of food had been stacked up, apparently untouched, but he looked healthy. Dirty but healthy. And his eyes... Lillian looked at them and had the strangest feeling of being very heavy, of wanting to relax and just let the current take her...but something in her mind tugged her back before she fell into the onyx pools. She wanted to ask how he knew she was there before he saw her, but she knew that would make her look weak. She was afraid of him, and he probably already knew that too, but she didn't have to show it.

"You're fairly chipper for someone who's going to see his end soon." It was a bold threat but certainly not an empty one.

"Ah, Your Highness, no need to put yourself down with the trolls. I can understand your hostility, but I assure you, our conversation can be quite civil. You've come to ask me some questions, I believe."

Lillian did her best to hide the effect of his unnerving prophesying.

He's only reading the situation. Of course you're here to ask him questions. Why else would you be here?

"Who are you?" she asked.

"I have many faces, as you've gathered, and go by many names, one just as good as any."

"That's not what I meant."

His arrogant smile made her sick.

"Of course not. I apologize, Your Highness, I *do* like to play games." He gave a small bow of atonement. "Do you know what a magician's true trick is?" He waited for a moment but continued when Lillian didn't answer. "Misdirection," he said proudly. "It was always a gift of mine. Making people focus their attention where I chose. And I never get tired of fooling them. Seeing the surprised, dumbfounded looks on their faces." He paused, his face twisting into a contemptuous sneer. "As I said, I have had many names but currently, I am known as Zands. The form you see before you is my—ah, how should I put it—my truest form. The one I am in the most. I have lived a very long time."

"Are you Zoldaine?"

Zands chuckled. "You flatter me, Highness. I have only a fraction of power the master does. No, I am not Zoldaine. I am merely one of his servants. Granted, more revered than most, but a servant nonetheless."

"Why are you—*is he*—trying to kidnap me? What does he want with me?"

"I wish I could say. My master only gives the orders. He does not indulge me with his motives."

"How is it possible he's still alive? My father and the other kings killed Zoldaine ten years ago. How does he give you your orders?"

"His survival was never in question for his true followers. We only waited for his return. As far as his instructions, that's nothing you need to concern yourself with."

"You haven't seen him, have you? So, you really don't know if it's him?"

Lillian felt the gleam start to tug at her.

Zands said, "One does not need to see something to know it's there. A sensation I gather you are becoming more familiar with. One that has become stronger since you met him."

This time Lillian could not hide her reaction.

How does he know about Alexander? How does he know about our connection? Is Alexander involved with him somehow? Even by accident?

"You are worried about him. He hasn't returned yet."

"What have you done with him? What have you done with Alexander?" she lashed out. She hated herself for revealing he got to her, but he had hit her square in the emotions.

"Calm yourself, Highness. I'd hate for the guards to interrupt our pleasant conversation," he said as if they were taking tea together.

Zands was so collected. He knew he had the upper hand, even being locked up.

I'd like to open this cell door and jab an arrow into that smug mouth.

"My apologies for upsetting you. It was not my intention. Your friend is fine. Although…from what I understand, he has become more than a friend."

"You don't know *anything* about him."

Does he?

"Oh, don't I?"

The way he said it sent chills down Lillian's spine.

"I know he's a brilliant archer. Has a nice set of Calderan steel arrows. Rides a black horse called Winston."

Every fiber in Lillian was trying to deny what he was saying right now.

"Is that supposed to impress me? Anyone could know that."

"But does everyone know his secret recipe for thackleberry bread?" he said airily. "Tapera does have a nice crop of Dewdrop Daisies this time of year."

Lillian's stomach was suddenly filled with lead.

It can't be. It's not possible.

"You're lying."

"Well now, what would I be lying about?"

"You're not him. You're not!"

"Of course not. How could *I* possibly be *Alexander*?" His name dripped off Zands' tongue. "For only *he* would know about the Forge. About how you didn't get any fish your first try, or the swimming hole and diving off the rocks together. The strange scar over his chest." He paused, looking straight at her. "About how good it felt to hold you the night you snuck out..." He let the words hang between them, a cruel smirk cracking across his face. "What is it they say, 'things only a mother would know?'" He raised a brow. "Or in this case...things only *I* would know."

Lillian simply tried to keep breathing. "I don't believe you." She tried to hold on to what she'd felt about Alexander. His goodness...

"I know, I know. Seeing is believing. I would show you, of course, but they took my ring. It does as well as a necklace, I've found. Glows nicely in the moonlight. Red always did look better on me than purple..." Zands let the last thought trail off as he looked directly at Lillian.

Lillian's resolve was being tested to its limit. He was lying. She knew he was. She hoped he was.

He has to be.

"But then how does he know all those things?"

The voice of reason beckoned again.

I don't know, but he is.

"Zands wasn't there. It was just you and Alexander."

Stop it. He's not Alexander.

"Then how do you explain why Alexander disappears the very night Zands is captured?"

I can't. But I know my Alexander, and this monster is not him.

She shoved the doubt away.

She would sort through the specifics later, but she could not have this internal battle in front of Zands. Lillian had to change the subject or she wouldn't be able to continue. "So, why would your almighty master allow one of his 'revered' servants to be captured?"

"Have you ever played chess, Your Highness?"

"I'm familiar with the game."

"Good. It will make this simpler. In the game of chess, the most important piece is the king. Some would argue it's the queen, but the game is only won when the king is captured. My favorite was always the pawn. Inconspicuously making its way into enemy territory to save one of its comrades…" Zands trailed off as if thinking of a particular time he had used this tactic, then quickly continued. "Now, there are of course other pieces. Knights. Bishops, rooks, and so forth. Sometimes certain pieces need to be sacrificed in order to protect the king. It's unfortunate but that's the game."

"So, you're saying you're some knight in a game that had to be sacrificed?"

"I didn't have to be, but regrettably for me, that's how the game has played out. And I gladly accept my role to protect my king."

As morbid as his explanation sounded, it made sense to Lillian. She knew her father's men and the other king's men had fallen in their battle with Zoldaine. They sacrificed themselves for their king.

"So, why now? Why is your master playing the game now?"

Zands' shrewd eyes bored into hers as he arrogantly sauntered up to the bars, his hands folded in front. "Why, the answer is simple, dear Princess. The only reason one plays against someone who has beat them before is vengeance." He leaned forward. "Vengeance, and the resolute knowledge you can beat them."

CHAPTER 37: Preparations
August 7

itful sleep was all Lillian had for the past week. Nightmares of Zands turning into Alexander, her father being murdered by a shadowy figure, Rogues rushing into her room and taking her. She was exhausted. What made matters worse is the scouts the king had sent to find Alexander's farm had come back empty-handed. They found a farm, but no one was there. It looked recently abandoned. With each passing day that Alexander didn't show up, her doubting voice grew stronger.

"You know where he is. You saw him the other day."

She fought back each time, but it got harder and harder to disbelieve. She didn't eat and couldn't sleep. She was just hollow. Lillian had started to slip into a mild depression, which had prompted the queen's interference. Her mom had recruited her to help with the festival preparations.

"Lillian, sweetie, have you heard from Talula yet? She was supposed to give us her menu listing to go on the flyer." Snow White was sifting through a pile of papers, getting them organized. The queen glanced over at her daughter.

Lillian was gazing out the window. Zands' words had haunted her every day. *Vengeance, and the resolute knowledge you can beat them. Resolute knowledge you can beat them.* She thought they'd have gone away once her father had come back a couple of days ago, but they didn't.

Officially, the threat was over now that Zands had been captured. Her dad had come back from his meeting in Tapera, and all kingdoms were reporting back the same thing. Since Zands' capture, factions of Rogues had been captured all over as well. Zands was seemingly the head of the snake. And from the king's last meeting, Lillian's information about his other forms were evidenced in Tapera and Caldera. A middle-aged woman and an ancient old man, both seen with a purple cloth of some sort and a magic ring. Each had been under observation but were very elusive—and neither had been seen for over a week. Whatever he and his "master" were planning had fallen apart. But Lillian could not get Zands' arrogant face out of her mind.

"Lillian, honey?"

"Huh? Sorry, Mom, what did you need?"

"Talula's menu. Has she sent it yet?"

"Yeah, I saw it over here on the other table."

The queen watched her daughter slowly walk over to the table and bring her the menu. She could tell being cooped up in the castle was not helping. "Sweetie, why don't you head into the village and see how things are coming with Jafria? It would do you some good to get some fresh air."

"Are you sure, Mom? It's really okay. You can't do all this alone."

"I'm fine, sweetie. I've got my own system going here. Plus, if I need anything, I'll drag your brother down here."

Lillian hugged her mom. "Thanks, Mom. I'm really sorry I'm not in better spirits right now, I just…" Tears shone in Lillian's eyes.

The queen held her daughter. "Oh, Lillian, it's okay."

"I just don't understand, Mom. Where could he be? This isn't like him. Something is wrong, I know it," she cried as tears poured down her cheeks.

Preparations

"Shhh, it's going to be okay, Lillian. He's going to be okay. Look, I know you and your father share this feeling thing about situations and people. You can tell when things are off. But usually that's the short term. The immediate. Your mother, however, has a gift too. Mine isn't as precise, but I do get feelings. More about the general—and I have a *good feeling* about your friend. About Alexander. I believe you that something is amiss right now, but eventually everything *will* work out. *I know it*." She wiped the tears from her daughter's face and kissed her on the cheek.

"Thanks, Mom. So much." Lillian wasn't sure if her mom was telling the truth or not, but she appreciated what she was trying to do. And surprisingly, it did make her feel better.

The fresh air and high spirits of the village took the edge off her pain. Lillian couldn't remember a time the town looked busier. She wasn't sure if it was because of the ten-year anniversary, or because the mood had been so dampened by the recent events, but everyone was smiling and bustling hurriedly to get things ready in three days. Most of the traffic was gathered around the hub of Falloren Fountain. There were carts funneling in from every direction carrying various supplies of food, building materials, and barrels. Most were heading out of the village to the south field where the festival would be held. Adults were barking at children to get out of the way, while kids were celebrating early with Dragon Poppers and Zipping Lizards, which were giving the horses fits. Eventually, the kids were shooed away to cause havoc elsewhere. To the left, Lillian could see the artists gathering their various paintings and sculptures to peddle alongside the designers, with their newest fashions.

To the right, she could smell the samples of delicacies baking to tempt passersby into purchasing some to take home.

The commotion didn't die down as she headed toward the field to find Jafria. There were makeshift stands springing up all around, as well as official game areas being roped off. Children scurried toward the field, hoping to get an early glimpse of what was to come. Several men were carting down blue barrels of water to set next to stands for emergency use, a practice implemented after the second festival when one of Galen's smokers got knocked over. It was quite by accident, and no one was hurt. But the fallen smoker did manage to take out half the kiosks and set off Grayson's finale a little early. Lillian was so engrossed with what she saw that she didn't see a person hurrying back into the village and bumped into him.

"Oh, I'm so sorry, I didn't see...Doc!" No matter what mood she was in, Doc always put a smile on her face.

"Oh my goodness, Your 'ighness, my utmost apologies. I should've watched where I was going. We've been in such a rush to get the rides together. I brought the wrong gears for the Wind Spinner."

The dwarves were always in charge of the amusements. They usually were able to put together four or five attractions with enough preparation, but with such short notice, they were hustling to get three. The Wind Spinner must be their newest contraption because Lillian didn't remember that one. They always tried to bring back the favorites and then some crazy new way to thrill people. Last year, it was the Flip-Up. A tiny, yet effective mechanism that rocked the passengers back and forth until eventually it did a full flip.

"Wind Spinner? Is that your latest creation, Doc?"

"My design, but Erwyn inspired it. 'E was out spinning himself silly one day, and I thought it might make for a good time. So, we got these small platforms people will strap onto to 'old them in place while it spins them around. We only got to test it out once. It should be interesting. It's the width of a goblin whisker, though, between makin' them dizzy and makin' them sick." Doc grimaced.

"Well, good luck with that. Let me know when you work out the kinks, and I might try it."

"Aye, Princess, now if you'll excuse me, I better get going or I'll get a tongue lashing from Byme."

And with that, the old dwarf hobbled off back into the village to their shop.

The path had a small slope down to the field. Lillian took advantage of the height difference to scout out where Jafria was setting up. She found her friend's area easily and headed that direction.

Along the way, she stopped and talked to a few friendly faces who were setting up. Galen had brought down one of his smokers. Talula was there too. Madame LeMarc stopped her briefly to pass along a message to Pierre that this year was her year for the pastry contest.

As Lillian made her way to the arts and fashion section, Jafria was doing what she did best, taking charge. "No, no, not over there, here. The stairs go over here." Jafria walked over and pointed to make sure she was clear.

"So, how's it going?" Lillian glanced over the stage Jafria was having built for her fashion show.

"Lillian! How are you doing?" Jafria grabbed her friend in a tight embrace. "Well, it's actually going pretty good. Gwen, Carissa, Sophie, and Lizzy are all back at my place figuring out what outfits they're going to wear. That's probably where the most chaos is right now." She laughed. "But as long as they don't tear any of my clothes, I don't care who wears what. That's the beauty of my new line. It's flattering to any size or shape."

"I can't wait to see it, Jafria. It's really exciting. Hey, can I talk to you for a second?"

Jafria could see the concerned look in her friend's eyes. "Sure, sweetie, let's go over here." The two walked back behind the stage, where they were relatively alone. "What's got you bothered?"

"I talked to Zands."

"You *what*?"

"I said I talked…"

"I heard what you said. Have you gone completely over the wall? Well, are you okay? Is that why you've been so off lately? *What* were you thinking?"

"Bring your voice down," Lillian hissed. "I'm fine. And no, I have not gone over the wall. I just had to talk to him. I needed to know."

"Okay, look, I'm sorry. I get it. I'm sure I would have done the same thing. So, what'd he say?"

Lillian gave her friend the abridged version but couldn't begin to convey the sensation she felt being around him. She shared what Zands knew of her and Alexander, the details of the unique gems, and the information that Zands divulged. Everything. When she finished, Jafria just stood there. "Well?"

"Wow, girl, I…" Jafria, for once, was speechless.

"Well? What about," Lillian hated to say it, "what about Zands being Alexander? Do you think it's possible?"

"Lillian, I don't know." Jafria saw the dread cross Lillian's face. "But there's no way, right? It's just coincidence. It *has* to be." Jafria thought for a moment. "I'm sorry, Lil', I wish I could be more help."

A worker called out, needing Jafria's attention for a display.

"Look. I'll let you get back to this. Thanks for listening. I'll let you know if I find out anything else."

"Anytime, Lillian. You know I'm always here for you."

Lillian headed back to the castle but used the path to the west, around the village. It was relatively deserted except for a lone cart coming her way about halfway down the road, being pulled by a huge silhouette. It stopped for a minute but then continued her direction. Whatever it was, it was big and covered. As it got closer, she realized it was Moose pulling the cart, being led by an even more familiar face.

"Seth! What are you doing over here?" Lillian picked up her pace.

"Hey, Lillian, I was wondering who that was. I was about to turn back but worried that would raise more suspicion. I'm glad it's you since you kind of already know about it."

"Oh, is that the secret you were working on for Grayson?"

"Yes, ma'am. I'm just glad Zands was caught, because otherwise it would have been a complete waste of a month's time. It's so incredible. I can't wait to show it off. I just hope it works; there are a lot of mechanics involved. But it will be the most amazing grand finale ever. It will blow people away." Seth's eyes widened in excitement. "And good thing you brought this beastie in," he patted Moose, "otherwise, I'm not sure how I would have gotten this thing down there. It's mostly metal."

At that moment, a huge gust blew the tarp off from a where a rope was loose, revealing a corner of Seth's grand invention. Lillian only caught a brief glimpse of several metal tubes of different sizes angled up in different boxes before Seth quickly gathered up the tarp and tied it back down.

"It's okay, Seth. I'm not going to tell anyone. You're right, it looks impressive."

He finished the knot. "Well, that's the plan. A big impact for the big anniversary festival. Thanks for your discretion, Lillian. Grayson really wants to surprise everybody. He's never attempted something like this before."

"Sure, Seth, but may I be so bold to take a guess that it has something to do with his crackling stars?" Seth pursed his lips. "I'll take *that* as a yes. Well, I can't wait to see what you and he have put together. Careful getting it down there. It's pretty busy."

"Thanks, Lil', I'll see you later." Seth flicked Moose's reins and started back down to the field.

Lillian watched him descend. When the tarp blew up earlier, she had had a moment of déjà vu. She knew she couldn't have seen it before because he had just finished it, but she just couldn't shake this feeling. It reminded her of something she had seen recently, but she couldn't pluck the memory from her mind.

Lillian slumbered fitfully again that night. Eventually, she got up and wandered to the kitchen to get a glass of milk and a piece of bread to help settle her stomach. Her knife was poised over the loaf when she felt the thrumming sensation of Alexander. He was back. He was at their rock. Doubts and worries of the past weeks were tossed aside as she sprinted off.

She was outside in no time. Her gleam allowed her to move swiftly, growing stronger as she cleared the castle. There was not a pinprick of light in the sky. She flew to their spot so fast that she seemed to have skipped sections of the path. She ran even faster still once she saw Alexander's silhouette sitting on a rock.

"*Alexander!*" She hurtled toward him.

He stood up just in time to receive Lillian as she threw her arms around him, nearly knocking him to the ground.

"Oof! Oh, I'm glad to see you too. I was hoping our connection here was strong enough for you to find me."

She stood back to take him all in. "Where have you been? I've had the entire *kingdom* looking for you. Guards went to your farm, but they said it was abandoned."

"I know, I'm sorry. There was nothing I could do. I barely got my mother to safety before they came for me."

"*Came* for you? Alexander, what are you talking…" She realized something peculiar. "Alexander, where's your necklace?"

"They took it. Look, Lillian, we don't have much time. Any minute your brother is going to wake you up and I have something important to tell you."

"Wake me up? Alexander, I don't understand." She started backing away from him, leery this was another of Zands' tricks.

"Please Lillian, you have to listen. You *need* to talk to Sir Laurel. It's important."

"Laurel? Alexander, he's been captured. So has Zands. Everything's fine now, you can…"

Alexander grew impatient. "Lillian, you're not listening to me. I'm not really here. Neither are you. This is a dream—of sorts. I'm focusing all I can to keep you here, but you have to listen."

"A dream? That's impossible. I ran all the way from the…" She almost fainted as she turned around. The castle was gone. So was most of the landscape. Her knees became weak beneath her, and Alexander caught her.

He turned her to look directly in her eyes. "Lillian, you have to talk to Sir Laurel. When you wake up, you have to remember that. Talk to Laurel."

Suddenly there was a foggy knock coming from all around. "Alexander, what is that? I'm scared." She was floating back toward the nonexistent castle. "*Alexander! Wait!*" She reached her arms out in desperation, but she was being pulled backward as if caught in a current.

Alexander was running after her. "Don't forget, Lillian. Talk to Laurel!"

Knock, knock, knock.

She was flying back faster now, losing sight of Alexander but his voice still trailed after her in an echo. "Talk to Laaaaauuurrel!"

Knock, knooooo. . .

. . .ooock, knock.

"Lillian, Mom needs you in the kitchen." Andrew was outside her door. "Lillian, are you awake?"

Lillian found herself in her bed.

But I was just outside…wasn't I?

The dream she was having, like most dreams, was quickly slipping away.

*I was with someone…*Alexander! *He was here!*

Lillian jumped out of bed, dashing to the window, and looked out toward their rock. But there was no *A*.

It was a dream. He had said that. That and something else…

"Lillian, are you in there?" Andrew beckoned again.

"Uh, yeah, Andrew, I'll be down in a minute." Lillian sat down. The more she thought about her dream, the more she forgot. Andrew's final interruption had muddled her memories of the dream. Whatever Alexander had imparted to her was lost for now. She just hoped it wasn't that important.

CHAPTER 38: Betrayal
August 8

nce the day of the festival had arrived, the castle was incredibly quiet. Most of the servants had the day off to enjoy the festivities. Lillian had decided to stay behind for a while just in case Alexander should show up, but she promised her parents she wouldn't stay all day. Jafria's show was around dusk, and she couldn't miss that.

It was rather nice having the castle to herself. Well, there was one person she would have liked to have shared it with. It had been over two weeks since she'd seen Alexander. If she didn't have evidence to prove it, she wouldn't even be sure he'd ever existed. She knew Zands had to be involved. She *knew* he was lying. Since her conversation with Zands, she had been focusing her gleam on Alexander. And she'd finally decided that although she still didn't know where he was, she could feel he wasn't in the dungeon. Actually, when she gleamed, she felt the opposite coming from the dungeon, much like she had felt when she'd approached Zands that day, as if an invisible force was pushing back at her. She felt the same sensation now, fighting against her search for Alexander. She found, however, that holding the arrows he had made her helped. They were the only tangible connection she had to him.

But before she knew it, it was time for her to get ready. Not that she thought Alexander would really appear, but her heart was still heavy at his absence.

The evening would be warm but would chill quickly once the sun set. So, Lillian chose a pale-blue linen dress and topped it with a thin jacket of sapphire satin. And while, as the princess, her clothes would always be of exceptional quality, she hated to be ostentatious when mixing directly with her subjects. She had always followed her parents' penchant for trying to appear approachable rather than pompous. She didn't even bother with her better shoes. She just wanted her comfortable boots for trekking over grassy terrain. She was on her way out when she saw a servant carrying a tray of food toward the east wing. She thought it was odd at first since the castle was empty, but then realized the food was for the guards posted there. The unfortunates who drew the short straws had to stay back to keep an eye on the Rogues who had recently been rounded up. About a dozen servants and even another knight had failed the faeries' spell. Some of them had tried to deny the accusation; others had shouted their loyalty to Zoldaine, perhaps believing he might reach down and save them himself.

Their deceitful faces passed through Lillian's mind. Several she had had dealings with nearly on a daily basis. The thought of them being so close to her for so long made her shudder. Even the king hadn't realized their underlying deception, and two of them were knights sworn to protect his life. Both, of course, had been stripped of their titles. Laurel and...

Sir Laurel!

Lillian's dream from last night came crashing back into her mind. *"Talk to Sir Laurel."* Alexander's last words to her. *"Don't forget, Lillian. Talk to Sir Laurel."*

Oh! Oh, no!

She had never gotten around to talking to him. She hadn't seen the point. Whether it had been Laurel or someone else who had left the letters, he had been incriminated on other charges. And she had reached her fill of anyone with malicious intent toward her, after talking with Zands.

But now she had a different reason for talking to Laurel. Somehow, he was the key to finding Alexander. She whirled around and headed for the east wing.

"Good evening, Your Highness. How can we help you?" a stocky guard asked her.

"I need to speak to Laurel." Lillian was straightforward.

A thinner guard inquired, "Right now, Your Highness? But the festival is…"

She cut him off. "The festival can wait. I need to speak with him *now*." She put all the authority she had into her statement. She had no time to wait for dallying.

"I'll fetch him right away, my lady," the stockier one said. He had no intention of keeping her waiting. "Will you be using the inquiry chamber?"

"Yes, thank you."

Lillian crossed the hall to a small chamber that was once probably quite cozy but had lately become a makeshift interrogation room for the Dainian cohorts who had been captured. A few minor changes had been made to suit its needs, such as iron rings and some manacles set into the floor, and it suited its purpose for the king or anyone else who might have questions. Right now, Lillian only had one, and she hoped it was enough for whatever the gleam wanted her to know.

The door opened and the guard walked in with Laurel cuffed in manacles on his wrists and ankles. It had been just shy of three weeks since Laurel had been locked up, but he looked like he hadn't seen a day of civilization in his life. A simple brown outfit had replaced his usual knightly garb. His once-luxurious hair was matted and dull. Lillian couldn't tell the difference between his stubble and the dirt that clung to his face. He shuffled in, barely glancing up as the guard sat him in the chair across from Lillian and secured his shackles to the floor.

"Thank you," Lillian addressed the guard. Her voice prompted Laurel to look up. "You may leave us now."

"We'll be just outside should you need anything, Your Highness." The guard eyed Laurel before leaving but saw no need for concern from the disheveled ex-knight.

"Hello, Laurel. How are you?" She tried not to sound patronizing.

His usual disposition came across in his voice. "Princess, as you can see, I'm the belle of the ball." He smoothed a dirty lock of his hair back from his face, chains clinking against his manacles. "Why aren't you at the festival? Needed to make yourself feel good, eh? Make sure I was still locked up so I couldn't hurt anyone?"

She could tell he was going to be unpleasant, so she got right to the point. "Was it you who left the notes for me?"

Laurel stared at her with confused disdain. "Is that another accusation? Doesn't your father have enough lies on me already?" Laurel spat.

Lillian understood why he was angry. Even if he was guilty, he had been stripped of his lavish lifestyle and his customary glass—or five—of wine. But she *was* the princess, and approachable or not, she demanded a certain amount of respect from subjects and certainly from prisoners. Niceties were over.

"I am not here to quibble with you about what you did or didn't do, according to my father. I am here to find out something for myself. And *if* you cooperate, I might be compelled to talk to my father on your behalf."

Laurel looked at the princess and apparently determined he had nothing left to lose.

"All right. What was it you wanted to know?"

"The notes. Did you leave them?"

"I'm sorry, Princess, but I've found that in my current sober state, I'm having trouble recalling some details, so if you could be a tad more specific."

"A little over a month ago, Andrew brought me a letter from someone who knew about my kidnapping. There was a second note left during the dinner party that told me who to look for. We had no idea who left either one, but Seth saw you walking from the stables during the party. The letters ultimately led to the discovery of a rogue Dainian faction in the kingdom that you have now been associated with." Lillian paused to make sure it all sank in. "*Those* notes. Did you leave them?"

She definitely had Laurel's attention. "Where did Andrew get the first note?" he asked.

"What do you mean?"

"I mean where did he get it? Did he find it? Did someone give it to him?" Laurel was getting agitated.

"Seth found it in the stables when he had stepped out for a minute, and he gave it to Andrew. Same as the second note, but Seth happened to see you coming from that direction of the stables that time."

Laurel just shook his head, oblivious to Lillian's underlying allegation. "I knew it," he snarled.

"I'm sorry?" Lillian didn't follow.

Laurel tore into explanation, his animated gestures causing his chains to jangle wildly. "I wasn't sure at first— all I knew was something strange was going on in the stables. I didn't think much of it at first because I don't know when deliveries are made—*but*—I *did* think it was rather odd for one to come in the middle of the night. And then, when I saw the second one, I just got a feeling that something wasn't right. And I was *right*! I still don't know who it is, but *they* have to be the ones who put those plans in my quarters. I need to talk to your father *right* now." Laurel tried to get up, but the chains jerked him back down.

Lillian jumped up and backed away. "Whoa! *Whoa!* Slow down, Laurel. You need to calm yourself. You're not making any sense. Just stay seated and go over everything with me slowly, and I might get my father."

Laurel was shaking with frustration but took a couple of breaths. "Sorry, Your Highness, I didn't mean to startle you."

He wasted no time, which Lillian was grateful for.

"You see, a few months ago, I was returning from," he hesitated and looked embarrassed, "from being out. It was late. Maybe three in the morning? I was coming in from the west side when I saw a cart roll up. All the torches were out, but the moon was full, thank the Fae, so I could still make out shadows. Someone came out of the stables, the silhouette was short and tiny, and it appeared to have a ponytail, so I'm assuming it was a girl. Anyway, she guided them in and they started unloading these crates and kegs. I didn't think much of it at the time, but something just didn't sit well."

I'd bet a dragon's horde the girl was Hayden—if he's telling the truth.

"And I'm sure you were sober when you witnessed all of this?" Lillian's disdain was thick.

Laurel looked hurt by the jab but shook his head as though he understood. "Your Highness, I won't deny I've acted shamefully in your father's service. He did me a great honor in taking a chance on a potential enemy, and I have squandered it. I resent my actions. And not just because of my current situation. This has merely served to give me time to reflect upon my disgrace without distraction. As for my frivolous and indecent conduct, I am sorry. But I swear to you—I am telling the truth now."

Lillian could see the contriteness and sincerity in the man's eyes before her. She could honestly say she felt like she was finally looking at Laurel's true self. "Continue."

"Wait. You, you believe me?" Laurel was taken aback.

"I haven't decided yet."

"Oh." Laurel quickly resumed. "Well, I was curious, so I went back a couple more nights before leaving for the tournament in Tapera to see if there were any other late-night deliveries and there were. Again, it was close to three in the morning, a cart pulled up, same girlish figure came out, and they unloaded more of the same. Crates and kegs."

"Who brought the delivery?"

"The first was by a tall, skinny guy. Quick attitude. I didn't know it at the time, but I'm almost sure it was the guy involved in your kidnapping."

Daxon.

"The second was someone different. I didn't get a good look at him because I think he knew I was there."

"So, when Seth saw you coming back from the stables during the dinner party…"

"I was looking for what the shipment was. I figured everyone would be preoccupied with the party, including him."

Well, he was busy getting ready for me, but you don't need to know that.

Laurel continued. "I told a couple other guards to keep a close eye on the stables while I was gone to let me know if anything was moved from there or any more shipments came in. They never saw anything suspicious, which told me whatever those crates and kegs were, still had to be there. Once I got back, I continued to watch for shipments and when I thought it was safe, I searched around for the previous deliveries."

Lillian had to give Laurel credit. He was more intuitive than he looked or certainly acted.

"So, what did you find?"

Laurel slammed his fists against his thighs in frustration. "Nothing! I looked all over. I checked every stall, every bin, every stack of hay, and there wasn't a single crate or keg."

"But why didn't you go to Sir Alger or my father about all this?"

"Because I knew how this would sound, especially coming from me. They would have dismissed me then, and now that I've been affiliated with the Rogues, they definitely would. I need evidence. And unfortunately, whoever she, or they, were, must have seen me the night of the second shipment and set me up. But who's everyone going to believe? Their own eyes? Or a washed-up charity-case knight who no one's ever seen sober?" His voice trailed off, croaking with emotion. His head bowed.

Lillian could see his logic.

Laurel lifted his head and looked at her squarely. "They put those plans in my room. I hadn't ever seen them before. I *swear*."

"Then why didn't you pass the faeries' spell?"

Lillian had asked the one question he didn't have an answer to. His face became bleak and pained. "I don't know," he said softly.

"You realize you still haven't given me anything to go on. As you said, all you have is your word, which isn't worth much currently, against a substantial amount of evidence, both physical and magical." Lillian was slowly beginning to think this conversation was a waste of time, though she wasn't ready to write him off yet. The gleam left her feeling as if it was not done weaving connections Lillian wasn't aware of yet.

"What was on the plans?"

Laurel thought for a moment. "I'm not really sure, just a bunch of sketches of something, but I couldn't tell what."

"Could you draw it?"

Laurel laughed. "In my sleep. They kept pushing them in my face during their interrogation, asking me what they were and what they were for."

Lillian grabbed a piece of parchment and pencil from the nearby desk. "Here."

Laurel took the pencil and positioned his awkward manacles and set to work on the parchment. After a moment, he slid it back over to her. "I'm not an artist, but that's pretty close to what it was."

Laurel was right. It was a rough drawing, but it was enough. Her body went numb. Her vision blurred as flashes of memory came flooding back to Lillian. The sketch in front of her took her back to the caves a month ago. She was being rushed out of a burning cavern and only caught a glimpse, but this is what she had seen on the table as Preston pulled her from the room—a machine of some kind. Lillian's blood ran cold.

It was Seth's machine. That's why the glimpse earlier had seemed to stir something in her memory.

But there was something else you saw. Another paper next to it.

Laurel's voice was far off, barely registering in the fog Lillian was in. "Princess? Princess? *Lillian*, are you okay?"

She was trying desperately to hold on to the memory, but Laurel kept bringing her back to the present.

She lost it, angry he had disrupted her.

"What was in them?" she demanded.

"Sorry, what?"

"The kegs and crates, Laurel! What was in them? What did they look like?"

"I'm not sure what was in the crates. But the kegs, they're what concerned me more. They had the red skull painted on them." He paused, contemplating whether or not to make his next statement. "Since it was all happening in the stables, just for a brief moment, I thought Seth might be involved somehow."

Lillian raised her eyebrow skeptically.

"I know, I know, it was foolish. I've known Seth since before the liberation. His family was very influential in Drod, but even I couldn't believe he would be involved with whatever was going on. He and I have conversed several times about how much better life is here. He enjoyed working with his hands. He talked about how blessed he was to have such a loving adoptive family. But I did ask him if he knew anything about the shipments. He didn't, of course. He said he was going to have some delivered closer to the Dawning Festival, if we were having one, though, but it would only be a couple of kegs, three at most, because he and Grayson were working on a really special show for the ten-year anniversary. I told him to keep a lookout for anything suspicious. I talked to him the night before they arrested me, and he hadn't seen anything."

Lillian felt like she had just taken a turn on Doc's new ride, her thoughts spinning so fast she felt a little sick.

Seth doesn't know the Rogues have his plans for the machine. And he's all but given it to them on a silver platter, with a side of black powder included! They're going to steal it for something, but what? Could these other shipments of kegs be used with it somehow?

Something else was still nagging at Lillian though. "Why, then, is it that only *you* saw the shipments come in and not any of the guards?"

Laurel got wide-eyed, like she had just helped him prove his point. "I *thought* about that, because I was also wondering if maybe that's how they were hiding the crates and kegs. So, I talked to Switwick about concealment spells. He said for stationary items, if you knew where to look and got close enough, you would eventually see them, and I searched every inch and never saw anything. But for something that's moving, it's trickier. He said, depending on the spell, they could affect a variety of distances. I figure for this one, I must have been out of the spell's range, but it obscured the cart and people for anyone closer in the castle."

"Well, that's convenient." Lillian realized how spiteful she sounded and regretted it.

"I don't find it very convenient at all, Princess."

"I'm sorry, Laurel, I didn't mean…"

"It's okay. Trust me, I've been running this through in my head for the last three weeks. I know how it sounds *to me*. I can only imagine what you think." Laurel's eyes suddenly began to tear. "I do care for this kingdom and its people, Your Highness. I won't lie, it hurt at how quickly I was cast aside and labeled a traitor, but most of it is my fault, I admit. If I am exonerated, I promise to bring honor to my family name and make your father proud."

Lillian wanted so desperately to believe him, but all he had given her was a good story. "Laurel," she said seriously, "is there anything, *anything* else at all you can tell me that might be of help."

"Perhaps. I never got a chance to tell your dad or Sir Alger what worried me the most." Laurel shook his head in uneasiness. "I've seen how much powder Grayson uses for his shows before, and at *best*, it's one to two kegs. The dwarves only go through three kegs a day if they're doing solid blasting. But from those two shipments alone, I counted forty kegs. Forty. That's why I went looking for them. I couldn't conceive of anything they could be doing with that much powder, and I'm not sure if that was even all of it. There's no telling how many more shipments came before or after."

Lillian knew there were about half as many kegs in the caves. When they had exploded, the damage was devastating. Dragon's Wrath was nothing more than charred remains now—and it was on the *other* side of the portal.

Suddenly her mind flashed back to the caves again. This time she would not let go.

I saw it. I saw the parchment of the machine, but what was the other one?

The gleam was helping her. She replayed the scene in her head.

She was running out of the cavern, Preston was pulling her, she glanced down at the table and saw...

There!

As soon as the parchments came into view, the movement in her vision slowed to a crawl, just like when she was in the grove.

I can do this. Focus.

She saw the machine sketches next to another paper with drawings that looked like a map. *But a map of what?*

Lillian dug deeper, her haze lifting. The lines and colors becoming crisp. The diagram wasn't the map of the tunnels they had found in Laurel's chambers, but a map of the village. A map with a number of red skulls placed evenly about the buildings.

No. Oh, no. No, no. NO!

Lillian snapped back to the present like the crack of a whip. "Guards!" Lillian yelled. She was done with Laurel and was up and heading out before two guards entered the room. "Take Laurel back."

"What? But, wait! What about everything I've told you?" Laurel was confused and offended.

She didn't answer him. She couldn't. Too many things were running through her head as she barreled headlong down the corridor to get to the nearest tower.

Please, Fae, please let me be wrong.

She tried to hold back her tears, afraid if she cried, it would somehow make the horror real.

Don't let it be true.

Betrayal

Yet as much as she wanted to deny everything she had just heard, the pieces in her mind were clicking together, creating a frightening conclusion. Somehow, whether it was the part of her father, the gleam, or Alexander's urgency from her dream, she knew. She knew Laurel was telling the truth, and that's what scared Lillian the most. If she was right, the kingdom, *her* kingdom, was in grave danger. She ran even faster.

I just pray it's not too late.

The only memory she had knowledge about, that Laurel didn't mention, was the map of the village she'd recently recalled from the caves. No one had mentioned that map, which meant no one had *seen* that map.

She needed to see the village from above. She reached the northeast tower and bolted up the stairs, taking two at a time, to get higher ground.

Please don't let me be right. Please don't let me be right. Please don't let me be right.

She made it three stories up and dashed out onto the connecting wall. Dusk had just started to settle, but Lillian still had just enough light. She could hear the merriment of the festival carried along on the wind as she scrutinized the village. Then suddenly the world dropped away and sounds muted like she'd just been caught in a secret sphere. She had to lean against the wall to keep herself from falling as her legs buckled.

Though the festival was taking place at the field outside of town, most of its tenants had still decorated facades of their buildings. However, one "decoration" was not part of the festivities.

Adorning nearly a quarter of the rooftops were groupings of kegs—all bearing a red skull.

CHAPTER 39: End Game

ood times were being had by all as the festival was in full swing. No one the wiser of the peril their village was in. The crowd was thick but not so much that Lillian had to be rude to make her way through. She was focused on finding just a few individuals. Her father, Sir Alger, Henry, and Seth. Anyone else she wasn't convinced she could trust.

I can't believe this is happening.

Lillian felt like she was caught in a nightmare. She was in a familiar place, but it wasn't the same. She knew the people but didn't recognize the faces.

Am I really warning my father that the village is about to explode? But how? There aren't enough Rogues to set off all those kegs. They're all locked up in the castle.

She didn't think it was possible for her life to get turned upside down any more than it already was. Maybe she was naïve, but for a while, she had thought her life was getting back to normal. Just a few short weeks ago, she had looked forward to Alexander meeting her parents so he didn't have to hide. She'd been hoping to go to the festival together. She imagined he'd never seen half of the food, the outfits, the games, and especially the rides. She wanted to watch his overcast eyes sparkle as the wonders of the festival whirled around him.

Alexander, where are you? I really need you right now.

Screams in the distance brought Lillian back from her daydream. For a moment, she thought she was too late, but quickly realized it was just Doc's Wind Spinner delighting, thrilling, and scaring several riders.

Guess they worked out the kinks.

Lillian stopped for a moment to think. She couldn't just walk around hoping to find them.

Okay, where would Dad be right now?

She was running through his various vices of food and entertainment when a large cheer came up from a crowd of people.

Jafria's fashion show, of course!

Lillian headed toward the colored orbs of light decorating Jafria's stage, scanning the crowd along the way. Seth was probably out with the machine, so there was no point in looking for him.

Fae, protect him from the Rogues.

Her dad and Sir Alger were tall, which helped, but they weren't the only tall ones in tonight's crowd. *Please, Fae, I need you. I have to find someone now.*

Apparently the Fae were listening.

"Lillian! I was wondering when you'd get down here." Seth came up to hug her. "Your parents said you were still up at the castle."

She welcomed the embrace to tether her back to humanity and hope. "Oh, Seth, I'm so glad you're okay."

Seth stepped back, giving her a quizzical look. "Of course I'm okay. Why wouldn't I be?"

"No, no reason. Just a bad dream I had last night." Lillian felt like she should tell him about what Laurel said, but she didn't want to worry him before his machine's big debut.

But will there be a big debut? What if the Rogues have it already?

She needed him to take her to the machine without alerting him. "Hey, Seth, where is the big show going to come from?"

"Funny you should ask because I was actually coming to find you. I need your help with something. One of the gears came loose yesterday on the ride down. I need someone to hold a lever up while I slip it back into place. It's not hard, but you and Grayson are the only ones who know about it."

Oh, thank the Fae.

"Sure I'll help. But we better hurry."

Before it's too late.

"If I miss Jafria's show, she'll make me wear the Clencher for a year."

"Wear the what?"

"Nothing. Come on, let's go."

Seth led her through the crowd and between a couple of art stands. The last sliver of sun had disappeared beneath the horizon. Lillian could barely make out the silhouette of the machine, which was set up two hundred paces away from the rest of the festivities. The air was pleasantly warm, yet an abrupt chill ran through Lillian's body.

We're not alone. Someone else is out here with us.

Lillian quickened her pace.

"So, how exactly does this thing work anyhow?"

Seth squinted his eyes and pursed his lips. "Well, I guess there's no harm in telling you now since you'll be seeing it soon." He thought for a second. "Basically, you put the payload of crackling stars into the pipes, adjust the gears to where you want them to shoot, start the timer for the fuses, and enjoy the show."

"Sounds fairly simple."

"Ha! Well, yeah, it is now, but believe me, it wasn't simple to make. I'll show you the workings when we get there. I've been dying to brag about it anyhow. When I finally revealed it to Grayson, he simply stroked his beard and said, 'Oh, yes, that should do just fine.' Fine? Fine! My greatest creation is not just 'fine'. With all the individual gears, the pipes can be aimed quite accurately to mix the stars' colors and designs. It's going to be so amazing, it'll bring the people to their knees. 'Fine!' He's lucky I'm letting him watch the show. Although, he was the one who suggested the timing mechanism. He said it might be best if we had some distance between it and us in case things didn't quite work out the way we planned. After seeing all the powder he was using, I agreed. If something did go wrong, it would clear a fifty-foot area, putting a small crater in the ground."

"Wow, Seth, no wonder you've been so secretive about your creation. The machine sounds very impressive."

What would the Rogues do with a mobile crackling-star spectacle, or potential bomb? There are easier ways to blow stuff up...

Once they reached the machine, Seth began to untie the rest of the tarp that covered it. Lillian could still feel whoever it was close by and getting closer. She glanced around but didn't see anyone besides Seth.

Where could they be?

"It's right here." Seth waved to her. "Just hold this lever up so I can slip the gear into place."

Lillian walked around and grabbed the lever. She needed both hands to hold it up, which prevented her from looking behind her.

"I'll just be a second. I have to go around to the other side where the gear is. I'll be right back."

Lillian felt uneasy. "Seth, Jafria's show is going to start any minute," Lillian called after him, concerned for him as well, but he was already around the corner.

"It'll only take a second," he called back.

She examined the machine since she had the chance. Seth hadn't exaggerated when he talked about the amount of powder being used. From all the pipes, Lillian estimated they had used about seven kegs' worth of the demolition mix.

The pipes…why do they look like…?

"Seth?" Lillian called, "Where is the show supposed to be? Because right now, it looks like the crackling stars are going to be shot right at the festival."

And the village. The kegs! OH!

Lillian suddenly saw stars, but they were not Grayson's. She slumped down to the ground, darkness closing in around her.

Lillian's head throbbed. She struggled to come to, but her brain felt sluggish. She knew there was something important she should be doing. She needed to move…

But her attempt proved futile, as she quickly realized her hands were bound to a chair behind her back. The haze of her surroundings slowly came into focus. A worktable lay off to her left with a rack of tools on the wall. Leftover pipes and gears from the machine were piled in a corner. The smell of hay and horses lingered.

The stables? Why am I back here? What happened to Seth?

"Seth," she called out weakly, "*Seth!*" Her voice was stronger this time.

"Ah, I see you're awake," Seth said, strolling in from behind her. "I wasn't sure when you'd come around. I hit you a little harder than I'd intended, but I needed you to be out for the trip."

Her pounding head did not make it any easier for Lillian to understand what was going on. "Seth, why am I tied up? What are you doing?"

"Oh please, Princess, we can stop the charade. There's no one here but us. Everyone is at the festival just like he planned."

Charade?

She had known Seth for most of her life. They had played together as children, shared scars, summer swims; her friends were right, he was like a brother. But the gleam was revealing the distortion. And while his strength wasn't nearly as strong, Lillian could feel the same rancid power that had oozed out of Zands fighting against her now. And any lingering doubts about Seth vanished as her skin prickled up the back of her neck.

Her heart was torn. Tears, unbidden, ran down her cheeks. This vile force he emitted was literally repulsive. It pushed her away, dissolving ten years of kinship, and left her wondering how he had fooled everyone for so long and how she had ever felt any amity for him at all. She tried her best to keep her voice from cracking. "Why?"

"Why?" He turned and came closer to her. "Why? You really are as naïve as Hayden said you were." He walked back around the stables, kicking hay around. "Do you know how long I have been waiting for my master to be ready? To finally put into action what would bring him back into power—*us* back into power. My family ruled their district. I was to inherit all that my parents had and more. Zoldaine had already begun grooming me to become a member of his court. But thanks to your father and the other royals, all I inherited was ten years of cleaning up after your horses." His last words dripped with disdain. "I will say, though, you have definitely made things interesting. You have a knack for getting out of traps. That's why master finally had me take care of you personally. I don't make mistakes."

Lillian wasn't sure what she was going to do, but she knew she had to keep him talking and hope that not everyone was at the festival, that someone would find her. "What do you mean, I have a knack for getting out of traps?"

"Well, it was supposed to be nice and clean. The day of your birthday celebration, the day you went out on the bridge? You were *supposed* to fall into a portal waiting below. But your boyfriend showed up and rescued you. So the next attempt, your kidnapping, was planned more carefully. Thanks, by the way, for keeping me up to date on your social events. But once again, Mr. Archer saved the day. Master was not pleased. Your 'hero' would have to be dealt with, as I'm sure you've realized by now."

Anger and fear were a tempest inside of Lillian. "What have you done with him? Where is Alexander?" she shouted. "You tell me right now, or by the Fae, I'll…"

Seth rushed up so fast he almost knocked her chair over. "You'll *what*, Princess?" he challenged. "There's nothing you can do for him. He's far, far away where he most *certainly* cannot liberate you this time."

As Seth pulled away, Lillian noticed something. His palm was purple.

He couldn't have. No one knows about that passage. It's not possible.

Blood rushed out of her head, fading her vision. Quick, short breaths attempted to fill her tightening chest. *This is not happening. This is* not *happening.*

She had imagined enough horror already without considering what travesty Zands would pile on top. Memory of his words echoed in her mind. *"My favorite was always the pawn. Inconspicuously making its way into enemy territory to save one of its comrades."*

"So, it was you all along. You wrote the notes. You set up Laurel."

Seth laughed and clapped his hands. "Bravo, Princess, bravo. Seems like there are some gears turning in there after all. Too bad they didn't start clicking sooner. Just like

Laurel's. He was almost as naïve as you were. But not quite enough. Who would have thought that drunken, self-absorbed knight would cause any issues? He thought he was being inconspicuous, but I caught him snooping around my stables looking for those shipments he saw come in. *He* wasn't as easy to fool, yet a couple of potion drops in his wine to falsify the faeries' spell and a few parchments I had no more use for was enough to fool everyone else. But you," Seth said, shaking his finger at her, "you might as well be one of us. Everything that's happening tonight is because of you."

"I would never help you."

"But you already have. Why do you think Hayden gave you the information to have Zands captured? He needed to be caught so your father and the other kingdoms would have the Dawning Festival. Why do you think I gave you the knife? We planned your escape to happen. Not in the way that it did, mind you. We're still trying to figure out who helped you. And, of course, the meddlesome archer blew up a stash of our powder kegs, so we borrowed a few from the dwarves. But what's a plan without a little improvisation?" He clapped his hands together. "Everyone is still exactly where we want them to be. You are with me. The Rogues are safely in the castle. And everyone else is neatly rounded up in one location—the festival. And in about half an hour, my machine will shoot lit powder bags at the village rooftops and kiosk water barrels."

"The water barrels are…?"

"Not filled with water, I'm afraid. Your father managed to round up most of us, but there were enough Rogues left to carry out Zoldaine's plans. Just as he anticipated."

Lillian remembered seeing the blue barrels being spread out all around the festival. If anyone survived, it would be a miracle.

Lillian knew it was a long shot but had to try. "Seth, whatever it is Zoldaine has told you, whatever you have planned tonight, you don't have to go through with it. You have a good life here. You don't have to remain a stable boy. From the look of your machine, you should be working with the dwarves in engineering. No one has gotten hurt yet. I'm sure my father would—"

The slap took Lillian completely by surprise.

"Don't patronize me, Princess. Your father would have me slaughtered just like my parents were. Now, sit there and be good. I need to remove any traces before we leave, and I'd hate to have to knock you out again."

Seth walked over to the wall of tools. He twisted a pair of blacksmith tongs. Lillian heard a latch release and saw him lift up a section of the "dirt" floor and step down into a large opening.

Well, I know why Laurel didn't find anything.

Lillian knew this was her only chance to try and escape. Seth had reminded her that she still had his knife in her boot. It wasn't easy, but she managed to bring her left leg back just enough for her hand to reach inside.

She slowly worked the blade up and down against the rope while keeping an eye on the stall. She could feel her bonds getting looser. They released at the same instant as Seth came back up with a powder keg.

"This should take care of any evidence we were here." He set it down underneath his bench and shut the opening. He pulled out a long fuse, stuck it in the top of the keg, and lit it. "There, that'll give us plenty of time." He took a bottle off the bench and dabbed a rag with its contents. "Before I tied Grayson up, he assured me this potion would keep someone asleep for days. It definitely put him out."

Lillian was terrified.

I have to get out of here now! Her eyes darted around wildly. There was no way she could get past Seth.

You know what has to be done.

"I wish I didn't have to do this," Seth said, feigning concern, "but we have a long journey ahead of us and master wants you unharmed. He probably won't be pleased I hit you. I'll be reprimanded, I'm sure. Though I won't say it wasn't worth it." He walked toward her. "But this time, I promise you won't feel a thing."

She closed her eyes and reached for the gleam, letting all the fear and worry and anger of the past few months flow from her. It came to her in a rush, as completely as it had that night at the grove. Behind her back, she gripped the knife solidly in her hand.

I've only got one chance at this.

She "saw" Seth approaching. Heard the crunch of hay underneath his feet. Felt his malicious aura repelling hers, getting stronger as he drew closer.

Almost...wait...NOW!

She swung her hand around, landing a stabbing blow to Seth's thigh.

Seth howled in pain and rage. He stumbled back. Lillian lunged out of the chair, shoving Seth out of the way and down to the ground. She made it two steps before he was able to grab her foot and bring her down too. She reached for anything to gain leverage. He pulled her toward him, climbing on top of her, the rag still in his hand. Lillian saw the knife was still sticking out of his leg, so she twisted around and kicked it. He screamed and his grip loosened just enough for her to wriggle free. But he was still blocking her way out.

Hide. Hide in the stables and maybe I can slip past him.
Lillian gave Seth one more punt to his face and dashed to the stables.

She frantically hunted for a stall to hide in.

"Lillian!" Seth's poisonous voice called.

She heard him coming fast. She darted into a stall in the middle and crouched in a corner.

Please, Fae, let him start in the back.

She heard Seth enter the stable row.

"Princess, I don't think you want to be here when the keg goes off. We don't have time to play hide 'n' seek."

She was panicking. There was nothing in her stall but hay.

What am I going to do, stuff him to death?

She heard the stall gate next to her open.

"Come out, come out, wherever you are."

Lillian's skin crawled at his sick crooning.

Her stall was next.

I'm trapped. The kingdom is about to be destroyed. My citizens murdered. My parents...oh...NO! It will not end like this!

She poised herself to spring at him when he came in.

Your master doesn't want you to hurt me? Well, you're going to have to kill me before I go with you.

"You know, I can feel your presence." She heard the gate latch release. "Just like you," he said as she saw the sharp blade of a sickle enter the stall, her chance of escape plummeting, "can feel me." He stepped into the enclosed space, blood trickling down his leg, smears of it across his face. His eyes were wild with fury, one hand still clutching the elixir-soaked rag.

Suddenly, a bright red flash filled the stables. Lillian balled up, knowing it was the keg going off. But the only noise she heard was a small thud in front of her. She opened her eyes to see Seth lying face down, completely unconscious. Then she felt a very positive force join hers.

Grayson!

"Lillian! Dear, are you okay?" a very wise, warm voice called out to her.

"I'm here, Grayson!" She raised up and ran to the old wizard, grabbing him tightly. "Oh, Grayson!"

"Careful now with these old bones. You might grind them to powder."

Powder? The keg!

"Grayson! There's a keg in the workroom. It's about…"

He raised a long, wizened hand to stop her. "I took care of it, it's okay. Now, can you please tell me what's going on? Seth managed to catch me off guard when I was explaining my slumber potion. Then he had the audacity to use a wizard's own concoction on him. Foolish boy. Barely lasted an hour with his energy. When I woke up, my third eye was ringing my head like the alarm bells telling me to come here. I could feel you. I've always had a small sense for your family, but your energy has been awakened, and it's potent. I thought I felt it a few weeks ago, but I hadn't felt anything that strong again until tonight."

Lillian motioned to Seth's body. "What about Seth? Will he…be okay?" She was revolted by him but still concerned at least as to whether he was still alive.

"He'll be fine. Probably have a nasty headache and be a little surprised he's in shackles." And with that, Grayson waved his staff and a pair of chains came down from the wall and wrapped around Seth, securing him tightly.

"Could you feel Seth too? I don't understand; why couldn't I sense his real aura before? How did he hide his intentions for so long?" Lillian's mouth spilling forth questions her mind was running through.

"Seth had help. Powerful help. Even I couldn't feel him until tonight, so don't be too hard on yourself. This is *old* magic. Not even Zands was that strong."

Lillian had forgotten about Seth's hand in the commotion. Her immediate death thwarted, the sense of urgency came flooding back.

Zands. I have to find him. And the villagers have to be warned.

Lillian looked at the wizard. "Grayson, I promise to tell you everything later."

He arched a woolly white brow.

"*Everyone* at the festival is about to die. There are powder kegs placed all over the village, and the water barrels at the festival aren't filled with water. Your machine is prepped to go off anytime, and it's rigged to set them off."

The air crackled with power and the hairs on Lillian's arms raised. She realized she was gaining a glimpse of Grayson's true potential.

"Why, that insolent little…turning something beautiful and magical against the kingdom. Something I created…" Grayson looked at the incapacitated Seth, the wizard's eyes were electric. He raised his staff.

"Grayson!" Lillian yelled, "You have to get to the machine *now*!"

The light left the wizard's eyes, and he turned to Lillian.

Her heart was beating in her throat. "I can get the castle guards to the village. Can you slide down there to stop it?"

Grayson wrinkled his woolly brow. "Step back."

Lillian did. Grayson murmured some words then struck his staff on the ground with finality. A translucent double image of Grayson materialized where the wizard had just been standing, along with a long, blue line in the air. His first form slid into the line, disappearing behind it like a doorway. The second image hovered for a moment, then followed the first. The blue line dissolved, and any trace of Grayson was gone.

Fae be with you, Grayson.

Lillian raced to the east wing where most of the guards were. She advised them of the situation and sent as many as could be spared to begin removing the kegs. Once she was certain the guards were in order, she dashed back to the stables, thinking about her family and friends.

She had to get down to the festival and help Grayson. Her whole life was down there. She wanted to look for Zands but realized the futility of it.

I can't feel him anymore, and he could be anywhere.
She knew Zands was a huge threat, but he would have to wait.

How much time had passed?
She couldn't tell, but she hadn't heard any explosions yet. With each passing second, she felt both relief and the tension of anticipation.

She rushed to Patches' stall and noticed a folded piece of parchment tucked between the top hinges of the gate. As she walked over to it, she could feel Zands' residual energy lingering. She was leery to even touch the note, let alone read it, afraid it might zap her with a magic spell or worse. Her name was written on the outside.

He knew I'd be coming. He wrote this for me.

My dearest Lillian, if you are reading this note, which I suspected you would be doing, it means you have eluded yet another effort to secure you. Nevertheless, pieces were moved long ago to account for this contingency, as the master's pawn has sacrificed itself for me. That's the beauty of the game; there's never just one strategy in play at any moment.

As I'm sure you've guessed, we've captured your friend as well. Whether you see him again is entirely up to you. I'm sure you're asking yourself right now if you can trust me. The answer is of course not, but what choice do you have? You have been checked, and the move is yours and yours alone. In two days' time, your presence is required at the location marked on the map. Should you fail to show. . .well, let's say you may end up forfeiting your noble knight.

I do wish I could have seen your surprised face tonight. As I said, it's one of my greatest joys to see the confounded expressions that appear when I have deceived my audience through misdirection. But ironically, my attention was called elsewhere. I look forward to seeing you soon, Princess. ˉZ

Lillian examined the small map sketched on the bottom of the letter. The location was in Drod.

Of course it is. Where else would it be?

She looked at the map again. The location was in the northernmost part of the country.

But if I'm to get there in two days...

Lillian was in her room frantically packing. Each passing moment, she expected to hear an explosion destroying everything she held dear, but none came.

Everyone is safe—everyone except Alexander. I'm all he has.

The letter gave no indication as to how long she'd be gone, but every second counted if she was to make it to Alexander in time, so she had little allowance to vacillate on the particulars. She stuffed her pack with a variety of items she thought would come in handy, including a few leftover vials of Hair Hue and her disguise from the dinner party.

I may be a princess, but I don't have to look like one.

She had no reason to believe any villages or towns existed in Drod, but she took what few coins she had stashed away just in case.

Someone, or something, is up there though. Seth's words echoed in her mind once again, *"If you think about it, what better place to kidnap someone and start a revolt than somewhere no one wants to go."* She grabbed her bow and quiver from the corner, praying to the Fae she didn't have to use it like Alexander did the night she was kidnapped.

She finished by writing a note to her parents. It was short. There was nothing she could say that wouldn't keep them from going spiral, and she apologized for that. She hoped they would understand.

She left the note in the kitchen, where she took a few provisions and a sheepskin for water. She wasn't sure how long the bread and dried meat would last, but they would have to do.

At least I can catch fish.

Her body was as tense as a drawn bow, the agonizing fear of what could happen any second making her hands shake and breath come fast. But the blasts from the powder kegs never came, which meant Grayson and the guards must have succeeded, Fae be praised. She wasn't sure she could leave if her kingdom was burning down in flames and all her family and friends had just perished.

Her last stop was the stables. She passed by Patches, giving him a rub on the nose. "Sorry, old friend. This journey may be too much for you." She continued to the far end of the stables. "Hello, Moose."

The night air rushing against her face was cool but refreshing. No noise could be heard over the gallop of Moose's hooves, which Lillian was thankful for. If she had heard one sound reminding her of what she was leaving behind, she wasn't sure she'd have the resolve to keep going.

She put her hand in her pocket and caressed the letter from Zands. She distracted herself from the reality of her situation by imagining how she would put an arrow through that smug heart of his.

Lillian wasn't sure how she was going to save Alexander. But she knew she had to try. She now understood the feeling others had told her about, the sentiment that made people do foolish things. The sensation one couldn't explain but simply knew when it was found. The emotional bond between two individuals where one would do anything for the other. She would sacrifice herself for him just as surely as she knew he would do the same. All logic and reason in her mind screamed at her, *"No! Why are you doing this?"* Her answer was simple.

Because I love him.

CONTINENT
— OF —
AZSHURA

VALANTI

Harry & Snow White
Charming

Lillian
May 11th (18)

Andrew
March 30th (10)

TAPERA

Louis & Cinderella
Charming

Marcus
February 25th (21)

Olivia
December 10th (16)

CALDERA

Phillip & Aurora
Perrault

Jaccob
June 17th (20)

Avery
January 11th (17)

Layla
October 12th (9)

CASTLE & MISCELLANEOUS

Alondra Watersworth
Maid servant to Lillian

Henry Watersworth
Head advisor to the King

Seth Hamilton
Stable boy, all-around chores

Sir Braelyn Alger
Head security, former archer

Pierre
Royal head chef

Ophelia
Castle seamstress

Sir Laurel
An attractive less chivalrous knight

Grayson
Wizard and castle healer

Richard Burkhardt
Lillian's current suitor

Jafria, Sophie, Elizabeth (Lizzy)
Lillian's closest friends

Barrett, Gage, Brock
Current suitors to Lillian's closest friends

Gwendolyn, Carissa, Hannah,
& Camellia
Lillian's other friends

Note from C.M. Healy

Thank you so much for reading my first full-length novel. I hope you enjoyed the journey reading it as much as I did writing it. Being my first novel, I would love to hear from you, my audience and faithful fans. Feel free to email me and let me know what you think.

I promise this intricate tale does have closure…in the fourth book. For now, the story will develop in the next Beyond the After book. Princess Olivia is sought after by unscrupulous creatures for reasons yet discovered. New and familiar characters will intertwine as the conspiracy of the Rogues plagues the Tapera Kingdom. More questions arise. Secrets are revealed. Relationships are found.

Don't forget to check out my website and sign up for my newsletter for giveaways and exclusive Beyond the After content (full color illustration of map, cover variants, etc.).

Once again, I appreciate you taking a chance on an unknown (for now) author.

Other books by C.M. Healy
Young Adult
Beyond the After: Princess Olivia (Book 2)

Children's with YouTube read along (C.M. Healy)
The Different Little Lion
If Mom Became an Octopus
Missing Numbers
I Can't
Penelope Rose
The Other Side
The Lion & the Red Balloon and Other Silly Stories

About the Author

C.M. Healy currently lives in Texas with his wife, baby girl, dog, and two giant cats where he teaches science. When he's not busy with writing and visiting schools, he enjoys building Lego sets, playing video games, reading comic books (The Flash is his favorite), and watching TV with his best buddy, his wife. He earned the distinguished award of Eagle Scout during high school and went on to obtain his masters in child development from Oklahoma State University. He has been working with and entertaining children of all ages ever since.

www.authorcmhealy.com
authorcmhealy@gmail.com
Instagram & Twitter @authorcmhealy
Facebook CM Healy

Map by Barry Fuxa
BarryFuxa.com | @barryfuxa
http://www.facebook.com/barryfuxa

Made in USA - Kendallville, IN
72304_9781948577007
03.20.2023 1327